## THE QUIET AMERICAN

*Text and Criticism*

GRAHAM GREENE was born in 1904. On coming down from Balliol College, Oxford, he worked for four years as subeditor on *The Times*. He established his reputation with his fourth novel, *Stamboul Train*. In 1935 he made a journey across Liberia, described in *Journey Without Maps*, and on his return was appointed film critic of the *Spectator*. In 1926 he had been received into the Roman Catholic Church and he visited Mexico in 1938 to report on the religious persecution there. As a result he wrote *The Lawless Roads* and, later, his famous novel *The Power and the Glory*.

*Brighton Rock* was published in 1938 and in 1940 he became literary editor of the *Spectator*. The next year he undertook work for the Foreign Office and was stationed in Sierra Leone from 1941 to 1943. This later produced his novel *The Heart of the Matter*, set in West Africa. Other novels include *The End of the Affair*, *The Quiet American*, *Travels With My Aunt*, *The Honorary Consul*, and *The Captain and the Enemy*.

As well as his many novels, Graham Greene wrote several collections of short stories, four travel books, six plays, two books of autobiography, *A Sort of Life* and *Ways of Escape*, two of biography, and four books for children. He also contributed hundreds of essays, and film and book reviews, some of which appear in the collection *Reflections*. Many of his novels and stories have been filmed and *The Third Man* was written as a film treatment. Graham Greene was a member of the Order of Merit and a Companion of Honour.

Graham Greene died in April 1991. Among the many people who paid tribute to him on his death were Kingsley Amis: "He will be missed all over the world. Until today, he was our greatest living novelist"; Alec Guinness: "He was a great writer who spoke brilliantly to a whole generation. He was almost prophet-like with a surprising humility"; and William Golding: "Graham Greene was in a class by himself. . . . He will be read and remembered as the ultimate chronicler of twentieth-century man's consciousness and anxiety."

JOHN CLARK PRATT served twenty years in the United States Air Force, retiring with the rank of lieutenant colonel. He was both a jet instructor pilot and professor of English at the U.S. Air Force Academy. During his tour in Southeast Asia, he commanded the Thailand detachment of Project CHECO (Contemporary Historical Examination of Combat Operations), and it was in Thailand that he wrote four book-length analyses of air operations in the war, flew 101 combat hours in nine different kinds of aircraft, and supervised the microfilming of documents relative to the war. He has written or edited numerous articles and twelve books, among which are *Vietnam Voices: Perspectives on the War Years, 1941–1982*; *The Laotian Fragments* (a Vietnam War novel); *The Meaning of Modern Poetry*; *John Steinbeck*; *George Eliot's "Middlemarch" Notebooks* (with Victor Neufeldt); *Reading the Wind: The Literature of the Vietnam War* (with Tim Lomperis); the Viking Critical Edition of Ken Kesey's *One Flew Over the Cuckoo's Nest*; and *Writing from Scratch: The Essay*. He conceived and was the general editor of the Writing from Scratch series and is president of his own on-demand publishing company. The recipient of a Ph.D. from Princeton University, he has taught American literature in Thailand, Portugal, and the Soviet Union. Mr. Pratt was for five years chairman of the English Department at Colorado State University, where he is at present professor of English.

*Winesburg, Ohio*
Sherwood Anderson
Edited by John H. Ferres

*The Quiet American*
Graham Greene
Edited by John Clark Pratt

*A Portrait of the Artist
as a Young Man*
James Joyce
Edited by Chester G. Anderson

*Dubliners*
James Joyce
Edited by Robert Scholes
and A. Walton Litz

*One Flew Over the Cuckoo's Nest*
Ken Kesey
Edited by John Clark Pratt

*Sons and Lovers*
D. H. Lawrence
Edited by Julian
Moynahan

*The Crucible*
Arthur Miller
Edited by Gerald Weales

*Death of a Salesman*
Arthur Miller
Edited by Gerald Weales

*The Grapes of Wrath*
John Steinbeck
Edited by Peter Lisca
Updated with Kevin Hearle

THE VIKING CRITICAL LIBRARY

# GRAHAM GREENE

## The Quiet American

*TEXT AND CRITICISM*

EDITED BY

John Clark Pratt

PENGUIN BOOKS

PENGUIN BOOKS
Published by the Penguin Group
Penguin Books USA Inc., 375 Hudson Street, New York,
New York 10014, U.S.A.
Penguin Books Ltd, 27 Wrights Lane, London W8 5TZ, England
Penguin Books Australia Ltd, Ringwood, Victoria, Australia
Penguin Books Canada Ltd, 10 Alcorn Avenue, Toronto, Ontario,
Canada M4V 3B2
Penguin Books (N.Z.) Ltd, 182–190 Wairau Road, Auckland 10,
New Zealand

Penguin Books Ltd, Registered Offices: Harmondsworth, Middlesex, England

The Quiet American first published in Great Britain by
William Heinemann Ltd 1955
First published in the United States of America by The Viking Press 1956
The Viking Critical Library The Quiet American published in
Penguin Books 1996

10

LIBRARY OF CONGRESS CATALOGING IN PUBLICATION DATA
Greene, Graham, 1904–
The quiet American/Graham Greene; text and criticism edited by
John Clark Pratt.
p.   cm.—(The Viking critical library)
Includes bibliographical references (p.      ).
ISBN 0 14 02.4350 X
1. Indochinese War, 1946–1954—Journalists—Fiction.   2. War
correspondents—Fiction.   3. Indochina—Politics and
government—1945-   —Fiction.   4. Vietnam—Politics and
government—1945–1975—Fiction.   I. Pratt, John Clark.   II. Title.
III. Series.
PR6013.R44Q5   1996
823'.912—dc20      95–23183

Printed in the United States of America
Set in Elante
Designed by Kate Nichols

# Contents

# Contents

# Introduction

> To the Frenchman war is just a part of human life: it
> can be pleasant or unpleasant, like adultery. *"La vie
> sportive"*—that is how a French commandant described
> to me his life on a small landing craft in the delta south
> of Saigon.
>
> GRAHAM GREENE, *Ways of Escape*

One of the best and most productive writers of the twentieth
century, Graham Greene also wrote more about his own work
than has almost any other significant author. His letters to various newspapers (usually to "educate" a reviewer), his inter-
views in print and on radio, and his published journal extracts,
essays, articles and autobiographical writings provide scholars
with remarkable documentation not only of the personality that
created his literary works, but also of the factual material behind many of them.

Consequently, the major problem that a reader faces when
dealing with a Greene novel—and this problem is excruciat-
ingly apparent with *The Quiet American*—is how to approach
the work both in and out of its historical context. Like so many
of his other novels, *The Quiet American* resulted from Greene's
participation in many of the events it depicts, and also as happened with some of his other works, critics have had difficulty
differentiating between the author and the novel's protagonist-
hero, Thomas Fowler—like Greene himself in the early to mid-
1950s, a British journalist observing a war.

Of course, the events of history—most noticeably, the outcome of the Second Indo-China War—have radically changed
critics' perceptions of this novel and what has come to be called
Greene's "ominous prophecy." In order to understand *The
Quiet American*'s true place in Greene's canon and also in that

of the more than 500 other novels about Americans at war in Southeast Asia, one must consider not only biographical and critical information but also historical and political matters that were apparent in 1956 to few English-speaking readers—and sometimes not even to Greene himself.

An example of one of the problems: altogether too many readers (and some critics as well) have misunderstood the function of the dates (March 1952–June 1955) at the end of the text. After all, during the years 1955 (the date of publication in England) and 1956 (publication of the American edition), neither the American nor British publics knew or cared much about events in Southeast Asia. It was the Soviet Union that preoccupied most Westerners. And even now, the facts of the early days of the Second Indo-China War have become obfuscated in light of the tragic aftermath. The dates that Greene appended to the manuscript are those of the writing of the book; the actual time frame of *The Quiet American* is about six months—from September of 1951 (Pyle's arrival, p. 23) to February–March, 1952 (Pyle's death, p. 11). That these dates also include Greene's second visit (his first "winter") in Vietnam certainly impacts the accuracy of what some critics call the "reportage" element in the novel. Also, the 1951–52 period predates the arrival of American Colonel Edward Lansdale, who many critics believe (even though Greene constantly denied it) was the model for Alden Pyle.

This Critical Edition is designed to offer both context and commentary to provide a modern reader with some of the tools necessary for a more complete understanding of the greatness of *The Quiet American*. Some of the selections detail the American presence in Vietnam during the early years; others offer the views of North Vietnamese President Ho Chi Minh and South Vietnamese officials. Some—but only some—of Greene's writings on Indo-China are included, and the Literary Criticism section demonstrates the wide range of interpretations of the novel that appeared in the forty years after its publication. Also in this edition are a plot summary of the

American film version, which Greene called the "treachery of Joseph Mankiewicz" (*Ways of Escape*, p. 17) and Greene's other reactions to the Hollywood version.

Referred to often by Greene's critics are the early reviews of the book, only one of which is reprinted here. I think that most of the subsequent analyses overstate the American–British dichotomy: that Americans disliked the book but British reviewers praised it. Certainly, *The New York Herald Tribune*'s reviewer speculated that the "fantastic" characters represented "an elaborate leg-pulling," and A. J. Liebling's *New Yorker* essay (p. 347) is a classic put-down that produced a comment by John Atkins that "If *The Quiet American* is a good novel, Liebling's article is a better review" (GG, 235). But the *Saturday Review* found it "a superb fiction," the *New Republic* lauded Greene's "mastery of story-telling," and the *Atlantic* called it "continuously intriguing." Some religious publications—*The Christian Science Monitor, Christian Century, Commonweal*— attacked the novel for various reasons without belaboring its anti-Christian theme, but in general many of the first American reviews seemed supportive, as was, of course, much of the British press. The *Spectator* called it "a very fine novel indeed," and to *The* [London] *Times*, the novel's "particular excellence . . . [is] powerful and long-lasting." However, because some of the other British reviewers were hardly as praising, I think it is wrong to infer unanimity from either critical camp.

The literary criticism that followed was also a mixed bag, with many Greene scholars seeming unsure of exactly where to place *The Quiet American*. Was it one of his "entertainments"? Was it merely an anti-American tract? With America fully involved in the Vietnam War, however, some critics began to see in this novel a paradigm for all that was apparently going wrong with the American cause, and in almost everything written about Greene since the early 1970s, *The Quiet American* has been elevated to the status of one of Greene's major works. In the 80s and 90s, given the failure of the United States to prevail in Vietnam, a flood of Greene scholarship from Britain, India,

Canada, and the United States (much of it using Greene's own published comments on his novel and about his Vietnam experiences) provides an illuminating discourse about the sources and possible meanings of this work.

Predominant, I think, is the attention now being given to *The Quiet American* as another example of Greene's analyses of "the human condition," and some critics even see a positive movement toward a religious affirmation. Significant, too, is the realization by many analysts that Thomas Fowler is to be seen as a flawed, ironic narrator instead of merely a literal spokesman for the author—even though Fowler is, as Greene was, a British journalist estranged from his wife. Some early reviewers, for instance, chastised Greene for a flat portrayal of Phuong and an inconsistent characterization of Alden Pyle, but a reader must realize that it is Fowler who describes them to us—that it is Fowler who sees Phuong as childlike and Pyle as clumsily innocent. In fact, it is what Fowler does *not* understand about her that makes Phuong fascinating, and his misreading of Pyle (who, after all, is probably a rather well trained CIA agent) leads to his own involvement and responsibility. Fowler's final wish for someone to whom he might apologize becomes ultimately saddening, for he must now be a very quiet Englishman, like Pyle another involved Westerner who has failed to heed Kipling's warning not to "hustle the East."

Also, as any great work of fiction demands, there has in recent years been more scholarly attention paid to the backgrounds and sources for this novel, and of all the selections reprinted in this edition, Judith Adamson's work stands out as an excellent example of what some moderns might call the "new historicism" (some of us prefer to see it as a return to the "old" criticism). Her work both in film (she notes how "badly distorted" the movie version is [p. 88]) and fiction provides precisely the contextuality that is necessary for understanding *The Quiet American*. Other critics have been more speculative: that U.S. Colonel Edward Lansdale was the model for Pyle is widely believed, but according to Greene, he and

Lansdale never met. Lansdale arrived incognito in Saigon in June of 1953, stayed a month, then came back for two years in 1954 to head the Saigon Military Mission for the CIA. The admitted model for at least two other fictional characters (Colonel Hillandale in *The Ugly American* and Colonel Teryman in Jean Larteguy's *Yellow Fever*), Lansdale told me in 1983 that he knew Greene had him in mind as Alden Pyle because Pyle, too, had a dog. Lansdale also commented in a later letter, "Incidentally, Graham Greene also shares the French hatred for Trinh Minh Thé, who had one of their generals blown up (by grenade). I was his [Thé's] American friend and the French used to mock me about him, *in the presence of Greene*" (emphasis added). Regardless of whether they actually met, Lansdale no doubt saw his close relationship with the real General Thé as a possible source—but he did not meet Thé until the fall of 1954, after Greene had left Vietnam and was well into his novel. Hardly as "innocent" as Pyle, Lansdale was an experienced, mature undercover operative with perhaps the best understanding ever possessed by any American of Vietnamese politics and intrigue. Then again, given the outcome of the American presence in Vietnam, perhaps Lansdale *should* have been the model after all. Much as Pyle might have done, Lansdale helped convince the producer of the film version to make the American presence seem positive (see pp. 299 and 307).

Other critics have speculated on additional models for the novel's characters, most notably James Hazen in an essay I could not include here. Believing that Greene "seems clearly to admire the American press," Hazen thinks that the name Alden Pyle derives from Ernie Pyle, the World War II American correspondent, and Priscilla Alden "from Longfellow's poem" (p. 16). He does not, however, make the perfectly proper association between the role of John Alden and that of Thomas Fowler as an ironic go-between for someone else's romance. Another critic, Harry Rudman, has identified the Clough and Byron quotations that introduce the novel, and he also notes A. C. Clough as the "adult poet in the nineteenth century" whom Fowler quotes on page 177. In *Dipsychus* (lines 124–29), these words, Rudman notes, are spoken by the Mephistophelean spirit (VN, p. 15), an identification that certainly does further characterize Greene's narrator.

In addition, many of the novel's characters were drawn from life, as Greene's official biographer, Norman Sherry, notes. Phuong seems to have been inspired by a "ravingly beautiful" woman Greene met one night in Saigon (p. 410); Vigot by a M. Moret of the French Sureté (p. 410); and Granger by the American Pulitzer prizewinning journalist Larry Allen, who was "once called 'the most shot-at United States Foreign correspondent'" (p. 399).

Interestingly, no one except Jonathan Nashel (see p. 313) seems to have investigated possible sources for York Harding, the Asian "expert" on whose theories Alden Pyle so depends. There are many other candidates. During the late 1940s and early 1950s, for instance, American Robert Payne was one of many Western political scientists concerned with the growing global influence of Communism, and his *Red Storm Over Asia* (1951) contains his vision of what America's role should be. Discussing what had gone wrong in Asia as the Communist influence had increased from 1948–50, Payne states that "An almost nihilistic opportunism became inevitable in all countries where a moderate 'third force' either failed to take power or found itself with no means of exercising its power" (p. 3). Payne pleads for "an extension of the social arm of America until it reaches the villages of Asia" (p. 202), and then he deplores in Vietnam "the absence of any real [French] intention to create a social revolution in the South" (p. 203). These are words that would have indeed excited Alden Pyle.

In general, then, *The Quiet American* has sparked a remarkable critical output, and the essays in this edition consider the novel as reportage, as political statement, as detective story, as allegory, and as romance. Some find it existential, others affirmative. That few of the later critics can find much fault with the book testifies to its increasing influence. Indeed, students who might not otherwise be exposed to Greene are reading *The Quiet American* in history and political science courses that deal with the Vietnam War, and I have met almost no writer of serious Vietnam War fiction who does not admire this novel. As shown by the selection from *Into a Black Sun* (p. 340), perhaps Mr. Heng was still advising foreigners in 1964, and in Desmond Meiring's *The Brinkman*, a novel about the French failure in Vietnam, one of the characters, Jeanette, has a copy of *The Quiet American* prominently displayed on her bookshelf in early 1960s Vientiane, Laos (p. 187). In addition, a stage version was even performed in Moscow, a play that Greene told Philip Stratford was "a fairly honest version but terribly long running to nearly four hours . . . with out-of-date gestures . . . and costumes" (GG to PS, 15 February 1982).

One hopes, then, that with the opportunity to consider *The Quiet American* in context, readers far removed from the events of 1951–52 can not only see what causes a great novel to last but also reflect upon and ponder the nature of involvement itself, both political and personal—the subject that *The Quiet American* is ultimately about. As Thomas Fowler finds out from Mr. Heng, what we must never forget in an increasingly complex and mystifying world is that "Sooner or later . . . one has to take sides. If one is to remain human" (p. 174).

—John Clark Pratt
Vietnam, Laos, Thailand, 1969–70

## WORKS CITED IN INTRODUCTION

### Reviews

*Atlantic* 197 (March, 1956): 82.
*Christian Century* 73 (1 August 1956): 901.
*Christian Science Monitor* (22 March 1956).
*Commonweal* 63 (16 March 1956): 622.
*New Republic* 134 (12 March 1956): 26.
*New York Herald Tribune Book Review* (11 March 1956).

*The New York Times* (11 March 1956).
*Saturday Review* 39 (10 March 1956): 12.
*The Spectator* (9 December 1955).
*The Times* (London) *Literary Supplement* (9 December 1955).


**Other**

Adamson, Judith. *Graham Greene and Cinema*. Norman, Okla.:
    Pilgrim Books, 1984.

Atkins, John. *Graham Greene*. London: Calder and Boyars,
    1966.

Greene, Graham. *Ways of Escape*. New York: Simon and Schus-
    ter, 1980.

Hazen, James. "The Greeneing of America," in *Essays in
    Graham Greene*, ed. Peter Wolfe, Vol. 1. Greenwood, Fla.:
    Penkevill Publishing Company, 1987, 1–24.

Letter. Graham Greene to Philip Stratford, 15 February 1982.

Letter. Maj. Gen. Edward G. Lansdale to John Clark Pratt,
    6 February 1985.

Meiring, Desmond. *The Brinkman*. Boston: Houghton Mifflin,
    1965.

Payne, Robert. *Red Storm Over Asia*. New York: Macmillan,
    1951.

Rudman, Harry W. "Clough and Graham Greene's *The Quiet
    American*," in *The Victorian Newsletter* 19 (Spring 1961):
    14–15.

Sherry, Norman. *The Life of Graham Greene*. Vol. II, 1939–55.
    London: Jonathan Cape, 1994.

# Chronology

[Editor's note: Because of the large number of Greene's works, only a few relevant ones are noted here. For a complete listing, see R. A. Wobbe, *Graham Greene: A Bibliography and Guide to Research* (1979); "Graham Greene," in *Contemporary Authors*, CANR 35 (1992): 179–88; and Neil Brennan and Alan R. Redway, eds., *A Bibliography of Graham Greene* (1990).]

## INDOCHINA

**1627**

Vietnamese language adapted to Roman alphabet by French missionary, Alexandre de Rhodes.

**1820**

First American visitor, Captain John White, arrives in Vietnam. Like Alden Pyle in *TQA* he is from Massachusetts.

**1861**

French capture and occupy Saigon.

## GRAHAM GREENE

1862

French treaty with emperor of
Vietnam insures broad French
rights.

1887

France establishes "Indochinese
Union" consisting of Vietnam
(Cochinchina, Annam, Tonkin)
and Cambodia.

1890

Ho Chi Minh born.

1904

Graham Greene born on 2 October at Berkhamstead, Hert-
fordshire.

1911

Ho Chi Minh leaves Vietnam
for the next thirty years.

1918–24

Ho is in Paris, where he joins
French Communist Party.

1922–25

Greene at Balliol College, Oxford.

1924

Ho Chi Minh leaves Paris for
Moscow.

1925

Greene publishes first book,
*Babbling April* (poetry).

## 1930

Indochinese Communist Party formed by Ho Chi Minh in Hong Kong.

Greene publishes a second novel, *The Name of Action*.

## 1932

Bao Dai returns to Saigon from school in France to ascend throne as Emperor.

Greene's first "entertainment," *Stamboul Train*.

### 1932–39

Greene publishes seven books of fiction and nonfiction.

## 1940

Japan occupies Indochina, interns French forces but allows French to administer the territories.

Publishes *The Power and the Glory*.

## 1941–45: World War II

### 1941

Ho returns to Vietnam, forms Vietminh. Fights Japanese and French.

Greene is attached to British Foreign Office. Wins Hawthornden prize for *The Power and the Glory*.

### 1942–43

Greene serves with British Secret Service. Writes *Ministry of Fear*.

### 1944

Vietminh Army created. Vo Nguyen Giap is commander.

1945

April. OSS Major Patti meets
secretly with Ho Chi Minh and
establishes U.S. advisory mission to help fight the Japanese.

25 August. After Japan's surrender, Ho declares the Democratic Republic of Vietnam is a
"republic" in the French union.

23 September. French forces
overthrow DRV government in
Saigon.

1946

Heavy fighting between French        Greene publishes first children's
and Vietminh forces in Hai-          book, *The Little Train*.
phong. Ho flees to the hills and
declares war against France on
20 December.

### 1946–54: First Indochina War

1947

France agrees to "limited independence" for Vietnam under
Emperor Bao Dai, who is living
in Hong Kong.

1948

Publishes *The Heart of the Matter*. Writes film scripts for
*Brighton Rock* and *Fallen Idol*.

## 1949

Bao Dai signs agreement with France to make Vietnam an "Associated State" within the French Union. Ho Chi Minh does not agree and intensifies guerrilla war.

Writes film script for *The Third Man*.

## 1950–53: Korean War

## 1950

Ho names the Democratic Republic of Vietnam (DRV) as the sole legal government of Vietnam. USSR and China recognize DRV. United States recognizes Bao Dai government and sends $10,000,000 in aid to France. In May, the first U.S. economic Mission established in Saigon. In December, General Jean de Lattre de Tassigny takes command of French forces.

*The Third Man* and *Fallen Idol* published as novels.

## 1951

After numerous successes in battles against the Vietminh, General de Lattre is diagnosed as having cancer and leaves late in the year. U.S. military aid to France tops $500,000,000. In February and March, U.S. delivers ninety F-8F "Bearcat" fighters to Saigon (see *TQA*, pp. 11, 19).

Greene in Malaya and Kenya as correspondent. Publishes *The End of the Affair*. In January, pays first visit to Vietnam. Is guest of Trevor Wilson, British Consul in Hanoi. Returns in October and spends first winter in Vietnam. Meets de Lattre and has idea for a novel set in Vietnam.

1952

De Lattre dies in Paris, 11 January (see *TQA*, pp. 72, 155). U.S. Legation in Saigon elevated to an Embassy. From U.S. perspective, the war has become one between communism and the Free World.

1953

20 June: U.S. CIA officer Colonel Edward Lansdale visits Saigon for the first time. French occupy Dien Bien Phu in November to form "enclave" to block Vietminh in north. Vietminh forces invade Laos in December.

Greene's play *The Living Room* performed and published in London. In December, Greene returns to Vietnam for two months as correspondent for *New Republic*.

1954

13 March: the battle of Dien Bien Phu begins. U.S. refuses French request for intervention. French defeated by 7 May. In June, Colonel Lansdale returns to Saigon as Chief of CIA-run Saigon Military Mission and Bao Dai appoints Ngo Dinh Diem as Prime Minister of Vietnam. On 21 July, the Paris Peace accords between France and Vietnam are signed, temporarily partitioning Vietnam into two areas. U.S. suspends military aid to France for Vietnam operations. Total so far: more than two billion dollars.

Greene leaves Vietnam in February after visiting Dien Bien Phu in January. *Twenty-One Stories* published.

## 1955

United States begins direct aid program to Diem government of South Vietnam. Ho Chi Minh secures commitments of aid from the Soviet Union and China. Diem in Saigon wins rigged referendum and declares South Vietnam a republic with himself as president. Colonel Lansdale becomes his primary U.S. adviser. French transfer control of the South Vietnamese economy, military training, and foreign aid to the United States. French Expeditionary Corps withdraws from Vietnam.

In the spring, Greene returns to Hanoi and has tea with Ho Chi Minh. Published are *Loser Take All* and, in December, *The Quiet American*. During the rest of his life, Greene will publish dozens of novels, plays, screenplays, essays, and memoirs. He will become one of the best-known and respected authors of the twentieth century. He dies on 3 April 1991 in Switzerland.

**1955–75: The United States Involvement in Vietnam and the Second Indochina War.**

I

# The Text

# THE QUIET AMERICAN

*paratext*
*Is this part of the novel?*
*or outside of it?*

*Dear Réné and Phuong,*

I have asked permission to dedicate this book to you not only in memory of the happy evenings I have spent with you in Saigon over the last five years, but also because I have quite shamelessly borrowed the location of your flat to house one of my characters, and your name, Phuong, for the convenience of readers because it is simple, beautiful and easy to pronounce, which is not true of all your country-women's names. You will both realize I have borrowed little else, certainly not the characters of anyone in Viet Nam. Pyle, Granger, Fowler, Vigot, Joe—these have had no originals in the life of Saigon or Hanoi, and General Thé is dead: shot in the back, so they say. Even the historical events have been in at least one case rearranged. For example, the big bomb near the Continental preceded and did not follow the bicycle bombs. I have no scruples about such small changes. <u>This is a story and not a piece of history</u>, and I hope that as a story about a few imaginary characters it will pass for both of you-one hot Saigon evening.

Yours affectionately,
*Graham Greene*

*calling attn to that which*
*it denies*

I do not like being moved: for the will is excited; and action
Is a most dangerous thing; I tremble for something factitious,
Some malpractice of heart and illegitimate process;
We're so prone to these things, with our terrible notions of duty.

—A. H. CLOUGH

This is the patent age of new inventions
For killing bodies, and for saving souls,
All propagated with the best intentions.

—BYRON

# PART ONE

# CHAPTER 1

After dinner I sat and waited for Pyle in my room over the rue Catinat; he had said, "I'll be with you at latest by ten," and when midnight struck I couldn't stay quiet any longer and went down into the street. A lot of old women in black trousers squatted on the landing: it was February and I suppose too hot for them in bed. One trishaw driver pedalled slowly by towards the river-front and I could see lamps burning where they had disembarked the new American planes. There was no sign of Pyle anywhere in the long street.

Of course, I told myself, he might have been detained for some reason at the American Legation, but surely in that case he would have telephoned to the restaurant—he was very meticulous about small courtesies. I turned to go indoors when I saw a girl waiting in the next doorway. I couldn't see her face, only the white silk trousers and the long flowered robe, but I knew her for all that. She had so often waited for me to come home at just this place and hour.

"Phuong," I said—which means Phoenix, but nothing nowadays is fabulous and nothing rises from its ashes. I knew before she had time to tell me that she was waiting for Pyle too. "He isn't here."

"*Je sais. Je t'ai vu seul à la fenêtre.*"

"You may as well wait upstairs," I said. "He will be coming soon."

"I can wait here."

"Better not. The police might pick you up."

She followed me upstairs. I thought of several ironic and unpleasant jests I might make, but neither her English nor her French would have been good enough for her to understand the irony, and, strange to say, I had no desire to hurt her or even to hurt myself. When we reached the landing all the old women turned their heads, and as soon as we had passed their voices rose and fell as though they were singing together.

"What are they talking about?"

"They think I have come home."

Inside my room the tree I had set up weeks ago for the Chinese New Year had shed most of its yellow blossoms. They had fallen between the keys of my typewriter. I picked them out. *"Tu es troublé,"* Phuong said.

"It's unlike him. He's such a punctual man."

I took off my tie and my shoes and lay down on the bed. Phuong lit the gas stove and began to boil the water for tea. It might have been six months ago. "He says you are going away soon now," she said.

"Perhaps."

"He is very fond of you."

"Thank him for nothing," I said.

I saw that she was doing her hair differently, allowing it to fall black and straight over her shoulders. I remembered that Pyle had once criticized the elaborate hairdressing which she thought became the daughter of a mandarin. I shut my eyes and she was again the same as she used to be: she was the hiss of steam, the clink of a cup, she was a certain hour of the night and the promise of rest.

"He will not be long," she said as though I needed comfort for his absence.

I wondered what they talked about together. Pyle was very earnest and I had suffered from his lectures on the Far East, which he had known for as many months as I had years. Democracy was another subject of his—he had pronounced and aggravating views on what the United States was doing for the world. Phuong on the other hand was wonderfully ignorant; if Hitler had come into the conversation she would have interrupted to ask who he was. The explanation would be all the more difficult because she had never met a German or a Pole and had only the vaguest knowledge of European geography, though about Princess Margaret of course she knew more than I. I heard her put a tray down on the end of the bed.

"Is he still in love with you, Phuong?"

To take an Annamite to bed with you is like taking a bird: they twitter and sing on your pillow. There had been a time when I thought none of their voices sang like Phuong's. I put out my hand and touched her arm—their bones too were as fragile as a bird's.

"Is he, Phuong?"

She laughed and I heard her strike a match. "In love?"—perhaps it was one of the phrases she didn't understand.

"May I make your pipe?" she asked.

When I opened my eyes she had lit the lamp and the tray was already prepared. The lamplight made her skin the colour of dark amber as she bent over the flame with a frown of concentration, heating the small paste of opium, twirling her needle.

"Does Pyle still not smoke?" I asked her.

"No."

"You ought to make him or he won't come back." It was a superstition among them that a lover who smoked would always return, even from France. A man's sexual capacity might be injured by smoking, but they would always prefer a faithful to a potent lover. Now she was kneading the little ball of hot paste on the convex margin of the bowl and I could smell the opium. There is no smell like it. Beside the bed my alarm-clock showed twelve-twenty, but already my tension was over. Pyle had diminished. The lamp lit her face as she tended the long pipe, bent over it with the serious attention she might have given to a child. I was fond of my pipe: more than two feet of straight bamboo, ivory at either end. Two-thirds of the way down was the bowl, like a convolvulus reversed, the convex margin polished and darkened by the frequent kneading of the opium. Now with a flick of the wrist she plunged the needle into the tiny cavity, released the opium and reversed the bowl over the flame, holding the pipe steady for me. The bead of opium bubbled gently and smoothly as I inhaled.

The practised inhaler can draw a whole pipe down in one breath, but I always had to take several pulls. Then I lay back, with my neck on the leather pillow, while she prepared the second pipe.

I said, "You know, really, it's as clear as daylight. Pyle knows I smoke a few pipes before bed, and he doesn't want to disturb me. He'll be round in the morning."

In went the needle and I took my second pipe. As I laid it down, I said, "Nothing to worry about. Nothing to worry about at all." I took a sip of tea and held my hand in the pit of her arm. "When you left me," I said, "it was lucky I had this to fall back on. There's a good house in the rue d'Ormay. What a fuss we Europeans make about nothing. You shouldn't live with a man who doesn't smoke, Phuong."

"But he's going to marry me," she said. "Soon now."

"Of course, that's another matter."

"Shall I make your pipe again?"

"Yes."

I wondered whether she would consent to sleep with me that night if Pyle never came, but I knew that when I had smoked four pipes I would no longer want her. Of course it would be agreeable to feel her thigh beside me in the bed—she always slept on her back, and when I woke in the morning I could start the day with a pipe, instead of with my own company. "Pyle won't come now," I said. "Stay here, Phuong." She held the pipe out to me and shook her head. By the time I had drawn the opium in, her presence or absence mattered very little.

"Why is Pyle not here?" she asked.

"How do I know?" I said.

"Did he go to see General Thé?"

"I wouldn't know."

"He told me if he could not have dinner with you, he wouldn't come here."

"Don't worry. He'll come. Make me another pipe." When she bent over the flame the poem of Baudelaire's came into my mind: *"Mon enfant, ma soeur . . ."* How did it go on?

> *Aimer à loisir,*
> *Aimer et mourir*
> *Au pays qui te ressemble.*

Out on the waterfront slept the ships, *"dont l'humeur est vagabonde."* I thought that if I smelt her skin it would have the faintest fragrance of opium, and her colour was that of the small flame. I had seen the flowers on her dress beside the canals in the north, she was indigenous like a herb, and I never wanted to go home.

"I wish I were Pyle," I said aloud, but the pain was limited and bearable—the opium saw to that. Somebody knocked on the door.

"Pyle," she said.

"No. It's not his knock."

Somebody knocked again impatiently. She got quickly up, shaking the yellow tree so that it showered its petals again over my typewriter. The door opened. "Monsieur Fowlair," a voice commanded.

"I'm Fowler," I said. I was not going to get up for a police-man—I could see his khaki shorts without lifting my head.

He explained in almost unintelligible Vietnamese French that I was needed immediately—at once—rapidly—at the Sureté.

"At the French Sureté or the Vietnamese?"

"The French." In his mouth the word sounded like *"Françung."*

"What about?"

He didn't know: it was his orders to fetch me.

*"Toi aussi,"* he said to Phuong.

"Say *vous* when you speak to a lady," I told him. "How did you know she was here?"

He only repeated that they were his orders.

"I'll come in the morning."

*"Sur le chung,"* he said, a little, neat, obstinate figure. There wasn't any point in arguing, so I got up and put on my tie and shoes. Here the police had the last word: they could with-draw my order of circulation: they could have me barred from Press Conferences: they could even, if they chose, refuse me an exit permit. These were the open legal methods, but le-gality was not essential in a country at war. I knew a man who had suddenly and inexplicably lost his cook—he had traced him to the Vietnamese Sureté, but the officers there assured him that he had been released after questioning. His family never saw him again. Perhaps he had joined the Communists; perhaps he had been enlisted in one of the private armies which flourished round Saigon—the Hoa-Haos or the Caoda-ists or General Thé. Perhaps he was in a French prison. Per-haps he was happily making money out of girls in Cholon,

the Chinese suburb. Perhaps his heart had given way when they questioned him. I said, "I'm not going to walk. You'll have to pay for a trishaw." One had to keep one's dignity.

That was why I refused a cigarette from the French officer at the Sureté. After three pipes I felt my mind clear and alert: it could take such decisions easily without losing sight of the main question—what do they want from me? I had met Vigot before several times at parties—I had noticed him because he appeared incongruously in love with his wife, who ignored him, a flashy and false blonde. Now it was two in the morning and he sat tired and depressed in the cigarette smoke and the heavy heat, wearing a green eye-shade, and he had a volume of Pascal open on his desk to while away the time. When I refused to allow him to question Phuong without me he gave way at once, with a single sigh that might have represented his weariness with Saigon, with the heat, or with the whole human condition.

He said in English, "I'm so sorry I had to ask you to come."

"I wasn't asked. I was ordered."

"Oh, these native police—they don't understand." His eyes were on a page of *Les Pensées* as though he were still absorbed in those sad arguments. "I wanted to ask you a few questions —about Pyle."

"You had better ask him the questions."

He turned to Phuong and interrogated her sharply in French. "How long have you lived with Monsieur Pyle?"

"A month—I don't know," she said.

"How much has he paid you?"

"You've no right to ask her that," I said. "She's not for sale."

"She used to live with you, didn't she?" he asked abruptly. "For two years."

"I'm a correspondent who's supposed to report your war— when you let him. Don't ask me to contribute to your scandal sheet as well."

"What do you know about Pyle? Please answer my questions, Monsieur Fowler. I don't want to ask them. But this is serious. Please believe me it is very serious."

"I'm not an informer. You know all I can tell you about

Pyle. Age thirty-two, employed in the Economic Aid Mission, nationality American."

"You sound like a friend of his," Vigot said, looking past me at Phuong. A native policeman came in with three cups of black coffee.

"Or would you rather have tea?" Vigot asked.

"I *am* a friend," I said. "Why not? I shall be going home one day, won't I? I can't take her with me. She'll be all right with him. It's a reasonable arrangement. And he's going to marry her, he says. He might, you know. He's a good chap in his way. Serious. Not one of those noisy bastards at the Continental. A quiet American," I summed him precisely up as I might have said, "a blue lizard," "a white elephant."

Vigot said, "Yes." He seemed to be looking for words on his desk with which to convey his meaning as precisely as I had done. "A very quiet American." He sat there in the little hot office waiting for one of us to speak. A mosquito droned to the attack and I watched Phuong. Opium makes you quick-witted —perhaps only because it calms the nerves and stills the emotions. Nothing, not even death, seems so important. Phuong, I thought, had not caught his tone, melancholy and final, and her English was very bad. While she sat there on the hard office chair, she was still waiting patiently for Pyle. I had at that moment given up waiting, and I could see Vigot taking those two facts in.

"How did you meet him first?" Vigot asked me.

Why should I explain to him that it was Pyle who had met me? I had seen him last September coming across the square towards the bar of the Continental: an unmistakably young and unused face flung at us like a dart. With his gangly legs and his crew-cut and his wide campus gaze he seemed incapable of harm. The tables on the street were most of them full. "Do you mind?" he had asked with serious courtesy. "My name's Pyle. I'm new here," and he had folded himself around a chair and ordered a beer. Then he looked quickly up into the hard noon glare.

"Was that a grenade?" he asked with excitement and hope.

"Most likely the exhaust of a car," I said, and was suddenly sorry for his disappointment. One forgets so quickly one's own youth: once I was interested myself in what for want of a better term they call news. But grenades had staled on me; they were something listed on the back page of the local paper—so many last night in Saigon, so many in Cholon: they never made the European Press. Up the street came the lovely flat figures—the white silk trousers, the long tight jackets in pink and mauve patterns slit up the thigh. I watched them with the nostalgia I knew I would feel when I had left these regions for ever. "They are lovely, aren't they?" I said over my beer, and Pyle cast them a cursory glance as they went up the rue Catinat.

"Oh, sure," he said indifferently: he was a serious type. "The Minister's very concerned about these grenades. It would be very awkward, he says, if there was an incident—with one of us, I mean."

"With one of you? Yes, I suppose that would be serious. Congress wouldn't like it." Why does one want to tease the innocent? Perhaps only ten days ago he had been walking back across the Common in Boston, his arms full of the books he had been reading in advance on the Far East and the problems of China. He didn't even hear what I said; he was absorbed already in the dilemmas of Democracy and the responsibilities of the West; he was determined—I learnt that very soon—to do good, not to any individual person but to a country, a continent, a world. Well, he was in his element now with the whole universe to improve.

"Is he in the mortuary?" I asked Vigot.

"How did you know he was dead?" It was a foolish policeman's question, unworthy of the man who read Pascal, unworthy also of the man who so strangely loved his wife. You cannot love without intuition.

"Not guilty," I said. I told myself that it was true. Didn't Pyle always go his own way? I looked for any feeling in myself, even resentment at a policeman's suspicion, but I could find none. No one but Pyle was responsible. Aren't we all better dead? the opium reasoned within me. But I looked cautiously at Phuong, for it was hard on her. She must have loved him in her way: hadn't she been fond of me and hadn't she left me for Pyle? She had attached herself to youth and hope and seriousness and now they had failed her more than age and despair. She sat there looking at the two of us and I thought she had not yet understood. Perhaps it would be a good thing if I could get her away before the fact got home. I was ready to answer any questions if I could bring the interview quickly and ambiguously to an end, so that I might tell her later, in private, away from a policeman's eye and the hard office chairs and the bare globe where the moths circled.

I said to Vigot, "What hours are you interested in?"

"Between six and ten."

"I had a drink at the Continental at six. The waiters will remember. At six forty-five I walked down to the quay to watch the American planes unloaded. I saw Wilkins of the Associated News by the door of the Majestic. Then I went into the cinema next door. They'll probably remember—they had to get me change. From there I took a trishaw to the Vieux Moulin—I suppose I arrived about eight thirty—and had dinner by myself. Granger was there—you can ask him. Then I took a trishaw back about a quarter to ten. You could probably find the driver. I was expecting Pyle at ten, but he didn't turn up."

"Why were you expecting him?"

"He telephoned me. He said he had to see me about something important."

"Have you any idea what?"

"No. Everything was important to Pyle."

"And this girl of his?—do you know where she was?"

"She was waiting for him outside at midnight. She was anxious. She knows nothing. Why, can't you see she's waiting for him still?"

"Yes," he said.

"And you can't really believe I killed him for jealousy—or she for what? He was going to marry her."

"Yes."

"Where did you find him?"

"He was in the water under the bridge to Dakow."

The Vieux Moulin stood beside the bridge. There were armed police on the bridge and the restaurant had an iron grille to keep out grenades. It wasn't safe to cross the bridge at night, for all the far side of the river was in the hands of the Vietminh after dark. I must have dined within fifty yards of his body.

"The trouble was," I said, "he got mixed up."

"To speak plainly," Vigot said, "I am not altogether sorry. He was doing a lot of harm."

"God save us always," I said, "from the innocent and the good."

"The good?"

"Yes, good. In his way. You're a Roman Catholic. You wouldn't recognize his way. And anyway, he was a damned Yankee."

"Would you mind identifying him? I'm sorry. It's a routine, not a very nice routine."

I didn't bother to ask him why he didn't wait for someone from the American Legation, for I knew the reason. French methods are a little old-fashioned by our cold standards: they believe in the conscience, the sense of guilt, a criminal should be confronted with his crime, for he may break down and betray himself. I told myself again I was innocent, while he went down the stone stairs to where the refrigerating plant hummed in the basement.

They pulled him out like a tray of ice-cubes, and I looked at him. The wounds were frozen into placidity. I said, "You see, they don't re-open in my presence."

"*Comment?*"

"Isn't that one of the objects? Ordeal by something or other? But you've frozen him stiff. They didn't have deep freezes in the Middle Ages."

"You recognize him?"

"Oh yes."

He looked more than ever out of place: he should have stayed at home. I saw him in a family snapshot album, riding on a dude ranch, bathing on Long Island, photographed with his colleagues in some apartment on the twenty-third floor. He belonged to the skyscraper and the express elevator, the ice-cream and the dry Martinis, milk at lunch, and chicken sandwiches on the Merchant Limited.

"He wasn't dead from this," Vigot said, pointing at a wound in the chest. "He was drowned in the mud. We found the mud in his lungs."

"You work quickly."

"One has to in this climate."

They pushed the tray back and closed the door. The rubber padded.

"You can't help us at all?" Vigot asked.

"Not at all."

I walked back with Phuong towards my flat. I was no longer on my dignity. Death takes away vanity—even the vanity of the cuckold who mustn't show his pain. She was still unaware of what it was about, and I had no technique for telling her slowly and gently. I was a correspondent: I thought in headlines. "American official murdered in Saigon." Working on a newspaper one does not learn the way to break bad news, and even now I had to think of my paper and to ask her, "Do you mind stopping at the cable office?" I left her in the street and sent my wire and came back to her. It was only a gesture: I knew too well that the French correspondents would already be informed, or if Vigot had played fair (which was possible), then the censors would hold my telegram till the French had filed theirs. My paper would get the news first under a Paris dateline. Not that Pyle was very important. It wouldn't have done to cable the details of his true career, that before he died he had been responsible for at least fifty deaths, for it would have damaged Anglo-American relations, the Minister would have been upset. The Minister had a great respect for Pyle—Pyle had taken a good degree in—well, one of those subjects Americans can take degrees in: perhaps public relations or theatrecraft, perhaps even Far Eastern studies (he had read a lot of books).

"Where is Pyle?" Phuong asked. "What did they want?"

"Come home," I said.

"Will Pyle come?"

"He's as likely to come there as anywhere else."

The old women were still gossiping on the landing, in the relative cool. When I opened my door I could tell my room had been searched: everything was tidier than I ever left it.

"Another pipe?" Phuong asked.

"Yes."

I took off my tie and my shoes; the interlude was over; the night was nearly the same as it had been. Phuong crouched at the end of the bed and lit the lamp. *Mon enfant, ma soeur*— skin the colour of amber. *Sa douce langue natale.*

"Phuong," I said. She was kneading the opium on the bowl. *"Il est mort*, Phuong." She held the needle in her hand and looked up at me like a child trying to concentrate, frowning. *"Tu dis?"*

"Pyle *est mort. Assassiné."*

She put the needle down and sat back on her heels, looking at me. There was no scene, no tears, just thought—the long private thought of somebody who has to alter a whole course of life.

"You had better stay here tonight," I said.

She nodded and taking up the needle again began to heat the opium. That night I woke from one of those short deep opium sleeps, ten minutes long, that seem a whole night's rest, and found my hand where it had always lain at night, between her legs. She was asleep and I could hardly hear her breathing. Once again after so many months I was not alone, and yet I thought suddenly with anger, remembering Vigot and his eye-shade in the police station and the quiet corridors of the Legation with no one about and the soft hairless skin under my hand, "Am I the only one who really cared for Pyle?"

# CHAPTER 2

1

The morning Pyle arrived in the square by the Continental I had seen enough of my American colleagues of the Press, big, noisy, boyish and middle-aged, full of sour cracks against the French, who were, when all was said, fighting this war. Periodically, after an engagement had been tidily finished and the casualties removed from the scene, they would be summoned to Hanoi, nearly four hours' flight away, addressed by the Commander-in-Chief, lodged for one night in a Press Camp where they boasted that the barman was the best in Indo-China, flown over the late battlefield at a height of 3,000 feet (the limit of a heavy machine-gun's range) and then delivered safely and noisily back, like a school-treat, to the Continental Hotel in Saigon.

Pyle was quiet, he seemed modest, sometimes that first day I had to lean forward to catch what he was saying. And he was very, very serious. Several times he seemed to shrink up within himself at the noise of the American Press on the terrace above—the terrace which was popularly believed to be safer from hand-grenades. But he criticized nobody.

"Have you read York Harding?" he asked.

"No. No, I don't think so. What did he write?"

He gazed at a milk-bar across the street and said dreamily, "That looks like a soda-fountain." I wondered what depth of homesickness lay behind his odd choice of what to observe in a scene so unfamiliar. But hadn't I on my first walk up the rue Catinat noticed first the shop with the Guerlain perfume and comforted myself with the thought that, after all, Europe was only distant thirty hours? He looked reluctantly away from the milk-bar and said, "York wrote a book called *The Advance of Red China*. It's a very profound book."

"I haven't read it. Do you know him?"

He nodded solemnly and lapsed into silence. But he broke it again a moment later to modify the impression he had given. "I don't know him well," he said. "I guess I only met him twice." I liked him for that—to consider it was boasting to claim acquaintance with—what was his name?—York Harding. I was to learn later that he had an enormous respect for what he called serious writers. That term excluded novelists, poets and dramatists unless they had what he called a contemporary theme, and even then it was better to read the straight stuff as you got it from York.

I said, "You know, if you live in a place for long you cease to read about it."

"Of course I always like to know what the man on the spot has to say," he replied guardedly.

"And then check it with York?"

"Yes." Perhaps he had noticed the irony, because he added with his habitual politeness, "I'd take it as a very great privilege if you could find time to brief me on the main points. You see, York was here more than two years ago."

· I liked his loyalty to Harding—whoever Harding was. It was a change from the denigrations of the Pressmen and their immature cynicism. I said, "Have another bottle of beer and I'll try to give you an idea of things."

I began, while he watched me intently like a prize pupil, by explaining the situation in the north, in Tonkin, where the French in those days were hanging on to the delta of the Red River, which contained Hanoi and the only northern port, Haiphong. Here most of the rice was grown, and when the harvest was ready the annual battle for the rice always began.

"That's the north," I said. "The French may hold, poor devils, if the Chinese don't come to help the Vietminh. A war of jungle and mountain and marsh, paddy fields where you wade shoulder-high and the enemy simply disappear, bury their arms, put on peasant dress. But you can rot comfortably in the damp in Hanoi. They don't throw bombs there. God knows why. You could call it a regular war."

"And here in the south?"

"The French control the main roads until seven in the evening: they control the watch towers after that, and the towns —part of them. That doesn't mean you are safe, or there wouldn't be iron grilles in front of the restaurants."

How often I had explained all this before. I was a record always turned on for the benefit of newcomers—the visiting Member of Parliament, the new British Minister. Sometimes I would wake up in the night saying, "Take the case of the Caodaists." Or the Hoa-Haos or the Binh Xuyen, all the private armies who sold their services for money or revenge. Strangers found them picturesque, but there is nothing picturesque in treachery and distrust.

"And now," I said, "there's General Thé. He was Caodaist Chief of Staff, but he's taken to the hills to fight both sides, the French, the Communists . . ."

"York," Pyle said, "wrote that what the East needed was a Third Force." Perhaps I should have seen that fanatic gleam, the quick response to a phrase, the magic sound of figures: Fifth Column, Third Force, Seventh Day. I might have saved all of us a lot of trouble, even Pyle, if I had realized the direction of that indefatigable young brain. But I left him with arid bones of background and took my daily walk up and down the rue Catinat. He would have to learn for himself the real background that held you as a smell does: the gold of the rice-fields under a flat late sun: the fishers' fragile cranes hovering over the fields like mosquitoes: the cups of tea on an old abbot's platform, with his bed and his commercial calendars, his buckets and broken cups and the junk of a lifetime washed up around his chair: the mollusc hats of the girls repairing the road where a mine had burst: the gold and the young green and the bright dresses of the south, and in the north the deep browns and the black clothes and the circle of enemy mountains and the drone of planes. When I first came I counted the days of my assignment, like a schoolboy marking off the days of term; I thought I was tied to what was left of a Bloomsbury square and the 73 bus passing the portico of Euston and springtime in the local in Torrington Place. Now the bulbs would be out in the square garden, and I didn't care a damn. I wanted a day punctuated by those quick reports that might be car-exhausts or might be grenades, I wanted to keep the sight of those silk-trousered figures moving with grace through the humid noon, I wanted Phuong, and my home had shifted its ground eight thousand miles.

I turned at the High Commissioner's house, where the Foreign Legion stood on guard in their white képis and their scarlet epaulettes, crossed by the Cathedral and came back by the dreary wall of the Vietnamese Sureté that seemed to smell of urine and injustice. And yet that too was a part of home, like the dark passages on upper floors one avoided in childhood. The new dirty magazines were out on the bookstalls near the quay—*Tabu* and *Illusion*, and the sailors were drinking beer on the pavement, an easy mark for a home-made bomb. I thought of Phuong, who would be haggling over the price of fish in the third street down on the left before going for her elevenses to the milk-bar (I always knew where she was in those days), and Pyle ran easily and naturally out of my mind. I didn't even mention him to Phuong, when we sat down to lunch together in our room over the rue Catinat and she wore her best flowered silk robe because it was two years to a day since we had met in the Grand Monde in Cholon.

2

Neither of us mentioned him when we woke on the morning after his death. Phuong had risen before I was properly awake and had our tea ready. One is not jealous of the dead, and it seemed easy to me that morning to take up our old life together.

"Will you stay tonight?" I asked Phuong over the *croissants* as casually as I could.

"I will have to fetch my box."

"The police may be there," I said. "I had better come with you." It was the nearest we came that day to speaking of Pyle.

Pyle had a flat in a new villa near the rue Duranton, off one of those main streets which the French continually subdivided in honour of their generals—so that the rue de Gaulle became after the third intersection the rue Leclerc, and that again sooner or later would probably turn abruptly into the rue de Lattre. Somebody important must have been arriving from Europe by air, for there was a policeman facing the pavement every twenty yards along the route to the High Commissioner's Residence.

On the gravel drive to Pyle's apartment were several motor-cycles and a Vietnamese policeman examined my press-card. He wouldn't allow Phuong into the house, so I went in search of a French officer. In Pyle's bathroom Vigot was washing his hands with Pyle's soap and drying them on Pyle's towel. His tropical suit had a stain of oil on the sleeve—Pyle's oil, I supposed.

"Any news?" I asked.

"We found his car in the garage. It's empty of petrol. He must have gone off last night in a trishaw—or in somebody else's car. Perhaps the petrol was drained away."

"He might even have walked," I said. "You know what Americans are."

"Your car was burnt, wasn't it?" he went thoughtfully on. "You haven't a new one yet?"

"No."

"It's not an important point."

"No."

"Have you any views?" he asked.

"Too many," I said.

"Tell me."

"Well, he might have been murdered by the Vietminh. They have murdered plenty of people in Saigon. His body was found in the river by the bridge to Dakow—Vietminh territory when your police withdraw at night. Or he might have been killed by the Vietnamese Sureté—it's been known. Perhaps they didn't like his friends. Perhaps he was killed by Caodaists because he knew General Thé."

"Did he?"

"They say so. Perhaps he was killed by General Thé because he knew the Caodaists. Perhaps he was killed by the Hoa-Haos for making passes at the General's concubines. Perhaps he was just killed by someone who wanted his money."

"Or a simple case of jealousy," Vigot said.

"Or perhaps by the French Sureté," I continued, "because they didn't like his contacts. Are you really looking for the people who killed him?"

"No," Vigot said. "I'm just making a report, that's all. So long as it's an act of war—well, there are thousands killed every year."

"You can rule me out," I said. "I'm not involved. Not involved," I repeated. It had been an article of my creed. The human condition being what it was, let them fight, let them love, let them murder, I would not be involved. My fellow journalists called themselves correspondents; I preferred the title of reporter. I wrote what I saw. I took no action—even an opinion is a kind of action.

"What are you doing here?"

"I've come for Phuong's belongings. Your police wouldn't let her in."

"Well, let us go and find them."

"It's nice of you, Vigot."

Pyle had two rooms, a kitchen and bathroom. We went to the bedroom. I knew where Phuong would keep her box—under the bed. We pulled it out together; it contained her picture books. I took her few spare clothes out of the wardrobe, her two good robes and her spare trousers. One had a sense that they had been hanging there for a few hours only and didn't belong, they were in passage like a butterfly in a room. In a drawer I found her small triangular *culottes* and her collection of scarves. There was really very little to put in the box, less than a week-end visitor's at home.

In the sitting-room there was a photograph of herself and Pyle. They had been photographed in the botanical gardens beside a large stone dragon. She held Pyle's dog on a leash—a black chow with a black tongue. A too black dog. I put the photograph in her box. "What's happened to the dog?" I said.

"It isn't here. He may have taken it with him."

"Perhaps it will return and you can analyse the earth on its paws."

"I'm not Lecoq, or even Maigret, and there's a war on."

I went across to the bookcase and examined the two rows of books—Pyle's library. *The Advance of Red China, The Challenge to Democracy, The Rôle of the West*—these, I suppose, were the complete works of York Harding. There were a lot of Congressional Reports, a Vietnamese phrase book, a history of the War in the Philippines, a Modern Library Shakespeare. On what did he relax? I found his light reading on another shelf: a portable Thomas Wolfe and a

mysterious anthology called *The Triumph of Life* and a selection
of American poetry. There was also a book of chess problems.
It didn't seem much for the end of the working day, but, after
all, he had had Phuong. Tucked away behind the anthology
there was a paper-backed book called *The Physiology of Marriage*. Perhaps he was studying sex, as he had studied the East,
on paper. And the keyword was marriage. Pyle believed in being
involved.

His desk was quite bare. "You've made a clean sweep," I
said.

"Oh," Vigot said, "I had to take charge of these on behalf
of the American Legation. You know how quickly rumour
spreads. There might have been looting. I had all his papers
sealed up." He said it seriously without even smiling.

"Anything damaging?"

"We can't afford to find anything damaging against an
ally," Vigot said.

"Would you mind if I took one of these books—as a
keepsake?"

"I'll look the other way."

I chose York Harding's *The Rôle of the West* and packed it
in the box with Phuong's clothes.

"As a friend," Vigot said, "is there nothing you could tell
me in confidence? My report's all tied up. He was murdered by
the Communists. Perhaps the beginning of a campaign against
American aid. But between you and me—listen, it's dry talking,
what about a vermouth cassis round the corner?"

"Too early."

"He didn't confide anything to you the last time he saw
you?"

"No."

"When was that?"

"Yesterday morning. After the big bang."

He paused to let my reply sink in—to my mind, not to his:
he interrogated fairly. "You were out when he called on you
last night?"

"Last night? I must have been. I didn't think . . ."

"You may be wanting an exit visa. You know we could delay
it indefinitely."

"Do you really believe," I said, "that I want to go home?"

Vigot looked through the window at the bright cloudless day. He said sadly, "Most people do."

"I like it here. At home there are—problems."

"*Merde*," Vigot said, "here's the American Economic Attaché." He repeated with sarcasm, "Economic Attaché."

"I'd better be off. He'll want to seal me up too."

Vigot said wearily, "I wish you luck. He'll have a terrible lot to say to me."

The Economic Attaché was standing by his Packard when I came out, trying to explain something to his driver. He was a stout middle-aged man with an exaggerated bottom and a face that looked as if it never needed a razor. He called out, "Fowler. Could you explain to this darned driver . . . ?"

I explained.

He said, "But that's just what I told him, but he always pretends not to understand French."

"It may be a matter of accent."

"I was three years in Paris. My accent's good enough for one of these darned Vietnamese."

"The voice of Democracy," I said.

"What's that?"

"I expect it's a book by York Harding."

"I don't get you." He took a suspicious look at the box I carried. "What've you got there?" he said.

"Two pairs of white silk trousers, two silk robes, some girl's underpants—three pairs, I think. All home products. No American aid."

"Have you been up there?" he asked.

"Yes."

"You heard the news?"

"Yes."

"It's a terrible thing," he said, "terrible."

"I expect the Minister's very disturbed."

"I should say. He's with the High Commissioner now, and he's asked for an interview with the President." He put his hand on my arm and walked me away from the cars. "You knew young Pyle well, didn't you? I can't get over a thing like that happening to him. I knew his father. Professor Harold C. Pyle—you'll have heard of him?"

"No."

"He's the world authority on underwater erosion. Didn't you see his picture on the cover of *Time* the other month?"

"Oh, I think I remember. A crumbling cliff in the background and gold-rimmed glasses in the foreground."

"That's him. I had to draft the cable home. It was terrible. I loved that boy like he was my son."

"That makes you closely related to his father."

He turned his wet brown eyes on me. He said, "What's getting you? That's not the way to talk when a fine young fellow . . ."

"I'm sorry," I said. "Death takes people in different ways." Perhaps he had really loved Pyle. "What did you say in your cable?" I asked.

He replied seriously and literally, " 'Grieved to report your son died a soldier's death in cause of Democracy.' The Minister signed it."

"A soldier's death," I said. "Mightn't that prove a bit confusing? I mean to the folks at home. The Economic Aid Mission doesn't sound like the Army. Do you get Purple Hearts?"

He said in a low voice, tense with ambiguity, "He had special duties."

"Oh yes, we all guessed that."

"He didn't talk, did he?"

"Oh no," I said, and Vigot's phrase came back to me, "He was a very quiet American."

"Have you any hunch," he asked, "why they killed him? and who?"

Suddenly I was angry; I was tired of the whole pack of them with their private stores of Coca-Cola and their portable hospitals and their too wide cars and their not quite latest guns. I said, "Yes. They killed him because he was too innocent to live. He was young and ignorant and silly and he got involved. He had no more of a notion than any of you what the whole affair's about, and you gave him money and York

Harding's books on the East and said, 'Go ahead. Win the East for Democracy.'" He never saw anything he hadn't heard in a lecture-hall, and his writers and his lecturers made a fool of him. When he saw a dead body he couldn't even see the wounds. A Red menace, a soldier of democracy.'"

"I thought you were his friend," he said in a tone of reproach.

"I *was* his friend. I'd have liked to see him reading the Sunday supplements at home and following the baseball. I'd have liked to see him safe with a standardized American girl who subscribed to the Book Club."

He cleared his throat with embarrassment. "Of course," he said, "I'd forgotten that unfortunate business. I was quite on your side, Fowler. He behaved very badly. I don't mind telling you I had a long talk with him about the girl. You see, I had the advantage of knowing Professor and Mrs. Pyle."

I said, "Vigot's waiting," and walked away. For the first time he spotted Phuong and when I looked back at him he was watching me with pained perplexity: an eternal brother who didn't understand.

# CHAPTER 3

## 1

The first time Pyle met Phuong was again at the Continental, perhaps two months after his arrival. It was the early evening, in the momentary cool which came when the sun had just gone down, and the candles were lit on the stalls in the side streets. The dice rattled on the tables where the French were playing *Quatre Cent Vingt-et-un* and the girls in the white silk trousers bicycled home down the rue Catinat. Phuong was drinking a glass of orange juice and I was having a beer and we sat in silence, content to be together. Then Pyle came tentatively across, and I introduced them. He had a way of staring hard at a girl as though he hadn't seen one before and then blushing. "I was wondering whether you and your lady," Pyle said, "would step across and join my table. One of our attachés . . ."

It was the Economic Attaché. He beamed down at us from the terrace above, a great warm welcoming smile, full of confidence, like the man who keeps his friends because he uses the right deodorants. I had heard him called Joe a number of times, but I had never learnt his surname. He made a noisy show of pulling out chairs and calling for the waiter, though all that activity could possibly produce at the Continental was a choice of beer, brandy-and-soda or vermouth cassis. "Didn't expect to see you here, Fowler," he said. "We are waiting for the boys back from Hanoi. There seems to have been quite a battle. Weren't you with them?"

"I'm tired of flying four hours for a Press Conference," I said.

He looked at me with disapproval. He said, "These guys are real keen. Why, I expect they could earn twice as much in business or on the radio without any risk."

"They might have to work," I said.

"They seem to sniff the battle like war-horses," he went on exultantly, paying no attention to words he didn't like. "Bill Granger—you can't keep him out of a scrap."

"I expect you're right. I saw him in one the other evening at the bar of the Sporting."

"You know very well I didn't mean that."

Two trishaw drivers came pedalling furiously down the rue Catinat and drew up in a photo-finish outside the Continental. In the first was Granger. The other contained a small, grey, silent heap which Granger now began to pull out on to the pavement. "Oh, come on, Mick," he said, "come on." Then he began to argue with his driver about the fare. "Here," he said, "take it or leave it," and flung five times the correct amount into the street for the man to stoop for.

The Economic Attaché said nervously, "I guess these boys deserve a little relaxation."

Granger flung his burden on to a chair. Then he noticed Phuong. "Why," he said, "you old so-and-so, Joe. Where did you find her? Didn't know you had a whistle in you. Sorry, got to find the can. Look after Mick."

"Rough soldierly manners," I said.

Pyle said earnestly, blushing again, "I wouldn't have invited you two over if I'd thought . . ."

The grey heap stirred in the chair and the head fell on the table as though it wasn't attached. It sighed, a long whistling sigh of infinite tedium, and lay still.

"Do you know him?" I asked Pyle.

"No. Isn't he one of the Press?"

"I heard Bill call him Mick," the Economic Attaché said.

"Isn't there a new U.P. correspondent?"

"It's not him. I know him. What about your Economic Mission? You can't know all your people—there are hundreds of them."

"I don't think he belongs," the Economic Attaché said. "I can't recollect him."

"We might find his identity card," Pyle suggested.

"For God's sake don't wake him. One drunk's enough. Anyway Granger will know."

But he didn't. He came gloomily back from the lavatory. "Who's the dame?" he asked morosely.

"Miss Phuong is a friend of Fowler's," Pyle said stiffly. "We want to know who . . ."

"Where'd he find her? You got to be careful in this town."
He added gloomily, "Thank God for penicillin."

"Bill," the Economic Attaché said, "we want to know who
Mick is."

"Search me."

"But you brought him here."

"The Frogs can't take Scotch. He passed out."

"Is he French? I thought you called him Mick."

"Had to call him something," Granger said. He leant over
to Phuong and said, "Here. You. Have another glass of orange?
Got a date tonight?"

I said, "She's got a date every night."

The Economic Attaché said hurriedly, "<u>How's the war, Bill?</u>"

"Great victory north-west of Hanoi. French recaptured two
villages they never told us they'd lost. Heavy Vietminh casualties. Haven't been able to count their own yet but will let us
know in a week or two."

The Economic Attaché said, "There's a rumour that the
Vietminh have broken into Phat Diem, burned the Cathedral,
chased out the Bishop."

"They wouldn't tell us about that in Hanoi. That's not a
victory."

"One of our medical teams couldn't get beyond Nam
Dinh," Pyle said.

"You didn't get down as far as that, Bill?" the Economic
Attaché asked.

"Who do you think I am? I'm a correspondent with an
*Ordre de Circulation* which shows when I'm out of bounds. I
fly to Hanoi airport. They give us a car to the Press Camp.
They lay on a flight over the two towns they've recaptured and
show us the tricolour flying. It might be any darned flag at that
height. Then we have a Press Conference and a colonel explains
to us what we've been looking at. Then we file our cables with
the censor. Then we have drinks. Best barman in Indo-China.
Then we catch the plane back."

Pyle frowned at his beer.

"You underrate yourself, Bill," the Economic Attaché said.
"Why, that account of Road 66—what did you call it? Highway
to Hell—that was worthy of the Pulitzer. You know the

*representation*

story I mean—the man with his head blown off kneeling in the ditch, and that other you saw walking in a dream . . ."

"Do you think I'd really go near their stinking highway? Stephen Crane could describe a war without seeing one. Why shouldn't I? It's only a damned colonial war anyway. Get me another drink. And then let's go and find a girl. You've got a piece of tail. I want a piece of tail too."

I said to Pyle, "Do you think there's anything in the rumour about Phat Diem?"

"I don't know. Is it important? I'd like to go and have a look," he said, "if it's important."

"Important to the Economic Mission?"

"Oh, well," he said, "you can't draw hard lines. Medicine's a kind of weapon, isn't it? These Catholics, they'd be pretty strong against the Communists, wouldn't they?"

"They trade with the Communists. The Bishop gets his cows and the bamboo for his building from the Communists. I wouldn't say they were exactly York Harding's Third Force," I teased him.

"Break it up," Granger was shouting. "Can't waste the whole night here. I'm off to the House of Five Hundred Girls."

"If you and Miss Phuong would have dinner with me . . ." Pyle said.

"You can eat at the Chalet," Granger interrupted him, "while I'm knocking the girls next door. Come on, Joe. Anyway you're a man."

I think it was then, wondering what a man is, that I felt my first affection for Pyle. He sat a little turned away from Granger, twisting his beer mug, with an expression of determined remoteness. He said to Phuong, "I guess you get tired of all this shop—about your country, I mean?"

"*Comment?*"

"What are you going to do with Mick?" the Economic Attaché asked.

"Leave him here," Granger said.

"You can't do that. You don't even know his name."

"We could bring him along and let the girls look after him."

The Economic Attaché gave a loud communal laugh. He looked like a face on television. He said, "You young people can do what you want, but I'm too old for games. I'll take him home with me. Did you say he was French?"

"He spoke French."

"If you can get him into my car . . ."

After he had driven away, Pyle took a trishaw with Granger, and Phuong and I followed along the road to Cholon. Granger had made an attempt to get into the trishaw with Phuong, but Pyle diverted him. As they pedalled us down the long suburban road to the Chinese town a line of French armoured cars went by, each with its jutting gun and silent officer motionless like a figurehead under the stars and the black, smooth, concave sky—trouble again probably with a private army, the Binh Xuyen, who ran the Grand Monde and the gambling halls of Cholon. This was a land of rebellious barons. It was like Europe in the Middle Ages. But what were the Americans doing here? Columbus had not yet discovered their country. I said to Phuong, "I like that fellow, Pyle."

"He's quiet," she said, and the adjective which she was the first to use stuck like a schoolboy name, till I heard even Vigot use it, sitting there with his green eye-shade, telling me of Pyle's death.

I stopped our trishaw outside the Chalet and said to Phuong, "Go in and find a table. I had better look after Pyle." That was my first instinct—to protect him. It never occurred to me that there was greater need to protect myself. Innocence always calls mutely for protection when we would be so much wiser to guard ourselves against it: innocence is like a dumb leper who has lost his bell, wandering the world, meaning no harm.

When I reached the House of the Five Hundred Girls, Pyle and Granger had gone inside. I asked at the military police post just inside the doorway, *"Deux Américains?"*

He was a young Foreign Legion corporal. He stopped cleaning his revolver and jutted his thumb towards the doorway beyond, making a joke in German. I couldn't understand it.

It was the hour of rest in the immense courtyard which lay open to the sky. Hundreds of girls lay on the grass or sat on their heels talking to their companions. The curtains were undrawn in the little cubicles around the square—one tired girl lay alone on a bed with her ankles crossed. There was trouble in Cholon and the troops were confined to quarters and there was no work to be done: the Sunday of the body. Only a knot of fighting, scrabbling, shouting girls showed me where custom was still alive. I remembered the old Saigon story of the distinguished visitor who had lost his trousers fighting his way back to the safety of the police post. There was no protection here for the civilian. If he chose to poach on military territory, he must look after himself and find his own way out.

I had learnt a technique—to divide and conquer. I chose one in the crowd that gathered round me and edged her slowly towards the spot where Pyle and Granger struggled.

"*Je suis un vieux*," I said. "*Trop fatigué.*" She giggled and pressed. "*Mon ami,*" I said, "*il est très riche, très vigoureux.*"

"*Tu es sale,*" she said.

I caught sight of Granger flushed and triumphant; it was as though he took this demonstration as a tribute to his manhood. One girl had her arm through Pyle's and was trying to tug him gently out of the ring. I pushed my girl in among them and called to him, "Pyle, over here."

He looked at me over their heads and said, "It's terrible. Terrible." It may have been a trick of the lamplight, but his face looked haggard. It occurred to me that he was quite possibly a virgin.

"Come along, Pyle," I said. "Leave them to Granger." I saw his hand move towards his hip pocket. I really believe he intended to empty his pockets of piastres and greenbacks. "Don't be a fool, Pyle," I called sharply. "You'll have them fighting." My girl was turning back to me and I gave her another push into the inner ring round Granger. "*Non, non,*" I said, "*je suis un Anglais, pauvre, très pauvre.*" Then I got hold of Pyle's sleeve and dragged him out, with the girl hanging on to his other arm like a hooked fish. Two or three girls tried to intercept us before we got to the gateway where the corporal stood watching, but they were half-hearted.

"What'll I do with this one?" Pyle said.

"She won't be any trouble," and at that moment she let go his arm and dived back into the scrimmage round Granger.

"Will he be all right?" Pyle asked anxiously.

"He's got what he wanted—a bit of tail."

The night outside seemed very quiet with only another squadron of armoured cars driving by like people with a purpose. He said, "It's terrible. I wouldn't have believed . . ." He said with sad awe, "They were so pretty." He was not envying Granger, he was complaining that anything good—and prettiness and grace are surely forms of goodness—should be marred or ill-treated. Pyle could see pain when it was in front of his eyes. (I don't write that as a sneer; after all there are many of us who can't.)

I said, "Come back to the Chalet. Phuong's waiting."

"I'm sorry," he said. "I quite forgot. You shouldn't have left her."

"*She* wasn't in danger."

"I just thought I'd see Granger safely . . ." He dropped again into his thoughts, but as we entered the Chalet he said with obscure distress, "I'd forgotten how many men there are . . ."

2

Phuong had kept us a table at the edge of the dance-floor and the orchestra was playing some tune which had been popular in Paris five years ago. Two Vietnamese couples were dancing, small, neat, aloof, with an air of civilization we couldn't match. (I recognized one, an accountant from the Banque de l'Indo-Chine and his wife.) They never, one felt, dressed carelessly, said the wrong word, were a prey to untidy passion. If the war seemed medieval, they were like the eighteenth-century future. One would have expected Mr. Pham-Van-Tu to write Augustans in his spare time, but I happened to know he was a student of Wordsworth and wrote nature poems. His holidays he spent at Dalat, the nearest he could get to the atmosphere of the English lakes. He bowed slightly as he came round. I wondered how Granger had fared fifty yards up the road.

Pyle was apologizing to Phuong in bad French for having kept her waiting. "*C'est impardonable*," he said.

"Where have you been?" she asked him.

He said, "I was seeing Granger home."

"Home?" I said and laughed, and Pyle looked at me as though I were another Granger. Suddenly I saw myself as he saw me, a man of middle age, with eyes a little bloodshot, beginning to put on weight, ungraceful in love, less noisy than Granger perhaps but more cynical, less innocent, and I saw Phuong for a moment as I had seen her first, dancing past my table at the Grand Monde in a white ball-dress, eighteen years old, watched by an elder sister who had been determined on a good European marriage. An American had bought a ticket and asked her for a dance: he was a little drunk—not harmfully, and I suppose he was new to the country and thought the hostesses of the Grand Monde were whores. He held her much too close as they went round the floor the first time, and then suddenly there she was, going back to sit with her sister, and he was left, stranded and lost among the dancers, not knowing what had happened or why. And the girl whose name I didn't know sat quietly there, occasionally sipping her orange juice, owning herself completely.

"*Peut-on avoir l'honneur?*" Pyle was saying in his terrible accent, and a moment later I saw them dancing in silence at the other end of the room, Pyle holding her so far away from him that you expected him at any moment to sever contact. He was a very bad dancer, and she had been the best dancer I had ever known in her days at the Grand Monde.

It had been a long and frustrating courtship. If I could have offered marriage and a settlement everything would have been easy, and the elder sister would have slipped quietly and tactfully away whenever we were together. But three months passed before I saw her so much as momentarily alone, on a balcony at the Majestic, while her sister in the next room kept on asking when we proposed to come in. A cargo boat from France was being unloaded in Saigon River by the light of flares, the trishaw bells rang like telephones, and I might have been a young and inexperienced fool for all I found to say. I went back hopelessly to my bed in the rue Catinat and never dreamed that four months later she would be lying beside me, a little out of breath, laughing as though with surprise because nothing had been quite what she expected.

"Monsieur Fowlair." I had been watching them dance and hadn't seen her sister signalling to me from another table. Now she came over and I reluctantly asked her to sit down. We had never been friends since the night she was taken ill in the Grand Monde and I had seen Phuong home.

"I haven't seen you for a whole year," she said.

"I am away so often at Hanoi."

"Who is your friend?" she asked.

"A man called Pyle."

"What does he do?"

"He belongs to the American Economic Mission. You know the kind of thing—electrical sewing machines for starving seamstresses."

"Are there any?"

"I don't know."

"But they don't use sewing machines. There wouldn't be any electricity where they live." She was a very literal woman.

"You'll have to ask Pyle," I said.

"Is he married?"

I looked at the dance-floor. "I should say that's as near as he ever got to a woman."

"He dances very badly," she said.

"Yes."

"But he looks a nice reliable man."

"Yes."

"Can I sit with you for a little? My friends are very dull."

The music stopped and Pyle bowed stiffly to Phuong, then led her back and drew out her chair. I could tell that his formality pleased her. I thought how much she missed in her relation to me.

"This is Phuong's sister," I said to Pyle. "Miss Hei."

"I'm very glad to meet you," he said and blushed.

"You come from New York?" she asked.

"No. From Boston."

"That is in the United States too?"

"Oh yes. Yes."

"Is your father a business man?"

"Not really. He's a professor."

"A teacher?" she asked with a faint note of disappointment.

"Well, he's a kind of authority, you know. People consult him."

"About health? Is he a doctor?"

"Not that sort of doctor. He's a doctor of engineering though. He understands all about underwater erosion. You know what that is?"

"No."

Pyle said with a dim attempt at humour, "Well, I'll leave it to Dad to tell you about that."

"He is here?"

"Oh no."

"But he is coming?"

"No. That was just a joke," Pyle said apologetically.

"Have you got another sister?" I asked Miss Hei.

"No. Why?"

"It sounds as though you were examining Mr. Pyle's marriageability."

"I have only one sister," Miss Hei said, and she clamped her hand heavily down on Phuong's knee, like a chairman with his gavel marking a point of order.

"She's a very pretty sister," Pyle said.

"She is the most beautiful girl in Saigon," Miss Hei said, as though she were correcting him.

"I can believe it."

I said, "It's time we ordered dinner. Even the most beautiful girl in Saigon must eat."

"I am not hungry," Phuong said.

"She is delicate," Miss Hei went firmly on. There was a note of menace in her voice. "She needs care. She deserves care. She is very, very loyal."

"My friend is a lucky man," Pyle said gravely.

"She loves children," Miss Hei said.

I laughed and then caught Pyle's eye; he was looking at me with shocked surprise, and suddenly it occurred to me that he was genuinely interested in what Miss Hei had to say. While I was ordering dinner (though Phuong had told me she was not hungry, I knew she could manage a good steak tartare with two raw eggs and etceteras), I listened to him seriously discussing the question of children. "I've always thought I'd like a lot of children," he said. "A big family's a wonderful interest. It makes for the stability of marriage. And it's good for the children too. I was an only child. It's a great disadvantage being an only child." I had never heard him talk so much before.

"How old is your father?" Miss Hei asked with gluttony.

"Sixty-nine."

"Old people love grandchildren. It is very sad that my sister has no parents to rejoice in her children. When the day comes," she added with a baleful look at me.

"Nor you either," Pyle said, rather unnecessarily I thought.

"Our father was of a very good family. He was a mandarin in Hué."

I said, "I've ordered dinner for all of you."

"Not for me," Miss Hei said. "I must be going to my friends. I would like to meet Mr. Pyle again. Perhaps you could manage that."

"When I get back from the north," I said.

"Are you going to the north?"

"I think it's time I had a look at the war."

"But the Press are all back," Pyle said.

"That's the best time for me. I don't have to meet Granger."

"Then you must come and have dinner with me and my sister when Monsieur Fowlair is gone." She added with morose courtesy, "To cheer her up."

After she had gone Pyle said, "What a very nice cultivated woman. And she spoke English so well."

"Tell him my sister was in business once in Singapore," Phuong said proudly.

"Really? What kind of business?"

I translated for her. "Import, export. She can do shorthand."

"I wish we had more like her in the Economic Mission."

"I will speak to her," Phuong said. "She would like to work for the Americans."

After dinner they danced again. I am a bad dancer too and I hadn't the unselfconsciousness of Pyle—or had I possessed it, I wondered, in the days when I was first in love with Phuong? There must have been many occasions at the Grand Monde before the memorable night of Miss Hei's illness when I had danced with Phuong just for an opportunity to speak to her. Pyle was taking no such opportunity as they came round the floor again; he had relaxed a little, that was all, and was holding her less at arm's length, but they were both silent. Suddenly watching her feet, so light and precise and mistress of his shuffle, I was in love again. I could hardly believe that in an hour, two hours, she would be coming back to me to that dingy room with the communal closet and the old women squatting on the landing.

I wished I had never heard the rumour about Phat Diem, or that the rumour had dealt with any other town than the one place in the north where my friendship with a French naval officer would allow me to slip in, uncensored, uncontrolled. A newspaper scoop? Not in those days when all the world wanted to read about was Korea. A chance of death? Why should I want to die when Phuong slept beside me every night? But I knew the answer to that question. From childhood I had never believed in permanence, and yet I had longed for it. Always I was afraid of losing happiness. This month, next year, Phuong would leave me. If not next year, in three years. Death was the only absolute value in my world. Lose life and one would lose nothing again for ever. I envied those who could believe in a God and I distrusted them. I felt they were keeping their courage up with a fable of the changeless and the permanent. Death was far more certain than God, and with death there would be no longer the daily possibility of love dying. The nightmare of a future of boredom and indifference would lift. I could never have been a pacifist. To kill a man was surely to grant him an immeasurable benefit. Oh yes, people always, everywhere, loved their enemies. It was their friends they preserved for pain and vacuity.

"Forgive me for taking Miss Phuong from you," Pyle's voice said.

"Oh, I'm no dancer, but I like watching her dance." One

always spoke of her like that in the third person as though she were not there. Sometimes she seemed invisible like peace.

The first cabaret of the evening began: a singer, a juggler, a comedian—he was very obscene, but when I looked at Pyle he obviously couldn't follow the argot. He smiled when Phuong smiled and laughed uneasily when I laughed. "I wonder where Granger is now," I said, and Pyle looked at me reproachfully.

Then came the turn of the evening: a troupe of female impersonators. I had seen many of them during the day in the rue Catinat walking up and down, in old slacks and sweaters, a bit blue about the chin, swaying their hips. Now in low-cut evening dresses, with false jewellery and false breasts and husky voices, they appeared at least as desirable as most of the European women in Saigon. A group of young Air Force officers whistled to them and they smiled glamorously back. I was astonished by the sudden violence of Pyle's protest. "Fowler," he said, "let's go. We've had enough, haven't we? This isn't a bit suitable for *her*."

# CHAPTER 4

## 1

From the bell tower of the Cathedral the battle was only picturesque, fixed like a panorama of the Boer War in an old *Illustrated London News*. An aeroplane was parachuting supplies to an isolated post in the *calcaire*, those strange weather-eroded mountains on the Annam border that look like piles of pumice, and because it always returned to the same place for its glide, it might never have moved, and the parachute was always there in the same spot, half-way to earth. From the plain the mortar-bursts rose unchangingly, the smoke as solid as stone, and in the market the flames burnt palely in the sunlight. The tiny figures of the parachutists moved in single file along the canals, but at this height they appeared stationary. Even the priest who sat in a corner of the tower never changed his position as he read in his breviary. The war was very tidy and clean at that distance.

I had come in before dawn in a landing-craft from Nam Dinh. We couldn't land at the naval station because it was cut off by the enemy who completely surrounded the town at a range of six hundred yards, so the boat ran in beside the flaming market. We were an easy target in the light of the flames, but for some reason no one fired. Everything was quiet, except for the flop and crackle of the burning stalls. I could hear a Senegalese sentry on the river's edge shift his stance.

I had known Phat Diem well in the days before the attack—the one long narrow street of wooden stalls, cut up every hundred yards by a canal, a church and a bridge. At night it had been lit only by candles or small oil lamps (there was no electricity in Phat Diem except in the French officers' quarters), and day or night the street was packed and noisy. In its strange medieval way, under the shadow and protection of the Prince Bishop, it had been the most living town in all the country, and now when I landed and walked up to the officers' quarters it was the most dead. Rubble and broken glass and the smell of burnt paint and plaster, the long street empty as far as the sight could reach, it reminded me of a London thoroughfare in the early morning after an all-clear: one expected to see a placard, "Unexploded Bomb."

The front wall of the officers' house had been blown out, and the houses across the street were in ruins. Coming down the river from Nam Dinh I had learnt from Lieutenant Peraud what had happened. He was a serious young man, a Free-mason, and to him it was like a judgement on the superstitions of his fellows. The Bishop of Phat Diem had once visited Europe and acquired there a devotion to Our Lady of Fatima—that vision of the Virgin which appeared, so Roman Catholics believe, to a group of children in Portugal. When he came home, he built a grotto in her honour in the Cathedral precincts, and he celebrated her feast-day every year with a procession. Relations with the colonel in charge of the French and Vietnamese troops had always been strained since the day when the authorities had disbanded the Bishop's private army. This year the colonel—who had some sympathy with the Bishop, for to each of them his country was more important than Catholicism—made a gesture of amity and walked with his senior officers in the front of the procession. Never had a greater crowd gathered in Phat Diem to do honour to Our Lady of Fatima. Even many of the Buddhists—who formed about half the population—could not bear to miss the fun, and those who had belief in neither God nor Buddha believed that somehow all these banners and incense-burners and the golden monstrance would keep war from their homes. All that was left of the Bishop's army—his brass band—led the procession, and the French officers, pious by order of the colonel, followed like choirboys through the gateway into the Cathedral precincts, past the white statue of the Sacred Heart that stood on an island in the little lake before the Cathedral, under the bell tower with spreading oriental wings and into the carved wooden Cathedral with its gigantic pillars formed out of single trees and the scarlet lacquer work of the altar, more Buddhist than Christian. From all the villages between the canals, from that Low Country landscape where young green rice-shoots and golden harvests take the place of tulips and churches of windmills, the people poured in.

Nobody noticed the Vietminh agents who had joined the procession too, and that night as the main Communist battalion moved through the passes in the *calcaire,* into the Tonkin plain, watched helplessly by the French outpost in the mountains above, the advance agents struck in Phat Diem.

Now after four days, with the help of parachutists, the enemy had been pushed back half a mile around the town. This was a defeat: no journalists were allowed, no cables could be sent, for the papers must carry only victories. The authorities would have stopped me in Hanoi if they had known of my purpose, but the further you get from headquarters, the looser becomes the control until, when you come within range of the enemy's fire, you are a welcome guest—what has been a menace for the *Etat Major* in Hanoi, a worry for the full colonel in Nam Dinh, to the lieutenant in the field is a joke, a distraction, a mark of interest from the outer world, so that for a few blessed hours he can dramatize himself a little and see in a false heroic light even his own wounded and dead.

The priest shut his breviary and said, "Well, that's finished." He was a European, but not a Frenchman, for the Bishop would not have tolerated a French priest in his diocese. He said apologetically, "I have to come up here, you understand, for a bit of quiet from all those poor people." The sound of the mortar-fire seemed to be closing in, or perhaps it was the enemy at last replying. The strange difficulty was to find them: there were a dozen narrow fronts, and between the canals, among the farm buildings and the paddy fields, innumerable opportunities for ambush.

Immediately below us stood, sat and lay the whole population of Phat Diem. Catholics, Buddhists, pagans, they had all packed their most valued possessions—a cooking-stove, a lamp, a mirror, a wardrobe, some mats, a holy picture—and moved into the Cathedral precincts. Here in the north it would be bitterly cold when darkness came, and already the Cathedral was full: there was no more shelter; even on the stairs to the bell tower every step was occupied, and all the time more people crowded through the gates, carrying their babies and household goods. They believed, whatever their religion, that here they would be safe. While we watched, a young man with a rifle in Vietnamese uniform pushed his way through: he was stopped by a priest, who took his rifle from him. The father at my side said in explanation, "We are neutral here. This is God's territory." I thought, "It's a strange poor population God has in his kingdom, frightened, cold, starving—'I don't know how we are going to feed these people,' the priest told me—you'd think a great King would do better than that." But then I thought, "It's always the same wherever one goes—it's not the most powerful rulers who have the happiest populations."

Little shops had already been set up below. I said, "It's like an enormous fair, isn't it, but without one smiling face."

The priest said, "They were terribly cold last night. We have to keep the monastery gates shut or they would swamp us."

"You all keep warm in here?" I asked.

"Not very warm. And we would not have room for a tenth of them." He went on, "I know what you are thinking. But it is essential for some of us to keep well. We have the only hospital in Phat Diem, and our only nurses are these nuns."

"And your surgeon?"

"I do what I can." I saw then that his soutane was speckled with blood.

He said, "Did you come up here to find me?"

"No. I wanted to get my bearings."

"I asked you because I had a man up here last night. He wanted to go to confession. He had got a little frightened, you see, with what he had seen along the canal. One couldn't blame him."

"It's bad along there?"

"The parachutists caught them in a cross-fire. Poor souls. I thought perhaps you were feeling the same."

"I'm not a Roman Catholic. I don't think you could even call me a Christian."

"It's strange what fear does to a man."

"It would never do that to me. If I believed in any God at

all, I should still hate the idea of confession. Kneeling in one of your boxes. Exposing myself to another man. You must excuse me, Father, but to me it seems morbid—unmanly even."

"Oh," he said lightly, "I expect you are a good man. I don't suppose you've ever had much to regret."

I looked along the churches, where they ran down evenly spaced between the canals, towards the sea. A light flashed from the second tower. I said, "You haven't kept all your churches neutral."

"It isn't possible," he said. "The French have agreed to leave the Cathedral precincts alone. We can't expect more. That's a Foreign Legion post you are looking at."

"I'll be going along. Good-bye, Father."

"Good-bye and good luck. Be careful of the snipers."

I had to push my way through the crowd to get out, past the lake and the white statue with its sugary outspread arms, into the long street. I could see for nearly three quarters of a mile each way, and there were only two living beings in all that length besides myself—two soldiers with camouflaged helmets going slowly away up the edge of the street, their sten guns at the ready. I say the living because one body lay in a doorway with its head in the road. The buzz of flies collecting there and the squelch of the soldiers' boots growing fainter and fainter were the only sounds. I walked quickly past the body, turning my head the other way. A few minutes later when I looked back I was quite alone with my shadow and there were no sounds except the sounds I made. I felt as though I were a mark on a firing range. It occurred to me that if something happened to me in this street it might be many hours before I was picked up: time for the flies to collect.

When I had crossed two canals, I took a turning that led to a church. A dozen men sat on the ground in the camouflage of parachutists, while two officers examined a map. Nobody paid me any attention when I joined them. One man, who wore the long antennae of a walkie-talkie, said, "We can move now," and everybody stood up.

I asked them in my bad French whether I could accompany

them. An advantage of this war was that a European face proved in itself a passport on the field: a European could not be suspected of being an enemy agent. "Who are you?" the lieutenant asked.

"I am writing about the war," I said.

"American?"

"No, English."

He said, "It is a very small affair, but if you wish to come with us . . ." He began to take off his steel helmet. "No, no," I said, "that is for combatants."

"As you wish."

We went out behind the church in single file, the lieutenant leading, and halted for a moment on a canal-bank for the soldier with the walkie-talkie to get contact with the patrols on either flank. The mortar shells tore over us and burst out of sight. We had picked up more men behind the church and were now about thirty strong. The lieutenant explained to me in a low voice, stabbing a finger at his map, "Three hundred have been reported in this village here. Perhaps massing for tonight. We don't know. No one has found them yet."

"How far?"

"Three hundred yards."

Words came over the wireless and we went on in silence, to the right the straight canal, to the left low scrub and fields and scrub again. "All clear," the lieutenant whispered with a reassuring wave as we started. Forty yards on, another canal, with what was left of a bridge, a single plank without rails, ran across our front. The lieutenant motioned to us to deploy and we squatted down facing the unknown territory ahead, thirty feet off, across the plank. The men looked at the water and then, as though by a word of command, all together, they looked away. For a moment I didn't see what they had seen, but when I saw, my mind went back, I don't know why, to the Chalet and the female impersonators and the young soldiers whistling and Pyle saying, "This isn't a bit suitable."

The canal was full of bodies: I am reminded now of an Irish stew containing too much meat. The bodies overlapped: one head, seal-grey, and anonymous as a convict with a shaven scalp, stuck up out of the water like a buoy. There was

no blood: I suppose it had flowed away a long time ago. I have
no idea how many there were: they must have been caught in
a cross-fire, trying to get back, and I suppose every man of us
along the bank was thinking, "Two can play at that game." I
too took my eyes away; we didn't want to be reminded of how
little we counted, how quickly, simply and anonymously death
came. Even though my reason wanted the state of death, I was
afraid like a virgin of the act. I would have liked death to come
with due warning, so that I could prepare myself. For what? I
didn't know, nor how, except by taking a look around at the
little I would be leaving.

The lieutenant sat beside the man with the walkie-talkie
and stared at the ground between his feet. The instrument
began to crackle instructions and with a sigh as though he had
been roused from sleep he got up. There was an odd comrade-
liness about all their movements, as though they were equals
engaged on a task they had performed together times out of
mind. Nobody waited to be told what to do. Two men made
for the plank and tried to cross it, but they were unbalanced
by the weight of their arms and had to sit astride and work
their way across a few inches at a time. Another man had found
a punt hidden in some bushes down the canal and he worked
it to where the lieutenant stood. Six of us got in and he began
to pole towards the other bank, but we ran on a shoal of bodies
and stuck. He pushed away with his pole, sinking it into this
human clay, and one body was released and floated up all its
length beside the boat like a bather lying in the sun. Then we
were free again, and once on the other side we scrambled out,
with no backward look. No shots had been fired: we were alive:
death had withdrawn perhaps as far as the next canal. I heard
somebody just behind me say with great seriousness, "*Gott sei
dank.*" Except for the lieutenant they were most of them
Germans.

Beyond was a group of farm-buildings; the lieutenant went
in first, hugging the wall, and we followed at six-foot intervals
in single file. Then the men, again without an order, scattered
through the farm. Life had deserted it—not so much as a hen
had been left behind, though hanging on the walls of what had
been the living room where two hideous oleographs of the

Sacred Heart and the Mother and Child which gave the whole ramshackle group of buildings a European air. One knew what these people believed even if one didn't share their belief: they were human beings, not just grey drained cadavers.

So much of the war is sitting around and doing nothing, waiting for somebody else. With no guarantee of the amount of time you have left it doesn't seem worth starting even a train of thought. Doing what they had done so often before, the sentries moved out. Anything that stirred ahead of us now was enemy. The lieutenant marked his map and reported our position over the radio. A noonday hush fell: even the mortars were quiet and the air was empty of planes. One man doodled with a twig in the dirt of the farmyard. After a while it was as if we had been forgotten by war. I hoped that Phuong had sent my suits to the cleaners. A cold wind ruffled the straw of the yard, and a man went modestly behind a barn to relieve himself. I tried to remember whether I had paid the British Consul in Hanoi for the bottle of whisky he had allowed me.

Two shots were fired to our front, and I thought, "This is it. Now it comes." It was all the warning I wanted. I awaited, with a sense of exhilaration, the permanent thing.

But nothing happened. Once again I had "over-prepared the event." Only long minutes afterwards one of the sentries entered and reported something to the lieutenant. I caught the phrase, "Deux civils."

The lieutenant said to me, "We will go and see," and following the sentry we picked our way along a muddy overgrown path between two fields. Twenty yards beyond the farm buildings, in a narrow ditch, we came on what we sought: a woman and a small boy. They were very clearly dead: a small neat clot of blood on the woman's forehead, and the child might have been sleeping. He was about six years old and he lay like an embryo in the womb with his little bony knees drawn up. "Mal chance," the lieutenant said. He bent down and turned the child over. He was wearing a holy medal round his neck, and I said to myself, "The juju doesn't work." There was a gnawed piece of loaf under his body. I thought, "I hate war."

The lieutenant said, "Have you seen enough?" speaking

savagely, almost as though I had been responsible for these deaths. Perhaps to the soldier the civilian is the man who employs him to kill, who includes the guilt of murder in the pay-envelope and escapes responsibility. We walked back to the farm and sat down again in silence on the straw, out of the wind, which like an animal seemed to know that dark was coming. The man who had doodled was relieving himself, and the man who had relieved himself was doodling. I thought how in those moments of quiet, after the sentries had been posted, they must have believed it safe to move from the ditch. I wondered whether they had lain there long—the bread had been very dry. This farm was probably their home.

The radio was working again. The lieutenant said wearily, "They are going to bomb the village. Patrols are called in for the night." We rose and began our journey back, punting again around the shoal of bodies, filing past the church. We hadn't gone very far, and yet it seemed a long enough journey to have made with the killing of those two as the only result. The planes had gone up, and behind us the bombing began.

Dark had fallen by the time I reached the officers'' quarters, where I was spending the night. The temperature was only a degree above zero, and the sole warmth anywhere was in the blazing market. With one wall destroyed by a bazooka and the doors buckled, canvas curtains couldn't shut out the draughts. The electric dynamo was not working, and we had to build barricades of boxes and books to keep the candles burning. I played *Quatre Cent Vingt-et-un* for Communist currency with a Captain Sorel: it wasn't possible to play for drinks as I was a guest of the mess. The luck went wearisomely back and forth. I opened my bottle of whisky to try to warm us a little, and the others gathered round. The colonel said, "This is the first glass of whisky I have had since I left Paris."

A lieutenant came in from his round of the sentries. "Perhaps we shall have a quiet night," he said.

"They will not attack before four," the colonel said. "Have you a gun?" he asked me.

"No."

"I'll find you one. Better keep it on your pillow." He added courteously, "I am afraid you will find your mattress rather hard. And at three-thirty the mortar-fire will begin. We try to break up any concentrations."

"How long do you suppose this will go on?"

"Who knows? We can't spare any more troops from Nam Dinh. This is just a diversion. If we can hold out with no more help than we got two days ago, it is, one may say, a victory."

The wind was up again, prowling for an entry. The canvas curtain sagged (I was reminded of Polonius stabbed behind the arras) and the candle wavered. The shadows were theatrical. We might have been a company of barnstormers.

"Have your posts held?"

"As far as we know." He said with an effect of great tiredness, "This is nothing, you understand, an affair of no importance compared with what is happening a hundred kilometres away at Hoa Binh. That is a battle."

"Another glass, Colonel?"

"Thank you, no. It is wonderful, your English whisky, but it is better to keep a little for the night in case of need. I think, if you will excuse me, I will get some sleep. One cannot sleep after the mortars start. Captain Sorel, you will see that Monsieur Fowlair has everything he needs, a candle, matches, a revolver." He went into his room.

It was the signal for all of us. They had put a mattress on the floor for me in a small store-room and I was surrounded by wooden cases. I stayed awake only a very short time—the hardness of the floors was like rest. I wondered, but oddly without jealousy, whether Phuong was at the flat. The possession of a body tonight seemed a very small thing—perhaps that day I had seen too many bodies which belonged to no one, not even to themselves. We were all expendable. When I fell asleep I dreamed of Pyle. He was dancing all by himself on a stage, stiffly, with his arms held out to an invisible partner, and I sat and watched him from a seat like a music-stool with a gun in my hand in case anyone should interfere with his dance. A programme set up by the stage, like the numbers in an English music-hall, read, "The Dance of Love. 'A' certificate." Somebody moved at the back of the theatre and I held my gun tighter. Then I woke.

My hand was on the gun they had lent me, and a man stood in the doorway with a candle in his hand. He wore a steel helmet which threw a shadow over his eyes, and it was only when he spoke that I knew he was Pyle. He said shyly, "I'm awfully sorry to wake you up. They told me I could sleep in here."

I was still not fully awake. "Where did you get that helmet?" I asked.

"Oh, somebody lent it to me," he said vaguely. He dragged in after him a military kitbag and began to pull out a wool-lined sleeping-bag.

"You are very well equipped," I said, trying to recollect why either of us should be here.

"This is the standard travelling kit," he said, "of our medical aid teams. They lent me one in Hanoi." He took out a thermos and a small spirit stove, a hair-brush, a shaving-set and a tin of rations. I looked at my watch. It was nearly three in the morning.

2

Pyle continued to unpack. He made a little ledge of cases, on which he put his shaving-mirror and tackle. I said, "I doubt if you'll get any water."

"Oh," he said, "I've enough in the thermos for the morning." He sat down on his sleeping-bag and began to pull off his boots.

"How on earth did you get here?" I asked.

"They let me through as far as Nam Dinh to see our trachoma team, and then I hired a boat."

"A boat?"

"Oh, some kind of a punt—I don't know the name for it. As a matter of fact I had to buy it. It didn't cost much."

"And you came down the river by yourself?"

"It wasn't really difficult, you know. The current was with me."

"You are crazy."

"Oh no. The only real danger was running aground."

"Or being shot up by a naval patrol, or a French plane. Or having your throat cut by the Vietminh."

He laughed shyly. "Well, I'm here anyway," he said.

"Why?"

"Oh, there are two reasons. But I don't want to keep you awake."

"I'm not sleepy. The guns will be starting soon."

"Do you mind if I move the candle? It's a little too bright here." He seemed nervous.

"What's the first reason?"

"Well, the other day you made me think this place was rather interesting. You remember when we were with Granger . . . and Phuong."

"Yes?"

"I thought I ought to take a look at it. To tell you the truth, I was a little ashamed of Granger."

"I see. As simple as all that."

"Well, there wasn't any real difficulty, was there?" He began to play with his bootlaces, and there was a long silence. "I'm not being quite honest," he said at last.

"No?"

"I really came to see you."

"You came here to see me?"

"Yes."

"Why?"

He looked up from his bootlaces in an agony of embarrassment. "I had to tell you—I've fallen in love with Phuong."

I laughed. I couldn't help it. He was so unexpected and serious. I said, "Couldn't you have waited till I got back? I shall be in Saigon next week."

"You might have been killed," he said. "It wouldn't have been honourable. And then I don't know if I could have stayed away from Phuong all that time."

"You mean, you *have* stayed away?"

"Of course. You don't think I'll tell *her*—without you knowing?"

"People do," I said. "When did it happen?"

"I guess it was that night at the Chalet, dancing with her."

"I didn't think you ever got close enough."

He looked at me in a puzzled way. If his conduct seemed crazy to me, mine was obviously inexplicable to him. He said,

"You know, I think it was seeing all those girls in that house. They were so pretty. Why, she might have been one of them. I wanted to protect her."

"I don't think she's in need of protection. Has Miss Hei invited you out?"

"Yes, but I haven't gone. I've kept away." He said gloomily, "It's been terrible. I feel such a heel, but you do believe me, don't you, that if you'd been married—why, I wouldn't ever come between a man and his wife."

"You seem pretty sure you *can* come between," I said. For the first time he had irritated me.

"Fowler," he said, "I don't know your Christian name . . . ?"

"Thomas. Why?"

"I can call you Tom, can't I? I feel in a way this has brought us together. Loving the same woman, I mean."

"What's your next move?"

He sat up enthusiastically against the packing-cases. "Everything seems different now that you know," he said. "I shall ask her to marry me, Tom."

"I'd rather you called me Thomas."

"She'll just have to choose between us, Thomas. That's fair enough." But was it fair? I felt for the first time the premonitory chill of loneliness. It was all fantastic, and yet . . . He might be a poor lover, but I was the poor man. He had in his hand the infinite riches of respectability.

He began to undress and I thought, "He has youth too." How sad it was to envy Pyle.

I said, "I can't marry her. I have a wife at home. She would never divorce me. She's High Church—if you know what that means."

"I'm sorry, Thomas. By the way, my name's Alden, if you'd care . . ."

"I'd rather stick to Pyle," I said. "I think of you as Pyle."

He got into his sleeping-bag and stretched his hand out for the candle. "Whew," he said, "I'm glad that's over, Thomas. I've been feeling awfully bad about it." It was only too evident that he no longer did.

When the candle was out, I could just see the outline of his crew-cut against the light of the flames outside. "Goodnight,

Thomas. Sleep well," and immediately at those words like a bad comedy cue the mortars opened up, whirring, shrieking, exploding.

"Good God," Pyle said, "is it an attack?"

"They are trying to stop an attack."

"Well, I suppose there'll be no sleep for us now?"

"No sleep."

"Thomas, I want you to know what I think of the way you've taken all this—I think you've been swell, swell, there's no other word for it."

"Thank you."

"You've seen so much more of the world than I have. You know, in some ways Boston is a bit—cramping. Even if you aren't a Lowell or a Cabot. I wish you'd advise me, Thomas."

"What about?"

"Phuong."

"I wouldn't trust my advice if I were you. I'm biased. I want to keep her."

"Oh, but I know you're straight, absolutely straight, and we both have her interests at heart."

Suddenly I couldn't bear his boyishness any more. I said, "I don't care that for her interests. You can have her interests. I only want her body. I want her in bed with me. I'd rather ruin her and sleep with her than, than . . . look after her damned interests."

He said, "Oh," in a weak voice, in the dark.

I went on, "If it's only her interests you care about, for God's sake leave Phuong alone. Like any other woman she'd rather have a good . . ." The crash of a mortar saved Boston ears from the Anglo-Saxon word.

But there was a quality of the implacable in Pyle. He had determined I was behaving well and I had to behave well. He said, "I know what you are suffering, Thomas."

"I'm not suffering."

"Oh yes, you are. I know what I'd suffer if I had to give up Phuong."

"But I haven't given her up."

"I'm pretty physical too, Thomas, but I'd give up all hope of that if I could see Phuong happy."

"She is happy."

"She can't be—not in her situation. She needs children."

"Do you really believe all that nonsense her sister . . ."

"A sister sometimes knows better . . ."

"She was just trying to sell the notion to you, Pyle, because she thinks you have more money. And, my God, she has sold it all right."

"I've only got my salary."

"Well, you've got a favourable rate of exchange anyway."

"Don't be bitter, Thomas. These things happen. I wish it had happened to anybody else but you. Are those our mortars?"

"Yes, 'our' mortars. You talk as though she was leaving me, Pyle."

"Of course," he said without conviction, "she may choose to stay with you."

"What would you do then?"

"I'd apply for a transfer."

"Why don't you just go away, Pyle, without causing trouble?"

"It wouldn't be fair to her, Thomas," he said quite seriously. I never knew a man who had better motives for all the trouble he caused. He added, "I don't think you quite understand Phuong."

And waking that morning months later with Phuong beside me, I thought, "And did you understand her either? Could you have anticipated this situation? Phuong so happily asleep beside me and you dead?" Time has its revenges, but revenges seem so often sour. Wouldn't we all do better not trying to understand, accepting the fact that no human being will ever understand another, not a wife a husband, a lover a mistress, nor a parent a child? Perhaps that's why men have invented God —a being capable of understanding. Perhaps if I wanted to be understood or to understand I would bamboozle myself into belief, but I am a reporter; God exists only for leader-writers.

"Are you sure there's anything much to understand?" I asked Pyle. "Oh, for God's sake, let's have a whisky. It's too noisy to argue."

"It's a little early," Pyle said.

"It's damned late."

I poured out two glasses and Pyle raised his and stared through the whisky at the light of the candle. His hand shook whenever a shell burst, and yet he had made that senseless trip from Nam Dinh.

Pyle said, "It's a strange thing that neither of us can say 'Good luck.'" So we drank saying nothing.

# CHAPTER 5

I had thought I would be only one week away from Saigon, but it was nearly three weeks before I returned. In the first place it proved more difficult to get out of the Phat Diem area than it had been to get in. The road was cut between Nam Dinh and Hanoi and aerial transport could not be spared for one reporter who shouldn't have been there anyway. Then when I reached Hanoi the correspondents had been flown up for briefing on the latest victory and the plane that took them back had no seat left for me. Pyle got away from Phat Diem the morning he arrived: he had fulfilled his mission—to speak to me about Phuong, and there was nothing to keep him. I left him asleep when the mortar-fire stopped at five-thirty and when I returned from a cup of coffee and some biscuits in the mess he wasn't there. I assumed that he had gone for a stroll—after punting all the way down the river from Nam Dinh a few snipers would not have worried him; he was as incapable of imagining pain or danger to himself as he was incapable of conceiving the pain he might cause others. On one occasion—but that was months later—I lost control and thrust his foot into it, into the pain I mean, and I remember how he turned away and looked at his stained shoe in perplexity and said, "I must get a shine before I see the Minister." I knew then he was already forming his phrases in the style he had learnt from York Harding. Yet he was sincere in his way: it was coincidence that the sacrifices were all paid by others, until that final night under the bridge to Dakow.

It was only when I returned to Saigon that I learnt how Pyle, while I drank my coffee, had persuaded a young naval officer to take him on a landing-craft which after a routine patrol dropped him surreptitiously at Nam Dinh. Luck was with him and he got back to Hanoi with his trachoma team twenty-four hours before the road was officially regarded as cut. When I reached Hanoi he had already left for the south, leaving me a note with the barman at the Press Camp.

"Dear Thomas," he wrote, "I can't begin to tell you how swell you were the other night. I can tell you my heart was in my mouth when I walked into that room to find you." (Where had it been on the long boat-ride down the river?) "There are not many men who would have taken the whole thing so calmly. You were great, and I don't feel half as mean as I did, now that I've told you." (Was he the only one that mattered? I wondered angrily, and yet I knew that he didn't intend it that way. To him the whole affair would be happier as soon as he didn't feel mean—I would be happier, Phuong would be happier, the whole world would be happier, even the Economic Attaché and the Minister. Spring had come to Indo-China now that Pyle was mean no longer.) "I waited for you here for twenty-four hours, but I shan't get back to Saigon for a week if I don't leave today, and my real work is in the south. I've told the boys who are running the trachoma teams to look you up—you'll like them. They are great boys and doing a man-size job. Don't worry in any way that I'm returning to Saigon ahead of you. I promise you I won't see Phuong until you return. I don't want you to feel later that I've been unfair in any way. Cordially yours, Alden."

Again that calm assumption that "later" it would be I who would lose Phuong. Is confidence based on a rate of exchange? We used to speak of sterling qualities. Have we got to talk now about a dollar love? A dollar love, of course, would include marriage and Junior and Mother's Day, even though later it might include Reno or the Virgin Islands or wherever they go nowadays for their divorces. A dollar love had good intentions, a clear conscience, and to Hell with everybody. But my love had no intentions: it knew the future. All one could do was try to make the future less hard, to break the future gently when it came, and even opium had its value there. But I never foresaw that the first future I would have to break to Phuong would be the death of Pyle.

I went—for I had nothing better to do—to the Press Conference. Granger, of course, was there. A young and too

beautiful French colonel presided. He spoke in French and a
junior officer translated. The French correspondents sat together like a rival football-team. I found it hard to keep my
mind on what the colonel was saying: all the time it wandered
back to Phuong and the one thought—suppose Pyle is right
and I lose her: where does one go from here?

The interpreter said, "The colonel tells you that the enemy
has suffered a sharp defeat and severe losses—the equivalent
of one complete battalion. The last detachments are now making their way back across the Red River on improvised rafts.
They are shelled all the time by the Air Force." The colonel
ran his hand through his elegant yellow hair and, flourishing
his pointer, danced his way down the long maps on the wall.
An American correspondent asked, "What are the French
losses?"

The colonel knew perfectly well the meaning of the
question—it was usually put at this stage of the conference,
but he paused, pointer raised with a kind smile like a popular
schoolmaster, until it was interpreted. Then he answered with
patient ambiguity.

"The colonel says our losses have not been heavy. The exact
number is not yet known."

This was always the signal for trouble. You would have
thought that sooner or later the colonel would have found a
formula for dealing with his refractory class, or that the head-
master would have appointed a member of his staff more efficient at keeping order.

"Is the colonel seriously telling us," Granger said, "that's
he's had time to count the enemy dead and not his own?"

Patiently the colonel wove his web of evasion, which he
knew perfectly well would be destroyed again by another question. The French correspondents sat gloomily silent. If the
American correspondents stung the colonel into an admission
they would be quick to seize it, but they would not join in
baiting their countryman.

"The colonel says the enemy forces are being over-run. It
is possible to count the dead behind the firing-line, but while
the battle is still in progress you cannot expect figures from the
advancing French units."

"It's not what *we* expect," Granger said, "it's what the *Etat Major* knows or not. Are you seriously telling us that platoons do not report their casualties as they happen by walkie-talkie?"

The colonel's temper was beginning to fray. If only, I thought, he had called our bluff from the start and told us firmly that he knew the figures but wouldn't say. After all it was their war, not ours. We had no God-given right to information. We didn't have to fight Left-Wing deputies in Paris as well as the troops of Ho Chi Minh between the Red and the Black Rivers. We were not dying.

The colonel suddenly snapped out the information that French casualties had been in a proportion of one to three, then turned his back on us, to stare furiously at his map. These were his men who were dead, his fellow officers, belonging to the same class at St. Cyr—not numerals as they were to Granger. Granger said, "Now we are getting somewhere," and stared round with oafish triumph at his fellows; the French with heads bent made their sombre notes.

"That's more than can be said in Korea," I said with deliberate misunderstanding, but I had only given Granger a new line.

"Ask the colonel," he said, "what the French are going to do next? He says the enemy's on the run across the Black River . . ."

"Red River," the interpreter corrected him.

"I don't care what the colour of the river is. What we want to know is what the French are going to do now."

"The enemy are in flight."

"What happens when they get to the other side? What are you going to do then? Are you just going to sit down on the other bank and say that's over?" The French officers listened with gloomy patience to Granger's bullying voice. Even humility is required today of the soldier. "Are you going to drop them Christmas cards?"

The captain interpreted with care, even to the phrase, "*cartes de Noël.*" The colonel gave us a wintry smile. "Not Christmas cards," he said.

I think the colonel's youth and beauty particularly irritated Granger. The colonel wasn't—at least not by Granger's interpretation—a man's man. He said, "You aren't dropping much else."

The colonel spoke suddenly in English, good English. He said, "If the supplies promised by the Americans had arrived, we should have more to drop." He was really in spite of his elegance a simple man. He believed that a newspaper correspondent cared for his country's honour more than for news. Granger said sharply (he was efficient: he kept dates well in his head), "You mean that none of the supplies promised for the beginning of September have arrived?"

"No."

Granger had got his news: he began to write.

"I am sorry," the colonel said, "that is not for printing: that is for background."

"But colonel," Granger protested, "that's news. We can help you there."

"No, it is a matter for the diplomats."

"What harm can it do?"

The French correspondents were at a loss: they could speak very little English. The colonel had broken the rules. They muttered angrily together.

"I am no judge," the colonel said. "Perhaps the American newspapers would say, 'Oh, the French are always complaining, always begging.' And in Paris the Communists would accuse, 'The French are spilling their blood for America and America will not even send a second-hand helicopter.' It does no good. At the end of it we should still have no helicopters, and the enemy would still be there, fifty miles from Hanoi."

"At least I can print that, can't I, that you need helicopters bad?"

"You can say," the colonel said, "that six months ago we had three helicopters and now we have one. One," he repeated with a kind of amazed bitterness. "You can say that if a man is wounded in this fighting, not seriously wounded, just wounded, he knows that he is probably a dead man. Twelve hours, twenty-four hours perhaps, on a stretcher to the ambulance, then bad tracks, a breakdown, perhaps an ambush, gangrene. It is better to be killed outright." The French correspondents leant forward, trying to understand. "You can write that," he said, looking all the more venomous for his physical beauty. "*Interprétez,*" he ordered, and walked out of the room leaving the captain the unfamiliar task of translating from English into French.

"Got him on the raw," said Granger with satisfaction, and he went into a corner by the bar to write his telegram. Mine didn't take long: there was nothing I could write from Phat Diem that the censors would pass. If the story had seemed good enough I could have flown to Hong Kong and sent it from there, but was any news good enough to risk expulsion? I doubted it. Expulsion meant the end of a whole life, it meant the victory of Pyle, and there, when I returned to my hotel, waiting in my pigeon-hole, was in fact his victory, the end of the affair—a congratulatory telegram of promotion. Dante never thought up that turn of the screw for his condemned lovers. Paolo was never promoted to Purgatory.

I went upstairs to my bare room and the dripping cold-water tap (there was no hot water in Hanoi) and sat on the edge of my bed with the bundle of the mosquito-net like a swollen cloud overhead. I was to be the new foreign editor, arriving every afternoon at half past three, at that grim Victorian building near Blackfriars station with a plaque of Lord Salisbury by the lift. They had sent the good news on from Saigon, and I wondered whether it had already reached Phuong's ears. I was to be a reporter no longer: I was to have opinions, and in return for that empty privilege I was deprived of my last hope in the contest with Pyle. I had experience to match his virginity, age was as good a card to play in the sexual game as youth, but now I hadn't even the limited future of twelve more months to offer, and a future was trumps. I envied the most homesick officer condemned to the chance of death. I would have liked to weep, but the ducts were as dry as the hot-water pipes. Oh, they could have home—I only wanted my room in the rue Catinat.

It was cold after dark in Hanoi and the lights were lower than those of Saigon, more suited to the darker clothes of the women and the fact of war. I walked up the rue Gambetta to the Pax Bar—I didn't want to drink in the Metropole with the senior French officers, their wives and their girls, and as I reached the bar I was aware of the distant drumming of the guns out towards Hoa Binh. In the day they were drowned in traffic-noises, but everything was quiet now except for the tring of bicycle-bells where the trishaw drivers plied for hire. Pietri sat in his usual place. He had an odd elongated skull which sat on his shoulders like a pear on a dish; he was a Sureté officer and was married to a pretty Tonkinese who owned the Pax Bar. He was another man who had no particular desire to go home. He was a Corsican, but he preferred Marseilles, and to Marseilles he preferred any day his seat on the pavement in the rue Gambetta. I wondered whether he already knew the contents of my telegram.

"*Quatre Cent Vingt-et-un?*" he asked.

"Why not?"

We began to throw and it seemed impossible to me that I could ever have a life again, away from the rue Gambetta and the rue Catinat, the flat taste of vermouth cassis, the homely click of dice, and the gunfire travelling like a clock-hand around the horizon.

I said, "I'm going back."

"Home?" Pietri asked, throwing a four-to-one.

"No. England."

# PART TWO

# CHAPTER 1

Pyle had invited himself for what he called a drink, but I knew very well he didn't really drink. After the passage of weeks that fantastic meeting in Phat Diem seemed hardly believable: even the details of the conversation were less clear. They were like the missing letters on a Roman tomb and I the archaeologist filling in the gaps according to the bias of my scholarship. It even occurred to me that he had been pulling my leg, and that the conversation had been an elaborate and humorous disguise for his real purpose, for it was already the gossip of Saigon that he was engaged in one of those services so ineptly called secret. Perhaps he was arranging American arms for a Third Force— the Bishop's brass band, all that was left of his young scared unpaid levies. The telegram that awaited me in Hanoi I kept in my pocket. There was no point in telling Phuong, for that would be to poison the few months we had left with tears and quarrels. I wouldn't even go for my exit-permit till the last moment in case she had a relation in the immigration-office.

I told her, "Pyle's coming at six."

"I will go and see my sister," she said.

"I expect he'd like to see you."

"He does not like me or my family. When you were away he did not come once to my sister, although she had invited him. She was very hurt."

"You needn't go out."

"If he wanted to see me, he would have asked us to the Majestic. He wants to talk to you privately—about business."

"What is his business?"

"People say he imports a great many things."

"What things?"

"Drugs, medicines . . ."

"Those are for the trachoma teams in the north."

"Perhaps. The Customs must not open them. They are dip-lomatic parcels. But once there was a mistake—the man was discharged. The First Secretary threatened to stop all imports."

"What was in the case?"

"Plastic."

"You don't mean bombs?"

"No. Just plastic."

When Phuong had gone, I wrote home. A man from Reuters' was leaving for Hong Kong in a few days and he could mail my letter from there. I knew my appeal was hopeless, but I was not going to reproach myself later for not taking every possible measure. I wrote to the Managing Editor that this was the wrong moment to change their correspondent. General de Lattre was dying in Paris: the French were about to withdraw altogether from Hoa Binh: the north had never been in greater danger. I wasn't suitable, I told him, for a foreign editor—I was a reporter, I had no real opinions about anything. On the last page I even appealed to him on personal grounds, although it was unlikely that any human sympathy could survive under the strip-light, among the green eye-shades and the stereotyped phrases—"the good of the paper," "the situation demands . . ."

I wrote: "For private reasons I am very unhappy at being moved from Vietnam. I don't think I can do my best work in England, where there will be not only financial but family strains. Indeed, if I could afford it I would resign rather than return to the U.K. I only mention this as showing the strength of my objection. I don't think you have found me a bad correspondent, and this is the first favour I have ever asked of you." Then I looked over my article on the battle of Phat Diem, so that I could send it out to be posted under a Hong Kong dateline. The French would not seriously object now—the siege had been raised: a defeat could be played as a victory. Then I tore up the last page of my letter to the editor. It was no use—the "private reasons" would become only the subject of sly jokes. Every correspondent, it was assumed, had his local girl. The editor would joke to the night-editor, who would take the envious thought back to his semi-detached villa in Streatham and climb into bed with it beside the faithful wife he had carried with him years back from Glasgow. I could see so well the kind of house that has no mercy—a broken tricycle stood in the hall and somebody had broken his favourite pipe; and there was a child's shirt in the living-room waiting for a button to be sewn on. "Private reasons": drinking in the Press Club I wouldn't want to be reminded by their jokes of Phuong.

There was a knock on the door. I opened it to Pyle and his black dog walked in ahead of him. Pyle looked over my shoulder and found the room empty. "I'm alone," I said, "Phuong is with her sister." He blushed. I noticed that he was wearing a Hawaii shirt, even though it was comparatively restrained in colour and design. I was surprised: had he been accused of un-American activities? He said, "I hope I haven't interrupted . . ."

"Of course not. Have a drink?"

"Thanks. Beer?"

"Sorry. We haven't a frig—we send out for ice. What about a Scotch?"

"A small one, if you don't mind. I'm not very keen on hard liquor."

"On the rocks?"

"Plenty of soda—if you aren't short."

I said, "I haven't seen you since Phat Diem."

"You got my note, Thomas?"

When he used my Christian name, it was like a declaration that he hadn't been humorous, that he hadn't been covering up, that he was here to get Phuong. I noticed that his crewcut had recently been trimmed; was even the Hawaii shirt serving the function of male plumage?

"I got your note," I said. "I suppose I ought to knock you down."

"Of course," he said, "you've every right, Thomas. But I boxed at college—and I'm so much younger."

"No, it wouldn't be a good move for me, would it?"

"You know, Thomas (I'm sure you feel the same), I don't like discussing Phuong behind her back. I thought she would be here."

"Well, what shall we discuss—plastic?" I hadn't meant to surprise him.

He said, "You know about that?"

"Phuong told me."

"How could she . . . ?"

"You can be sure it's all over the town. What's so important about it? Are you going into the toy business?"

"We don't like the details of our aid to get around. You know what Congress is like—and then one has visiting Senators. We had a lot of trouble about our trachoma teams because they were using one drug instead of another."

"I still don't understand the plastic."

His black dog sat on the floor taking up too much room, panting; its tongue looked like a burnt pancake. Pyle said vaguely, "Oh, you know, we want to get some of these local industries on their feet, and we have to be careful of the French. They want everything bought in France."

"I don't blame them. A war needs money."

"Do you like dogs?"

"No."

"I thought the British were great dog-lovers."

"We think Americans love dollars, but there must be exceptions."

"I don't know how I'd get along without Duke. You know sometimes I feel so darned lonely . . ."

"You've got a great many companions in your branch."

"The first dog I ever had was called Prince. I called him after the Black Prince. You know, the fellow who . . ."

"Massacred all the women and children in Limoges."

"I don't remember that."

"The history books gloss it over."

I was to see many times that look of pain and disappointment touch his eyes and mouth when reality didn't match the romantic ideas he cherished, or when someone he loved or admired dropped below the impossible standard he had set. Once, I remember, I caught York Harding out in a gross error of fact, and I had to comfort him: "It's human to make mistakes." He had laughed nervously and said, "You must think me a fool, but—well, I almost thought him infallible."

He added, "My father took to him a lot the only time they met, and my father's darned difficult to please."

The big black dog called Duke, having panted long enough to establish a kind of right to the air, began to poke about the room. "Could you ask your dog to be still?" I said.

"Oh, I'm so sorry. Duke. Duke. Sit down, Duke." Duke sat down and began noisily to lick his private parts. I filled our glasses and managed in passing to disturb Duke's toilet. The quiet lasted a very short time; he began to scratch himself.

"Duke's awfully intelligent," said Pyle.

"What happened to Prince?"

"We were down on the farm in Connecticut and he got run over."

"Were you upset?"

"Oh, I minded a lot. He meant a great deal to me, but one has to be sensible. Nothing could bring him back."

"And if you lose Phuong, will you be sensible?"

"Oh yes, I hope so. And you?"

"I doubt it. I might even run amok. Have you thought about that, Pyle?"

"I wish you'd call me Alden, Thomas."

"I'd rather not. Pyle has got—associations. Have you thought about it?"

"Of course I haven't. You're the straightest guy I've ever known. When I remember how you behaved when I barged in . . ."

"I remember thinking before I went to sleep how convenient it would be if there were an attack and you were killed. A hero's death. For Democracy."

"Don't laugh at me, Thomas." He shifted his long limbs uneasily. "I must seem a bit dumb to you, but I know when you're kidding."

"I'm not."

"I know if you come clean you want what's best for her."

It was then I heard Phuong's step. I had hoped against hope that he would have gone before she returned. He heard it too and recognized it. He said, "There she is," although he had had only one evening to learn her footfall. Even the dog got up and stood by the door, which I had left open for coolness, almost as though he accepted her as one of Pyle's family. I was an intruder.

Phuong said, "My sister was not in," and looked guardedly at Pyle.

I wondered whether she were telling the truth or whether her sister had ordered her to hurry back.

"You remember Monsieur Pyle?" I said.

"*Enchantée.*" She was on her best behaviour.

"I'm so pleased to see you again," he said, blushing.

"*Comment?*"

"Her English is not very good," I said.

"I'm afraid my French is awful. I'm taking lessons though. And I can understand—if Phuong will speak slowly."

"I'll act as interpreter," I said. "The local accent takes some getting used to. Now what do you want to say? Sit down, Phuong. Monsieur Pyle has come specially to see you. Are you sure," I added to Pyle, "that you wouldn't like me to leave you two alone?"

"I want you to hear everything I have to say. It wouldn't be fair otherwise."

"Well, fire away."

He said solemnly, as though this part he had learned by heart, that he had a great love and respect for Phuong. He had felt it ever since the night he had danced with her. I was reminded a little of a butler showing a party of tourists over a "great house." The great house was his heart, and of the private apartments where the family lived we were given only a rapid and surreptitious glimpse. I translated for him with meticulous care—it sounded worse that way, and Phuong sat quiet with her hands in her lap as though she were listening to a movie.

"Has she understood that?" he asked.

"As far as I can tell. You don't want me to add a little fire to it, do you?"

"Oh no," he said, "just translate. I don't want to sway her emotionally."

"I see."

"Tell her I want to marry her."

I told her.

"What was that she said?"

"She asked me if you were serious. I told her you were the serious type."

"I suppose this is an odd situation," he said. "Me asking you to translate."

"Rather odd."

"And yet it seems so natural. After all you are my best friend."

"It's kind of you to say so."

"There's nobody I'd go to in trouble sooner than you," he said.

"And I suppose being in love with my girl is a kind of trouble?"

"Of course. I wish it was anybody but you, Thomas."

"Well, what do I say to her next. That you can't live without her?"

"No, that's too emotional. It's not quite true either. I'd have to go away, of course, but one gets over everything."

"While you are thinking what to say, do you mind if I put in a word for myself?"

"No, of course not, it's only fair, Thomas."

"Well, Phuong," I said, "are you going to leave me for him? He'll marry you. I can't. You know why."

"Are you going away?" she asked, and I thought of the editor's letter in my pocket.

"No."

"Never?"

"How can one promise that? He can't either. Marriages break. Often they break quicker than an affair like ours."

"I do not want to go," she said, but the sentence was not comforting; it contained an unexpressed "but."

Pyle said, "I think I ought to put all my cards on the table. I'm not rich. But when my father dies I'll have about fifty thousand dollars. I'm in good health—I've got a medical certificate only two months old, and I can let her know my blood-group."

"I don't know how to translate that. What's it for?"

"Well, to make certain we can have children together."

"Is that how you make love in America—figures of income and blood-group?"

"I don't know, I've never done it before. Maybe at home my mother would talk to her mother."

"About your blood-group?"

"Don't laugh at me, Thomas. I expect I'm old-fashioned. You know I'm a little lost in this situation."

"So am I. Don't you think we might call it off and dice for her?"

"Now you are pretending to be tough, Thomas. I know you love her in your way as much as I do."

"Well, go on, Pyle."

"Tell her I don't expect her to love me right away. That will come in time, but tell her what I offer is security and respect. That doesn't sound very exciting, but perhaps it's better than passion."

"She can always get passion," I said, "with your chauffeur when you are away at the office."

Pyle blushed. He got awkwardly to his feet and said, "That's a dirty crack. I won't have her insulted. You've no right . . ."

"She's not your wife yet."

"What can you offer her?" he asked with anger. "A couple of hundred dollars when you leave for England, or will you pass her on with the furniture?"

"The furniture isn't mine."

"She's not either. Phuong, will you marry me?"

"What about the blood-group?" I said. "And a health certificate. You'll need hers, surely? Maybe you ought to have mine too. And her horoscope—no, that's an Indian custom."

"Will you marry me?"

"Say it in French," I said. "I'm damned if I'll interpret for you any more."

I got to my feet and the dog growled. It made me furious. "Tell your damned Duke to be quiet. This is my home, not his."

"Will you marry me?" he repeated. I took a step towards Phuong and the dog growled again.

I said to Phuong, "Tell him to go away and take his dog with him."

"Come away with me now," Pyle said. "*Avec moi.*"

"No," Phuong said, "no." Suddenly all the anger in both of us vanished; it was a problem as simple as that: it could be solved with a word of two letters. I felt an enormous relief; Pyle stood there with his mouth a little open and an expression of bewilderment on his face. He said, "She said no."

"She knows that much English." I wanted to laugh now: what fools we had both made of each other. I said, "Sit down and have another Scotch, Pyle."

"I think I ought to go."

"One for the road."

"Mustn't drink all your whisky," he muttered.

"I get all I want through the Legation." I moved towards the table and the dog bared its teeth.

Pyle said furiously, "Down, Duke. Behave yourself." He wiped the sweat off his forehead. "I'm awfully sorry, Thomas, if I said anything I shouldn't. I don't know what came over me." He took the glass and said wistfully, "The best man wins. Only please don't leave her, Thomas."

"Of course I shan't leave her," I said.

Phuong said to me, "Would he like to smoke a pipe?"

"Would you like to smoke a pipe?"

"No, thank you. I don't touch opium and we have strict rules in the service. I'll just drink this up and be off. I'm sorry about Duke. He's very quiet as a rule."

"Stay to supper."

"I think, if you don't mind, I'd rather be alone." He gave an uncertain grin. "I suppose people would say we'd both behaved rather strangely. I wish you could marry her, Thomas."

"Do you really?"

"Yes. Ever since I saw that place—you know, that house near the Chalet—I've been so afraid."

He drank his unaccustomed whisky quickly, not looking at Phuong, and when he said good-bye he didn't touch her hand, but gave an awkward little bobbing bow. I noticed how her eyes followed him to the door and as I passed the mirror I saw myself: the top button of my trousers undone, the beginning of a paunch. Outside he said, "I promise not to see her, Thomas. You won't let this come between us, will you? I'll get a transfer when I finish my tour."

"When's that?"

"About two years."

I went back to the room and I thought. "What's the good? I might as well have told them both that I was going." He had only to carry his bleeding heart for a few weeks as a decoration . . . My lie would even ease his conscience.

"Shall I make you a pipe?" Phuong asked.

"Yes, in a moment. I just want to write a letter."

It was the second letter of the day, but I tore none of this up, though I had as little hope of a response. I wrote: "Dear Helen, I am coming back to England next April to take the job of foreign editor. You can imagine I am not very happy about it. England is to me the scene of my failure. I had intended our marriage to last quite as much as if I had shared your Christian beliefs. To this day I'm not certain what went wrong (I know we both tried), but I think it was my temper. I know how cruel and bad my temper can be. Now I think it's a little better—the East has done that for me—not sweeter, but quieter. Perhaps it's simply that I'm five years older—at the end of life when five years becomes a high proportion of what's left. You have been very generous to me, and you have never reproached me once since our separation. Would you be even more generous? I know that before we married you warned me there could never be a divorce. I accepted the risk and I've nothing to complain of. At the same time I'm asking for one now."

Phuong called out to me from the bed that she had the tray ready.

"A moment," I said.

"I could wrap this up," I wrote, "and make it sound more honourable and more dignified by pretending it was for someone else's sake. But it isn't, and we always used to tell each other the truth. It's for my sake and only mine. I love someone very much, we have lived together for more than two years, she has been very loyal to me, but I know I'm not essential to her. If I leave her, she'll be a little unhappy I think, but there won't be any tragedy. She'll marry someone else and have a family. It's stupid of me to tell you this. I'm putting a reply into your mouth. But because I've been truthful so far, perhaps you'll believe me when I tell you that to lose her will be, for me, the beginning of death. I'm not asking you to be 'reasonable' (reason is all on your side) or to be merciful. It's too big a word for my situation and anyway I don't particularly deserve mercy. I suppose what I'm really asking you is to behave, all of a sudden, irrationally, out of character. I want you to feel" (I hesitated over the word and then I didn't get it right) "affection and to act before you have time to think. I know that's easier done over a telephone than over eight thousand miles. If only you'd just cable me 'I agree'!"

When I had finished I felt as though I had run a long way and strained unconditioned muscles. I lay down on the bed while Phuong made my pipe. I said, "He's young."

"Who?"

"Pyle."

"That's not so important."

"I would marry you if I could, Phuong."

"I think so, but my sister does not believe it."

"I have just written to my wife and I have asked her to divorce me. I have never tried before. There is always a chance."

"A big chance?"

"No, but a small one."

"Don't worry. Smoke."

I drew in the smoke and she began to prepare my second pipe. I asked her again, "Was your sister really not at home, Phuong?"

"I told you—she was out." It was absurd to subject her to this passion for truth, an Occidental passion, like the passion for alcohol. Because of the whisky I had drunk with Pyle, the effect of the opium was lessened. I said, "I lied to you, Phuong. I have been ordered home."

She put the pipe down. "But you won't go?"

"If I refused, what would we live on?"

"I could come with you. I would like to see London."

"It would be very uncomfortable for you if we were not married."

"But perhaps your wife will divorce you."

"Perhaps."

"I will come with you anyway," she said. She meant it, but I could see in her eyes the long train of thoughts begin, as she lifted the pipe again and began to warm the pellet of opium. She said, "Are there skyscrapers in London?" and I loved her for the innocence of her question. She might lie from politeness, from fear, even for profit, but she would never have the cunning to keep her lie concealed.

"No," I said, "you have to go to America for them."

She gave me a quick look over the needle and registered her mistake. Then as she kneaded the opium she began to talk at random of what clothes she would wear in London, where we should live, of the tube-trains she had read about in a novel, and the double-decker buses: would we fly or go by sea? "And the Statue of Liberty . . ." she said.

"No, Phuong, that's American too."

# CHAPTER 2

## 1

At least once a year the Caodaists hold a festival at the Holy See in Tanyin, which lies eighty kilometres to the north-west of Saigon, to celebrate such and such a year of Liberation, or of Conquest, or even a Buddhist, Confucian or Christian festival. Caodaism was always the favourite chapter of my briefing to visitors. Caodaism, the invention of a Cochin civil servant, was a synthesis of the three religions. The Holy See was at Tanyin. A Pope and female cardinals. Prophecy by planchette. Saint Victor Hugo. Christ and Buddha looking down from the roof of the Cathedral on a Walt Disney fantasia of the East, dragons and snakes in technicolour. Newcomers were always delighted with the description. How could one explain the dreariness of the whole business: the private army of twenty-five thousand men, armed with mortars made out of the exhaust-pipes of old cars, allies of the French who turned neutral at the moment of danger? To these celebrations, which helped to keep the peasants quiet, the Pope invited members of the Government (who would turn up if the Caodaists at the moment held office), the Diplomatic Corps (who would send a few second secretaries with their wives or girls) and the French Commander-in-Chief, who would detail a two-star general from an office job to represent him.

Along the route to Tanyin flowed a fast stream of staff and C.D. cars, and on the more exposed sections of the road Foreign Legionaries threw out cover across the rice-fields. It was always a day of some anxiety for the French High Command and perhaps a certain hope for the Caodaists, for what could more painlessly emphasize their own loyalty than to have a few important guests shot outside their territory?

Every kilometre a small mud watch tower stood up above the flat fields like an exclamation-mark, and every ten kilometres there was a larger fort manned by a platoon of Legionaries, Moroccans or Senegalese. Like the traffic into New York

the cars kept one pace—and as with the traffic into New York
you had a sense of controlled impatience, watching the next
car ahead and in the mirror the car behind. Everybody wanted
to reach Tanyin, see the show and get back as quickly as possible: curfew was at seven.

One passed out of the French-controlled rice-fields into the
rice-fields of the Hoa-Haos and thence into the rice-fields of
the Caodaists, who were usually at war with the Hoa-Haos: only
the flags changed on the watch towers. Small naked boys sat
on the buffaloes which waded genital-deep among the irrigated
fields; where the gold harvest was ready the peasants in their
hats like limpets winnowed the rice against little curved shelters
of plaited bamboo. The cars drove rapidly by, belonging to another world.

Now the churches of the Caodaists would catch the attention of strangers in every village; pale blue and pink plasterwork
and a big eye of God over the door. Flags increased: troops of
peasants made their way along the road: we were approaching
the Holy See. In the distance the sacred mountain stood like a
green bowler hat above Tanyin—that was where General Thé
held out, the dissident Chief of Staff who had recently declared
his intention of fighting both the French and the Vietminh.
The Caodaists made no attempt to capture him, although he
had kidnapped a cardinal, but it was rumoured that he had
done it with the Pope's connivance.

It always seemed hotter in Tanyin than anywhere else in
the Southern Delta; perhaps it was the absence of water, perhaps it was the sense of interminable ceremonies which made
one sweat vicariously, sweat for the troops standing to attention
through the long speeches in a language they didn't understand, sweat for the Pope in his heavy chinoiserie robes. Only
the female cardinals in their white silk trousers chatting to the
priests in sun-helmets gave an impression of coolness under the
glare; you couldn't believe it would ever be seven o'clock and
cocktail-time on the roof of the Majestic, with a wind from
Saigon river.

After the parade I interviewed the Pope's deputy. I didn't
expect to get anything out of him and I was right: it was a
convention on both sides. I asked him about General Thé.

"A rash man," he said and dismissed the subject. He began his set speech, forgetting that I had heard it two years before —it reminded me of my own gramophone records for newcomers. Caodaism was a religious synthesis . . . the best of all religions . . . missionaries had been despatched to Los Angeles . . . the secrets of the Great Pyramid . . . He wore a long white soutane and he chain-smoked. There was something cunning and corrupt about him: the word "love" occurred often. I was certain he knew that all of us were there to laugh at his movement; our air of respect was as corrupt as his phoney hierarchy, but we were less cunning. Our hypocrisy gained us nothing— not even a reliable ally, while theirs had procured arms, supplies, even cash down.

"Thank you, your Eminence." I got up to go. He came with me to the door, scattering cigarette-ash.

"God's blessing on your work," he said unctuously. "Remember God loves the truth."

"Which truth?" I asked.

"In the Caodaist faith all truths are reconciled and truth is love."

He had a large ring on his finger, and when he held out his hand I really think he expected me to kiss it, but I am not a diplomat.

Under the bleak vertical sunlight I saw Pyle; he was trying in vain to make his Buick start. Somehow, during the last two weeks, at the bar of the Continental, in the only good bookshop in the rue Catinat, I had continually run into Pyle. The friendship which he had imposed from the beginning he now emphasized more than ever. His sad eyes would inquire with fervour after Phuong, while his lips expressed with even more fervour the strength of his affection and of his admiration— God save the mark—for me.

A Caodaist commandant stood beside the car talking rapidly. He stopped when I came up. I recognized him—he had been one of Thé's assistants before Thé took to the hills.

"Hullo, commandant," I said, "how's the General?"

"Which general?" he asked with a shy grin.

"Surely in the Caodaist faith," I said, "all generals are reconciled."

"I can't make this car move, Thomas," Pyle said.

"I will get a mechanic," the commandant said, and left us.

"I interrupted you."

"Oh, it was nothing," Pyle said. "He wanted to know how much a Buick cost. These people are so friendly when you treat them right. The French don't seem to know how to handle them."

"The French don't trust them."

Pyle said solemnly, "A man becomes trustworthy when you trust him." It sounded like a Caodaist maxim. I began to feel the air of Tanyin was too ethical for me to breathe.

"Have a drink," Pyle said.

"There's nothing I'd like better."

"I brought a thermos of lime-juice with me." He leant over and busied himself with a basket in the back.

"Any gin?"

"No, I'm awfully sorry. You know," he said encouragingly, "lime-juice is very good for you in this climate. It contains—I'm not sure which vitamins." He held out a cup to me and I drank.

"Anyway, it's wet," I said.

"Like a sandwich? They're really awfully good. A new sandwich-spread called Vit-Health. My mother sent it from the States."

"No, thanks, I'm not hungry."

"It tastes rather like Russian salad—only sort of drier."

"I don't think I will."

"You don't mind if I do?"

"No, no, of course not."

He took a large mouthful and it crunched and crackled. In the distance Buddha in white and pink stone rode away from his ancestral home and his valet—another statue—pursued him running. The female cardinals were drifting back to their house and the Eye of God watched us from above the Cathedral door.

"You know they are serving lunch here?" I said.

"I thought I wouldn't risk it. The meat—you have to be careful in this heat."

"You are quite safe. They are vegetarian."

"I suppose it's all right—but I like to know what I'm eating." He took another munch at his Vit-Health. "Do you think they have any reliable mechanics?"

"They know enough to turn your exhaust pipe into a mortar. I believe Buicks make the best mortars."

The commandant returned and, saluting us smartly, said he had sent to the barracks for a mechanic. Pyle offered him a Vit-Health sandwich, which he refused politely. He said with a man-of-the-world air, "We have so many rules here about food." (He spoke excellent English.) "So foolish. But you know what it is in a religious capital. I expect it is the same thing in Rome—or Canterbury," he added with a neat natty little bow to me. Then he was silent. They were both silent. I had a strong impression that my company was not wanted. I couldn't resist the temptation to tease Pyle—it is, after all, the weapon of weakness and I was weak. I hadn't youth, seriousness, integrity, a future. I said, "Perhaps after all I'll have a sandwich."

"Oh, of course," Pyle said, "of course." He paused before turning to the basket in the back.

"No, no," I said. "I was only joking. You two want to be alone."

"Nothing of the kind," Pyle said. He was one of the most inefficient liars I have ever known—it was an art he had obviously never practised. He explained to the commandant, "Thomas here's the best friend I have."

"I know Mr. Fowler," the commandant said.

"I'll see you before I go, Pyle." And I walked away to the Cathedral. I could get some coolness there.

Saint Victor Hugo in the uniform of the French Academy with the halo round his tricorn hat pointed at some noble sentiment Sun Yat Sen was inscribing on a tablet, and then I was in the nave. There was nowhere to sit except in the Papal chair, round which a plaster cobra coiled, the marble floor glittered like water and there was no glass in the windows. We make a cage for air with holes, I thought, and man makes a cage for his religion in much the same way—with doubts left open to the weather and creeds opening on innumerable interpretations. My wife had found her cage with holes and sometimes I envied her. There is a conflict between sun and air: I lived too much in the sun.

I walked the long empty nave—this was not the Indo-China I loved. The dragons with lion-like heads climbed the pulpit: on the roof Christ exposed his bleeding heart. Buddha sat, as Buddha always sits, with his lap empty. Confucius's beard hung meagrely down like a waterfall in the dry season. This was play-acting: the great globe above the altar was ambition: the basket with the movable lid in which the Pope worked his prophecies was trickery. If this Cathedral had existed for five centuries instead of two decades, would it have gathered a kind of convincingness with the scratches of feet and the erosion of weather? Would somebody who was convincible like my wife find here a faith she couldn't find in human beings? And if I had really wanted faith would I have found it in her Norman church? But I had never desired faith. The job of a reporter is to expose and record. I had never in my career discovered the inexplicable. The Pope worked his prophecies with a pencil in a movable lid and the people believed. In any vision somewhere you could find the planchette. I had no visions or miracles in my repertoire of memory.

I turned my memories over at random like pictures in an album: a fox I had seen by the light of an enemy flare over Orpington stealing along beside a fowl run, out of his russet place in the marginal country: the body of a bayoneted Malay which a Gurkha patrol had brought at the back of a lorry into a mining camp in Pahang, and the Chinese coolies stood by and giggled with nerves, while a brother Malay put a cushion under the dead head: a pigeon on a mantelpiece, poised for flight in a hotel bedroom: my wife's face at a window when I came home to say good-bye for the last time. My thoughts had begun and ended with her. She must have received my letter more than a week ago, and the cable I did not expect had not come. But they say if a jury remains out for long enough there is hope for the prisoner. In another week, if no letter arrived, could I begin to hope? All round me I could hear the cars of the soldiers and the diplomats revving up: the party was over for another year. The stam-

pede back to Saigon was beginning, and curfew called. I went
out to look for Pyle.

He was standing in a patch of shade with his commandant,
and no one was doing anything to his car. The conversation
seemed to be over, whatever it had been about, and they stood
silently there, constrained by mutual politeness. I joined them.

"Well," I said, "I think I'll be off. You'd better be leaving
too if you want to be in before curfew."

"The mechanic hasn't turned up."

"He will come soon," the commandant said. "He was in
the parade."

"You could spend the night," I said. "There's a special
Mass—you'll find it quite an experience. It lasts three hours."

"I ought to get back."

"You won't get back unless you start now." I added unwillingly, "I'll give you a lift if you like and the commandant
can have your car sent in to Saigon tomorrow."

"You need not bother about curfew in Caodaist territory,"
the commandant said smugly. "But beyond .... Certainly I will
have your car sent tomorrow."

"Exhaust intact," I said, and he smiled brightly, neatly, ef-
ficiently, a military abbreviation of a smile.

## 2

The procession of cars was well ahead of us by the time we
started. I put on speed to try to overtake it, but we had passed
out of the Caodaist zone into the zone of the Hoa-Haos with
not even a dust cloud ahead of us. The world was flat and
empty in the evening.

It was not the kind of country one associates with ambush,
but men could conceal themselves neck-deep in the drowned
fields within a few yards of the road.

Pyle cleared his throat and it was the signal for an approaching intimacy. "I hope Phuong's well," he said.

"I've never known her ill." One watch tower sank behind,
another appeared, like weights on a balance.

"I saw her sister out shopping yesterday."

"And I suppose she asked you to look in," I said.

"As a matter of fact she did."

"She doesn't give up hope easily."

"Hope?"

"Of marrying you to Phuong."

"She told me you are going away."

"These rumours get about."

Pyle said, "You'd play straight with me, Thomas, wouldn't you?"

"Straight?"

"I've applied for a transfer," he said. "I wouldn't want her to be left without either of us."

"I thought you were going to see your time out."

He said without self-pity, "I found I couldn't stand it."

"When are you leaving?"

"I don't know. They thought something could be arranged in six months."

"You can stand six months?"

"I've got to."

"What reason did you give?"

"I told the Economic Attaché—you met him—Joe—more or less the facts."

"I suppose he thinks I'm a bastard not to let you walk off with my girl."

"Oh no, he rather sided with you."

The car was spluttering and heaving—it had been spluttering for a minute, I think, before I noticed it, for I had been examining Pyle's innocent question: "Are you playing straight?" It belonged to a psychological world of great simplicity, where you talked of Democracy and Honor without the *u* as it's spelt on old tombstones, and you meant what your father meant by the same words. I said, "We've run out."

"Gas?"

"There was plenty. I crammed it full before I started. Those bastards in Tanyin have syphoned it out. I ought to have noticed. It's like them to leave us enough to get out of their zone."

"What shall we do?"

"We can just make the next watch tower. Let's hope they have a little."

But we were out of luck. The car reached within thirty yards of the tower and gave up. We walked to the foot of the tower and I called up in French to the guards that we were friends, that we were coming up. I had no wish to be shot by a Vietnamese sentry. There was no reply: nobody looked out. I said to Pyle, "Have you a gun?"

"I never carry one."

"Nor do I."

The last colours of sunset, green and gold like the rice, were dripping over the edge of the flat world: against the grey neutral sky the watch tower looked as black as print. It must be nearly the hour of curfew. I shouted again and nobody answered.

"Do you know how many towers we passed since the last fort?"

"I wasn't noticing."

"Nor was I." It was probably at least six kilometres to the next fort—an hour's walk. I called a third time, and silence repeated itself like an answer.

I said, "It seems to be empty: I'd better climb up and see." The yellow flag with red stripes faded to orange showed that we were out of the territory of the Hoa-Haos and in the territory of the Vietnamese army.

Pyle said, "Don't you think if we waited here a car might come?"

"It might, but *they* might come first."

"Shall I go back and turn on the lights? For a signal."

"Good God, no. Let it be." It was dark enough now to stumble, looking for the ladder. Something cracked under foot; I could imagine the sound travelling across the fields of paddy, listened to by whom? Pyle had lost his outline and was a blur at the side of the road. Darkness, when once it fell, fell like a stone. I said, "Stay there until I call." I wondered whether the guard would have drawn up his ladder, but there it stood—though an enemy might climb it, it was their only way of escape. I began to mount.

I have read so often of people's thoughts in the moment of fear: of God, or family, or a woman. I admire their control. I thought of nothing, not even of the trap-door above me: I ceased, for those seconds, to exist: I was fear taken neat. At the top of the ladder I banged my head because fear couldn't count steps, hear, or see. Then my head came over the earth floor and nobody shot at me and fear seeped away.

3

A small oil lamp burned on the floor and two men crouched against the wall, watching me. One had a sten gun and one a rifle, but they were as scared as I'd been. They looked like schoolboys, but with the Vietnamese age drops suddenly like the sun—they are boys and then they are old men. I was glad that the colour of my skin and the shape of my eyes were a passport—they wouldn't shoot now even from fear.

I came up out of the floor, talking to reassure them, telling them that my car was outside, that I had run out of petrol. Perhaps they had a little I could buy. It didn't seem likely as I stared around. There was nothing in the little round room except a box of ammunition for the sten gun, a small wooden bed, and two packs hanging on a nail. A couple of pans with the remains of rice and some wooden chopsticks showed they had been eating without much appetite.

"Just enough to get us to the next fort?" I asked.

One of the men sitting against the wall—the one with the rifle—shook his head.

"If you can't we'll have to stay the night here."

"C'est défendu."

"Who by?"

"You are a civilian."

"Nobody's going to make me sit out there on the road and have my throat cut."

"Are you French?"

Only one man had spoken. The other sat with his head turned sideways, watching the slit in the wall. He could have seen nothing but a postcard of sky: he seemed to be listening and I began to listen too. The silence became full of sound:

noises you couldn't put a name to—a crack, a creak, a rustle, something like a cough, and a whisper. Then I heard Pyle: he must have come to the foot of the ladder. "You all right, Thomas?"

"Come up," I called back. He began to climb the ladder and the silent soldier shifted his sten gun—I don't believe he'd heard a word of what we'd said: it was an awkward, jumpy movement. I realized that fear had paralysed him. I rapped out at him like a sergeant-major, "Put that gun down!" and I used the kind of French obscenity I thought he would recognize. He obeyed me automatically. Pyle came up into the room. I said, "We've been offered the safety of the tower till morning."

"Fine," Pyle said. His voice was a little puzzled. He said, "Oughtn't one of those mugs to be on sentry?"

"They prefer not to be shot at. I wish you'd brought something stronger than lime-juice."

"I guess I will next time," Pyle said.

"We've got a long night ahead." Now that Pyle was with me, I didn't hear the noises. Even the two soldiers seemed to have relaxed a little.

"What happens if the Viets attack them?" Pyle asked.

"They'll fire a shot and run. You read it every morning in the *Extrême Orient*. 'A post south-west of Saigon was temporarily occupied last night by the Vietminh.'"

"It's a bad prospect."

"There are forty towers like this between us and Saigon. The chances always are that it's the other chap who's hurt."

"We could have done with those sandwiches," Pyle said. "I do think one of them should keep a look-out."

"He's afraid a bullet might look in." Now that we too had settled on the floor, the Vietnamese relaxed a little. I felt some sympathy for them: it wasn't an easy job for a couple of ill-trained men to sit up here night after night, never sure of when the Viets might creep up on the road through the fields of paddy. I said to Pyle, "Do you think they know they are fighting for Democracy? We ought to have York Harding here to explain it to them."

"You always laugh at York," said Pyle.

"I laugh at anyone who spends so much time writing about what doesn't exist—mental concepts."

"They exist for him. Haven't you got any mental concepts? God, for instance?"

"I've no reason to believe in a God. Do you?"

"Yes. I'm a Unitarian."

"How many hundred million Gods do people believe in? Why, even a Roman Catholic believes in quite a different God when he's scared or happy or hungry."

"Maybe, if there is a God, he'd be so vast he'd look different to everyone."

"Like the great Buddha in Bangkok," I said. "You can't see all of him at once. Anyway *he* keeps still."

"I guess you're just trying to be tough," Pyle said. "There's something you must believe in. Nobody can go on living without some belief."

"Oh, I'm not a Berkeleian. I believe my back's against this wall. I believe there's a sten gun over there."

"I didn't mean that."

"I believe what I report, which is more than most of your correspondents do."

"Cigarette?"

"I don't smoke—except opium. Give one to the guards. We'd better stay friends with them." Pyle got up and lit their cigarettes and came back. I said, "I wish cigarettes had a symbolic significance like salt."

"Don't you trust them?"

"No French officer," I said, "would care to spend the night alone with two scared guards in one of these towers. Why, even a platoon have been known to hand over their officers. Sometimes the Viets have a better success with a megaphone than a bazooka. I don't blame them. They don't believe in anything either. You and your like are trying to make a war with the help of people who just aren't interested."

"They don't want Communism."

"They want enough rice," I said. "They don't want to be shot at. They want one day to be much the same as another. They don't want our white skins around telling them what they want."

"If Indo-China goes . . ."

"I know the record. Siam goes. Malaya goes. Indonesia goes. What does 'go' mean? If I believed in your God and another life, I'd bet my future harp against your golden crown that in five hundred years there may be no New York or London, but they'll be growing paddy in these fields, they'll be carrying their produce to market on long poles wearing their pointed hats. The small boys will be sitting on the buffaloes. I like the buffaloes, they don't like our smell, the smell of Europeans. And remember—from a buffalo's point of view you are a European too."

"They'll be forced to believe what they are told, they won't be allowed to think for themselves."

"Thought's a luxury. Do you think the peasant sits and thinks of God and Democracy when he gets inside his mud hut at night?"

"You talk as if the whole country were peasant. What about the educated? Are they going to be happy?"

"Oh no," I said, "we've brought them up in *our* ideas. We've taught them dangerous games, and that's why we are waiting here, hoping we don't get our throats cut. We deserve to have them cut. I wish your friend York was here too. I wonder how he'd relish it."

"York Harding's a very courageous man. Why, in Korea . . ."

"He wasn't an enlisted man, was he? He had a return ticket. With a return ticket courage becomes an intellectual exercise, like a monk's flagellation. How much can I stick? Those poor devils can't catch a plane home. Hi," I called to them, "what are your names?" I thought that knowledge somehow would bring them into the circle of our conversation. They didn't answer: just lowered back at us behind the stumps of their cigarettes. "They think we are French," I said.

"That's just it," Pyle said. "You shouldn't be against York, you should be against the French. Their colonialism."

"Isms and ocracies. Give me facts. A rubber planter beats his labourer—all right, I'm against him. He hasn't been instructed to do it by the Minister of the Colonies. In France I expect he'd beat his wife. I've seen a priest, so poor he hasn't a change of trousers, working fifteen hours a day from hut to hut in a cholera epidemic, eating nothing but rice and salt fish, saying his Mass with an old cup—a wooden platter. I don't believe in God and yet I'm for that priest. Why don't you call that colonialism?"

"It *is* colonialism. York says it's often the good administrators who make it hard to change a bad system."

"Anyway the French are dying every day—that's not a mental concept. They aren't leading these people on with half-lies like your politicians—and ours. I've been in India, Pyle, and I know the harm liberals do. We haven't a liberal party any more—liberalism's infected all the other parties. We are all either liberal conservatives or liberal socialists: we all have a good conscience. I'd rather be an exploiter who fights for what he exploits, and dies with it. Look at the history of Burma. We go and invade the country: the local tribes support us: we are victorious: but like you Americans we weren't colonialists in those days. Oh no, we made peace with the king and we handed him back his province and left our allies to be crucified and sawn in two. They were innocent. They thought we'd stay. But we were liberals and we didn't want a bad conscience."

"That was a long time ago."

"We shall do the same thing here. Encourage them and leave them with a little equipment and a toy industry."

"Toy industry?"

"Your plastic."

"Oh yes, I see."

"I don't know what I'm talking politics for. They don't interest me and I'm a reporter. I'm not *engagé*."

"Aren't you?" Pyle said.

"For the sake of an argument—to pass this bloody night, that's all. I don't take sides. I'll be still reporting, whoever wins."

"If they win, you'll be reporting lies."

"There's usually a way round, and I haven't noticed much regard for truth in our papers either."

I think the fact of our sitting there talking encouraged the two soldiers: perhaps they thought the sound of our white voices—for voices have a colour too, yellow voices sing and black voices gargle, while ours just speak—would give an impression of numbers and keep the Viets away. They picked up their pans and began to eat again, scraping with their chopsticks, eyes watching Pyle and me over the rim of the pan.

"So you think we've lost?"

"That's not the point," I said. "I've no particular desire to see you win. I'd like those two poor buggers there to be happy—that's all. I wish they didn't have to sit in the dark at night scared."

"You have to fight for liberty."

"I haven't seen any Americans fighting around here. And as for liberty, I don't know what it means. Ask them." I called across the floor in French to them. *"La liberté—qu'est-ce que c'est la liberté?"* They sucked in the rice and stared back and said nothing.

Pyle said, "Do you want everybody to be made in the same mould? You're arguing for the sake of arguing. You're an intellectual. You stand for the importance of the individual as much as I do—or York."

"Why have we only just discovered it?" I said. "Forty years ago no one talked that way."

"It wasn't threatened then."

"Ours wasn't threatened, oh no, but who cared about the individuality of the man in the paddy field—and who does now? The only man to treat him as a man is the political commissar. He'll sit in his hut and ask his name and listen to his complaints; he'll give up an hour a day to teaching him—it doesn't matter what, he's being treated like a man, like someone of value. Don't go on in the East with that parrot cry about a threat to the individual soul. Here you'd find yourself on the wrong side—it's they who stand for the individual and we just stand for Private 23987, unit in the global strategy."

"You don't mean half what you are saying," Pyle said uneasily.

"Probably three quarters. I've been here a long time. You know, it's lucky I'm not *engagé*, there are things I might be tempted to do—because here in the East—well, I don't like

Ike. I like—well, these two. This is their country. What's the
time? My watch has stopped."

"It's turned eight-thirty."

"Ten hours and we can move."

·     "It's going to be quite chilly," Pyle said and shivered. "I
never expected that."

"There's water all round. I've got a blanket in the car. That
will be enough."

"Is it safe?"

"It's early for the Viets."

"Let me go."

"I'm more used to the dark."

When I stood up the soldiers stopped eating. I told them,
"*Je reviens, tout de suite.*" I dangled my legs over the trap door,
found the ladder and went down. It is odd how reassuring conversation is, especially on abstract subjects: it seems to normalize the strangest surroundings. I was no longer scared: it
was as though I had left a room and would be returning there
to pick up the argument—the watch tower was the rue Catinat,
the bar of the Majestic, or even a room off Gordon Square.

I stood below the tower for a minute to get my vision back.
There was starlight, but no moonlight. Moonlight reminds me
of a mortuary and the cold wash of an unshaded globe over a
marble slab, but starlight is alive and never still, it is almost as
though someone in those vast spaces is trying to communicate
a message of good will, for even the names of the stars are
friendly. Venus is any woman we love, the Bears are the bears
of childhood, and I suppose the Southern Cross, to those, like
my wife, who believe, may be a favourite hymn or a prayer
beside the bed. Once I shivered as Pyle had done. But the night
was hot enough, only the shallow stretch of water on either side
gave a kind of icing to the warmth. I started out towards the
car, and for a moment when I stood on the road I thought it
was no longer there. That shook my confidence, even after I
remembered that it had petered out thirty yards away. I
couldn't help walking with my shoulders bent: I felt more unobtrusive that way.

I had to unlock the boot to get the blanket and the click

and squeak startled me in the silence. I didn't relish being the only noise in what must have been a night full of people. With the blanket over my shoulder I lowered the boot more carefully than I had raised it, and then, just as the catch caught, the sky towards Saigon flared with light and the sound of an explosion came rumbling down the road. A bren spat and spat and was quiet again before the rumbling stopped. I thought, "Somebody's had it," and very far away heard voices crying with pain or fear or perhaps even triumph. I don't know why, but I had thought all the time of an attack coming from behind, along the road we had passed, and I had a moment's sense of unfairness that the Viets should be there ahead, between us and Saigon. It was as though we had been unconsciously driving towards danger instead of away from it, just as I was now walking in its direction, back towards the tower. I walked because it was less noisy than to run, but my body wanted to run.

At the foot of the ladder I called up to Pyle, "It's me—Fowler." (Even then I couldn't bring myself to use my Christian name to him.) The scene inside the hut had changed. The pans of rice were back on the floor; one man held his rifle on his hip and sat against the wall staring at Pyle and Pyle knelt a little way out from the opposite wall with his eyes on the sten gun which lay between him and the second guard. It was as though he had begun to crawl towards it but had been halted. The second guard's arm was extended towards the gun: no one had fought or even threatened, it was like that child's game when you mustn't be seen to move or you are sent back to base to start again.

"What's going on?" I said.

The two guards looked at me and Pyle pounced, pulling the sten to his side of the room.

"Is it a game?" I asked.

"I don't trust him with the gun," Pyle said, "if they are coming."

"Ever used a sten?"

"No."

"That's fine. Nor have I. I'm glad it's loaded—we wouldn't know how to reload it."

The guards had quietly accepted the loss of the gun. The one lowered his rifle and laid it across his thighs; the other slumped against the wall and shut his eyes as though like a child he believed himself invisible in the dark. Perhaps he was glad to have no more responsibility. Somewhere far away the bren started again—three bursts and then silence. The second guard screwed his eyes closer shut.

"They don't know we can't use it," Pyle said.

"They are supposed to be on our side."

"I thought you didn't have a side."

"*Touché*," I said. "I wish the Viets knew it."

"What's happening out there?"

I quoted again tomorrow's *Extrême Orient*: "A post fifty kilometres outside Saigon was attacked and temporarily captured last night by Vietminh irregulars."

"Do you think it would be safer in the fields?"

"It would be terribly wet."

"You don't seem worried," Pyle said.

"I'm scared stiff—but things are better than they might be. They don't usually attack more than three posts in a night. Our chances have improved."

"What's that?"

It was the sound of a heavy car coming up the road, driving towards Saigon. I went to the rifle slit and looked down, just as a tank went by.

"The patrol," I said. The gun in the turret shifted now to this side, now to that. I wanted to call out to them, but what was the good? They hadn't room on board for two useless civilians. The earth floor shook a little as they passed, and they had gone. I looked at my watch—eight fifty-one—and waited, straining to read when the light flapped. It was like judging the distance of lightning by the delay before the thunder. It was nearly four minutes before the gun opened up. Once I thought I detected a bazooka replying, then all was quiet again.

"When they come back," Pyle said, "we could signal them for a lift to the camp."

An explosion set the floor shaking. "If they come back," I said. "That sounded like a mine." When I looked at my watch again it had passed nine fifteen and the tank had not returned. There had been no more firing.

I sat down beside Pyle and stretched out my legs. "We'd better try to sleep," I said. "There's nothing else we can do."

"I'm not happy about the guards," Pyle said.

"They are all right so long as the Viets don't turn up. Put the sten under your leg for safety." I closed my eyes and tried to imagine myself somewhere else—sitting up in one of the fourth-class compartments the German railways ran before Hitler came to power, in the days when one was young and sat up all night without melancholy, when waking dreams were full of hope and not of fear. This was the hour when Phuong always set about preparing my evening pipes. I wondered whether a letter was waiting for me—I hoped not, for I knew what a letter would contain, and so long as none arrived I could day-dream of the impossible.

"Are you asleep?" Pyle asked.

"No."

"Don't you think we ought to pull up the ladder?"

"I begin to understand why they don't. It's the only way out."

"I wish that tank would come back."

"It won't now."

I tried not to look at my watch except at long intervals, and the intervals were never as long as they had seemed. Nine forty, ten five, ten twelve, ten thirty-two, ten forty-one.

"You awake?" I said to Pyle.

"Yes."

"What are you thinking about?"

He hesitated. "Phuong," he said.

"Yes?"

"I was just wondering what she was doing."

"I can tell you that. She'll have decided that I'm spending the night at Tanyin—it won't be the first time. She'll be lying on the bed with a joss stick burning to keep away the mosquitoes and she'll be looking at the pictures in an old *Paris-Match*. Like the French she has a passion for the Royal Family."

He said wistfully, "It must be wonderful to know exactly,"

and I could imagine his soft dog's eyes in the dark. They ought to have called him Fido, not Alden.

"I don't really know—but it's probably true. There's no good in being jealous when you can't do anything about it. 'No barricado for a belly.' "

"Sometimes I hate the way you talk, Thomas. Do you know how she seems to me? She seems fresh, like a flower."

"Poor flower," I said. "There are a lot of weeds around."

"Where did you meet her?"

"She was dancing at the Grand Monde."

"Dancing," he exclaimed, as though the idea were painful.

"It's a perfectly respectable profession," I said. "Don't worry."

"You have such an awful lot of experience, Thomas."

"I have an awful lot of years. When you reach my age . . ."

"I've never had a girl," he said, "not properly. Not what you'd call a real experience."

"A lot of energy with your people seems to go into whistling."

"I've never told anybody else."

"You're young. It's nothing to be ashamed of."

"Have you had a lot of women, Fowler?"

"I don't know what a lot means. Not more than four women have had any importance to me—or me to them. The other forty-odd—one wonders why one does it. A notion of hygiene, of one's social obligations, both mistaken."

"You think they *are* mistaken?"

"I wish I could have those nights back. I'm still in love, Pyle, and I'm a wasting asset. Oh, and there was pride, of course. It takes a long time before we cease to feel proud of being wanted. Though God knows why we should feel it, when we look around and see who is wanted too."

"You don't think there's anything wrong with me, do you, Thomas?"

"No, Pyle."

"It doesn't mean I don't *need* it, Thomas, like everybody else. I'm not—odd."

"Not one of us needs it as much as we say. There's an awful lot of self-hypnosis around. Now I know I need nobody—

except Phuong. But that's a thing one learns with time. I could go a year without one restless night if she wasn't there."

"But she *is* there," he said in a voice I could hardly catch.

"One starts promiscuous and ends like one's grandfather, faithful to one woman."

"I suppose it seems pretty naïve to start that way . . ."

"No."

"It's not in the Kinsey Report."

"That's why it's not naïve."

"You know, Thomas, it's pretty good being here, talking to you like this. Somehow it doesn't seem dangerous any more."

"We used to feel that in the blitz," I said, "when a lull came. But they always returned."

"If somebody asked you what your deepest sexual experience had been, what would you say?"

I knew the answer to that. "Lying in bed early one morning and watching a woman in a red dressing-gown brush her hair."

"Joe said it was being in bed with a Chink and a negress at the same time."

"I'd have thought that one up too when I was twenty."

"Joe's fifty."

"I wonder what mental age they gave him in the war."

"Was Phuong the girl in the red dressing-gown?"

I wished that he hadn't asked that question.

"No," I said, "that woman came earlier. When I left my wife."

"What happened?"

"I left her, too."

"Why?"

Why indeed? "We are fools," I said, "when we love. I was terrified of losing her. I thought I saw her changing—I don't know if she really was, but I couldn't bear the uncertainty any longer. I ran towards the finish just like a coward runs towards the enemy and wins a medal. I wanted to get death over."

"Death?"

"It was a kind of death. Then I came east."

"And found Phuong?"

"Yes."

"But don't you find the same thing with Phuong?"

"Not the same. You see, the other one loved me. I was afraid of losing love. Now I'm only afraid of losing Phuong." Why had I said that, I wondered? He didn't need encouragement from me.

"But she loves you, doesn't she?"

"Not like that. It isn't in their nature. You'll find that out. It's a cliché to call them children—but there's one thing which is childish. They love you in return for kindness, security, the presents you give them—they hate you for a blow or an injustice. They don't know what it's like—just walking into a room and loving a stranger. For an aging man, Pyle, it's very secure —she won't run away from home so long as the home is happy."

I hadn't meant to hurt him. I only realized I had done it when he said with muffled anger, "She might prefer greater security or more kindness."

"Perhaps."

"Aren't you afraid of that?"

"Not so much as I was of the other."

"Do you love her at all?"

"Oh yes, Pyle, yes. But that other way I've only loved once."

"In spite of the forty-odd women," he snapped at me.

"I'm sure it's below the Kinsey average. You know, Pyle, women don't want virgins. I'm not sure *we* do, unless we are a pathological type."

"I didn't mean I was a virgin," he said. All my conversations with Pyle seemed to take grotesque directions. Was it because of his sincerity that they so ran off the customary rails? His conversation never took the corners.

"You can have a hundred women and still be a virgin, Pyle. Most of your G.I.s who were hanged for rape in the war were virgins. We don't have so many in Europe. I'm glad. They do a lot of harm."

"I just don't understand you, Thomas."

"It's not worth explaining. I'm bored with the subject anyway. I've reached the age when sex isn't the problem so much as old age and death. I wake up with these in mind and not a woman's body. I just don't want to be alone in my last decade,

that's all. I wouldn't know what to think about all day long. I'd
sooner have a woman in the same room—even one I didn't
love. But if Phuong left me, would I have the energy to find
another . . . ?"

"If that's all she means to you . . ."

"All, Pyle? Wait until you're afraid of living ten years alone
with no companion and a nursing home at the end of it. Then
you'll start running in any direction, even away from that girl
in the red dressing-gown, to find someone, anyone, who will
last until you are through."

"Why don't you go back to your wife, then?"

"It's not easy to live with someone you've injured."

A sten gun fired a long burst—it couldn't have been more
than a mile away. Perhaps a nervous sentry was shooting at
shadows: perhaps another attack had begun. I hoped it was an
attack—it increased our chances.

"Are you scared, Thomas?"

"Of course I am. With all my instincts. But with my reason
I know it's better to die like this. That's why I came east. Death
stays with you." I looked at my watch. It had gone eleven. An
eight-hour night and then we could relax. I said, "We seem to
have talked about pretty nearly everything except God. We'd
better leave him to the small hours."

"You don't believe in Him, do you?"

"No."

"Things to me wouldn't make sense without Him."

"They don't make sense to me with him."

"I read a book once . . ."

I never knew what book Pyle had read. (Presumably it
wasn't York Harding or Shakespeare or the anthology of contemporary verse or *The Physiology of Marriage*—perhaps it was
*The Triumph of Life*.) A voice came right into the tower with
us, it seemed to speak from the shadows by the trap—a hollow
megaphone voice saying something in Vietnamese. "We're for
it," I said. The two guards listened, their faces turned to the
rifle slit, their mouths hanging open.

"What is it?" Pyle asked.

Walking to the embrasure was like walking through the
voice. I looked quickly out: there was nothing to be seen—I

couldn't even distinguish the road and when I looked back into the room the rifle was pointed, I wasn't sure whether at me or at the slit. But when I moved round the wall the rifle wavered, hesitated, kept me covered: the voice went on saying the same thing over again. I sat down and the rifle was lowered.

"What's he saying?" Pyle asked.

"I don't know. I expect they've found the car and are telling these chaps to hand us over or else. Better pick up that sten before they make up their minds."

"He'll shoot."

"He's not sure yet. When he is he'll shoot anyway."

Pyle shifted his leg and the rifle came up.

"I'll move along the wall," I said. "When his eyes waver get him covered."

Just as I rose the voice stopped: the silence made me jump. Pyle said sharply, "Drop your rifle." I had just time to wonder whether the sten was unloaded—I hadn't bothered to look—when the man threw his rifle down.

I crossed the room and picked it up. Then the voice began again—I had the impression that no syllable had changed. Perhaps they used a record. I wondered when the ultimatum would expire.

"What happens next?" Pyle asked, like a schoolboy watching a demonstration in the laboratory: he didn't seem personally concerned.

"Perhaps a bazooka, perhaps a Viet."

Pyle examined his sten. "There doesn't seem any mystery about this," he said. "Shall I fire a burst?"

"No, let them hesitate. They'd rather take the post without firing and it gives us time. We'd better clear out fast."

"They may be waiting at the bottom."

"Yes."

The two men watched us—I write men, but I doubt whether they had accumulated forty years between them. "And these?" Pyle asked, and he added with a shocking directness, "Shall I shoot them?" Perhaps he wanted to try the sten.

"They've done nothing."

"They were going to hand us over."

"Why not?" I said. "We've no business here. It's their country."

I unloaded the rifle and laid it on the floor. "Surely you're not leaving that," he said.

"I'm too old to run with a rifle. And this isn't my war. Come on."

It wasn't my war, but I wished those others in the dark knew that as well. I blew the oil-lamp out and dangled my legs over the trap, feeling for the ladder. I could hear the guards whispering to each other like crooners, in their language like a song. "Make straight ahead," I told Pyle, "aim for the rice. Remember there's water—I don't know how deep. Ready?"

"Yes."

"Thanks for the company."

"Always a pleasure," Pyle said.

I heard the guards moving behind us: I wondered if they had knives. The megaphone voice spoke peremptorily as though offering a last chance. Something shifted softly in the dark below us, but it might have been a rat. I hesitated. "I wish to God I had a drink," I whispered.

"Let's go."

Something was coming up the ladder: I heard nothing, but the ladder shook under my feet.

"What's keeping you?" Pyle said.

I don't know why I thought of it as something, that silent stealthy approach. Only a man could climb a ladder, and yet I couldn't think of it as a man like myself—it was as though an animal were moving in to kill, very quietly and certainly with the remorselessness of another kind of creation. The ladder shook and shook and I imagined I saw its eyes glaring upwards. Suddenly I could bear it no longer and I jumped, and there was nothing there at all but the spongy ground, which took my ankle and twisted it as a hand might have done. I could hear Pyle coming down the ladder; I realized I had been a frightened fool who could not recognize his own trembling, and I had believed I was tough and unimaginative, all that a truthful observer and reporter should be. I got on my feet and nearly fell again with the pain. I started out for the field dragging one foot after me and heard Pyle coming behind me. Then the bazooka shell burst on the tower and I was on my face again.

4

"Are you hurt?" Pyle said.

"Something hit my leg. Nothing serious."

"Let's get on," Pyle urged me. I could just see him because he seemed to be covered with a fine white dust. Then he simply went out like a picture on the screen when the lamps of the projector fail: only the soundtrack continued. I got gingerly up on to my good knee and tried to rise without putting any weight on my bad left ankle, and then I was down again breathless with pain. It wasn't my ankle: something had happened to my left leg. I couldn't worry—pain took away care. I lay very still on the ground hoping that pain wouldn't find me again. I even held my breath, as one does with toothache. I didn't think about the Viets who would soon be searching the ruins of the tower: another shell exploded on it—they were making quite sure before they came in. What a lot of money it costs, I thought as the pain receded, to kill a few human beings—you can kill horses so much cheaper. I can't have been fully conscious, for I began to think I had strayed into a knacker's yard which was the terror of my childhood in the small town where I was born. We used to think we heard the horses whinnying with fear and the explosion of the painless killer.

It was some while since the pain had returned, now that I was lying still and holding my breath—that seemed to me just as important. I wondered quite lucidly whether perhaps I ought to crawl towards the fields. The Viets might not have time to search far. Another patrol would be out by now trying to contact the crew of the first tank. But I was more afraid of the pain than of the partisans, and I lay still. There was no sound anywhere of Pyle: he must have reached the fields. Then I heard someone weeping. It came from the direction of the tower, or what had been the tower. It wasn't like a man weeping: it was like a child who is frightened of the dark and yet afraid to scream. I supposed it was one of the two boys—

perhaps his companion had been killed. I hoped that the Viets wouldn't cut his throat. One shouldn't fight a war with children and a little curled body in a ditch came back to mind. I shut my eyes—that helped to keep the pain away, too, and waited. A voice called something I didn't understand. I almost felt I could sleep in this darkness and loneliness and absence of pain.

Then I heard Pyle whispering, "Thomas. Thomas." He had learnt footcraft quickly; I had not heard him return.

"Go away," I whispered back.

He found me then and lay down flat beside me. "Why didn't you come? Are you hurt?"

"My leg. I think it's broken."

"A bullet?"

"No, no. Log of wood. Stone. Something from the tower. It's not bleeding."

"You've got to make an effort."

"Go away, Pyle. I don't want to, it hurts too much."

"Which leg?"

"Left."

He crept round to my side and hoisted my arm over his shoulder. I wanted to whimper like the boy in the tower and then I was angry, but it was hard to express anger in a whisper. "God damn you, Pyle, leave me alone. I want to stay."

"You can't."

He was pulling me half on to his shoulder and the pain was intolerable. "Don't be a bloody hero. I don't want to go."

"You've got to help," he said, "or we are both caught."

"You . . ."

"Be quiet or they'll hear you." I was crying with vexation —you couldn't use a stronger word. I hoisted myself against him and let my left leg dangle—we were like awkward contestants in a three-legged race and we wouldn't have stood a chance if, at the moment we set off, a bren had not begun to fire in quick short bursts somewhere down the road towards the next tower. Perhaps a patrol was pushing up or perhaps they were completing their score of three towers destroyed. It covered the noise of our slow and clumsy flight.

I'm not sure whether I was conscious all the time: I think for the last twenty yards Pyle must have almost carried my weight. He said, "Careful here. We are going in." The dry rice rustled around us and the mud squelched and rose. The water was up to our waists when Pyle stopped. He was panting and a catch in his breath made him sound like a bull-frog.

"I'm sorry," I said.

"Couldn't leave you," Pyle said.

The first sensation was relief; the water and mud held my leg tenderly and firmly like a bandage, but soon the cold set us chattering. I wondered whether it had passed midnight yet; we might have six hours of this if the Viets didn't find us.

"Can you shift your weight a little," Pyle said, "just for a moment?" And my unreasoning irritation came back—I had no excuse for it but the pain. I hadn't asked to be saved, or to have death so painfully postponed. I thought with nostalgia of my couch on the hard dry ground. I stood like a crane on one leg trying to relieve Pyle of my weight, and when I moved, the stalks of rice tickled and cut and crackled.

"You saved my life there," I said, and Pyle cleared his throat for the conventional response, "so that I could die here. I prefer dry land."

"Better not talk," Pyle said as though to an invalid.

"Who the hell asked you to save my life? I came east to be killed. It's like your damned impertinence . . ." I staggered in the mud and Pyle hoisted my arm around his shoulder. "Ease it off," he said.

"You've been seeing war-films. We aren't a couple of marines and you can't win a war-medal."

"Sh-sh." Footsteps could be heard, coming down to the edge of the field. The bren up the road stopped firing and there was no sound except the footsteps and the slight rustle of the rice when we breathed. Then the footsteps halted: they only seemed the length of a room away. I felt Pyle's hand on my good side pressing me slowly down; we sank together into the mud very slowly so as to make the least disturbance of the rice. On one knee, by straining my head backwards, I could just keep my mouth out of the water. The pain came back to my leg and I thought, "If I faint here I drown"—I had always hated and feared the thought of drowning. Why can't one choose one's death? There was no sound now: perhaps twenty feet away they were waiting for a rustle, a cough, a sneeze—"Oh God," I thought, "I'm going to sneeze." If only he had left me alone, I would have been responsible only for my own life—not his—and he wanted to live. I pressed my free fingers against my upper lip in that trick we learn when we are children playing at Hide and Seek, but the sneeze lingered, waiting to burst, and silent in the darkness the others waited for the sneeze. It was coming, coming, came . . .

But in the very second that my sneeze broke, the Viets opened with stens, drawing a line of fire through the rice—it swallowed my sneeze with its sharp drilling like a machine punching holes through steel. I took a breath and went under —so instinctively one avoids the loved thing, coquetting with death, like a woman who demands to be raped by her lover. The rice was lashed down over our heads and the storm passed. We came up for air at the same moment and heard the foot-steps going away back towards the tower.

"We've made it," Pyle said, and even in my pain I won-dered what we'd made: for me, old age, an editor's chair, lone-liness; and as for him, I know now that he spoke prematurely. Then in the cold we settled down to wait. Along the road to Tanyin a bonfire burst into life: it burnt merrily like a celebration.

"That's my car," I said.

Pyle said, "It's a shame, Thomas. I hate to see waste."

"There must have been just enough petrol in the tank to set it going. Are you as cold as I am, Pyle?"

"I couldn't be colder."

"Suppose we get out and lie flat on the road?"

"Let's give them another half hour."

"The weight's on you."

"I can stick it, I'm young." He had meant the claim hu-morously, but it struck as cold as the mud. I had intended to apologize for the way my pain had spoken, but now it spoke again. "You're young all right. You can afford to wait, can't you."

"I don't get you, Thomas."

We had spent what seemed to have been a week of nights together, but he could no more understand me than he could understand French. I said, "You'd have done better to let me be."

"I couldn't have faced Phuong," he said, and the name lay there like a banker's bid. I took it up.

"So it was for her," I said. What made my jealousy more absurd and humiliating was that it had to be expressed in the lowest of whispers—it had no tone, and jealousy likes histrionics. "You think these heroics will get her. How wrong you are. If I were dead you could have had her."

"I didn't mean that," Pyle said. "When you are in love you want to play the game, that's all." That's true, I thought, but not as he innocently means it. To be in love is to see yourself as someone else sees you, it is to be in love with the falsified and exalted image of yourself. In love we are incapable of honour—the courageous act is no more than playing a part to an audience of two. Perhaps I was no longer in love but I remembered.

"If it had been you, I'd have left you," I said.

"Oh no, you wouldn't, Thomas." He added with unbearable complacency, "I know you better than you do yourself." Angrily I tried to move away from him and take my own weight, but the pain came roaring back like a train in a tunnel and I leant more heavily against him, before I began to sink into the water. He got both arms round me and held me up, and then inch by inch he began to edge me to the bank and the roadside. When he got me there he lowered me flat in the shallow mud below the bank at the edge of the field, and when the pain retreated and I opened my eyes and ceased to hold my breath, I could see only the elaborate cypher of the constellations—a foreign cypher which I couldn't read: they were not the stars of home. His face wheeled over me, blotting them out. "I'm going down the road, Thomas, to find a patrol."

"Don't be a fool," I said. "They'll shoot you before they know who you are. If the Viets don't get you."

"It's the only chance. You can't lie in the water for six hours."

"Then lay me in the road."

"It's no good leaving you the sten?" he asked doubtfully.

"Of course it's not. If you are determined to be a hero, at least go slowly through the rice."

"The patrol would pass before I could signal it."

"You don't speak French."

"I shall call out '*Je suis Frongçais.*' Don't worry, Thomas. I'll be very careful." Before I could reply he was out of a whisper's range—he was moving as quietly as he knew how, with frequent pauses. I could see him in the light of the burning car, but no shot came; soon he passed beyond the flames and very soon the silence filled the footprints. Oh yes, he was being careful as he had been careful boating down the river into Phat Diem, with the caution of a hero in a boy's adventure-story, proud of his caution like a Scout's badge and quite unaware of the absurdity and the improbability of his adventure.

I lay and listened for the shots from the Viets or a Legion patrol, but none came—it would probably take him an hour or even more before he reached a tower, if he ever reached it. I turned my head enough to see what remained of our tower, a heap of mud and bamboo and struts which seemed to sink lower as the flames of the car sank. There was peace when the pain went—a kind of Armistice Day of the nerves: I wanted to sing. I thought how strange it was that men of my profession would make only two news-lines out of all this night—it was just a common-or-garden night and I was the only strange thing about it. Then I heard a low crying begin again from what was left of the tower. One of the guards must still be alive.

I thought, "Poor devil, if we hadn't broken down outside *his* post, he could have surrendered as they nearly all surrendered, or fled, at the first call from the megaphone. But we were there—two white men, and we had the sten and they didn't dare to move. When we left it was too late." I was responsible for that voice crying in the dark: I had prided myself on detachment, on not belonging to this war, but those wounds had been inflicted by me just as though I had used the sten, as Pyle had wanted to do.

I made an effort to get over the bank into the road. I wanted to join him. It was the only thing I could do, to share his pain. But my own personal pain pushed me back. I couldn't hear him any more. I lay still and heard nothing but my own pain beating like a monstrous heart and held my breath and prayed to the God I didn't believe in, "Let me die or faint. Let me die or faint"; and then I suppose I fainted and was aware of nothing until I dreamed that my eyelids had frozen together and someone was inserting a chisel to prise them apart, and I wanted to warn them not to damage the eyeballs beneath but couldn't speak and the chisel bit through and a torch was shining on my face.

"We made it, Thomas," Pyle said. I remember that, but I don't remember what Pyle later described to others: that I waved my hand in the wrong direction and told them there was a man in the tower and they had to see to him. Anyway I couldn't have made the sentimental assumption that Pyle made. I know myself, and I know the depth of my selfishness. I cannot be at ease (and to be at ease is my chief wish) if someone else is in pain, visibly or audibly or tactually. Sometimes this is mistaken by the innocent for unselfishness, when all I am doing is sacrificing a small good—in this case postponement in attending to my hurt—for the sake of a far greater good, a peace of mind when I need think only of myself.

They came back to tell me the boy was dead, and I was happy—I didn't even have to suffer much pain after the hypodermic of morphia had bitten my leg.

# CHAPTER 3

1

I came slowly up the stairs to the flat in the rue Catinat, pausing and resting on the first landing. The old women gossiped as they always had done, squatting on the floor outside the urinoir, carrying Fate in the lines of their faces as others on the palm. They were silent as I passed and I wondered what they might have told me, if I had known their language, of what had passed while I had been away in the Legion Hospital back on the road towards Tanyin. Somewhere in the tower and the fields I had lost my keys, but I had sent a message to Phuong which she must have received, if she was still there. That "if" was the measure of my uncertainty. I had had no news of her in hospital, but she wrote French with difficulty, and I couldn't read Vietnamese. I knocked on the door and it opened immediately and everything seemed to be the same. I watched her closely while she asked how I was and touched my splinted leg and gave me her shoulder to lean on, as though one could lean with safety on so young a plant. I said, "I'm glad to be home."

She told me that she had missed me, which of course was what I wanted to hear: she always told me what I wanted to hear, like a coolie answering questions, unless by accident. Now I awaited the accident.

"How have you amused yourself?" I asked.

"Oh, I have seen my sister often. She has found a post with the Americans."

"She has, has she? Did Pyle help?"

"Not Pyle, Joe."

"Who's Joe?"

"You know him. The Economic Attaché."

"Oh, of course, Joe."

He was a man one always forgot. To this day I cannot describe him, except his fatness and his powdered clean-shaven cheeks and his big laugh; all his identity escapes me—except that he was called Joe. There are some men whose names are always shortened.

With Phuong's help I stretched myself on the bed. "Seen any movies?" I asked.

"There is a very funny one at the Catinat," and immediately she began to tell me the plot in great detail, while I looked around the room for the white envelope that might be a telegram. So long as I didn't ask, I could believe that she had forgotten to tell me, and it might be there on the table by the typewriter, or on the wardrobe, perhaps put for safety in the cupboard-drawer where she kept her collection of scarves.

"The postmaster—I think he was the postmaster, but he may have been the mayor—followed them home, and he borrowed a ladder from the baker and he climbed through Corinne's window, but, you see, she had gone into the next room with François, but he did not hear Mme. Bompierre coming and she came in and saw him at the top of the ladder and thought . . ."

"Who was Mme. Bompierre?" I asked, turning my head to see the wash-basin, where sometimes she propped reminders among the lotions.

"I told you. She was Corinne's mother and she was looking for a husband because she was a widow . . ."

She sat on the bed and put her hand inside my shirt. "It was very funny," she said.

"Kiss me, Phuong." She had no coquetry. She did at once what I asked and she went on with the story of the film. Just so she would have made love if I had asked her to, straight away, peeling off her trousers without question, and afterwards have taken up the thread of Mme. Bompierre's story and the postmaster's predicament.

"Has a call come for me?"

"Yes."

"Why didn't you give it me?"

"It is too soon for you to work. You must lie down and rest."

"This may not be work."

She gave it me and I saw that it had been opened. It read:

"Four hundred words background wanted effect de Lattre's departure on military and political situation."

"Yes," I said. "It *is* work. How did you know? Why did you open it?"

"I thought it was from your wife. I hoped that it was good news."

"Who translated it for you?"

"I took it to my sister."

"If it had been bad news would you have left me, Phuong?"

She rubbed her hand across my chest to reassure me, not realizing that it was words this time I required, however untrue. "Would you like a pipe? There *is* a letter for you. I think perhaps it is from her."

"Did you open that too?"

"I don't open your letters. Telegrams are public. The clerks read them."

This envelope was among the scarves. She took it gingerly out and laid it on the bed. I recognized the hand-writing. "If this is bad news what will you . . . ?" I knew well that it could be nothing else but bad. A telegram might have meant a sudden act of generosity: a letter could only mean explanation, justification . . . so I broke off my question, for there was no honesty in asking for the kind of promise no one can keep.

"What are you afraid of?" Phuong asked, and I thought, "I'm afraid of the loneliness, of the Press Club and the bed-sitting room, I'm afraid of Pyle."

"Make me a brandy-and-soda," I said. I looked at the beginning of the letter, "Dear Thomas," and the end, "Affectionately, Helen," and waited for the brandy.

"It is from *her*?"

"Yes." Before I read it I began to wonder whether at the end I should lie or tell the truth to Phuong.

Dear Thomas,

I was not surprised to get your letter and to know that you were not alone. You are not a man, are you? to remain alone for very long. You pick up women like your coat picks up dust. Perhaps I would feel more sympathy with your case if I didn't feel that you would find consolation very easily when you return to London. I don't suppose you'll believe me, but what gives me pause and prevents me cabling you a simple No is the thought of the poor girl. We are apt to be more involved than you are.

I had a drink of brandy. I hadn't realized how open the sexual wounds remain over the years. I had carelessly—not choosing my words with skill—set hers bleeding again. Who could blame her for seeking my own scars in return? When we are unhappy we hurt.

"Is it bad?" Phuong asked.

"A bit hard," I said. "But she has the right . . ." I read on.

I always believed you loved Anne more than the rest of us until you packed up and went. Now you seem to be planning to leave another woman because I can tell from your letter that you don't really expect a "favourable" reply. "I'll have done my best"—aren't you thinking that? What would you do if I cabled "Yes"? Would you actually marry her? (I have to write "her"—you don't tell me her name.) Perhaps you would. I suppose like the rest of us you are getting old and don't like living alone. I feel very lonely myself sometimes. I gather Anne has found another companion. But you left her in time.

She had found the dried scab accurately. I drank again. An issue of blood—the phrase came into my mind.

"Let me make you a pipe," Phuong said.

"Anything," I said, "anything."

That is one reason why I ought to say No. (We don't need to talk about the religious reason, because you've never understood or believed in that.) Marriage doesn't prevent you leaving a woman, does it? It only delays the process, and it would be all the more unfair to the girl in this case if you lived with her as long as you lived with me. You would bring her back to England where she would be lost and a stranger, and when you left her, how terribly abandoned she would feel. I don't suppose she even uses a knife and fork, does she? I'm being harsh because I'm thinking of her good more than I am of yours. But, Thomas dear, I do think of yours too.

I felt physically sick. It was a long time since I had received a letter from my wife. I had forced her to write it and I could feel her pain in every line. Her pain struck at my pain: we were back at the old routine of hurting each other. If only it were possible to love without injury—fidelity isn't enough: I had been faithful to Anne and yet I had injured her. The hurt is in the act of possession: we are too small in mind and body to possess another person without pride or to be possessed without humiliation. In a way I was glad that my wife had struck out at me again—I had forgotten her pain for too long, and this was the only kind of recompense I could give her. Unfortunately the innocent are always involved in any conflict. Always, everywhere, there is some voice crying from a tower.

Phuong lit the opium lamp. "Will she let you marry me?"

"I don't know yet."

"Doesn't she say?"

"If she does, she says it very slowly."

I thought, "How much you pride yourself on being *dégagé*, the reporter, not the leader-writer, and what a mess you make behind the scenes. The other kind of war is more innocent than this. One does less damage with a mortar."

If I go against my deepest conviction and say "Yes," would it even be good for you? You say you are being recalled to England and I can realize how you will hate that and do anything to make it easier. I can see you marrying after a drink too many. The first time we really tried —you as well as me—and we failed. One doesn't try so hard the second time. You say it will be the end of life to lose this girl. Once you used exactly that phrase to me—I could show you the letter, I have it still —and I suppose you wrote in the same way to Anne. You say that we've always tried to tell the truth to each other, but, Thomas, your truth is always so temporary. What's the good of arguing with you, or trying to make you see reason? It's easier to act as my faith tells me to act—as you think unreasonably—and simply to write: I don't believe in divorce: my religion forbids it, and so the answer, Thomas, is no—no.

There was another half-page, which I didn't read, before "Affectionately, Helen." I think it contained news of the weather and an old aunt of mine I loved.

I had no cause for complaint, and I had expected this reply. There was a lot of truth in it. I only wished that she had not thought aloud at quite such length, when the thoughts hurt her as well as me.

"She says 'No'?"

I said with hardly any hesitation, "She hasn't made up her mind. There's still hope."

Phuong laughed. "—You say 'hope' with such a long face." She lay at my feet like a dog on a crusader's tomb, preparing the opium, and I wondered what I should say to Pyle. When I had smoked four pipes I felt more ready for the future and I told her the hope was a good one—my wife was consulting a lawyer. Any day now I would get the telegram of release.

"It would not matter so much. You could make a settlement," she said, and I could hear her sister's voice speaking through her mouth.

"I have no savings," I said. "I can't outbid Pyle."

"Don't worry. Something may happen. There are always ways," she said. "My sister says you could take out a life-insurance," and I thought how realistic it was of her not to minimize the importance of money and not to make any great and binding declarations of love. I wondered how Pyle over the years would stand that hard core, for Pyle was a romantic; but then of course in his case there would be a good settlement, the hardness might soften like an unused muscle when the need for it vanished. The rich had it both ways.

That evening, before the shops had closed in the rue Catinat, Phuong bought three more silk scarves. She sat on the bed and displayed them to me, exclaiming at the bright colours, filling a void with her singing voice, and then folding them carefully she laid them with a dozen others in her drawer: it was as though she were laying the foundation of a modest settlement. And I laid the crazy foundation of mine, writing a letter that very night to Pyle with the unreliable clarity and foresight of opium. This was what I wrote—I found it again the other day tucked into York Harding's *Rôle of the West.* He must have been reading the book when my letter arrived. Perhaps he had used it as a bookmark and then not gone on reading.

"Dear Pyle," I wrote, and was tempted for the only time to

write, "Dear Alden," for, after all, this was a bread-and-butter
letter of some importance and it differed from other bread-and-
butter letters in containing a falsehood:

"Dear Pyle, I have been meaning to write from the hospital
to say thank you for the other night. You certainly saved me
from an uncomfortable end. I'm moving about again now with
the help of a stick—I broke apparently in just the right place
and age hasn't yet reached my bones and made them brittle.
We must have a party together some time to celebrate." (My
pen stuck on that word, and then, like an ant meeting an ob-
stacle, went round it by another route.) "I've got something
else to celebrate and I know you will be glad of this, too, for
you've always said that Phuong's interests were what we both
wanted. I found a letter from my wife waiting when I got back,
and she's more or less agreed to divorce me. So you don't need
to worry any more about Phuong"—it was a cruel phrase, but
I didn't realize the cruelty until I read the letter over and then
it was too late to alter. If I were going to scratch that out, I
had better tear the whole letter up.

"Which scarf do you like best?" Phuong asked. "I love the
yellow."

"Yes. The yellow. Go down to the hotel and post this letter
for me."

She looked at the address. "I could take it to the Legation.
It would save a stamp."

"I would rather you posted it."

Then I lay back and in the relaxation of the opium I
thought, "At least she won't leave me now before I go, and
perhaps, somehow, tomorrow, after a few more pipes, I shall
think of a way to remain."

2

Ordinary life goes on—that has saved many a man's reason.
Just as in an air-raid it proved impossible to be frightened all
the time, so under the bombardment of routine jobs, of chance
encounters, of impersonal anxieties, one lost for hours together the personal fear. The thoughts of the coming April, of
leaving Indo-China, of the hazy future without Phuong, were

affected by the day's telegrams, the bulletins of the Vietnam Press, and by the illness of my assistant, an Indian called Domingues (his family had come from Goa by way of Bombay) who had attended in my place the less important Press Conferences, kept a sensitive ear open to the tones of gossip and rumour, and took my messages to the cable-offices and the censorship. With the help of Indian traders, particularly in the north, in Haiphong, Nam Dinh and Hanoi, he ran his own personal Intelligence Service for my benefit, and I think he knew more accurately than the French High Command the location of Vietminh battalions within the Tonkin delta.

And because we never used our information except when it became news, and never passed any reports to the French intelligence, he had the trust and the friendship of several Vietminh agents hidden in Saigon-Cholon. The fact that he was an Asiatic, in spite of his name, unquestionably helped.

I was fond of Domingues. Where other men carry their pride like a skin-disease on the surface, sensitive to the least touch, his pride was deeply hidden, and reduced to the smallest proportion possible, I think, for any human being. All that you encountered in daily contact with him was gentleness and humility and an absolute love of truth: you would have had to be married to him to discover the pride. Perhaps truth and humility go together; so many lies come from our pride—in my profession a reporter's pride, the desire to file a better story than the other man's, and it was Domingues who helped me not to care—to withstand all those telegrams from home asking why I had not covered so and so's story or the report of someone else which I knew to be untrue.

Now that he was ill I realized how much I owed him— why, he would even see that my car was full of petrol, and yet never once, with a phrase or a look, had he encroached on my private life. I believe he was a Roman Catholic, but I had no evidence for it beyond his name and the place of his origin— for all I knew from his conversation, he might have worshipped Krishna or gone on annual pilgrimages, pricked by a wire frame, to the Batu Caves. Now his illness came like a mercy, reprieving me from the treadmill of private anxiety. It was I now who had to attend the wearisome Press Conferences and hobble to my table at the Continental for a gossip with my colleagues; but I was less capable than Domingues of telling truth from falsehood, and so I formed the habit of calling in on him in the evenings to discuss what I had heard. Sometimes one of his Indian friends was there, sitting beside the narrow iron bed in the lodgings Domingues shared in one of the meaner streets off the Boulevard Galliéni. He would sit up straight in his bed with his feet tucked under him so that you had less the impression of visiting a sick man than of being received by a rajah or a priest. Sometimes when his fever was bad his face ran with sweat, but he never lost the clarity of his thought. It was as though his illness were happening to another person's body. His landlady kept a jug of fresh lime by his side, but I never saw him take a drink—perhaps that would have been to admit that it was his own thirst, and his own body which suffered.

Of all the days that I visited him I remember one in particular. I had given up asking him how he was for fear that the question sounded like a reproach, and it was always he who inquired with great anxiety about my health and apologized for the stairs I had to climb. Then he said, "I would like you to meet a friend of mine. He has a story you should listen to."

"Yes."

"I have his name written down because I know you find it difficult to remember Chinese names. We must not use it, of course. He has a warehouse on the Quai Mytho for junk metal."

"Important?"

"It might be."

"Can you give me an idea?"

"I would rather you heard from him. There is something strange, but I don't understand it." The sweat was pouring down his face, but he just let it run as though the drops were alive and sacred—there was that much of the Hindu in him, he would never have endangered the life of a fly. He said, "How much do you know of your friend Pyle?"

"Not very much. Our tracks cross, that's all. I haven't seen him since Tanyin."

"What job does he do?"

"Economic Mission, but that covers a multitude of sins. I think he's interested in home-industries—I suppose with an American business tie-up. I don't like the way they keep the French fighting and cut out their business at the same time."

"I heard him talking the other day at a party the Legation was giving to visiting Congressmen. They had put him on to brief them."

"God help Congress," I said, "he hasn't been in the country six months."

"He was talking about the old colonial powers—England and France, and how you two couldn't expect to win the confidence of the Asiatics. That was where America came in now with clean hands."

"Hawaii, Puerto Rico," I said, "New Mexico."

"Then someone asked him some stock question about the chances of the Government here ever beating the Vietminh and he said a Third Force could do it. There was always a Third Force to be found free from Communism and the taint of colonialism—national democracy he called it; you only had to find a leader and keep him safe from the old colonial powers."

"It's all in York Harding," I said. "He had read it before he came out here. He talked about it his first week and he's learned nothing."

"He may have found his leader," Domingues said.

"Would it matter?"

"I don't know. I don't know what he does. But go and talk to my friend on the Quai Mytho."

I went home to leave a note for Phuong in the rue Catinat and then drove down past the port as the sun set. The tables and chairs were out on the *quai* beside the steamers and the grey naval boats, and the little portable kitchens burned and bubbled. In the Boulevard de la Somme the hairdressers were busy under the trees and the fortune-tellers squatted against the walls with their soiled packs of cards. In Cholon you were in a different city where work seemed to be just beginning rather than petering out with the daylight. It was like driving into a pantomime set: the long vertical Chinese signs and the bright lights and the crowd of extras led you into the wings, where everything was suddenly so much darker and quieter. One such wing took me down again to the *quai* and a huddle of sampans, where the warehouses yawned in the shadow and no one was about.

I found the place with difficulty and almost by accident, the godown gates were open, and I could see the strange Picasso shapes of the junk-pile by the light of an old lamp: bedsteads, bathtubs, ashcans, the bonnets of cars, stripes of old colour where the light hit. I walked down a narrow track carved in the iron quarry and called out for Mr. Chou, but there was no reply. At the end of the godown a stair led up to what I supposed might be Mr. Chou's house—I had apparently been directed to the back door, and I supposed that Domingues had his reasons. Even the staircase was lined with junk, pieces of scrap-iron which might come in useful one day in this jackdaw's nest of a house. There was one big room on the landing and a whole family sat and lay about in it with the effect of a camp which might be struck at any moment. Small tea-cups stood about everywhere and there were lots of cardboard boxes full of unidentifiable objects and fibre suitcases ready strapped; there was an old lady sitting on a big bed, two boys and two girls, a baby crawling on the floor, three middle-aged women in old brown peasant-trousers and jackets, and two old men in a corner in blue silk mandarin coats playing mah jongg. They paid no attention to my coming; they played rapidly, identifying each piece by touch, and the noise was like shingle turning on a beach after a wave withdraws. No one paid any more attention than they did; only a cat leapt on to a cardboard box and a lean dog sniffed at me and withdrew.

"Monsieur Chou?" I asked, and two of the women shook their heads, and still no one regarded me, except that one of the women rinsed out a cup and poured tea from a pot which had been resting warm in its silk-lined box. I sat down on the end of the bed next the old lady and a girl brought me the cup: it was as though I had been absorbed into the community with the cat and the dog—perhaps they had turned up the first time as fortuitously as I had. The baby crawled across the floor and pulled at my laces and no one reproved it: one didn't in the East reprove children. Three commercial calendars were hanging on the walls, each with a girl in gay Chinese costume with bright pink cheeks. There was a big mirror mysteriously lettered Café de la Paix—perhaps it had got caught up accidentally in the junk: I felt caught up in it myself.

I drank slowly the green bitter tea, shifting the handleless cup from palm to palm as the heat scorched my fingers, and I wondered how long I ought to stay. I tried the family once in French, asking when they expected Monsieur Chou to return, but no one replied: they had probably not understood. When my cup was empty they refilled it and continued their own occupations: a woman ironing, a girl sewing, the two boys at their lessons, the old lady looking at her feet, the tiny crippled feet of old China—and the dog watching the cat, which stayed on the cardboard boxes.

I began to realize how hard Domingues worked for his lean living.

A Chinese of extreme emaciation came into the room. He seemed to take up no room at all: he was like the piece of greaseproof paper that divides the biscuits in a tin. The only thickness he had was in his striped flannel pyjamas. "Monsieur Chou?" I asked.

He looked at me with the indifferent gaze of a smoker: the sunken cheeks, the baby wrists, the arms of a small girl—many years and many pipes had been needed to whittle him down to these dimensions. I said, "My friend, Monsieur Domingues, said that you had something to show me. You *are* Monsieur Chou?"

Oh yes, he said, he was Monsieur Chou and waved me courteously back to my seat. I could tell that the object of my coming had been lost somewhere within the smoky corridors of his skull. I would have a cup of tea? he was much honoured by my visit. Another cup was rinsed on to the floor and put like a live coal into my hands—the ordeal by tea. I commented on the size of his family.

He looked round with faint surprise as though he had never seen it in that light before. "My mother," he said, "my wife,

my sister, my uncle, my brother, my children, my aunt's children." The baby had rolled away from my feet and lay on its
back kicking and crowing. I wondered to whom it belonged. No
one seemed young enough—or old enough—to have produced
that.

I said, "Monsieur Domingues told me it was important."

"Ah, Monsieur Domingues. I hope Monsieur Domingues is
well?"

"He has had a fever."

"It is an unhealthy time of year." I wasn't convinced that
he even remembered who Domingues was. He began to cough,
and under his pyjama jacket, which had lost two buttons, the
tight skin twanged like a native drum.

"You should see a doctor yourself," I said. A newcomer
joined us—I hadn't heard him enter. He was a young man
neatly dressed in European clothes. He said in English, "Mr.
Chou has only one lung."

"I am very sorry . . ."

"He smokes one hundred and fifty pipes every day."

"That sounds a lot."

"The doctor says it will do him no good, but Mr. Chou
feels much happier when he smokes."

I made an understanding grunt.

"If I may introduce myself, I am Mr. Chou's manager."

"My name is Fowler. Mr. Domingues sent me. He said that
Mr. Chou had something to tell me."

"Mr. Chou's memory is very much impaired. Will you have
a cup of tea?"

"Thank you, I have had three cups already." It sounded like
a question and an answer in a phrase-book.

Mr. Chou's manager took the cup out of my hand and held
it out to one of the girls, who after spilling the dregs on the
floor again refilled it.

"That is not strong enough," he said, and took it and tasted
it himself, carefully rinsed it and refilled it from a second teapot. "That is better?" he asked.

"Much better."

Mr. Chou cleared his throat, but it was only for an immense
expectoration into a tin spittoon decorated with pink blooms.

The baby rolled up and down among the tea-dregs and the cat leapt from a cardboard box on to a suitcase.

"Perhaps it would be better if you talked to me," the young man said. "My name is Mr. Heng."

"If you would tell me . . ."

"We will go down to the warehouse," Mr. Heng said. "It is quieter there."

I put out my hand to Mr. Chou, who allowed it to rest between his palms with a look of bewilderment, then gazed around the crowded room as though he were trying to fit me in. The sound of the turning shingle receded as we went down the stairs. Mr. Heng said, "Be careful. The last step is missing," and he flashed a torch to guide me.

We were back among the bedsteads and the bathtubs and Mr. Heng led the way down a side aisle. When he had gone about twenty paces he stopped and shone his light on to a small iron drum. He said, "Do you see that?"

"What about it?"

He turned it over and showed the trade mark: "Diolacton."

"It still means nothing to me."

He said, "I had two of those drums here. They were picked up with other junk at the garage of Mr. Phan-Van-Muoi. You know him?"

"No, I don't think so."

"His wife is a relation of General Thé."

"I still don't quite see . . . ?"

"Do you know what this is?" Mr. Heng asked, stooping and lifting a long concave object like a stick of celery which glistened chromium in the light of his torch.

"It might be a bath-fixture."

"It is a mould," Mr. Heng said. He was obviously a man who took a tiresome pleasure in giving instruction. He paused for me to show my ignorance again. "You understand what I mean by a mould?"

"Oh yes, of course, but I still don't follow . . ."

"This mould was made in U.S.A. Diolacton is an American trade name. You begin to understand?"

"Frankly, no."

"There is a flaw in the mould. That was why it was thrown away. But it should not have been thrown away with the junk —nor the drum either. That was a mistake. Mr. Muoi's manager came here personally. I could not find the mould, but I let him have back the other drum. I said it was all I had, and he told me he needed them for storing chemicals. Of course, he did not ask for the mould—that would have given too much away—but he had a good search. Mr. Muoi himself called later at the American Legation and asked for Mr. Pyle."

"You seem to have quite an Intelligence Service," I said. I still couldn't imagine what it was all about.

"I asked Mr. Chou to get in touch with Mr. Domingues."

"You mean you've established a kind of connection between Pyle and the General," I said. "A very slender one. It's not news anyway. Everybody here goes in for Intelligence."

Mr. Heng beat his heel against the black iron drum and the sound reverberated among the bedsteads. He said, "Mr. Fowler, you are English. You are neutral. You have been fair to all of us. You can sympathize if some of us feel strongly on whatever side."

I said, "If you are hinting that you are a Communist, or a Vietminh, don't worry. I'm not shocked. I have no politics."

"If anything unpleasant happens here in Saigon, it will be blamed on us. My Committee would like you to take a fair view. That is why I have shown you this and this."

"What is Diolacton?" I said. "It sounds like condensed milk."

"It has something in common with milk." Mr. Heng shone his torch inside the drum. A little white powder lay like dust on the bottom. "It is one of the American plastics," he said.

"I heard a rumour that Pyle was importing plastics for toys." I picked up the mould and looked at it. I tried in my mind to divine its shape. This was not how the object itself would look: this was the image in a mirror, reversed.

"Not for toys," Mr. Heng said.

"It is like parts of a rod."

"The shape is unusual."

"I can't see what it could be for."

Mr. Heng turned away. "I only want you to remember what

you have seen," he said, walking back in the shadows of the junk-pile. "Perhaps one day you will have a reason for writing about it. But you must not say you saw the drum here."

"Nor the mould?" I asked.

"Particularly not the mould."

## 3

It is not easy the first time to meet again one who has saved as they put it—one's life. I had not seen Pyle while I was in the Legion Hospital, and his absence and silence, easily accountable (for he was more sensitive to embarrassment than I), sometimes worried me unreasonably, so that at night before my sleeping drug had soothed me I would imagine him going up my stairs, knocking at my door, sleeping in my bed. I had been unjust to him in that, and so I had added a sense of guilt to my other more formal obligation. And then I suppose there was also the guilt of my letter. (What distant ancestors had given me this stupid conscience? Surely they were free of it when they raped and killed in their palaeolithic world.)

Should I invite my saviour to dinner, I sometimes wondered, or should I suggest a meeting for a drink in the bar of the Continental? It was an unusual social problem, perhaps depending on the value one attributed to one's life. A meal and a bottle of wine or a double whisky?—it had worried me for some days until the problem was solved by Pyle himself, who came and shouted at me through my closed door. I was sleeping through the hot afternoon, exhausted by the morning's effort to use my leg, and I hadn't heard his knock.

"Thomas, Thomas." The call dropped into a dream I was having of walking down a long empty road looking for a turning which never came. The road unwound like a tape-machine with a uniformity that would never have altered if the voice hadn't broken in—first of all like a voice crying in pain from a tower and then suddenly a voice speaking to me personally, "Thomas, Thomas."

Under my breath I said, "Go away, Pyle. Don't come near me. I don't want to be saved."

"Thomas." He was hitting at my door, but I lay possum as

though I were back in the rice-field and he was an enemy. Suddenly I realized that the knocking had stopped, someone was speaking in a low voice outside and someone was replying. Whispers are dangerous. I couldn't tell who the speakers were. I got carefully off the bed and with the help of my stick reached the door of the other room. Perhaps I had moved too hurriedly and they had heard me, because a silence grew outside. Silence like a plant put out tendrils: it seemed to grow under the door and spread its leaves in the room where I stood. It was a silence I didn't like, and I tore it apart by flinging the door open. Phuong stood in the passage and Pyle had his hands on her shoulders: from their attitude they might have parted from a kiss.

"Why, come in," I said, "come in."

"I couldn't make you hear," Pyle said.

"I was asleep at first, and then I didn't want to be disturbed. But I *am* disturbed, so come in." I said in French to Phuong, "Where did you pick him up?"

"Here. In the passage," she said. "I heard him knocking, so I ran upstairs to let him in."

"Sit down," I said to Pyle. "Will you have some coffee?"

"No, and I don't want to sit down, Thomas."

"I must. This leg gets tired. You got my letter?"

"Yes. I wish you hadn't written it."

"Why?"

"Because it was a pack of lies. I trusted you, Thomas."

"You shouldn't trust anyone when there's a woman in the case."

"Then you needn't trust me after this. I'll come sneaking up here when you go out, I'll write letters in typewritten envelopes. Maybe I'm growing up, Thomas." But there were tears in his voice, and he looked younger than he had ever done: "Couldn't you have won without lying?"

"No. This is European duplicity, Pyle. We have to make up for our lack of supplies. I must have been clumsy though. How did you spot the lies?"

"It was her sister," he said. "She's working for Joe now. I saw her just now. She knows you've been called home."

"Oh, that," I said with relief. "Phuong knows it too."

"And the letter from your wife? Does Phuong know about that? Her sister's seen it."

"How?"

"She came here to meet Phuong when you were out yesterday and Phuong showed it to her. You can't deceive her. She reads English."

"I see." There wasn't any point in being angry with anyone—the offender was too obviously myself, and Phuong had probably only shown the letter as a kind of boast—it wasn't a sign of mistrust.

"You knew all this last night?" I asked Phuong.

"Yes."

"I noticed you were quiet." I touched her arm. "What a fury you might have been, but you're Phuong—you are no fury."

"I had to think," she said, and I remembered how waking in the night I had told from the irregularity of her breathing that she was not asleep. I'd put my arm out to her and asked her *"Le cauchemar?"* She used to suffer from nightmares when she first came to the rue Catinat, but last night she had shaken her head at the suggestion: her back was turned to me and I had moved my leg against her—the first move in the formula of intercourse. I had noticed nothing wrong even then.

"Can't you explain, Thomas, why . . ."

"Surely it's obvious enough. I wanted to keep her."

"At any cost to her?"

"Of course."

"That's not love."

"Perhaps it's not your way of love, Pyle."

"I want to protect her."

"I don't. She doesn't need protection. I want her around, I want her in my bed."

"Against her will?"

"She wouldn't stay against her will, Pyle."

"She can't love you after this." His ideas were as simple as that. I turned to look for her. She had gone through to the bedroom and was pulling the counterpane straight where I had lain; then she took one of her picture books from a shelf and sat on the bed as though she were quite unconcerned with our talk. I could tell what book it was—a pictorial record of the Queen's life. I could see upside-down the state coach on the way to Westminster.

"Love's a Western word," I said. "We use it for sentimental reasons or to cover up an obsession with one woman. These people don't suffer from obsessions. You're going to be hurt, Pyle, if you aren't careful."

"I'd have beaten you up if it wasn't for that leg."

"You should be grateful to me—and Phuong's sister, of course. You can go ahead without scruples now—and you are very scrupulous in some ways, aren't you, when it doesn't come to plastics."

"Plastics?"

"I hope to God you know what you are doing there. Oh, I know your motives are good, they always are." He looked puzzled and suspicious. "I wish sometimes you had a few bad motives, you might understand a little more about human beings. And that applies to your country too, Pyle."

"I want to give her a decent life. This place—smells."

"We keep the smell down with joss sticks. I suppose you'll offer her a deep freeze and a car for herself and the newest television set and . . ."

"And children," he said.

"Bright young American citizens ready to testify."

"And what will you give her? You weren't going to take her home."

"No, I'm not that cruel. Unless I can afford her a return ticket."

"You'll just keep her as a comfortable lay until you leave."

"She's a human being, Pyle. She's capable of deciding."

"On faked evidence. And a child at that."

"She's no child. She's tougher than you'll ever be. Do you know the kind of polish that doesn't take scratches? That's Phuong. She can survive a dozen of us. She'll get old, that's all. She'll suffer from childbirth and hunger and cold and rheumatism, but she'll never suffer like we do from thoughts, obsessions—she won't scratch, she'll only decay." But even while I made my speech and watched her turn the page (a family group with Princess Anne), I knew I was inventing a character just as much as Pyle was. One never knows another human being; for all I could tell, she was as scared as the rest of us: she didn't have the gift of expression, that was all. And I remembered that first tormenting year when I had tried so passionately to understand her, when I had begged her to tell me what she thought and had scared her with my unreasoning anger at her silences. Even my desire had been a weapon, as though when one plunged one's sword towards the victim's womb, she would lose control and speak.

"You've said enough," I told Pyle. "You know all there is to know. Please go."

"Phuong," he called.

"Monsieur Pyle?" she inquired, looking up from the scrutiny of Windsor Castle, and her formality was comic and re-assuring at that moment.

"He's cheated you."

"*Je ne comprends pas.*"

"Oh, go away," I said. "Go to your Third Force and York Harding and the Rôle of Democracy. Go away and play with plastics."

Later I had to admit that he had carried out my instructions to the letter.

# PART THREE

# CHAPTER 1

1

It was nearly a fortnight after Pyle's death before I saw Vigot again. I was going up the Boulevard Charner when his voice called to me from Le Club. It was the restaurant most favoured in those days by members of the Sureté, who, as a kind of defiant gesture to those who hated them, would lunch and drink on the ground-floor while the general public fed upstairs out of the reach of a partisan with a hand-grenade. I joined him and he ordered me a vermouth cassis. "Play for it?"

"If you like," and I took out my dice for the ritual game of *Quatre Cent Vingt-et-un.* How those figures and the sight of dice bring back to mind the war-years in Indo-China. Anywhere in the world when I see two men dicing I am back in the streets of Hanoi or Saigon or among the blasted buildings of Phat Diem, I see the parachutists, protected like caterpillars by their strange markings, patrolling by the canals, I hear the sound of the mortars closing in, and perhaps I see a dead child.

"*Sans vaseline,*" Vigot said, throwing a four-two-one. He pushed the last match towards me. The sexual jargon of the game was common to all the Sureté; perhaps it had been invented by Vigot and taken up by his junior officers, who hadn't however taken up Pascal. "*Sous-lieutenant.*" Every game you lost raised you a rank—you played till one or other became a captain or a commandant. He won the second game as well and while he counted out the matches, he said, "We've found Pyle's dog."

"Yes?"

"I suppose it had refused to leave the body. Anyway they cut its throat. It was in the mud fifty yards away. Perhaps it dragged itself that far."

"Are you still interested?"

"The American Minister keeps bothering us. We don't have

the same trouble, thank God, when a Frenchman is killed. But then those cases don't have rarity value."

We played for the division of matches and then the real game started. It was uncanny how quickly Vigot threw a four-two-one. He reduced his matches to three and I threw the lowest score possible. "*Nanette*," Vigot said, pushing me over two matches. When he had got rid of his last match he said, "*Capitaine*," and I called the waiter for drinks. "Does anybody ever beat you?" I asked.

"Not often. Do you want your revenge?"

"Another time. What a gambler you could be, Vigot. Do you play any other game of chance?"

He smiled miserably, and for some reason I thought of that blonde wife of his who was said to betray him with his junior officers.

"Oh well," he said, "there's always the biggest of all."

"The biggest?"

" 'Let us weigh the gain and loss,' " he quoted, " 'in wagering that God is, let us estimate these two chances. If you gain, you gain all; if you lose you lose nothing.' "

I quoted Pascal back at him—it was the only passage I remembered. " 'Both he who chooses heads and he who chooses tails are equally at fault. They are both in the wrong. True course is not to wager at all.' "

" 'Yes; but you must wager. It is not optional. You are embarked.' You don't follow your own principles, Fowler. You're *engagé*, like the rest of us."

"Not in religion."

"I wasn't talking about religion. As a matter of fact," he said, "I was thinking about Pyle's dog."

"Oh."

"Do you remember what you said to me—about finding clues on its paws, analysing the dirt and so on?"

"And you said you weren't Maigret or Lecoq."

"I've not done so badly after all," he said. "Pyle usually took the dog with him when he went out, didn't he?"

"I suppose so."

"It was too valuable to let it stray by itself?"

"It wouldn't be very safe. They eat chows, don't they, in this country?" He began to put the dice in his pocket. "My dice, Vigot."

"Oh, I'm sorry. I was thinking . . ."

"Why did you say I was *engagé?*"

"When did you last see Pyle's dog, Fowler?"

"God knows. I don't keep an engagement-book for dogs."

"When are you due to go home?"

"I don't know exactly." I never like giving information to the police. It saves them trouble.

"I'd like—tonight—to drop in and see you. At ten? If you will be alone."

"I'll send Phuong to the cinema."

"Things all right with you again—with her?"

"Yes."

"Strange. I got the impression that you are—well— unhappy."

"Surely there are plenty of possible reasons for that, Vigot." I added bluntly, "You should know."

"Me?"

"You're not a very happy man yourself."

"Oh, I've nothing to complain about. 'A ruined house is not miserable.' "

"What's that?"

"Pascal again. It's an argument for being proud of misery. 'A tree is not miserable.' "

"What made you into a policeman, Vigot?"

"There were a number of factors. The need to earn a living, a curiosity about people, and—yes, even that, a love of Gaboriau."

"Perhaps you ought to have been a priest."

"I didn't read the right authors for that—in those days."

"You still suspect me, don't you, of being concerned?"

He rose and drank what was left of his vermouth cassis.

"I'd like to talk to you, that's all."

I thought after he had turned and gone that he had looked at me with compassion, as he might have looked at some prisoner, for whose capture he was responsible, undergoing his sentence for life.

2

I *had* been punished. It was as though Pyle, when he left my
flat, had sentenced me to so many weeks of uncertainty. Every
time that I returned home it was with the expectation of disaster. Sometimes Phuong would not be there, and I found it
impossible to settle to any work till she returned, for I always
wondered whether she would ever return. I would ask her where
she had been (trying to keep anxiety or suspicion out of my
voice) and sometimes she would reply the market or the shops
and produce her piece of evidence (even her readiness to confirm her story seemed at that period unnatural), and sometimes
it was the cinema, and the stub of her ticket was there to prove
it, and sometimes it was her sister's—that was where I believed
she met Pyle. I made love to her in those days savagely as
though I hated her, but what I hated was the future. Loneliness
lay in my bed and I took loneliness into my arms at night. She
didn't change; she cooked for me, she made my pipes, she gently and sweetly laid out her body for my pleasure (but it was no
longer a pleasure), and just as in those early days I wanted her
mind, now I wanted to read her thoughts, but they were hidden
away in a language I couldn't speak. I didn't want to question
her. I didn't want to make her lie (as long as no lie was spoken
openly I could pretend that we were the same to each other as
we had always been), but suddenly my anxiety would speak for
me, and I said, "When did you last see Pyle?"

She hesitated—or was it that she was really thinking back?
"When we came here," she said.

I began—almost unconsciously—to run down everything
that was American. My conversation was full of the poverty of
American literature, the scandals of American politics, the
beastliness of American children. It was as though she were
being taken away from me by a nation rather than by a man.
Nothing that America could do was right. I became a bore on
the subject of America, even with my French friends who were
ready enough to share my antipathies. It was as if I had been
betrayed, but one is not betrayed by an enemy.

It was just at that time that the incident occurred of the

bicycle bombs. Coming back from the Imperial Bar to an empty flat (was she at the cinema or with her sister?) I found that a note had been pushed under the door. It was from Domingues. He apologized for being still sick and asked me to be outside the big store at the corner of the Boulevard Charner around ten-thirty the next morning. He was writing at the request of Mr. Chou, but I suspected that Mr. Heng was the more likely to require my presence.

The whole affair, as it turned out, was not worth more than a paragraph, and a humorous paragraph at that. It bore no relation to the sad and heavy war in the north, those canals in Phat Diem choked with the grey days-old bodies, the pounding of the mortars, the white glare of napalm. I had been waiting for about a quarter of an hour by a stall of flowers when a truck-load of police drove up with a grinding of brakes and a squeal of rubber from the direction of the Sureté Headquarters in the rue Catinat; the men disembarked and ran for the store, as though they were charging a mob, but there was no mob—only a zareba of bicycles. Every large building in Saigon is fenced in by them—no university city in the West contains so many bicycle-owners. Before I had time to adjust my camera the comic and inexplicable action had been accomplished. The police had forced their way among the bicycles and emerged with three which they carried over their heads into the boulevard and dropped into the decorative fountain. Before I could intercept a single policeman they were back in their truck and driving hard down the Boulevard Bonnard.

"*Operation Bicyclette*," a voice said. It was Mr. Heng.

"What is it?" I asked. "A practice? For what?"

"Wait a while longer," Mr. Heng said.

A few idlers began to approach the fountain, where one wheel stuck up like a buoy as though to warn shipping away from the wrecks below: a policeman crossed the road shouting and waving his hands.

"Let's have a look," I said.

"Better not," Mr. Heng said, and examined his watch. The hands stood at four minutes past eleven.

"You're fast," I said.

"It always gains." And at that moment the fountain exploded over the pavement. A bit of decorative coping struck a window and the glass fell like the water in a bright shower. Nobody was hurt. We shook the water and glass from our clothes. A bicycle wheel hummed like a top in the road, staggered and collapsed. "It must be just eleven," Mr. Heng said.

"What on earth . . . ?"

"I thought you would be interested," Mr. Heng said. "I *hope* you were interested."

"Come and have a drink?"

"No, I am sorry. I must go back to Mr. Chou's, but first let me show you something." He led me to the bicycle park and unlocked his own machine. "Look carefully."

"A Raleigh," I said.

"No, look at the pump. Does it remind you of anything?" He smiled patronizingly at my mystification and pushed off. Once he turned and waved his hand, pedalling towards Cholon and the warehouse of junk. At the Sureté, where I went for information, I realized what he meant. The mould I had seen in his warehouse had been shaped like a half-section of a bicycle-pump. That day all over Saigon innocent bicycle-pumps had proved to contain bombs which had gone off at the stroke of eleven, except where the police, acting on information that I suspect emanated from Mr. Heng, had been able to anticipate the explosions. It was all quite trivial—ten explosions, six people slightly injured, and God knows how many bicycles. My colleagues—except for the correspondent of the *Extrême Orient*, who called it an "outrage"—knew they could only get space by making fun of the affair. "Bicycle Bombs" made a good headline. All of them blamed the Communists. I was the only one to write that the bombs were a demonstration on the part of General Thé, and my account was altered in the office. The General wasn't news. You couldn't waste space by identifying him. I sent a message of regret through Domingues to Mr. Heng—I had done my best. Mr. Heng sent a polite verbal reply. It seemed to me then that he—or his Vietminh Committee—had been unduly sensitive; no one held the affair seriously against the Communists.

Indeed, if anything could have done so, it would have given
them the reputation for a sense of humour. "What'll they think
of next?" people said at parties, and the whole absurd affair
was symbolized for me too in the bicycle-wheel gaily spinning
like a top in the middle of the boulevard. I never even mentioned to Pyle what I had heard of his connection with the
General. Let him play harmlessly with plastic moulds: it might
keep his mind off Phuong. All the same, because I happened
to be in the neighbourhood one evening, because I had nothing
better to do, I called in at Mr. Muoi's garage.

It was a small, untidy place, not unlike a junk warehouse
itself, in the Boulevard de la Somme. A car was jacked up in
the middle of the floor with its bonnet open, gaping like the
cast of some pre-historic animal in a provincial museum which
nobody ever visits. I don't believe anyone remembered it was
there. The floor was littered with scraps of iron and old boxes
—the Vietnamese don't like throwing anything away, any more
than a Chinese cook partitioning a duck into seven courses will
dispense with so much as a claw. I wondered why anybody had
so wastefully disposed of the empty drums and the damaged
mould—perhaps it was a theft by an employee making a few
piastres, perhaps somebody had been bribed by the ingenious
Mr. Heng.

Nobody seemed about, so I went in. Perhaps, I thought,
they are keeping away for a while in case the police call. It was
possible that Mr. Heng had some contact in the Sureté, but
even then it was unlikely that the police would act. It was better
from their point of view to let people assume that the bombs
were Communist.

Apart from the car and the junk strewn over the concrete
floor there was nothing to be seen. It was difficult to picture
how the bombs could have been manufactured at Mr. Muoi's.
I was very vague about how one turned the white dust I had
seen in the drum into plastic, but surely the process was too
complex to be carried out here, where even the two petrol
pumps in the street seemed to be suffering from neglect. I
stood in the entrance and looked out into the street. Under
the trees in the centre of the boulevard the barbers were
at work: a scrap of mirror nailed to a tree-trunk caught the

flash of the sun. A girl went by at a trot under her mollusc hat
carrying two baskets slung on a pole. The fortune-teller squatting against the wall of Simon Frères had found a customer,
an old man with a whisp of beard like Ho Chi Minh's who
watched impassively the shuffling and turning of the ancient
cards. What possible future had he got that was worth a pias-
tre? In the Boulevard de la Somme you lived in the open; everybody here knew all about Mr. Muoi, but the police had no
key which would unlock their confidence. This was the level of
life where everything was known, but you couldn't step down
to that level as you could step into the street. I remembered
the old women gossiping on our landing beside the communal
lavatory: they heard everything too, but I didn't know what they
knew.

I went back into the garage and entered a small office at
the back. There was the usual Chinese commercial calendar, a
littered desk—price-lists and a bottle of gum and an adding-
machine, some paper-clips, a teapot and three cups and a lot
of unsharpened pencils, and for some reason an unwritten
picture-postcard of the Eiffel Tower. York Harding might write
in graphic abstractions about the Third Force, but this was
what it came down to—this was it. There was a door in the
back wall; it was locked, but the key was on the desk among
the pencils. I opened the door and went through.

I was in a small shed about the size of the garage. It contained one piece of machinery that at first sight seemed like a
cage of rods and wires furnished with innumerable perches to
hold some wingless adult bird—it gave the impression of being
tied up with old rags, but the rags had probably been used for
cleaning when Mr. Muoi and his assistants had been called
away. I found the name of a manufacturer—somebody in Ly-
ons and a patent number—patenting what? I switched on the
current and the old machine came alive: the rods had a
purpose—the contraption was like an old man gathering his
last vital force, pounding down his fist, pounding down . . .
This thing was still a press, though in its own sphere it must
have belonged to the same era as the nickelodeon, but I suppose that in this country where nothing was ever wasted, and
where everything might be expected to come one day to

finish its career (I remembered seeing that ancient movie *The Great Train Robbery* jerking its way across a screen, giving entertainment, in a back-street in Nam Dinh), the press was still employable.

I examined the press more closely; there were traces of a white powder. Diolacton, I thought, something in common with milk. There was no sign of a drum or a mould. I went back into the office and into the garage. I felt like giving the old car a pat on the mudguard; it had a long wait ahead of it, perhaps, but it too one day . . . Mr. Muoi and his assistants were probably by this time somewhere among the rice-fields on the way to the sacred mountain where General Thé had his headquarters. When now at last I raised my voice and called "Monsieur Muoi!" I could imagine I was far away from the garage and the boulevard and the barbers, back among those fields where I had taken refuge on the road to Tanyin. "Monsieur Muoi!" I could see a man turn his head among the stalks of rice.

I walked home and up on my landing the old women burst into their twitter of the hedges which I could understand no more than the gossip of the birds. Phuong was not in—only a note to say that she was with her sister. I lay down on the bed—I still tired easily—and fell asleep. When I woke I saw the illuminated dial of my alarm pointing to one twenty-five and I turned my head expecting to find Phuong asleep beside me. But the pillow was undented. She must have changed the sheet that day—it carried the coldness of the laundry. I got up and opened the drawer where she kept her scarves, and they were not there. I went to the bookshelf—the pictorial Life of the Royal Family had gone too. She had taken her dowry with her.

In the moment of shock there is little pain; pain began about three A.M. when I began to plan the life I had still somehow to live and to remember memories in order somehow to eliminate them. Happy memories are the worst, and I tried to remember the unhappy. I was practised. I had lived all this before. I knew I could do what was necessary, but I was so much older—I felt I had little energy left to reconstruct.

3

I went to the American Legation and asked for Pyle. It was necessary to fill in a form at the door and give it to a military policeman. He said, "You haven't put the purpose of the visit."

"He'll know," I said.

"You're by appointment, then?"

"You can put it that way if you like."

"Seems silly to you, I guess, but we have to be very careful. Some strange types come around here."

"So I've heard." He shifted his chewing-gum to another side and entered the lift. I waited. I had no idea what to say to Pyle. This was a scene I had never played before. The policeman returned. He said grudgingly, "I guess you can go up. Room 12A. First floor."

When I entered the room I saw that Pyle wasn't there. Joe sat behind the desk: the Economic Attaché: I still couldn't remember his surname. Phuong's sister watched me from behind a typing desk. Was it triumph that I read in those brown acquisitive eyes?

"Come in, come in, Tom," Joe called boisterously. "Glad to see you. How's your leg? We don't often get a visit from you to our little outfit. Pull up a chair. Tell me how you think the new offensive's going. Saw Granger last night at the Continental. He's for the north again. That boy's *keen*. Where there's news there's Granger. Have a cigarette. Help yourself. You know Miss Hei? Can't remember all these names—too hard for an old fellow like me. I call her 'Hi, there!'—she likes it. None of this stuffy colonialism. What's the gossip of the market, Tom? You fellows certainly do keep your ears to the ground. Sorry to hear about your leg. Alden told me . . ."

"Where's Pyle?"

"Oh, Alden's not in the office this morning. Guess he's at home. Does a lot of his work at home."

"I know what he does at home."

"That boy's keen. Eh, what's that you said?"

"Anyway, I know one of the things he does at home."

"I don't catch on, Tom. Slow Joe—that's me. Always was. Always will be."

"He sleeps with my girl—your typist's sister."

"I don't know what you mean."

"Ask her. She fixed it. Pyle's taken my girl."

"Look here, Fowler, I thought you'd come here on business. We can't have scenes in the office, you know."

"I came here to see Pyle, but I suppose he's hiding."

"Now, you're the very last man who ought to make a remark like that. After what Alden did for you."

"Oh yes, yes, of course. He saved my life, didn't he? But I never asked him to."

"At great danger to himself. That boy's got guts."

"I don't care a damn about his guts. There are other parts of his body that are more à propos."

"Now we can't have any innuendoes like that, Fowler, with a lady in the room."

"The lady and I know each other well. She failed to get her rake-off from me, but she's getting it from Pyle. All right. I know I'm behaving badly, and I'm going to go on behaving badly. This is a situation where people do behave badly."

"We've got a lot of work to do. There's a report on the rubber output . . ."

"Don't worry, I'm going. But just tell Pyle if he phones that I called. He might think it polite to return the visit." I said to Phuong's sister, "I hope you've had the settlement witnessed by the notary public and the American Consul and the Church of Christ Scientist."

I went into the passage. There was a door opposite me marked Men. I went in and locked the door and sitting with my head against the cold wall I cried. I hadn't cried until now. Even their lavatories were air-conditioned, and presently the temperate tempered air dried my tears as it dries the spit in your mouth and the seed in your body.

4

I left affairs in the hands of Domingues and went north. At Haiphong I had friends in the Squadron Gascogne, and I would spend hours in the bar up at the airport, or playing bowls on the gravel-path outside. Officially I was at the front:

I could qualify for keenness with Granger, but it was of no more value to my paper than had been my excursion to Phat Diem. But if one writes about war, self-respect demands that occasionally one shares the risks.

It wasn't easy to share them for even the most limited period, since orders had gone out from Hanoi that I was to be allowed only on horizontal raids—raids in this war as safe as a journey by bus, for we flew above the range of the heavy machine-gun; we were safe from anything but a pilot's error or a fault in the engine. We went out by time-table and came home by time-table: the cargoes of bombs sailed diagonally down and the spiral of smoke blew up from the road-junction or the bridge, and then we cruised back for the hour of the aperitif and drove our iron bowls across the gravel.

One morning in the mess in the town, as I drank brandies-and-sodas with a young officer who had a passionate desire to visit Southend Pier, orders for a mission came in. "Like to come?" I said yes. Even a horizontal raid would be a way of killing time and killing thought. Driving out to the airport he remarked, "This is a vertical raid."

"I thought I was forbidden . . ."

"So long as you write nothing about it. It will show you a piece of country up near the Chinese border you will not have seen before. Near Lai Chau."

"I thought all was quiet there—and in French hands?"

"It was. They captured this place two days ago. Our parachutists are only a few hours away. We want to keep the Viets head down in their holes until we have recaptured the post. It means low diving and machine-gunning. We can only spare two planes—one's on the job now. Ever dive-bombed before?"

"No."

"It is a little uncomfortable when you are not used to it."

The Gascogne Squadron possessed only small B.26 bombers—the French called them prostitutes because with their short wing-span they had no visible means of support. I was crammed on to a little metal pad the size of a bicycle seat with my knees against the navigator's back. We came up the Red River, slowly climbing, and the Red River at this hour was really red. It was as though one had gone far back in time and saw it with the old geographer's eyes who had named it first, at just such an hour when the late sun filled it from bank to bank; then we turned away at 9,000 feet towards the Black River, really black, full of shadows, missing the angle of the light, and the huge majestic scenery of gorge and cliff and jungle wheeled around and stood upright below us. You could have dropped a squadron into those fields of green and grey and left no more trace than a few coins in a harvest-field. Far ahead of us a small plane moved like a midge. We were taking over.

We circled twice above the tower and the green-encircled village, then corkscrewed up into the dazzling air. The pilot—who was called Trouin—turned to me and winked. On his wheel were the studs that controlled the gun and the bomb-chamber. I had that loosening of the bowels, as we came into position for the dive, that accompanies any new experience—the first dance, the first dinner-party, the first love. I was reminded of the Great Racer at the Wembley Exhibition when it came to the top of the rise—there was no way to get out: you were trapped with your experience. On the dial I had just time to read 3,000 metres when we drove down. All was feeling now, nothing was sight. I was forced up against the navigator's back: it was as though something of enormous weight were pressing on my chest. I wasn't aware of the moment when the bombs were released; then the gun chattered and the cockpit was full of the smell of cordite, and the weight was off my chest as we rose, and it was the stomach that fell away, spiralling down like a suicide to the ground we had left. For forty seconds Pyle had not existed: even loneliness hadn't existed. As we climbed in a great arc I could see the smoke through the side window pointing at me. Before the second dive I felt fear—fear of humiliation, fear of vomiting over the navigator's back, fear that my ageing lungs would not stand the pressure. After the tenth dive I was aware only of irritation—the affair had gone on too long, it was time to go home. And again we shot steeply up out of machine-gun range and swerved away and the smoke pointed. The village was surrounded on all sides by mountains. Every time we had to make the same approach, through the same gap. There was no way to vary our attack. As we dived for the fourteenth time I thought, now that I was free from the fear of humiliation, "They have only to fix one machine-gun into position." We lifted our nose again into the safe air—perhaps they didn't even have a gun. The forty minutes of the patrol had seemed interminable, but it had been free from the discomfort of personal thought. The sun was sinking as we turned for home: the geographer's moment had passed: the Black River was no longer black, and the Red River was only gold.

Down we went again, away from the gnarled and fissured forest towards the river, flattening out over the neglected ricefields, aimed like a bullet at one small sampan on the yellow stream. The cannon gave a single burst of tracer, and the sampan blew apart in a shower of sparks: we didn't even wait to see our victims struggling to survive, but climbed and made for home. I thought again as I had thought when I saw the dead child at Phat Diem, "I hate war." There had been something so shocking in our sudden fortuitous choice of a prey—we had just happened to be passing, one burst only was required, there was no one to return our fire, we were gone again, adding our little quota to the world's dead.

I put on my earphones for Captain Trouin to speak to me. He said, "We will make a little detour. The sunset is wonderful on the *calcaire*. You must not miss it," he added kindly, like a host who is showing the beauty of his estate, and for a hundred miles we trailed the sunset over the Baie d'Along. The helmeted Martian face looked wistfully out, down the golden groves among the great humps and arches of porous stone, and the wounds of murder ceased to bleed.

5

Captain Trouin insisted that night on being my host in the opium house, though he would not smoke himself. He liked the smell, he said, he liked the sense of quiet at the end of the day, but in his profession relaxation could go no further. There were officers who smoked, but they were Army men— he had to have his sleep. We lay in a small cubicle in a row

of cubicles like a dormitory at school, and the Chinese propri-
etor prepared my pipes. I hadn't smoked since Phuong left me.
Across the way a *métisse* with long and lovely legs lay coiled
after her smoke reading a glossy woman's paper, and in the
cubicle next to her two middle-aged Chinese transacted business, sipping tea, their pipes laid aside.

I said, "That sampan—this evening—was it doing any
harm?"

Trouin said, "Who knows? In those reaches of the river we
have orders to shoot up anything in sight."

I smoked my first pipe. I tried not to think of all the pipes
I had smoked at home. Trouin said, "Today's affair—that is
not the worst for someone like myself. Over the village they
could have shot us down. Our risk was as great as theirs. What
I detest is napalm bombing. From 3,000 feet, in safety." He
made a hopeless gesture. "You see the forest catching fire. God
knows what you would see from the ground. The poor devils
are burnt alive, the flames go over them like water. They are
wet through with fire." He said with anger against a whole
world that didn't understand, "I'm not fighting a colonial war.
Do you think I'd do these things for the planters of Terre
Rouge? I'd rather be court-martialled. We are fighting all of
your wars, but you leave us the guilt."

"That sampan," I said.

"Yes, that sampan too." He watched me as I stretched out
for my second pipe. "I envy you your means of escape."

"You don't know what I'm escaping from. It's not from the
war. That's no concern of mine. I'm not involved."

"You will all be. One day."

"Not me."

"You are still limping."

"They had the right to shoot at me, but they weren't even
doing that. They were knocking down a tower. One should always avoid demolition squads. Even in Piccadilly."

"One day something will happen. You will take a side."

"No, I'm going back to England."

"That photograph you showed me once . . ."

"Oh, I've torn that one up. She left me."

"I'm sorry."

"It's the way things happen. One leaves people oneself and then the tide turns. It almost makes me believe in justice."

"I do. The first time I dropped napalm I thought, this is the village where I was born. That is where M. Dubois, my father's old friend, lives. The baker—I was very fond of the baker when I was a child—is running away down there in the flames I've thrown. The men of Vichy did not bomb their own country. I felt worse than them."

"But you still go on."

"Those are moods. They come only with the napalm. The rest of the time I think that I am defending Europe. And you know, those others—they do some monstrous things also. When they were driven out of Hanoi in 1946 they left terrible relics among their own people—people they thought had helped us. There was one girl in the mortuary—they had not only cut off her breasts, they had mutilated her lover and stuffed his . . ."

"That's why I won't be involved."

"It's not a matter of reason or justice. We all get involved in a moment of emotion and then we cannot get out. War and Love—they have always been compared." He looked sadly across the dormitory to where the *métisse* sprawled in her great temporary peace. He said, "I would not have it otherwise. *There* is a girl who was involved by her parents—what is her future when this port falls? France is only half her home . . ."

"Will it fall?"

"You are a journalist. You know better than I do that we can't win. You know the road to Hanoi is cut and mined every night. You know we lose one class of St. Cyr every year. We were nearly beaten in '50. De Lattre has given us two years of grace—that's all. But we are professionals: we have to go on fighting till the politicians tell us to stop. Probably they will get together and agree to the same peace that we could have had at the beginning, making nonsense of all these years." His ugly face which had winked at me before the dive wore a kind of professional brutality like a Christmas mask from which a child's eyes peer through the holes in the paper. "You would not understand the nonsense, Fowler. You are not one of us."

"There are other things in one's life which make nonsense of the years."

He put his hand on my knee with an odd protective gesture as though he were the older man. "Take her home," he said. "That is better than a pipe."

"How do you know she would come?"

"I have slept with her myself, and Lieutenant Perrin. Five hundred piastres."

"Expensive."

"I expect she would go for three hundred, but under the circumstances one does not care to bargain."

But his advice did not prove sound. A man's body is limited in the acts which it can perform and mine was frozen by memory. What my hands touched that night might be more beautiful than I was used to, but we are not trapped only by beauty. She used the same perfume, and suddenly at the moment of entry the ghost of what I'd lost proved more powerful than the body stretched at my disposal. I moved away and lay on my back and desire drained out of me.

"I am sorry," I said, and lied, "I don't know what is the matter with me."

She said with great sweetness and misunderstanding, "Don't worry. It often happens that way. It is the opium."

"Yes," I said, "the opium." And I wished to heaven that it had been.

# CHAPTER 2

## 1

It was strange, this first return to Saigon with nobody to welcome me. At the airport I wished there were somewhere else to which I could direct my taxi than the rue Catinat. I thought to myself: "Is the pain a little less than when I went away?" and tried to persuade myself that it was so. When I reached the landing I saw that the door was open, and I became breathless with an unreasonable hope. I walked very slowly towards the door. Until I reached the door hope would remain alive. I heard a chair creak, and when I came to the door I could see a pair of shoes, but they were not a woman's shoes. I went quickly in, and it was Pyle who lifted his awkward weight from the chair Phuong used to use.

He said, "Hullo, Thomas."

"Hullo, Pyle. How did you get in?"

"I met Domingues. He was bringing your mail. I asked him to let me stay."

"Has Phuong forgotten something?"

"Oh no, but Joe told me you'd been to the Legation. I thought it would be easier to talk here."

"What about?"

He gave a lost gesture, like a boy put up to speak at some school function who cannot find the grown-up words. "You've been away?"

"Yes. And you?"

"Oh, I've been travelling around."

"Still playing with plastics?"

He grinned unhappily. He said, "Your letters are over there."

I could see at a glance there was nothing which could interest me now: there was one from my office in London and several that looked like bills, and one from my bank. I said, "How's Phuong?"

His face lit up automatically like one of those electric toys which respond to a particular sound. "Oh, she's fine," he said, and then clamped his lips together as though he'd gone too far.

"Sit down, Pyle," I said. "Excuse me while I look at this. It's from my office."

I opened it. How inopportunely the unexpected can occur. The editor wrote that he had considered my last letter and that in view of the confused situation in Indo-China, following the death of General de Lattre and the retreat from Hoa Binh, he was in agreement with my suggestion. He had appointed a temporary foreign editor and would like me to stay on in Indo-China for at least another year. "We shall keep the chair warm for you," he reassured me with complete incomprehension. He believed I cared about the job, and the paper.

I sat down opposite Pyle and re-read the letter which had come too late. For a moment I had felt elation as on the instant of waking before one remembers.

"Bad news?" Pyle asked.

"No." I told myself that it wouldn't have made any difference anyway: a reprieve for one year couldn't stand up against a marriage settlement.

"Are you married yet?" I asked.

"No." He blushed—he had a great facility in blushing. "As a matter of fact I'm hoping to get special leave. Then we could get married at home—properly."

"Is it more proper when it happens at home?"

"Well, I thought—it's difficult to say these things to you, you are so darned cynical, Thomas, but it's a mark of respect. My father and mother would be there—she'd kind of enter the family. It's important in view of the past."

"The past?"

"You know what I mean. I wouldn't want to leave her behind there with any stigma . . ."

"Would you leave her behind?"

"I guess so. My mother's a wonderful woman—she'd take her around, introduce her, you know, kind of fit her in. She'd help her to get a home ready for me."

I didn't know whether to feel sorry for Phuong or not—she had looked forward so to the skyscrapers and the Statue of Liberty, but she had so little idea of all they would involve,

Professor and Mrs. Pyle, the women's lunch clubs; would they teach her Canasta? I thought of her that first night in the Grand Monde, in her white dress, moving so exquisitely on her eighteen-year-old feet, and I thought of her a month ago, bargaining over meat at the butcher's stores in the Boulevard de la Somme. Would she like those bright clean little New England grocery stores where even the celery was wrapped in cellophane? Perhaps she would. I couldn't tell. Strangely I found myself saying as Pyle might have done a month ago, "Go easy with her, Pyle. Don't force things. She can be hurt like you or me."

"Of course, of course, Thomas."

"She looks so small and breakable and unlike our women, but don't think of her as—as an ornament."

"It's funny, Thomas, how differently things work out. I'd been dreading this talk. I thought you'd be tough."

"I've had time to think, up in the north. There was a woman there . . . Perhaps I saw what you saw at that whorehouse. It's a good thing she went away with you. I might one day have left her behind with someone like Granger. A piece of tail."

"And we can remain friends, Thomas?"

"Yes, of course. Only I'd rather not see Phuong. There's quite enough of her around here as it is. I must find another flat—when I've got time."

He unwound his legs and stood up. "I'm so glad, Thomas. I can't tell you how glad I am. I've said it before, I know, but I do really wish it hadn't been you."

"I'm glad it's you, Pyle." The interview had not been the way I had foreseen: under the superficial angry schemes, at some deeper level, the genuine plan of action must have been formed. All the time that his innocence had angered me, some judge within myself had summed up in his favour, had compared his idealism, his half-baked ideas founded on the works of York Harding, with my cynicism. Oh, I was right about the facts, but wasn't he right too to be young and mistaken, and wasn't he perhaps a better man for a girl to spend her life with?

We shook hands perfunctorily, but some half-formulated fear made me follow him out to the head of the stairs and call after him. Perhaps there is a prophet as well as a judge in those interior courts where our true decisions are made. "Pyle, don't trust too much in York Harding."

"York!" He stared up at me from the first landing.

"We are the old colonial peoples, Pyle, but we've learnt a bit of reality, we've learned not to play with matches. This Third Force—it comes out of a book, that's all. General Thé's only a bandit with a few thousand men: he's not a national democracy."

It was as if he had been staring at me through a letter-box to see who was there and now, letting the flap fall, had shut out the unwelcome intruder. His eyes were out of sight. "I don't know what you mean, Thomas."

"Those bicycle bombs. They were a good joke, even though one man did lose a foot. But, Pyle, you can't trust men like Thé. They aren't going to save the East from Communism. We know their kind."

"We?"

"The old colonialists."

"I thought you took no sides."

"I don't, Pyle, but if someone has got to make a mess of things in your outfit, leave it to Joe. Go home with Phuong. Forget the Third Force."

"Of course I always value your advice, Thomas," he said formally. "Well, I'll be seeing you."

"I suppose so."

2

The weeks moved on, but somehow I hadn't yet found myself a new flat. It wasn't that I hadn't time. The annual crisis of the war had passed again: the hot wet *crachin* had settled on the north: the French were out of Hoa Binh, the rice-campaign was over in Tonkin and the opium-campaign in Laos. Domingues could cover easily all that was needed in the south. At last I did drag myself to see one apartment in a so-called modern building (Paris Exhibition 1934?) up at the other end of the rue Catinat beyond the Continental Hotel. It was the Saigon pied-à-terre of a rubber planter who was going home. He wanted to sell it lock, stock and barrel. I have always wondered what the barrels contain: as for the stock, there were a large number of engravings from the Paris Salon between 1880 and 1900. Their highest common factor was a big-bosomed woman with an extraordinary hair-do and gauzy draperies which somehow always exposed the great cleft buttocks and hid the field of battle. In the bathroom the planter had been rather more daring with his reproductions of Rops.

"You like art?" I asked and he smirked back at me like a fellow conspirator. He was fat with a little black moustache and insufficient hair.

"My best pictures are in Paris," he said.

There was an extraordinary tall ash-tray in the living-room made like a naked woman with a bowl in her hair, and there were china ornaments of naked girls embracing tigers, and one very odd one of a girl stripped to the waist riding a bicycle. In the bedroom facing his enormous bed was a great glazed oil painting of two girls sleeping together. I asked him the price of his apartment without his collection, but he would not agree to separate the two.

"You are not a collector?" he asked.

"Well, no."

"I have some books also," he said, "which I would throw in, though I intended to take these back to France." He unlocked a glass-fronted bookcase and showed me his library—there were expensive illustrated editions of *Aphrodite* and *Nana*, there was *La Garçonne*, and even several Paul de Kocks. I was tempted to ask him whether he would sell himself with his collection: he went with them: he was period too. He said, "If you live alone in the tropics a collection is company."

I thought of Phuong just because of her complete absence. So it always is: when you escape to a desert the silence shouts in your ear.

"I don't think my paper would allow me to buy an art-collection."

He said, "It would not, of course, appear on the receipt."

I was glad Pyle had not seen him: the man might have lent his features to Pyle's imaginary "old colonialist," who was repulsive enough without him. When I came out it was nearly half past eleven and I went down as far as the Pavillon for a glass of iced beer. The Pavillon was a coffee centre for European and American women and I was confident that I would not see Phuong there. Indeed I knew exactly where she would be at this time of day—she was not a girl to break her habits, and so, coming from the planter's apartment, I had crossed the road to avoid the milk-bar where at this time of day she had her chocolate malt. Two young American girls sat at the next table, neat and clean in the heat, scooping up ice-cream. They each had a bag slung on the left shoulder and the bags were identical, with brass eagle badges. Their legs were identical too, long and slender, and their noses, just a shade tilted, and they were eating their ice-cream with concentration as though they were making an experiment in the college laboratory. I wondered whether they were Pyle's colleagues: they were charming, and I wanted to send them home, too. They finished their ices and one looked at her watch. "We'd better be going," she said, "to be on the safe side." I wondered idly what appointment they had.

"Warren said we mustn't stay later than eleven twenty-five."

"It's past that now."

"It would be exciting to stay. I don't know what it's all about, do you?"

"Not exactly, but Warren said better not."

"Do you think it's a demonstration?"

"I've seen so many demonstrations," the other said wearily, like a tourist glutted with churches. She rose and laid on their table the money for the ices. Before going she looked around the café, and the mirrors caught her profile at every freckled angle. There was only myself left and a dowdy middle-aged Frenchwoman who was carefully and uselessly making up her face. Those two hardly needed make-up, the quick dash of lipstick, a comb through the hair. For a moment her glance had rested on me—it was not like a woman's glance, but a man's, very straightforward, speculating on some course of action. Then she turned quickly to her companion. "We'd better be off." I watched them idly as they went out side by side into the sun-splintered street. It was impossible to conceive either of them a prey to untidy passion: they did not belong to rumpled sheets and the sweat of sex. Did they take deodorants to bed with them? I found myself for a moment envying them their sterilized world, so different from this world that I inhabited—which suddenly inexplicably broke in pieces. Two of the mirrors on the wall flew at me and collapsed halfway. The dowdy Frenchwoman was on her knees in a wreckage of chairs and tables. Her compact lay open and unhurt in my lap and oddly enough I sat exactly where I had sat before, although my table had joined the wreckage around the Frenchwoman. A curious garden-sound filled the café: the regular drip of a fountain, and looking at the bar I saw rows of smashed bottles which let out their contents in a multi-coloured stream—the red of porto, the orange of cointreau, the green of chartreuse, the cloudy yellow of pastis, across the floor of the café. The Frenchwoman sat up and calmly looked around for her compact. I gave it her and she thanked me formally, sitting on the floor. I realized that I didn't hear her very well. The explosion had been so close that my ear-drums had still to recover from the pressure.

I thought rather petulantly, "Another joke with plastics: what does Mr. Heng expect me to write now?" but when I got into the Place Garnier, I realized by the heavy clouds of smoke that this was no joke. The smoke came from the cars burning in the car-park in front of the national theatre, bits of cars were scattered over the square, and a man without his legs lay twitching at the edge of the ornamental gardens. People were crowding in from the rue Catinat, from the Boulevard Bonnard. The sirens of police-cars, the bells of the ambulances and fireengines came at one remove to my shocked ear-drums. For one moment I had forgotten that Phuong must have been in the milk-bar on the other side of the square. The smoke lay between. I couldn't see through.

I stepped out into the square and a policeman stopped me. They had formed a cordon round the edge to prevent the crowd increasing, and already the stretchers were beginning to emerge. I implored the policeman in front of me, "Let me across. I have a friend . . ."

"Stand back," he said. "Everybody here has friends."

He stood on one side to let a priest through, and I tried to follow the priest, but he pulled me back. I said, "I am the Press," and searched in vain for the wallet in which I had my card, but I couldn't find it: had I come out that day without it? I said, "At least tell me what happened to the milk-bar": the smoke was clearing and I tried to see, but the crowd between was too great. He said something I didn't catch.

"What did you say?"

He repeated, "I don't know. Stand back. You are blocking the stretchers."

Could I have dropped my wallet in the Pavillon? I turned to go back and there was Pyle. He exclaimed, "Thomas."

"Pyle," I said, "for Christ's sake, where's your Legation pass? We've got to get across. Phuong's in the milk-bar."

"No, no," he said.

"Pyle, she is. She always goes there. At eleven thirty. We've got to find her."

"She isn't there, Thomas."

"How do you know? Where's your card?"

"I warned her not to go."

I turned back to the policeman, meaning to throw him to one side and make a run for it across the square: he might shoot: I didn't care—and then the word "warn" reached my consciousness. I took Pyle by the arm. "Warn?" I said. "What do you mean 'warn'?"

"I told her to keep away this morning."

The pieces fell together in my mind. "And Warren?" I said. "Who's Warren? He warned those girls too."

"I don't understand."

"There mustn't be any American casualties, must there?" An ambulance forced its way up the rue Catinat into the square and the policeman who had stopped me moved to one side to let it through. The policeman beside him was engaged in an argument. I pushed Pyle forward and ahead of me into the square before we could be stopped.

We were among a congregation of mourners. The police could prevent others entering the square; they were powerless to clear the square of the survivors and the first-comers. The doctors were too busy to attend to the dead, and so the dead were left to their owners, for one can own the dead as one owns a chair. A woman sat on the ground with what was left of her baby in her lap; with a kind of modesty she had covered it with her straw peasant hat. She was still and silent, and what struck me most in the square was the silence. It was like a church I had once visited during Mass—the only sounds came from those who served, except where here and there the Europeans wept and implored and fell silent again as though shamed by the modesty, patience and propriety of the East. The legless torso at the edge of the garden still twitched, like a chicken which has lost its head. From the man's shirt, he had probably been a trishaw driver.

Pyle said, "It's awful." He looked at the wet on his shoes and said in a sick voice, "What's that?"

"Blood," I said. "Haven't you ever seen it before?"

He said, "I must get them cleaned before I see the Minister." I don't think he knew what he was saying. He was seeing a real war for the first time: he had punted down into Phat Diem in a kind of schoolboy dream, and anyway in his eyes soldiers didn't count.

I forced him, with my hand on his shoulder, to look around. I said, "This is the hour when the place is always full of women and children—it's the shopping hour. Why choose that of all hours?"

He said weakly, "There was to have been a parade."

"And you hoped to catch a few colonels. But the parade was cancelled yesterday, Pyle."

"I didn't know."

"Didn't know!" I pushed him into a patch of blood where a stretcher had lain. "You ought to be better informed."

"I was out of town," he said, looking down at his shoes. "They should have called it off."

"And missed the fun?" I asked him. "Do you expect General Thé to lose his demonstration? This is better than a parade. Women and children are news, and soldiers aren't, in a war. This will hit the world's Press. You've put General Thé on the map all right, Pyle. You've got the Third Force and National Democracy all over your right shoe. Go home to Phuong and tell her about your heroic dead—there are a few dozen less of her people to worry about."

A small fat priest scampered by, carrying something on a dish under a napkin. Pyle had been silent a long while, and I had nothing more to say. Indeed I had said too much already. He looked white and beaten and ready to faint, and I thought, "What's the good? he'll always be innocent, you can't blame the innocent, they are always guiltless. All you can do is control them or eliminate them. Innocence is a kind of insanity."

He said, "Thé wouldn't have done this. I'm sure he wouldn't. Somebody deceived him. The Communists . . ."

He was impregnably armoured by his good intentions and his ignorance. I left him standing in the square and went on up the rue Catinat to where the hideous pink Cathedral blocked the way. Already people were flocking in: it must have been a comfort to them to be able to pray for the dead to the dead.

Unlike them, I had reason for thankfulness, for wasn't Phuong alive? Hadn't Phuong been "warned?" But what I remembered was the torso in the square, the baby on its mother's lap. They had not been warned: they had not been sufficiently important. And if the parade had taken place would they not have been there just the same, out of curiosity, to see the soldiers, and hear the speakers, and throw the flowers? A two-hundred-pound bomb does not discriminate. How many dead colonels justify a child's or a trishaw driver's death when you are building a national democratic front? I stopped a motor-trishaw and told the driver to take me to the Quai Mytho.

# PART FOUR

# CHAPTER 1

I had given Phuong money to take her sister to the cinema so that she would be safely out of the way. I went out to dinner myself with Domingues and was back in my room waiting when Vigot called sharp on ten. He apologized for not taking a drink—he said he was too tired and a drink might send him to sleep. It had been a very long day.

"Murder and sudden death?"

"No. Petty thefts. And a few suicides. These people love to gamble and when they have lost everything they kill themselves. Perhaps I would not have become a policeman if I had known how much time I would have to spend in mortuaries. I do not like the smell of ammonia. Perhaps after all I will have a beer."

"I haven't a refrigerator, I'm afraid."

"Unlike the mortuary. A little English whisky, then?"

I remembered the night I had gone down to the mortuary with him and they had slid out Pyle's body like a tray of ice-cubes.

"So you are not going home?" he asked.

"You've been checking up?"

"Yes."

I held the whisky out to him, so that he could see how calm my nerves were. "Vigot, I wish you'd tell me why you think I was concerned in Pyle's death. Is it a question of motive? That I wanted Phuong back? Or do you imagine it was revenge for losing her?"

"No. I'm not so stupid. One doesn't take one's enemy's book as a souvenir. There it is on your shelf. *The Rôle of the West*. Who is this York Harding?"

"He's the man you are looking for, Vigot. He killed Pyle—at long range."

"I don't understand."

"He's a superior sort of journalist—they call them diplomatic correspondents. He gets hold of an idea and then alters

every situation to fit the idea. Pyle came out here full of York
Harding's idea. Harding had been here once for a week on his
way from Bangkok to Tokyo. Pyle made the mistake of putting
his idea into practice. Harding wrote about a Third Force. Pyle
formed one—a shoddy little bandit with two thousand men
and a couple of tame tigers. He got mixed up."

"You never do, do you?"

"I've tried not to be."

"But you failed, Fowler." For some reason I thought of
Captain Trouin and that night which seemed to have happened
years ago in the Haiphong opium house. What was it he had
said? something about all of us getting involved sooner or later
in a moment of emotion. I said, "You would have made a good
priest, Vigot. What is it about you that would make it so easy
to confess—if there were anything to confess?"

"I have never wanted any confessions."

"But you've received them?"

"From time to time."

"Is it because like a priest it's your job not to be shocked,
but to be sympathetic? 'M. Flic, I must tell you exactly why I
battered in the old lady's skull.' 'Yes, Gustave, take your time
and tell me why it was.' "

"You have a whimsical imagination. Aren't you drinking,
Fowler?"

"Surely it's unwise for a criminal to drink with a police
officer?"

"I have never said you were a criminal."

"But suppose the drink unlocked even in me the desire to
confess? There are no secrets of the confessional in your profession."

"Secrecy is seldom important to a man who confesses: even
when it's to a priest. He has other motives."

"To cleanse himself?"

"Not always. Sometimes he only wants to see himself clearly
as he is. Sometimes he is just weary of deception. You are not
a criminal, Fowler, but I would like to know why you lied to
me. You saw Pyle the night he died."

"What gives you that idea?"

"I don't for a moment think you killed him. You would hardly have used a rusty bayonet."

"Rusty?"

"Those are the kind of details we get from an autopsy. I told you, though, that was not the cause of death. Dakow mud." He held out his glass for another whisky. "Let me see now. You had a drink at the Continental at six ten?"

"Yes."

"And at six forty-five you were talking to another journalist at the door of the Majestic?"

"Yes, Wilkins. I told you all this, Vigot, before. That night."

"Yes. I've checked up since then. It's wonderful how you carry such petty details in your head."

"I'm a reporter, Vigot."

"Perhaps the times are not quite accurate, but nobody could blame you, could they, if you were a quarter of an hour out here and ten minutes out there. You had no reason to think the times important. Indeed how suspicious it would be if you had been completely accurate."

"Haven't I been?"

"Not quite. It was at five to seven that you talked to Wilkins."

"Another ten minutes."

"Of course. As I said. And it had only just struck six when you arrived at the Continental."

"My watch is always a little fast," I said. "What time do you make it now?"

"Ten eight."

"Ten eighteen by mine. You see."

He didn't bother to look. He said, "Then the time you said you talked to Wilkins was twenty-five minutes out—by your watch. That's quite a mistake, isn't it?"

"Perhaps I readjusted the time in my mind. Perhaps I'd corrected my watch that day. I sometimes do."

"What interests me," Vigot said, "(could I have a little more soda?—you have made this rather strong) is that you are not at all angry with me. It is not very nice to be questioned as I am questioning you."

"I find it interesting, like a detective-story. And, after all, you know I didn't kill Pyle—you've said so."

Vigot said, "I know you were not present at his murder."

"I don't know what you hope to prove by showing that I was ten minutes out here and five there."

"It gives a little space," Vigot said, "a little gap in time."

"Space for what?"

"For Pyle to come and see you."

"Why do you want so much to prove that?"

"Because of the dog," Vigot said.

"And the mud between its toes?"

"It wasn't mud. It was cement. You see, somewhere that night, when it was following Pyle, it stepped into wet cement. I remembered that on the ground-floor of the apartment there are builders at work—they are still at work. I passed them to-night as I came in. They work long hours in this country."

"I wonder how many houses have builders in them—and wet cement. Did any of them remember the dog?"

"Of course I asked them that. But if they had they would not have told me. I am the police." He stopped talking and leant back in his chair, staring at his glass. I had a sense that some analogy had struck him and he was miles away in thought. A fly crawled over the back of his hand and he did not brush it away—any more than Domingues would have done. I had the feeling of some force immobile and profound. For all I knew, he might have been praying.

I rose and went through the curtains into the bedroom. There was nothing I wanted there, except to get away for a moment from that silence sitting in a chair. Phuong's picture-books were back on the shelf. She had stuck a telegram for me up among the cosmetics—some message or other from the London office. I wasn't in the mood to open it. Everything was as it had been before Pyle came. Rooms don't change, orna-ments stand where you place them: only the heart decays.

I returned to the sitting-room and Vigot put the glass to his lips. I said, "I've got nothing to tell you. Nothing at all."

"Then I'll be going," he said. "I don't suppose I'll trouble you again."

At the door he turned as though he were unwilling to

abandon hope—his hope or mine. "That was a strange picture for you to go and see that night. I wouldn't have thought you cared for costume drama. What was it? *Robin Hood?*"

"*Scaramouche*, I think. I had to kill time. And I needed distraction."

"Distraction?"

"We all have our private worries, Vigot," I carefully explained.

When Vigot was gone there was still an hour to wait for Phuong and living company. It was strange how disturbed I had been by Vigot's visit. It was as though a poet had brought me his work to criticize and through some careless action I had destroyed it. I was a man without a vocation—one cannot seriously consider journalism as a vocation, but I could recognize a vocation in another. Now that Vigot was gone to close his uncompleted file, I wished I had the courage to call him back and say, "You are right. I did see Pyle the night he died."

# CHAPTER 2

1

On the way to the Quai Mytho I passed several ambulances driving out of Cholon heading for the Place Garnier. One could almost reckon the pace of rumour from the expression of the faces in the street, which at first turned on someone like myself coming from the direction of the Place with looks of expectancy and speculation. By the time I entered Cholon I had outstripped the news: life was busy, normal, uninterrupted: nobody knew.

I found Mr. Chou's godown and mounted to Mr. Chou's house. Nothing had changed since my last visit. The cat and the dog moved from floor to cardboard box to suitcase, like a couple of chess knights who cannot get to grips. The baby crawled on the floor, and the two old men were still playing mah jongg. Only the young people were absent. As soon as I appeared in the doorway one of the women began to pour out tea. The old lady sat on the bed and looked at her feet.

"Monsieur Heng," I asked. I shook my head at the tea: I wasn't in the mood to begin another long course of that trivial bitter brew. *"Il faut absolument que je voie Monsieur Heng."* It seemed impossible to convey to them the urgency of my request, but perhaps the very abruptness of my refusal of tea caused some disquiet. Or perhaps like Pyle I had blood on my shoes. Anyway after a short delay one of the women led me out and down the stairs, along two bustling bannered streets and left me before what they would have called I suppose in Pyle's country a "funeral parlour," full of stone jars in which the resurrected bones of the Chinese dead are eventually placed. "Monsieur Heng," I said to an old Chinese in the doorway, "Monsieur Heng." It seemed a suitable halting place on a day which had begun with the planter's erotic collection and continued with the murdered bodies in the square. Somebody called from an inner room and the Chinese stepped aside and let me in.

Mr. Heng himself came cordially forward and ushered me into a little inner room lined with the black carved uncomfortable chairs you find in every Chinese ante-room, unused, unwelcoming. But I had the sense that on this occasion the chairs had been employed, for there were five little tea-cups on the table, and two were not empty. "I have interrupted a meeting," I said.

"A matter of business," Mr. Heng said evasively, "of no importance. I am always glad to see you, Mr. Fowler."

"I've come from the Place Garnier," I said.

"I thought that was it."

"You've heard . . ."

"Someone telephoned to me. It was thought best that I keep away from Mr. Chou's for a while. The police will be very active today."

"But you had nothing to do with it."

"It is the business of the police to find a culprit."

"It was Pyle again," I said.

"Yes."

"It was a terrible thing to do."

"General Thé is not a very controlled character."

"And bombs aren't for boys from Boston. Who is Pyle's chief, Heng?"

"I have the impression that Mr. Pyle is very much his own master."

"What is he? O.S.S.?"

"The initial letters are not very important. I think now they are different."

"What can I do, Heng? He's got to be stopped."

"You can publish the truth. Or perhaps you cannot?"

"My paper's not interested in General Thé. They are only interested in your people, Heng."

"You really want Mr. Pyle stopped, Mr. Fowler?"

"If you'd seen him, Heng. He stood there and said it was all a sad mistake, there should have been a parade. He said he'd have to get his shoes cleaned before he saw the Minister."

"Of course, you could tell what you know to the police."

"They aren't interested in Thé either. And do you think they would dare to touch an American? He has diplomatic privileges. He's a graduate of Harvard. The Minister's very fond of Pyle. Heng, there was a woman there whose baby—she kept it covered under her straw hat. I can't get it out of my head. And there was another in Phat Diem."

"You must try to be calm, Mr. Fowler."

"What'll he do next, Heng?"

"Would you be prepared to help us, Mr. Fowler?"

"He comes blundering in and people have to die for his mistakes. I wish your people had got him on the river from Nam Dinh. It would have made a lot of difference to a lot of lives."

"I agree with you, Mr. Fowler. He has to be restrained. I have a suggestion to make." Somebody coughed delicately behind the door, then noisily spat. He said, "If you would invite him to dinner tonight at the Vieux Moulin. Between eight thirty and nine thirty."

"What good . . . ?"

"We would talk to him on the way," Heng said.

"He may be engaged."

"Perhaps it would be better if you asked him to call on you—at six thirty. He will be free then: he will certainly come. If he is able to have dinner with you, take a book to your window as though you want to catch the light."

"Why the Vieux Moulin?"

"It is by the bridge to Dakow—I think we shall be able to find a spot and talk undisturbed."

"What will you do?"

"You do not want to know that, Mr. Fowler. But I promise you we will act as gently as the situation allows."

The unseen friends of Heng shifted like rats behind the wall. "Will you do this for us, Mr. Fowler?"

"I don't know," I said, "I don't know."

"Sooner or later," Heng said, and I was reminded of Captain Trouin speaking in the opium house, "one has to take sides. If one is to remain human."

## 2

I left a note at the Legation asking Pyle to come and then I went up the street to the Continental for a drink. The wreck-

age was all cleared away; the fire-brigade had hosed the square.
I had no idea then how the time and the place would become
important. I even thought of sitting there throughout the
evening and breaking my appointment. Then I thought that
perhaps I could frighten Pyle into inactivity by warning him
of his danger—whatever his danger was, and so I finished my
beer and went home, and when I reached home I began to
hope that Pyle would not come. I tried to read, but there
was nothing on my shelves to hold the attention. Perhaps I
should have smoked, but there was no one to prepare my
pipe. I listened unwillingly for footsteps and at last they came.
Somebody knocked. I opened the door, but it was only
Domingues.

I said, "What do you want, Domingues?"

He looked at me with an air of surprise. "Want?" He looked
at his watch. "This is the time I always come. Have you any
cables?"

"I'm sorry—I'd forgotten. No."

"But a follow-up on the bomb? Don't you want something
filed?"

"Oh, work one out for me, Domingues. I don't know how
it is—being there on the spot, perhaps I got a bit shocked. I
can't think of the thing in terms of a cable." I hit out at a
mosquito which came droning at my ear and saw Domingues
wince instinctively at my blow. "It's all right, Domingues, I
missed it." He grinned miserably. He could not justify this re-
luctance to take life: after all he was a Christian—one of those
who had learnt from Nero how to make human bodies into
candles.

"Is there anything I can do for you?" he asked. He didn't
drink, he didn't eat meat, he didn't kill—I envied him the
gentleness of his mind.

"No, Domingues. Just leave me alone tonight." I watched
him from the window, going away across the rue Catinat. A
trishaw driver had parked beside the pavement opposite my
window; Domingues tried to engage him, but the man shook
his head. Presumably he was waiting for a client in one of the
shops, for this was not a parking place for trishaws. When I
looked at my watch it was strange to see that I had been

waiting for little more than ten minutes, and, when Pyle knocked, I hadn't even heard his step.

"Come in." But as usual it was the dog that came in first.

"I was glad to get your note, Thomas. This morning I thought you were mad at me."

"Perhaps I was. It wasn't a pretty sight."

"You know so much now, it won't hurt to tell you a bit more. I saw Thé this afternoon."

"Saw him? Is he in Saigon? I suppose he came to see how his bomb worked."

"That's in confidence, Thomas. I dealt with him very severely." He spoke like the captain of a school-team who has found one of his boys breaking his training. All the same I asked him with a certain hope, "Have you thrown him over?"

"I told him that if he made another uncontrolled demonstration we would have no more to do with him."

"But haven't you finished with him already, Pyle?" I pushed impatiently at his dog which was nosing around my ankles.

"I can't. (Sit down, Duke.) In the long run he's the only hope we have. If he came to power with our help, we could rely on him . . ."

"How many people have to die before you realize . . . ?" But I could tell that it was a hopeless argument.

"Realize what, Thomas?"

"That there's no such thing as gratitude in politics."

"At least they won't hate us like they hate the French."

"Are you sure? Sometimes we have a kind of love for our enemies and sometimes we feel hate for our friends."

"You talk like a European, Thomas. These people aren't complicated."

"Is that what you've learned in a few months? You'll be calling them childlike next."

"Well—in a way."

"Find me an uncomplicated child, Pyle. When we are young we are a jungle of complications. We simplify as we get older." But what good was it to talk to him? There was an unreality in both our arguments. I was becoming a leader-writer before my time. I got up and went to the bookshelf.

"What are you looking for, Thomas?"

"Oh, just a passage I used to be fond of. Can you have dinner with me, Pyle?"

"I'd love to, Thomas. I'm so glad you aren't mad any longer. I know you disagree with me, but we can disagree, can't we, and be friends?"

"I don't know. I don't think so."

"After all, Phuong was much more important than this."

"Do you really believe that, Pyle?"

"Why, she's the most important thing there is. To me. And to you, Thomas."

"Not to me any longer."

"It was a terrible shock today, Thomas, but in a week, you'll see, we'll have forgotten it. We are looking after the relatives too."

"We?"

"We've wired to Washington. We'll get permission to use some of our funds."

I interrupted him. "The Vieux Moulin? Between nine and nine thirty?"

"Where you like, Thomas." I went to the window. The sun had sunk below the roofs. The trishaw driver still waited for his fare. I looked down at him and he raised his face to me.

"Are you waiting for someone, Thomas?"

"No. There was just a piece I was looking for." To cover my action I read, holding the book up to the last light:

> "I drive through the streets and I care not a damn,
> The people they stare, and they ask who I am;
> And if I should chance to run over a cad,
> I can pay for the damage if ever so bad.
>   So pleasant it is to have money, heigh ho!
>   So pleasant it is to have money."

"That's a funny kind of poem," Pyle said with a note of disapproval.

"He was an adult poet in the nineteenth century. There weren't so many of them." I looked down into the street again. The trishaw driver had moved away.

"Have you run out of drink?" Pyle asked.

"No, but I thought you didn't . . ."

"Perhaps I'm beginning to loosen up," Pyle said. "Your influence. I guess you're good for me, Thomas."

I got the bottle and glasses—I forgot one of them the first journey and then I had to go back for water. Everything that I did that evening took a long time. He said, "You know, I've got a wonderful family, but maybe they were a little on the strict side. We have one of those old houses in Chestnut Street, as you go up the hill on the right-hand side. My mother collects glass, and my father—when he's not eroding his old cliffs— picks up all the Darwin manuscripts and association-copies he can. You see, they live in the past. Maybe that's why York made such an impression on me. He seemed kind of open to modern conditions. My father's an isolationist."

"Perhaps I would like your father," I said. "I'm an isolationist too."

For a quiet man Pyle that night was in a talking mood. I didn't hear all that he said, for my mind was elsewhere. I tried to persuade myself that Mr. Heng had other means at his disposal but the crude and obvious one. But in a war like this, I knew, there is no time to hesitate: one uses the weapon to hand—the French the napalm bomb, Mr. Heng the bullet or the knife. I told myself too late that I wasn't made to be a judge—I would let Pyle talk awhile and then I would warn him. He could spend the night at my house. They would hardly break in there. I think he was speaking of the old nurse he had had—"She really meant more to me than my mother, and the blueberry pies she used to make!" when I interrupted him. "Do you carry a gun now—since that night?"

"No. We have orders in the Legation . . ."

"But you're on special duties?"

"It wouldn't do any good—if they wanted to get me, they always could. Anyway I'm as blind as a coot. At college they called me Bat—because I could see in the dark as well as they could. Once when we were fooling around . . ." He was off again. I returned to the window.

A trishaw driver waited opposite. I wasn't sure—they looked so much alike, but I thought he was a different one. Perhaps he really had a client. It occurred to me that Pyle would be safest at the Legation. They must have laid their plans, since my signal, for later in the evening: something that involved the Dakow bridge. I couldn't understand why or how: surely he would not be so foolish as to drive through Dakow after sunset and our side of the bridge was always guarded by armed police.

"I'm doing all the talking," Pyle said. "I don't know how it is, but somehow this evening . . ."

"Go on," I said, "I'm in a quiet mood, that's all. Perhaps we'd better cancel that dinner."

"No, don't do that. I've felt cut off from you, since . . . well . . ."

"Since you saved my life," I said and couldn't disguise the bitterness of my self-inflicted wound.

"No, I didn't mean that. All the same how we talked, didn't we, that night? As if it was going to be our last. I learned a lot about you, Thomas. I don't agree with you, mind, but for you maybe it's right—not being involved. You kept it up all right, even after your leg was smashed you stayed neutral."

"There's always a point of change," I said. "Some moment of emotion . . ."

"You haven't reached it yet. I doubt if you ever will. And I'm not likely to change either—except with death," he added merrily.

"Not even with this morning? Mightn't that change a man's views?"

"They were only war casualties," he said. "It was a pity, but you can't always hit your target. Anyway they died in the right cause."

"Would you have said the same if it had been your old nurse with her blueberry pie?"

He ignored my facile point. "In a way you could say they died for democracy," he said.

"I wouldn't know how to translate that into Vietnamese." I was suddenly very tired. I wanted him to go away quickly and die. Then I could start life again—at the point before he came in.

"You'll never take me seriously, will you, Thomas?" he

complained, with that schoolboy gaiety which he seemed to have kept up his sleeve for this night of all nights. "I tell you what—Phuong's at the cinema—what about you and me spending the whole evening together? I've nothing to do now." It was as though someone from outside were directing him how to choose his words in order to rob me of any possible excuse. He went on. "Why don't we go to the Chalet? I haven't been there since that night. The food is just as good as the Vieux Moulin, and there's music."

I said, "I'd rather not remember that night."

"I'm sorry. I'm a dumb fool sometimes, Thomas. What about a Chinese dinner in Cholon?"

"To get a good one you have to order in advance. Are you scared of the Vieux Moulin, Pyle? It's well wired and there are always police on the bridge. And you wouldn't be such a fool, would you, as to drive through Dakow?"

"It wasn't that. I just thought it would be fun tonight to make a long evening of it."

He made a movement and upset his glass, which smashed upon the floor. "Good luck," he said mechanically. "I'm sorry, Thomas." I began to pick up the pieces and pack them into the ash-tray. "What about it, Thomas?" The smashed glass reminded me of the bottles in the Pavillon bar dripping their contents. "I warned Phuong I might be out with you." How badly chosen was the word "warn." I picked up the last piece of glass. "I have got an engagement at the Majestic," I said, "and I can't manage before nine."

"Well, I guess I'll have to go back to the office. Only I'm always afraid of getting caught."

There was no harm in giving him that one chance. "Don't mind being late," I said. "If you do get caught, look in here later. I'll come back at ten, if you can't make dinner, and wait for you."

"I'll let you know . . ."

"Don't bother. Just come to the Vieux Moulin—or meet me here." I handed back the decision to that Somebody in whom I didn't believe: You can intervene if You want to: a telegram on his desk: a message from the Minister. You cannot exist unless you have the power to alter the future. "Go away now, Pyle. There are things I have to do." I felt a strange exhaustion, hearing him go away and the pad of his dog's paws.

3

There were no trishaw drivers nearer than the rue d'Ormay when I went out. I walked down to the Majestic and stood awhile watching the unloading of the American bombers. The sun had gone and they worked by the light of arc-lamps. I had no idea of creating an alibi, but I told Pyle I was going to the Majestic and I felt an unreasoning dislike of telling more lies than were needed.

"Evening, Fowler." It was Wilkins.

"Evening."

"How's the leg?"

"No trouble now."

"Got a good story filed?"

"I left it to Domingues."

"Oh, they told me you were there."

"Yes, I was. But space is tight these days. They won't want much."

"The spice has gone out of the dish, hasn't it?" Wilkins said. "We ought to have lived in the days of Russell and the old *Times*. Dispatches by balloon. One had time to do some fancy writing then. Why, he'd even have made a column out of *this*. The luxury hotel, the bombers, night falling. Night never falls nowadays, does it, at so many piastres a word." From far up in the sky you could faintly hear the noise of laughter: somebody broke a glass as Pyle had done. The sound fell on us like icicles. " 'The lamps shone o'er fair women and brave men,' " Wilkins malevolently quoted. "Doing anything tonight, Fowler? Care for a spot of dinner?"

"I'm dining as it is. At the Vieux Moulin."

"I wish you joy. Granger will be there. They ought to advertise special Granger nights. For those who like background noise."

I said good night to him and went into the cinema next door—Errol Flynn, or it may have been Tyrone Power (I don't know how to distinguish them in tights), swung on ropes and leapt from balconies and rode bareback into technicolour dawns. He rescued a girl and killed his enemy and led a charmed life. It was what they call a film for boys, but the sight of Oedipus emerging with his bleeding eyeballs from the palace at Thebes would surely give a better training for life today. No life is charmed. Luck had been with Pyle at Phat Diem and on the road from Tanyin, but luck doesn't last, and they had two hours to see that no charm worked. A French soldier sat beside me with his hand in a girl's lap, and I envied the simplicity of his happiness or his misery, whichever it might be. I left before the film was over and took a trishaw to the Vieux Moulin.

The restaurant was wired in against grenades and two armed policemen were on duty at the end of the bridge. The *patron*, who had grown fat on his own rich Burgundian cooking, let me through the wire himself. The place smelt of capons and melting butter in the heavy evening heat.

"Are you joining the party of M. Granjair?" he asked me.

"No."

"A table for one?" It was then for the first time that I thought of the future and the questions I might have to answer. "For one," I said, and it was almost as though I had said aloud that Pyle was dead.

There was only one room and Granger's party occupied a large table at the back; the *patron* gave me a small one closest to the wire. There were no window-panes, for fear of splintered glass. I recognized a few of the people Granger was entertaining, and I bowed to them before I sat down: Granger himself looked away. I hadn't seen him for months—only once since the night Pyle fell in love. Perhaps some offensive remark I had made that evening had penetrated the alcoholic fog, for he sat scowling at the head of the table while Madame Desprez, the wife of a public-relations officer, and Captain Duparc of the Press Liaison Service nodded and becked. There was a big man whom I think was an *hôtelier* from Pnom Penh and a French girl I'd never seen before and two or three other faces that I had only observed in bars. It seemed for once to be a quiet party.

I ordered a pastis because I wanted to give Pyle time to

come—plans go awry and so long as I did not begin to eat
my dinner it was as though I still had time to hope. And then
I wondered what I hoped for. Good luck to the O.S.S. or
whatever his gang were called? Long life to plastic bombs
and General Thé? Or did I—I of all people—hope for some
kind of miracle: a method of discussion arranged by Mr.
Heng which wasn't simply death? How much easier it would
have been if we had both been killed on the road from Tanyin.
I sat for twenty minutes over my pastis and then I ordered
dinner. It would soon be half past nine: he wouldn't come
now.

Against my will I listened: for what? a scream? a shot? some
movement by the police outside? but in any case I would probably hear nothing, for Granger's party was warming up. The
*hôtelier*, who had a pleasant untrained voice, began to sing and
as a new champagne cork popped others joined in, but not
Granger. He sat there with raw eyes glaring across the room at
me. I wondered if there would be a fight: I was no match for
Granger.

They were singing a sentimental song, and as I sat hungerless over my apology for a *Chapon duc Charles* I thought, for
almost the first time since I had known that she was safe, of
Phuong. I remembered how Pyle, sitting on the floor waiting
for the Viets, had said, "She seems fresh like a flower," and I
had flippantly replied, "Poor flower." She would never see New
England now or learn the secrets of Canasta. Perhaps she would
never know security: what right had I to value her less than the
dead bodies in the square? Suffering is not increased by numbers: one body can contain all the suffering the world can feel.
I had judged like a journalist in terms of quantity and I had
betrayed my own principles; I had become as *engagé* as Pyle,
and it seemed to me that no decision would ever be simple
again. I looked at my watch and it was nearly a quarter to ten.
Perhaps, after all, he had been caught; perhaps that "someone"
in whom he believed had acted on his behalf and he sat now
in his Legation room fretting at a telegram to decode, and soon
he would come stamping up the stairs to my room in the rue
Catinat. I thought, "If he does I shall tell him everything."

Granger suddenly got up from his table and came at me. He didn't even see the chair in his way and he stumbled and laid his hand on the edge of my table. "Fowler," he said, "come outside." I laid enough notes down and followed him. I was in no mood to fight with him, but at that moment I would not have minded if he had beaten me unconscious. We have so few ways in which to assuage the sense of guilt.

He leant on the parapet of the bridge and the two policemen watched him from a distance. He said, "I've got to talk to you, Fowler."

I came within striking distance and waited. He didn't move. He was like an emblematic statue of all I thought I hated in America—as ill-designed as the Statue of Liberty and as meaningless. He said without moving, "You think I'm pissed. You're wrong."

"What's up, Granger?"

"I got to talk to you, Fowler. I don't want to sit there with those Frogs tonight. I don't like you, Fowler, but you talk English. A kind of English." He leant there, bulky and shapeless in the half-light, an unexplored continent.

"What do you want, Granger?"

"I don't like Limies," Granger said. "I don't know why Pyle stomachs you. Maybe it's because he's Boston. I'm Pittsburgh and proud of it."

"Why not?"

"There you are again." He made a feeble attempt to mock my accent. "You all talk like poufs. You're so damned superior. You think you know everything."

"Good night, Granger. I've got an appointment."

"Don't go, Fowler. Haven't you got a heart? I can't talk to those Froggies."

"You're drunk."

"I've had two glasses of champagne, that's all, and wouldn't you be drunk in my place? I've got to go north."

"What's wrong in that?"

"Oh, I didn't tell you, did I? I keep on thinking everyone knows. I got a cable this morning from my wife."

"Yes?"

"My son's got polio. He's bad."

"I'm sorry."

"You needn't be. It's not your kid."

"Can't you fly home?"

"I can't. They want a story about some damned mopping-up operations near Hanoi and Connolly's sick." (Connolly was his assistant.)

"I'm sorry, Granger. I wish I could help."

"It's his birthday tonight. He's eight at half past ten our time. That's why I laid on a party with champagne before I knew. I had to tell someone, Fowler, and I can't tell these Froggies."

"They can do a lot for polio nowadays."

"I don't mind if he's crippled, Fowler. Not if he lives. Me, I'd be no good crippled, but he's got brains. Do you know what I've been doing in there while that bastard was singing? I was praying. I thought maybe if God wanted a life he could take mine."

"Do you believe in a God, then?"

"I wish I did," Granger said. He passed his whole hand across his face as though his head ached, but the motion was meant to disguise the fact that he was wiping tears away.

"I'd get drunk if I were you," I said.

"Oh, no, I've got to stay sober. I don't want to think afterwards I was stinking drunk the night my boy died. My wife can't drink, can she?"

"Can't you tell your paper . . . ?"

"Connolly's not really sick. He's off after a bit of tail in Singapore. I've got to cover for him. He'd be sacked if they knew." He gathered his shapeless body together. "Sorry I kept you, Fowler. I just had to tell someone. Got to go in now and start the toasts. Funny it happened to be you, and you hate my guts."

"I'd do your story for you. I could pretend it was Connolly."

"You wouldn't get the accent right."

"I don't dislike you, Granger. I've been blind to a lot of things . . ."

"Oh, you and me, we're cat and dog. But thanks for the sympathy."

Was I so different from Pyle, I wondered? Must I too have

my foot thrust in the mess of life before I saw the pain? Granger went inside and I could hear the voices rising to greet him. I found a trishaw and was pedalled home. There was nobody there, and I sat and waited till midnight. Then I went down into the street without hope and found Phuong there.

# CHAPTER 3

"Has Monsieur Vigot been to see you?" Phuong asked.

"Yes. He left a quarter of an hour ago. Was the film good?" She had already laid out the tray in the bedroom and now she was lighting the lamp.

"It was very sad," she said, "but the colours were lovely. What did Monsieur Vigot want?"

"He wanted to ask me some questions."

"What about?"

"This and that. I don't think he will bother me again."

"I like films with happy endings best," Phuong said. "Are you ready to smoke?"

"Yes." I lay down on the bed and Phuong set to work with her needle. She said, "They cut off the girl's head."

"What a strange thing to do."

"It was in the French Revolution."

"Oh. Historical. I see."

"It was very sad all the same."

"I can't worry much about people in history."

"And her lover—he went back to his garret—and he was miserable and he wrote a song—you see, he was a poet, and soon all the people who had cut off the head of his girl were singing his song. It was the Marseillaise."

"It doesn't sound very historical," I said.

"He stood there at the edge of the crowd while they were singing, and he looked very bitter and when he smiled you knew he was even more bitter and that he was thinking of her. I cried a lot and so did my sister."

"Your sister? I can't believe it."

"She is very sensitive. That horrid man Granger was there. He was drunk and he kept on laughing. But it was not funny at all. It was sad."

"I don't blame him," I said. "He has something to celebrate. His son's out of danger. I heard today at the Continental. I like happy endings too."

After I had smoked two pipes I lay back with my neck on the leather pillow and rested my hand in Phuong's lap. "Are you happy?"

"Of course," she said carelessly. I hadn't deserved a more considered answer.

"It's like it used to be," I lied, "a year ago."

"Yes."

"You haven't bought a scarf for a long time. Why don't you go shopping tomorrow?"

"It is a feast day."

"Oh yes, of course. I forgot."

"You have not opened your telegram," Phuong said.

"No. I'd forgotten that too. I don't want to think about work tonight. And it's too late to file anything now. Tell me more about the film."

"Well, her lover tried to rescue her from prison. He smuggled in boy's clothes and a man's cap like the one the gaoler wore, but just as she was passing the gate all her hair fell down and they called out '*Une aristocrate, une aristocrate.*' I think that was a mistake in the story. They ought to have let her escape. Then they would both have made a lot of money with his song and they would have gone abroad to America—or England," she added with what she thought was cunning.

"I'd better read the telegram," I said. "I hope to God I don't have to go north tomorrow. I want to be quiet with you."

She loosed the envelope from among the pots of cream and gave it to me. I opened it and read: "Have thought over your letter again stop am acting irrationally as you hoped stop have told my lawyer start divorce proceedings grounds desertion stop God bless you affectionately Helen."

"Do you have to go?"

"No," I said, "I don't have to go. I'll read it to you. Here's your happy ending."

She jumped from the bed. "But it is wonderful. I must go and tell my sister. She will be so pleased. I will say to her, 'Do you know who I am? I am the second Mrs. Fowlair.'"

Opposite me in the bookcase *The Rôle of the West* stood out like a cabinet portrait—of a young man with a crew-cut and a black dog at his heels. He could harm no one any more. I said to Phuong, "Do you miss him much?"

"Who?"

"Pyle." Strange how even now, even to her, it was impossible to use his first name.

"Can I go, please? My sister will be so excited."

"You spoke his name once in your sleep."

"I never remember my dreams."

"There was so much you could have done together. He was young."

"You are not old."

"The skyscrapers. The Empire State Building."

She said with a small hesitation, "I want to see the Cheddar Gorge."

"It isn't the Grand Canyon." I pulled her down on to the bed. "I'm sorry, Phuong."

"What are you sorry for? It is a wonderful telegram. My sister . . ."

"Yes, go and tell your sister. Kiss me first." Her excited mouth skated over my face, and she was gone.

I thought of the first day and Pyle sitting beside me at the Continental, with his eye on the soda-fountain across the way. Everything had gone right with me since he had died, but how I wished there existed someone to whom I could say that I was sorry.

*March 1952–June 1955*

# II

# The Author and His Work

# Graham Greene

*The following excerpts are from two of Greene's autobiographical works,* Ways of Escape *(1980) and* Reflections *(1990), edited by Judith Adamson. Most of the first selection appeared in a slightly shorter form as Greene's introduction to The Collected Edition of* The Quiet American *(1973).*

## From *WAYS OF ESCAPE*

It was quite by chance that I fell in love with Indo-China; nothing was further from my thoughts on my first visit than that I would one day set a novel there. An old friend of the war years, Trevor Wilson, was then our Consul in Hanoi, where another war had long been in progress, almost ignored by the British press, which took their reports from Reuters, or in the case of *The Times*, from Paris. So after Malaya I stopped off in Vietnam to see my friend, without any idea that all my winters would be spent there for several years to come. I had found Malaya, apart from the Emergency, as dull as a beautiful woman can sometimes be. People used to say to me, "You should have seen this country in peacetime," and I wanted to

From Graham Greene, *Ways of Escape*. New York: Simon and Schuster, 1980, 160–73, 184–92. Copyright © 1980 by Graham Greene. Reprinted by permission of Simon & Schuster, Inc., and David Higham Associates. Published in Great Britain by William Heinemann Ltd.

reply, "But all that interests me here is your war." Peacetime
Malaya would surely have been no more interesting than a
round of British clubs, of pink gins, of little scandals waiting
for a Maugham to record them.

. But in Indo-China I drained a magic potion, a loving cup
which I have shared since with many retired *colons* and officers
of the Foreign Legion, whose eyes light up at the mention of
Saigon and Hanoi.

The spell was first cast, I think, by the tall elegant girls in
white silk trousers; by the pewter evening light on flat paddy
fields, where the water buffaloes trudged fetlock-deep with a
slow primeval gait; by the French perfumeries in the rue Catinat, the Chinese gambling houses in Cholon; above all by that
feeling of exhilaration which a measure of danger brings to the
visitor with a return ticket: the restaurants wired against grenades, the watchtowers striding along the roads of the southern
delta with their odd reminders of insecurity: *"Si vous êtes ar-
rêtés ou attaqués en cours de route, prévenez le chef du premier
poste important."* (This brought to mind the notice, in the cool
style typical of British Railways, hung in the compartments of
the little train that ambled along the track from Singapore to
Kuala Lumpur.)

I stayed little more than a fortnight on that occasion, and
I crammed to the limit "the unforgiving minute." Hanoi is as
far from Saigon as London is from Rome, but I succeeded,
besides staying in those cities, in paying the first of many visits
in the southern delta to the strange religious sect the Caodaists,
whose saints include Victor Hugo, Christ, Buddha and Sun Yat-
sen, and to the little medieval state established in the marshes
of Bentre by the young half-caste Colonel Leroy, who read de
Tocqueville and struck, with the suddenness and cruelty of a
tiger, at the Communists in his region. Not so many years ago
he had been a small child riding a water buffalo in the rice
fields—now he was all but a king. I was glad years later to write
a preface to his autobiography, in which he did not attempt to
hide the tiger's face behind the smile—a rather small return

since he had probably saved my life. It was in 1955, when the French were evacuating the North and I was waiting in Saigon for permission to enter Hanoi, now in the hands of the Viet Minh. To pass the time I thought I would call on the "General" of one of the sects who fought their private wars in the South. I received a telephone call from Leroy asking me to come to him at his Saigon office. A Frenchman was there whom he introduced as the public relations officer of the "General." The General, he told me, had received my message and would be glad to see me at his headquarters for lunch. However, it would be better if I did not accept. The General had called for his files and he had found that, three years before, I had described him in *Paris-Match* as a former trishaw driver. This was libelous. He had never been a trishaw driver. He had been a bus conductor. Knowing that I was a friend of Leroy, the Frenchman had come to warn me that the General, though he would show me every courtesy at lunch, would make sure that an accident happened to me on the road back to Saigon.

I was anxious on this first visit in 1951 to pay a visit to Phat Diem, one of the two Prince Bishoprics of the North (the other, Bui-Chu, I knew some years later, and there I would have reached the end of my road if a mine had not been detected buried in the track at a point my jeep was about to pass). The two Bishops, like the Caodaist Pope, were allies rather than subjects of the French, and maintained small private armies. On this first occasion I was still basking in the favor of General de Lattre and he had put a little Morain plane at my disposal. He had expected me to fly round his own outposts on what were mistakenly called the lines of Hanoi: instead I went with Trevor Wilson to look at the little army of Phat Diem's Bishop. On the way back the plane was shot at well within the fictional lines and I made the mistake of mentioning the incident to the General at dinner that night. He was not amused. That evening our relations began to cool—an inconvenience to me, but a disaster to my friend.

The change was not immediately noticeable. I was the General's honored guest in Hanoi; he presented me with a shoulder flash of the First French Army, which he commanded at the fall of Strasbourg, and he brought me with him to a reunion of his old comrades. A few months before, all French families had been evacuated from Hanoi, the fall of the city was regarded as imminent, there was the demoralization of defeat. De Lattre had changed all that. In those days the General was able to cast a spell; I heard him tell his old comrades, "I am returning now to Saigon, but I am leaving with you my wife as a symbol that France will never, never leave Hanoi." It was the high summer of his success. It was impossible to imagine then that in little more than a year he would be dying of cancer in Paris, in the sadness of defeat, and that in less than four years I would be taking tea with President Ho Chi Minh in Hanoi.

I went back to England determined to return, but still unaware that I would find the subject for a novel in Vietnam. *Life* had been satisfied with my article on Malaya, so they agreed to send me to Vietnam the next autumn (they did not like the article I wrote there, but they generously allowed me to publish it in *Paris-Match*: I suspect my ambivalent attitude to the war was already perceptible—my admiration for the French Army, my admiration for their enemies, and my doubt of any final value in the war).

When I returned some eight months later, in October 1951, the changes were startling. De Lattre had lost his only son, ambushed with a Vietnamese battalion in the region of Phat Diem, and he was an altered man. His rhetoric of hope was wearing painfully thin; his colonels were openly critical of him, even to a foreigner. They were tired of his continual references to his own sacrifice—others had sacrificed their sons, too, and had not been able to fly the bodies home for a Paris funeral. The General had always suffered from a certain anglophobia and, in spite of the deep piety of his wife, he was highly suspicious of Catholicism. Now in a strange sick manner he linked the death of his son with my visit to Phat Diem and the fact that both Trevor Wilson and I were Catholics. He had shifted

onto us, in his poor guilt-ridden mind, the responsibility for his
son's death (he had sent his son to join a Vietnamese battalion
to break up his relationship with a Vietnamese girl who was a
former mistress of the Emperor). He reported to the Foreign
Office that Trevor Wilson, who had been decorated for his
services to France during the war, was no longer *persona grata*.
Trevor was thrown out of Indo-China, and the Foreign Office
lost a remarkable consul and the French a great friend of their
country. He was already gone when I returned to Hanoi, but
he was allowed to come back for two weeks to pack up his
effects.

In the meanwhile I found myself under the supervision of
the Sûreté, in the person of a gentleman whom I used to call
Monsieur Dupont. Alas, poor Monsieur Dupont, what anxieties
the two of us caused him when we were again temporarily together. We used to meet him at night in the Café de la Paix
in Hanoi and tell him our movements and plans for the morrow
and drink vermouth-cassis and play *quatre cent vingt-et-un*, at
which Trevor Wilson consistently threw the winning dice.

Monsieur Dupont had a rather weak head. He would return
home to his wife always a little the worse for wear, so that
domestic trouble was added to his official trouble, for his wife
refused to believe that his light and innocent tippling was all
in the cause of duty. On one sad occasion he accompanied
Trevor Wilson to Haiphong, where Trevor wanted to say good-
bye to his friends. Trevor had a passion for unfamiliar bath-
houses and he stopped Monsieur Dupont's official car at the
beginning of town, attracted by a board advertising a Chinese
bath. Monsieur Dupont took the cubicle next to his, as he was
bound in duty to do, but a Chinese bath includes an intimate
Chinese massage and Monsieur Dupont's heart was too weak
to stand it. He passed out and had to be revived by a lot of
whisky, to which he was equally unaccustomed. The next morning his *gueule du bois* had to be cured with a dose of Fernet
Branca, which he had never drunk before. (I am sure he considered that infernal spirit was part of the spy's plot.) To add

to all these worries he had lost track of me. I was in forbidden
Phat Diem with the martial Bishop.

I spread the story that I was writing a *roman policier* about
Indo-China and the title I had chosen in French was *Voilà,
Monsieur Dupont*, and so of an evening, sitting on the pavement outside the Café de la Paix, while the troops passed, and
the lovely drifting Tonkinoises, I would watch the approach of
nervous dutiful Monsieur Dupont, his eyes lifted towards mine
like a dog's, waiting for the next "tease."

The surveillance had started before Trevor's arrival. A few
days after I reached Hanoi, Monsieur Dupont came to call. He
brought with him two of my books in French editions, and I
signed them and drank a glass of lemonade with him. The next
day Monsieur Dupont arrived with another book—a *dédicace*
to his wife was required—and the next day he brought yet
others, for his friends. He had cleared every bookshop in Hanoi,
as I found when I tried to get a few copies to give away myself.
After that we dropped the pretense and arranged the evening
meetings, but it was odd how often in my daily strolls Monsieur
Dupont would crop up: in a café where I was drinking, in a
shop where I was buying some soap, in a long dull street along
which I was walking only for the sake of exercise. We became
genuinely fond of each other, and after Trevor's departure he
began to feel for me a paternal responsibility. I was smoking
then a little opium two or three times a week, and he would
plead with me earnestly that this night at least I would go home
quietly to bed after the game of *quatre cent vingt-et-un*.

The crisis of suspicion had come when an unsigned telegram was delivered to me in which Trevor announced his
imminent arrival from Paris. It was his eccentric economy never
unnecessarily to sign a telegram, but obviously to the censorship this was a deliberate attempt to deceive. I guessed matters
were coming to a head when I received, through the head of
the Sûreté in Vietnam, a command to have lunch with the
General. De Lattre was leaving for Paris the next day.

At lunch nothing was said. The guest of honor was a Swiss representative of the Red Cross who was trying to arrange an exchange of prisoners; I sat next to Mr. Tam, the head of the Vietnamese police, a man with a reputation for savagery since he had lost a wife, a son and a finger by enemy action. When lunch was over (it was the first occasion when I had seen de Lattre quiet at his own table) the General came to me. "*Ah, le pauvre Graham Greene*"—he had been unable to speak to me, I must come to his cocktail party that evening, and stay on to dinner. So back I went.

The cocktail party went on and on—it was de Lattre's farewell to Hanoi: there were rumors he would not return, and that the recent empty victory of Hoa Binh was the fairing he had expensively bought to take back with him to Paris. At last everybody left except the generals and colonels who were staying for dinner. There was some singing by a soldiers' choir, and General de Lattre sat on the sofa holding his wife's hand. If I had known he was a dying man perhaps I would have perceived in him again the hero I had met a year before. Now he seemed only the General whose speeches were too long, whose magic had faded, whom his colonels criticized—a dying flame looks as if it has never been anything but smoke.

At ten o'clock the singing stopped and the General turned to me. "And now, Graham Greene, why are you here?" His broken English had an abrupt boastful quality he did not intend. I said, "I have told you already. I am writing an article for *Life*."

"I understand," he said, while the two-starred generals, Linarès and Salan and Cogny, sat on the edges of their chairs pretending not to listen, "that you are a member of the British Secret Service."

I laughed.

"I understand you were in the Intelligence Service in the war. For three years."

I explained to the General that under National Service we

did not pick our job—nor continue it when the war was over.

"I understand that no one ever leaves the British Secret Service."

"That may be true of the Deuxième Bureau," I said. "It is not true with us." A servant announced dinner.

I sat next to the General and we talked polite small talk. Madame de Lattre eyed me sternly—I had disturbed the peace of a sick man whom she loved, on his last night in Hanoi, the scene of his triumph and his failure. Even though I was unaware how sick he was, I felt a meanness in myself. He deserved better company.

When we rose from the table I asked if I might see him alone. He told me to stay till the others had gone and at half past one in the morning he sent for me to his study. Madame de Lattre bade me a cold goodnight. Hadn't her husband enough to worry about?

I had prepared in my mind what I thought was a clear narration, which included even the amount I was being paid by *Life* for my article. He heard me out and then expressed his satisfaction with some grandiloquence (but that was his way). "I have told the Sûreté, Graham Greene is my friend. I do not believe what you say about him. Then they come again and tell me you have been here or there and I say, I do not believe. Graham Greene is my friend. And then again they come. . . ." He shook hands warmly, saying how glad he was to know that all was a mistake, but next day, before he left for Paris, his misgivings returned. I had received yet another dubious telegram, again unsigned—this time from my literary agent in Paris. "Your friend will arrive on Thursday. Dorothy under instruction from Philip."

The last sentence referred to my friend Dorothy Glover, the illustrator of my children's books, who had decided to become a Catholic, and Philip was Father Philip Caraman, the well-known London Jesuit, but it was obvious what the Sûreté made of it. "I knew he was a spy," de Lattre told one of his staff before boarding his plane. "Why should anyone come to this war for four hundred dollars?" I had forgotten how uncertain his English was—he had mislaid a zero.

I never wrote *Voilà, Monsieur Dupont*; instead the moment for *The Quiet American* struck as I was driving back to Saigon after spending the night with Colonel Leroy. Less than a year ago, when we had toured together his watery kingdom, it was in an armored boat with guns trained on the bank, but now as night fell we moved gently along the rivers in an unarmed barge furnished not with guns but with gramophones and dancing girls. He had built at Bentre a lake with a pagoda in imitation of the one at Hanoi; the night was full of strange cries from the zoo he had started for his people, and we dined on the island in the lake and the Colonel poured brandy down the throats of the girls to make the party go and played the Harry Lime theme of *The Third Man* on a gramophone in my honor.

I shared a room that night with an American attached to an economic aid mission—the members were assumed by the French, probably correctly, to belong to the C.I.A. My companion bore no resemblance at all to Pyle, the quiet American of my story—he was a man of greater intelligence and of less innocence, but he lectured me all the long drive back to Saigon on the necessity of finding a "third force in Vietnam." I had never before come so close to the great American dream which was to bedevil affairs in the East as it was to do in Algeria.

The only leader discernible for the "third force" was the self-styled General Thé. At the time of my first visit to the Caodaists he had been a colonel in the army of the Caodaist Pope—a force of twenty thousand men which theoretically fought on the French side. They had their own munitions factory in the Holy See at Tay Ninh; they supplemented what small arms they could squeeze out of the French with mortars made from the exhaust pipes of old cars. An ingenious people—it was difficult not to suspect their type of ingenuity in the bicycle bombs which went off in Saigon the following year. The time bombs were concealed in plastic containers made in the shape of bicycle pumps and the bicycles were left

in the parks outside the ministries and propped against walls.
. . . A bicycle arouses no attention in Saigon. It is as much a
bicycle city as Copenhagen.

Between my two visits General Thé (he had promoted himself) had deserted from the Caodaist Army with a few hundred
men and was now installed on the Holy Mountain, outside Tay
Ninh. He had declared war on both the French and the Communists. When my novel was eventually noticed in the *New
Yorker* the reviewer condemned me for accusing my "best
friends" (the Americans) of murder because I had attributed
to them the responsibility for the great explosion—far worse
than the trivial bicycle bombs—in the main square of Saigon,
in which many people lost their lives. But what are the facts,
of which the reviewer, needless to say, was ignorant? The *Life*
photographer at the moment of the explosion was so well
placed that he was able to take an astonishing and horrifying
photograph which showed the body of a trishaw driver still upright after his legs had been blown off. This photograph was
reproduced in an American propaganda magazine published in
Manila over the caption "The work of Ho Chi Minh," although
General Thé had promptly and proudly claimed the bomb as
his own. Who had supplied the material to a bandit who was
fighting French, Caodaists and Communists?

There was certainly evidence of contacts between the American services and General Thé. A jeep with the bodies of two
American women was found by a French rubber planter on the
route to the Holy Mountain—presumably they had been killed
by the Viet Minh, but what were they doing on the plantation?
The bodies were promptly collected by the American Embassy,
and nothing more was heard of the incident. Not a word appeared in the press. An American consul was arrested late at
night on the bridge to Dakow (where Pyle in my novel lost his
life) carrying plastic bombs in his car. Again the incident was
hushed up for diplomatic reasons.

So the subject of *The Quiet American* came to me during
that talk of a "third force" on the road through the delta, and

my characters quickly followed, all but one of them from the unconscious. The exception was Granger, the American newspaper correspondent. The press conference in Hanoi where he figures was recorded almost word for word in my journal at the time.

Perhaps there is more direct *reportage* in *The Quiet American* than in any other novel I have written. I had determined to employ again the experience I had gained with *The End of the Affair* in the use of the first person and the time shift, and my choice of a journalist as the "I" seemed to me to justify the use of *reportage*. The press conference is not the only example of direct reporting. I was in the dive-bomber (the pilot had broken an order of General de Lattre by taking me) which attacked the Viet Minh post and I was on the patrol of the Foreign Legion paras outside Phat Diem. I still retain the sharp image of the dead child couched in the ditch beside his dead mother. The very neatness of their bullet wounds made their death more disturbing than the indiscriminate massacre in the canals around.

I went back to Indochina for the fourth and last time in 1955, after the defeat of the French in the North, and with some difficulty I reached Hanoi—a sad city, abandoned by the French, where I drank the last bottle of beer left in the café which I used to frequent with Monsieur Dupont. I was feeling ill and tired and depressed. I sympathized with the victors, but I sympathized with the French too. The French classics were yet on view in a small secondhand bookshop which Monsieur Dupont had rifled a few years back, but a hundred years of French civilization had fled with the Catholic peasants to the South. The Metropole Hotel, where I used to stay, was in the hands of the International Commission. Viet Minh sentries stood outside the building where de Lattre had made his promise, "I leave you my wife as a symbol that France will never, never . . ."

Day after day passed while I tried to bully my way into the presence of Ho Chi Minh. It was the period of the *crachin* and my spirits sank with the thin daylong drizzle of warm rain. I told my contacts I could wait no longer—tomorrow I would return to what was left of French territory in the North. I don't know why my blackmail succeeded, but I was summoned suddenly to take tea with Ho Chi Minh, and now I felt too ill for the meeting. There was only one thing to be done. I went back to an old Chinese chemist's shop in the rue des Voiles which I had visited the year before. The owner, it was said, was "The Happiest Man in the World." There I was able to smoke a few pipes of opium while the mah-jong pieces rattled like gravel on a beach. I had a passionate desire for the impossible—a bottle of Eno's. A messenger was dispatched and before the pipes were finished I received the impossible. I had drunk the last bottle of beer in Hanoi. Was this the last bottle of Eno's? Anyway the Eno's and the pipes took away the sickness and the inertia and gave me the energy to meet Ho Chi Minh at tea.

Of those four winters which I passed in Indochina, opium has left the happiest memory, and as it played an important part in the life of Fowler, my character in *The Quiet American*, I add a few memories from my journal concerning it, for I am reluctant to leave Indo-China forever with only a novel to remember it by. . . .

*February 9, 1954. Saigon*

> After dinner at the Arc-en-Ciel, to the *fumerie* opposite the Casino above the school. I had only five pipes, but that night was very dopey. First I had a nightmare, then I was haunted by squares—architectural squares which reminded me of Angkor, equal distances, etc., and then mathematical squares—people's income, etc., square after square after square which seemed to go on all night. At last I woke and when I slept again I had a strange complete dream such as I have experienced only after opium. I was coming down the steps of a club in St. James's Street and on the steps I met the Devil who was wearing a tweed motoring coat and a deerstalker

cap. He had long black Edwardian moustaches. In the
street a girl, with whom I was apparently living, was
waiting for me in a car. The Devil stopped me and
asked whether I would like to have a year to live again
or to skip a year and see what would be happening to
me two years from now. I told him I had no wish to
live over any year again and I would like to have a
glimpse of two years ahead. Immediately the Devil vanished and I was holding in my hands a letter. I opened
the letter—it was from some girl whom I knew only
slightly. It was a very tender letter, and a letter of farewell. Obviously during that missing year we had reached
a relationship which she was now ending. Looking down
at the woman in the car I thought, "I must not show
her the letter, for how absurd it would be if she were
to be jealous of a girl whom I don't yet know." I went
into my room (I was no longer in the club) and tore
the letter into small pieces, but at the bottom of the
envelope were some beads which must have had a sentimental significance. I was unwilling to destroy these
and opening a drawer put them in and locked the
drawer. As I did so it suddenly occurred to me, "In two
years' time I shall be doing just this, opening a drawer,
putting away the beads, and finding the beads are already in the drawer." Then I woke.

There remains another memory which I find it difficult to
dispel, the doom-laden twenty-four hours I spent in Dien Bien
Phu in January 1954. Nine years later, when I was asked by *The
Sunday Times* to write on "a decisive battle of my choice," it
was Dien Bien Phu that came straightaway to my mind.

*Fifteen Decisive Battles of the World*—Sir Edward Creasy
gave that classic title to his book in 1851, but it is doubtful
whether any battle listed there was more decisive than Dien
Bien Phu in 1954. Even Sedan, which came too late for Creasy,
was only an episode in Franco-German relations, decisive for

the moment in a provincial dispute, but the decision was to be reversed in 1918, and that decision again in 1940.

Dien Bien Phu, however, was a defeat for more than the French Army. The battle marked virtually the end of any hope the Western Powers might have entertained that they could dominate the East. The French, with Cartesian clarity, accepted the verdict. So too, to a lesser extent, did the British: the independence of Malaya, whether the Malays like to think it or not, was won for them when the Communist forces of General Giap, an ex–geography professor at Hanoi University, defeated the forces of General Navarre, ex–cavalry officer, ex–Deuxième Bureau chief, at Dien Bien Phu. (That young Americans were still to die in Vietnam only shows that it takes time for the echoes even of a total defeat to encircle the globe.)

The battle itself, the heroic stand of Colonel de Castries's men while the conference of the Powers at Geneva dragged along, through the debates on Korea, towards the second item on the agenda—Indo-China—every speech in Switzerland punctuated by deaths in that valley in Tonkin—has been described many times. Courage will always find a chronicler, but what remains a mystery to this day is why the battle was ever fought at all, why twelve battalions of the French Army were committed to the defense of an armed camp situated in a hopeless geographical terrain—hopeless for defense and hopeless for the second objective, since the camp was intended to be the base of offensive operations. (For this purpose a squadron of ten tanks was assembled there, the components dropped by parachute.)

A commission of inquiry was appointed in Paris after the defeat, but no conclusion was ever reached. A battle of words followed the carnage. Monsieur Laniel, who was Prime Minister when the decision was taken to fight at Dien Bien Phu, published his memoirs, which attacked the strategy and conduct of General Navarre, and General Navarre published his memoirs attacking Monsieur Laniel and the politicians of Paris. Monsieur Laniel's book was called *Le Drame Indo-Chinois* and

General Navarre's *Agonie de l'Indo-Chine*, a difference in title which represents the difference between the war as seen from Paris and the war as seen in Hanoi.

For the future historian the difference between the titles will seem smaller than the contradictions in the works themselves. Accusations are bandied back and forth between the politician who had never visited the scene of war and the general who had known it only for a matter of months when the great error was made.

The war, which had begun in September 1946, was in 1953 reaching a period for the troops not so much of exhaustion as of cynicism and dogged pride—they believed in no solution but were not prepared for any surrender. In the southern delta around Saigon it had been for a long while a war of ambush and attrition—in Saigon itself of sudden attacks by hand grenades and bombs; in the North, in Tonkin, the French defense against the Viet Minh depended on the so-called lines of Hanoi, established by General de Lattre. The lines were not real lines; Viet Minh regiments would appear out of the rice fields in sudden attacks close to Hanoi itself before they vanished again into the mud. I was witness to one such attack at Phat Diem, and in Bui Chu, well within the lines, sleep was disturbed by mortar fire until dawn. While it was the avowed purpose of the High Command to commit the Viet Minh to a major action, it became evident with the French evacuation of Hoa Binh, which de Lattre had taken with the loss, it was popularly believed, of one man, that General Giap was no less anxious to commit the French Army, on ground of his own choosing.

Salan succeeded de Lattre, and Navarre succeeded Salan, and every year the number of officers killed was equal to a whole class at Saint-Cyr (the war was a drain mainly on French officers, for National Service troops were not employed in Indo-China on the excuse that this was not a war but a police action). Something somewhere had to give, and what gave was French intelligence in both senses of the word.

There is a bit of a schoolmaster in an Intelligence officer:

he imbibes information at second hand and passes it on too often as gospel truth. Giap being an ex-professor, it was thought suitable perhaps to send against him another schoolmaster, but Giap was better acquainted with his subject—the geography of his own northern country.

The French for years had been acutely sensitive to the Communist menace to the kingdom of Laos on their flank. The little umbrageous royal capital of Luang Prabang, on the banks of the Mekong, consisting mainly of Buddhist temples, was threatened every campaigning season by Viet Minh guerrilla regiments, but I doubt whether the threat was ever as serious as the French supposed. Ho Chi Minh can hardly have been anxious to add a Buddhist to a Catholic problem in the North, and Luang Prabang remained inviolate. But the threat served its purpose. The French left their "lines."

In November 1953 six parachute battalions dropped on Dien Bien Phu, a plateau ten miles by five, surrounded by thickly wooded hills, all in the hands of the enemy. When I visited the camp for twenty-four hours in January 1954, the huge logistic task had been accomplished: the airstrip was guarded by strong points on small hills; there were trenches, underground dugouts, and miles and miles and miles of wire. (General Navarre wrote with Maginot pride of his wire.) The number of battalions had been doubled, the tanks assembled, the threat to Luang Prabang had been contained, if such a threat really existed, but at what a cost.

It is easy to have hindsight, but what impressed me as I flew in on a transport plane from Hanoi, three hundred kilometers away, over mountains impassable to a mechanized force, was the vulnerability and the isolation of the camp. It could be reinforced—or evacuated—only by air, except by the route to Laos, and as we came down towards the landing strip I was uneasily conscious of flying only a few hundred feet above the invisible enemy.

General Navarre writes with naivety and pathos: "There was not one civil or military authority who visited the camp (French or foreign Ministers, French chiefs of staff, American generals) who was not struck by the strength of the defences. . . . To my knowledge no one expressed any doubt before the attack about the possibilities of resistance." Is anyone more isolated from human contact than a commander in chief?

One scene of evil augury comes back to my mind. We were drinking Colonel de Castries's excellent wine at lunch in the mess, and the Colonel, who had the nervy histrionic features of an old-time actor, overheard the commandant of his artillery discussing with another officer the evacuation of the French post of Na-San during the last campaigning season. De Castries struck his fist on the table and cried out with a kind of Shakespearian hysteria, "Be silent. I will not have Na-San mentioned in this mess. Na-San was a defensive post. This is an offensive one." There was an uneasy silence until de Castries's second-in-command asked me whether I had seen Claudel's *Christophe Colombe* as I passed through Paris. (The officer who had mentioned Na-San was to shoot himself during the siege.)

After lunch, as I walked round the intricate entrenchments, I asked an officer, "What did the Colonel mean? An offensive post?" He waved at the surrounding hills: "We should need a thousand mules—not a squadron of tanks—to take the offensive."

Monsieur Laniel writes of the unreal optimism which preceded the attack. In Hanoi optimism may have prevailed, but not in the camp itself. The defences were out of range of mortar fire from the surrounding hills, but not an officer doubted that heavy guns were on the way from the Chinese frontier (guns elaborately camouflaged, trundled in by bicycle along almost impassable ways by thousands of coolies—a feat more brilliant than the construction of the camp). Any night they expected a bombardment to open. It was no novelist's imagination which felt the atmosphere heavy with doom, for these men were aware of what they resembled—sitting ducks.

In the meanwhile, before the bombardment opened, the wives and sweethearts of officers visited them in the camp by transport plane for a few daylight hours: ardent little scenes took place in dugouts—it was pathetic and forgivable, even though it was not war. The native contingents, too, had their wives—more permanently—with them, and it was a moving sight to see a woman suckling her baby beside a sentry under waiting hills. It wasn't war, it wasn't optimism—it was the last chance.

The Viet Minh had chosen the ground for their battle by their menace to Laos. Monsieur Laniel wrote that it would have been better to have lost Laos for the moment than to have lost both Laos and the French Army, and he put the blame on the military command. General Navarre in return accused the French Government of insisting at all costs on the defence of Laos.

All reason for the establishment of the camp seems to disappear in the debate—somebody somewhere misunderstood, and passing the buck became after the battle a new form of logistics. Only the Viet Minh dispositions make sense, though even there a mystery remains. With their artillery alone the Communists could have forced the surrender of Dien Bien Phu. A man cannot be evacuated by parachute, and the airstrip was out of action a few days after the assault began.

A heavy fog, curiously not mentioned by either General Navarre or Monsieur Laniel, filled the cup among the hills every night around ten, and it did not lift again before eleven in the morning. (How impatiently I waited for it to lift after my night in a dugout.) During that period parachute supplies were impossible and it was equally impossible for planes from Hanoi to spot the enemy's guns. Under these circumstances why inflict on one's own army twenty thousand casualties by direct assault?

But the Great Powers had decided to negotiate, the conference of Geneva had opened in the last week of April with Korea first on the agenda, and individual lives were not considered important. It was preferable as propaganda for General Giap to capture the post by direct assault during the course of the Geneva Conference. The assault began on March 13, 1954, and Dien Bien Phu fell on May 7, the day before the delegates turned at last from the question of Korea to the question of Indo-China.

But General Giap could not be confident that the politicians of the West, who showed a certain guilt towards the defenders of Dien Bien Phu while they were discussing at such length the problem of Korea, would have continued to talk long enough to give him time to reduce Dien Bien Phu by artillery alone.

So the battle had to be fought with the maximum of human suffering and loss. Monsieur Mendès-France, who had succeeded Monsieur Laniel, needed his excuse for surrendering the North of Vietnam just as General Giap needed his spectacular victory by frontal assault before the Forum of the Powers to commit Britain and America to a division of the country.

> *The Sinister Spirit sneered:*
>   *"It had to be!"*
> *And again the Spirit of Pity*
>   *whispered, "Why?"*

# Graham Greene

*This selection from* Reflections *originally appeared in* Paris-Match, *12 July 1952. It is Greene's first publication on Vietnam and is not noted in Wobbe's otherwise excellent bibliography.*

## INDO-CHINA: FRANCE'S CROWN
## OF THORNS

The Indo-Chinese front is only one sector of a long line which crosses Korea, touches the limits of a still peaceful Hong Kong, cuts across Tongking, avoids—for the moment—Siam, and continues into the jungles of Malaya. If Indo-China falls, Korea will be isolated, Siam can be invaded in twenty-four hours and Malaya may have to be abandoned. In Tongking the French hold one sector of this vast front, and in the six years they have held it, the French army has lost more men than the Americans in Korea. This is the simple truth: war can sometimes appear to be simple.

From the bell tower of the cathedral of Phat Diem, 120 kilometres south-east of Hanoi, I could contemplate a panorama of war that was truly classical, the kind that historians or

From *Reflections* by Graham Greene, edited by Judith Adamson. New York: Penguin, 1990, 129–47. Copyright © 1990 by Graham Greene. Translation by Alan Adamson. Used by permission of Viking Penguin, a division of Penguin Books USA Inc.

war correspondents used to describe before the era of the camera. At a radius of 600 to 800 metres Phat Diem was encircled by rebel forces, but very peacefully; ahead of the parachutists, howitzer shells exploded in little clouds, hanging motionless for a moment in the calm air above the plain, as in a painting. On my left, above the profile of those strange mountains, sculptured and eroded by the elements, an aeroplane was supplying a small, isolated French post with ammunition, and when night fell the flames rising from the burning market of Phat Diem grew more vivid, adding an almost comforting element of colour to the landscape in the biting cold of this December night. Yes, war seemed very simple from the height of the bell tower.

Clearly it was an illusion—the only illusion of simplicity possible to retain in the midst of this confused struggle conducted on both sides by regulars and irregulars, by illustrious French generals and medieval warlords—one of them a kind of Buddhist prophet, another a cannibal who eats the liver of his enemy to strengthen his own body; elsewhere, a Catholic Bishop who commands his own army and hates the French more than the Communists; a new kind of Pope who preaches a dogma of synthesis and incorporates in his clergy a college of female cardinals; and (last but not least) the chief of a Third Force who makes war on everyone and places high-explosive bombs in the very centre of Saigon in order to kill innocent civilians. Western slogans and all that talk the politicians retail about the necessity of containing Communism seem here to apply only to a very small part of the picture. And it is even more difficult to fit in the oriental dragons and the fabulous serpents, different parts of a puzzle which form no part of any familiar design.

Vietnam, a creation of Western powers confronting the thrust of nationalism as much as Communism, is made up of three states: the old French colony of Cochin China, where members of the liberal professions take pride in their French citizenship, and the two ex-protectorates of Annam in the centre, and Tongking in the north. The Vietnamese government,

selected and appointed by the French administration, was until
recently presided over by Mr. Tran Van Huu, formerly chief
accountant of the *Crédit foncier d'Indochine*. He was never, and
still does not possess the authority of an elected government.
There is no national assembly. Under the wily Tran Van Huu's
presidency the government consisted of nothing but a group of
appointed individuals whose worth can be graded from simple
utility right up to the strictest and most capable executive of
them all, Mr. Nguyen Van Tam, Minister of Public Security,
who lost two sons—and one of his own fingers—to the Viet
Minh.

The Emperor Bao Dai, chief of state, has kept himself pru-
dently in the background. Just past forty, educated in France,
married to a Catholic (but the Empress lives in Cannes), he
sometimes gives the impression of showing more interest in
sports than in his somewhat nominal responsibilities. In fact,
he is an intelligent and subtle man, resolved not to compromise
himself, and to survive. Nevertheless, the death of General de
Lattre seems to have given him the opportunity of reappearing
on the scene, and the substitution of Mr. Nguyen Van Tam for
Mr. Tran Van Huu reinforced his administration significantly.
As chief of police, the new Prime Minister has been too involved in French policy to be able to adopt a very independent
line, but at least several of his ministers have been selected
from Tongking, the most independent state, and overtures have
been made to members of the Dai-Viet Party. This is the nationalist party of the north; it has always refused to collaborate
with Mr. Tran Van Huu, but its members enjoy a reputation
for integrity.

Their entry into the government will doubtless somewhat
soften the memory of the comparison General de Lattre made
on a visit to the United States between Vietnam in the French
Union and Australia in the Commonwealth. This remark was
not only erroneous, it lacked tact and served to irritate cultivated Vietnamese who realize, with bitterness, the fictitious
character of their independence. They might indeed ask if

Great Britain maintains a police organization in Canberra to parallel the Australian; if the British Governor-General expels diplomatic representatives of foreign powers without consulting the Australian government; or whether visitors must possess an English as well as an Australian visa.

General de Lattre was completely sincere when he stated that a French victory in this war would be followed by the withdrawal of his troops, but the Vietnamese would possibly have found more acceptable the policy of the English in Malaysia, provided with the same guarantees of good faith that were given India and Pakistan. They would have been better able to accept a slow and continuous progress towards independence than a show of independence, a show which costs them very dear: an uncontrolled and notoriously cruel local police force, a President who has never been elected and whom the Emperor can replace only with the consent of France. Until recently, the Emperor and the President have avoided any hint of a consultative assembly, and in a recent radio broadcast the Emperor would go no further than to suggest the creation of an assembly half of whose members he would name himself.

Who is the enemy? That is difficult to define. (Even the term Viet Minh is disconcerting for a foreigner who produces a smile or becomes suspect when he speaks of his Viet Minh friends instead of his Vietnam friends.) The Viet Minh is the nationalist government which, under the apparent direction of Ho Chi Minh, controls the greater part of Tongking and Annam. One of the most widely discussed subjects is how much authority is in the hands of the Communists, and the extent of Ho Chi Minh's personal power. Ho Chi Minh was indoctrinated in Moscow around 1920, but that doesn't necessarily make him a Stalinist to the death. There are few survivors of those first days of the Communist regime. There is some reason to believe that when he went to France in 1946 to carry on negotiations as the recognized Vietnamese chief of state, the stage was set for a shift of power to the Commander-in-Chief, Vo Nguyen Giap, an ex-lecturer in philosophy at the University of Hanoi, who, in Ho's absence, secured for himself command of Tongking.

At that time, Ho Chi Minh obtained from France conditions which would be difficult to improve upon today. They included the concession of real independence to Vietnam and the progressive withdrawal of French forces. Today, after six years of exhausting struggle and the death of 30,000 men, these are not the kind of demands that could be formulated on the battlefield.

It is difficult to believe that with such an accord in his pocket and the nation almost unanimously behind him, Ho Chi Minh decided to put everything he had achieved once more into question in the hope of rapid victory by force of arms. It is more probable that his hand was forced by Giap and other Communist leaders. There were few French troops in the north, 5,000 in Hanoi, some few thousands more in Lang Son and Haiphong, but two years later there would have been even fewer of them. Today at Lang Son Ho Chi Minh rules over nothing but ruins, and 160,000 men of the French army (including Moroccans, Senegalese and Legionaries) plus a Vietnamese army of 200,000 stand between him and the Hanoi–Haiphong delta, the essential bastion in the defence of Siam and Malaysia.

If Ho Chi Minh is really only the nominal head of the Viet Minh, who has taken his place? At the time of the battle for Hanoi, Giap was the military chief, but today the impression one gathers from reports of refugees from the Viet Minh zone is that power—civil as well as military—is in the hands of Dang Xuan Khu (alias Truongh Trinh), Secretary General of the Communist Party of Indo-China. Certain lawyers and doctors, who are sincere nationalists, have also reported that the growing pressure of Communist doctrine makes life intolerable for intellectuals. The churches still operate (for the moment the Viet Minh is more discreet towards Catholics and Buddhists since the latter's pacifism and lack of internal organization makes them more vulnerable) but persecution lies in wait just down the road. The evolution of the Viet Minh in this regard seems to be the same as in China in the first days of Communism. But one must remember that the numerous Catholic population of Tongking is almost entirely rural. They don't read European newspapers; indeed, they don't read at all. Ho Chi Minh, their great leader, teaches them by radio that the duty of Catholics is to be nationalists: no report reaches them of priests killed and nuns imprisoned in China. Propaganda is a one-way street. They could see the prudent behaviour of the Viet Minh soldiers when they penetrated the enclosure of the cathedral at Phat Diem last December, and since then they cannot understand the military necessity of the slow advance of the parachutists along the canals which cross their fields and the ruins of their abandoned farms.

It is clear that an element of idealism exists in the Viet Minh zone which is not at all Stalinist. Certain illusions still persist. A writer, taken prisoner and then released to teach literature in the schools, describes with nostalgia the life he led there. He and his pupils received the same rations as the troops. The daily distribution of rice was made with a simplicity and justice often absent in more developed countries. (Officers and their men were entitled to the same 600 grams of nourishment; a variance in treatment was only noticeable at the end of the month when wages were paid in money or in kind.) He spoke with regret of this school that moved with the troops. When they entered a village, they would select a big hut, a door taken off its hinges would make do for a desk, he and his pupils would sit down on the ground, their haversacks containing their daily rations slung across their shoulders. At the sound of a whistle announcing an air raid, they would take cover in a nearby forest. The weight of the haversack, the sound of the whistle, the feel of the improvised desk under the fingers, the flickers of the kitchen fires in the forest, such things can attach a man to a cause—until the weight of doctrine benumbs him with its monotony. Communism simplifies the war by eliminating the factors of pure nationalism.

I have written that Vietnam is composed of three states, but it would be more precise to say three countries, for the people of Cochin China differ much more from the Tongkinese than they do from the Siamese. Hanoi, the capital of Tongking, is a three-and-a-half hour flight from Saigon, and one shivers in Hanoi when one swelters in the heat of Saigon.

Each state has its own kind of war. Cochin China, along with Saigon, capital of Vietnam, is mainly held by the French and their allies. There the forces of the Viet Minh are composed of partisans, and the war is a guerrilla war. All the roads leading out of Saigon are guarded by watchtowers erected at one-kilometre intervals. More in form than in solidity, these lookouts are reminiscent of the watchtowers of French châteaux or English castles. Every evening at six traffic is suspended, for when night falls the adjacent rice fields become a no man's land.

In this flat, marshy country, all tender green or faded gold, held partly by the French and partly by their strange and often doubtful allies, a war of ambush is carried on. Even in Saigon it is a war of random assassination, of grenades thrown into cafés, nightclubs and cinemas. Life goes on, however, despite the grenades, although some people prefer to drink in an upstairs bar or dine in a restaurant protected by an iron grill, but these things are not major preoccupations. Unless one is unlucky, all one hears of the war is the occasional small explosion in the distance which might just as well be an automobile backfiring.

Nevertheless, ever since a local girl blew herself up with a party of sailors from a warship anchored in the Saigon river, one finds it quite natural in the big hotels to be advised against taking a Cochin Chinese woman to your room.

Of all France's allies in Indo-China, the most astonishing are the Caodaists, members of a religious sect founded around 1920. Their capital, which they call "The Holy See," is Tay Ninh, some 80 kilometres from Saigon, where their Pope lives surrounded by cardinals of both sexes. At the entrance to the fantastic, technicolour cathedral are hung the portraits of three minor saints of the Caodaist religion: Dr. Sun Yat Sen, Trang Trinh, a primitive Vietnamese poet, and Victor Hugo, attired in the uniform of a member of the Académie Française with a halo round his tricorn hat. In the nave of the cathedral, in the full Asiatic splendour of a Walt Disney fantasy, pastel dragons coil about the columns and pulpit; from every stained-glass window the great eye of God follows one, an enormous serpent forms the papal throne and high up under the arches are the effigies of the three major saints: Buddha, Confucius, and Christ displaying his Sacred Heart.

The saints, Victor Hugo in particular, still address the faithful through the medium of a pencil and a basket covered by a kind of movable Ouija board; the religious ceremonies are intolerably long, and a vegetarian diet is rigorously imposed. One should not therefore be surprised to learn that missionaries have been sent to Los Angeles.

The memory one retains of all this is phantasmagorical: a chain-smoking Pope discoursing hour after hour on Atlantis and the common origin of all religions, but who in fact makes use of this religious façade with all its pomp to support a solid army of 20,000 men with its own primitive arsenal to guard against an eventual stoppage of supply of French arms (mortars are fabricated from old exhaust pipes which, after a year of use, are given to the peasants for local defence). . . . Under the protection of this army, the pacifist Caodaist sect numbers a million and a half adherents. As Victor Hugo revealed to the faithful on 20 April 1930 at one o'clock in the morning: "Instruct the infidel by every available method."

But last summer a split occurred in the Caodaist ranks: the chief of the general staff, Colonel Trinh Minh Thé, went underground with 2,000 men. (The first indications of this dissidence were perhaps the champagne breakfasts to which he treated visiting journalists.) General Thé—as he has now promoted himself—states that he is as much the enemy of the Communists as of the French, but until now his exploits—

such as the assassination of General Chanson, one of the best young French generals, or setting off high-explosive bombs in Saigon—have all been directed against the latter. During a lunch at Tay Ninh last February, a Caodaist colonel complained to me about the difficulties General Thé was causing.

"The French want us to capture him," he said, "but that is obviously impossible."

"Why impossible?" I asked.

"Because he has not attacked any Caodaists!"

This seems to illustrate with subtlety and precision the nature of the alliance between the Caodaists and the Franco-Vietnamese administration. Since then General Trinh Minh Thé's headquarters has been attacked, but he succeeded in escaping, though severely wounded.

Another picturesque element among the French allies in South Vietnam is provided by the Hoa Haos, with a tougher army than the Caodaists, and also with its own form of religion founded on Buddhism. Their first prophet was a Viet Minh partisan but when he came under suspicion due to overweening ambition, he was assassinated and his disciples rallied to the French. Their present General, rumour has it, was a rickshaw driver in Saigon whose wife has established a women's army. (Its sole activity up to the present has been the "liquidation" of some of the General's concubines.)

Nor should one fail to mention the Binh-Xuyen. In theory, the authority of its commander is limited to the periphery of Cholon, Saigon's Chinese district, but since he has the gambling monopoly and owns establishments like "Le Grand Monde" with dancing, floor-shows, roulette and dice games, he has become, with the aid of his private police force, the real force responsible for keeping order in Cholon itself. (Cholon is no further from the centre of Saigon than Harlem from Fifth Avenue or Montmartre from the Champs-Elysées.) He runs a kind of Al Capone regime and last November the French were forced to send armoured cars to Cholon to dislodge him. Rumours circulated that de Lattre was anxious to get rid of the

Binh-Xuyen. Grenade attacks immediately became more frequent (a warning, no doubt, to the French and Vietnamese Sûretés, to stay out of the territory). In any case, the Binh-Xuyen still retains firm control of Cholon and its environs, holding out against the French as well as the Viet Minh.

The most reliable and also the happiest of the warlords in Cochin China is Colonel Leroy, founder of the Military Union for the Defence of Christianity (MUDC). When I visited him in February 1951 with a view to seeing the newly pacified region under his control, we had to travel protected by the armour plating of a landing barge. In February 1952 we were able to drift gently down the current in his personal boat, without even a rifle on board, to the sound of a Vietnamese orchestra.

Thirty-two years old, half French, half Annamite, Colonel Leroy is a curious and imposing personality. He quotes Proudhon, reads Montesquieu, discusses Pascal and Jansenism. He received me to the tune of *The Third Man* theme in a villa built in the middle of his new artificial lake, and, surrounded by dancing girls, treated me to a cognac. As far as social questions are concerned, he is much bolder than his own government: he advocates breaking up the great estates and distributing them to the peasants. With American aid, he has set up ninety-four first-aid stations in the territory under his administration (there are a total of ninety-six in all of Cochin China). In defiance of the President's orders he has instituted a system of local elections to a consultative assembly. Nor has he neglected the entertainment factor: he has built a free zoo around his lake with elegant Chinese pavilions, a bar, and neon lights shining all night long. What an astonishing contrast between this gay and rather bizarre Catholic state and the sober diocese of Phat Diem.

Annam, where the central cities like Hué, the former imperial capital, are controlled by Franco-Vietnamese forces, is accessible only by sea or air. The backcountry, a region of mountains and deep forests, is thinly populated and there the Viet Minh has established its bases. The highway and railroad which skirt the coast and link Saigon to Hanoi are cut off in the south by Quang-Ngai and in the north by Vinh. In these pockets the Viet Minh use certain sections of the railroad by night.

In the north, towards Hanoi, nothing remains but the trace of former tracks. In the Red River delta the road runs along the former railroad embankment but there is no longer even a sign of rails, although here and there you can still see an old station with its ticket-window, vaguely disguised as a farm building. At the edge of a rice paddy a signal raises its arm, permanently frozen; a water pipe swings gently to and fro like the trunk of an aged elephant. The magic of utter neglect has fallen over the line and one cannot imagine that trains will again run along its roadbed.

Further north, in Tongking, the war has become the business of armies. Here the population is physically more solid than in the south, the climate harsher, the clothing coarser, the women less pretty, and play is forbidden. People here still remember the great famines, like the one in 1944 which caused more than a million deaths: this is the country of Ho Chi Minh, the head of the Viet Minh.

If one sees Cochin China in colours of green and gold, one sees Tongking only in brown and black. Two-thirds of the country is held by the Viet Minh, and along the Chinese border the French have lost all their positions save one. Before the arrival of General de Lattre in December 1950, the entire Red River delta, with its capital Hanoi and its only port Haiphong, was seriously threatened.

There is no doubt that during this period of retreat General de Lattre fully earned his marshal's baton. He gave his troops their first tangible victory, and then dug them in. When I saw Tongking for the first time, in February 1951, two weeks after the victory of Vinh-Yen, a line of forts was being set up around the delta. By October 1951 it seemed impregnable; Hanoi was no longer besieged. Nevertheless, something had gone wrong. The enthusiasm raised by the arrival of the chief was seeping away. Still, one couldn't say morale was bad; the French continued to fight ferociously, tenaciously, without illusions.

I have noted that the French were losing more men in this war than the Americans in Korea. About a thousand officers, equal to two entire graduating classes from Saint-Cyr, had already been wiped out, among them many promising career officers and future five-star generals. De Lattre's son had been killed at Phat Diem; Leclerc's was a prisoner of war. Faith in a miracle had vanished. For a certain time after the General's arrival, the troops felt they were under proper leadership, and were able to believe in victory. They knew that the delta, so necessary to the strategic plans of the Europeans, could not fall—unless of course the Chinese intervened and Ho Chi Minh was supplied with aircraft and pilots—but they also felt that they could never again return to the Chinese frontier, and that it was perhaps unnecessary to hold it.

One could not even say they were fighting with their backs to the wall. There is a certain advantage in being able to get one's shoulders up against a wall. But behind that stubborn and heroic army was a hostile population and an irresponsible administration unworthy of trust. If free elections had been held in Tongking, the majority of French officials admitted that Ho Chi Minh would have received eighty percent of the vote (in the Vietnamese Assembly perhaps seventy percent). His face is the most familiar one in the whole of Indo-China (for one year de Lattre's was perhaps as well known). Without newspapers, billboards or books to broadcast it, the depreciated coins stamped with his effigy are alone enough to make him as familiar to everyone, peasant or intellectual, as Stalin or Churchill are in the West.

The Vietnamese military structure has for a long time been as unreliable as its political structure. Created by General de Lattre, it is treated neither to commendations or reviews and depends entirely for its training on French cadres. Ho Chi Minh's soldiers belong to the same race, but with them he has produced a courageous and disciplined force which possesses all the virtues of a revolutionary army: devotion to the cause (for most of its members, a nationalist rather than a Communist one), a beloved leader, officers who have moved up from the ranks (in the Vietnamese national army the indigenous officers are the sons of families of wealthy landowners who have no real affinity with the peasants they command: they speak French or Vietnamese with equal facility).

The national army's lack of depth was made apparent in disastrous fashion at the time of the spectacular and ill-fated offensive against Hoa-Binh last November. The capture of the city, some 50 kilometres south-west of Hanoi, was made without serious losses to either side, but it was the first time the French had broken the delta defence line, and for the next two terrible months Ho Chi Minh concerted all his efforts to drive them out. De Lattre's evident objective had been to cut the supply line between China and Annam, but last February, just as the French were preparing to evacuate their position, the Viet Minh put a new route into service. With insufficient equipment (only one helicopter was available, which in this mountainous and heavily wooded region meant that every seriously wounded man was condemned to death) and too few troops, it was an achievement for the French simply to hang on to the bitter fruit of this questionable offensive as long as possible. On the other hand, it was a moral victory for General Salan (whom one could only refuse to compare with his illustrious predecessor through ignorance or lack of generosity) to have had the sense to order the evacuation of Hoa-Binh before it was too late.

But while the French were sustaining one counterattack after another, the interior of the delta was being stripped of reserves. A propaganda campaign was undertaken to disguise this necessity. General Salan announced that the inner defence of the delta would henceforth be entrusted to the Vietnamese army. That was when the Viet Minh infiltrations began. During periods of calm at Hoa-Binh, the troops could hear bombs and shells exploding in their rear.

The case of Phat Diem is one example among many of an
infiltration that almost succeeded. I choose it because it illustrates so well the bizarre and confused nature of this conflict.
Phat Diem is a Catholic diocese situated on the delta plain not
far from the sea, a vulnerable point at the outer limit of territory held by the Viet Minh in Annam.

Since its foundation around 1890 by Père Six, a Catholic
Annamite priest who became the Emperor's regent (the same
Emperor who had had him tortured during religious persecu-
tions), Phat Diem has resembled nothing so much as a medieval episcopal principality. The Bishop conducts his own
foreign policy and has his own army, and it was only after the
Viet Minh attack of 19 June when it collapsed miserably and
the city was saved by French parachutists that this militia was
disbanded. Those of its members who had not fled were absorbed into the Vietnam army. The present Bishop is Monsi-
gnor Le Huu Tu, a former Trappist. He is an austere man with
the face of a sad, meditative monkey. He lives in the same
house built by Père Six and makes good use, one feels sure, of
the same unusual works of theology, and a dusty skull contem-
plates him from the other side of his desk. What experience
does he have of the outside world? He went to Europe once,
but his visits were limited almost exclusively to Rome, Lourdes,
and Fátima—a name which later must have had a sad resonance in Phat Diem. He is a nationalist and his number-one
enemy is the French, after which come the Communists. Even
with a foreigner, he makes no mystery of this order of preference. He knows the French (they took his army from him, the
army which he persists in believing saved Phat Diem). He
knows almost nothing of the Communists, save that the position of his diocese on the edge of the Viet Minh zone makes
certain neighbourly contacts inevitable: Ho Chi Minh's currency circulates in the Phat Diem market at a very low rate of
exchange (5 Vietnamese piastres for 2,500 Ho Chi Minh piastres). If he needs bamboo for a building or a milk cow for his
hospital, he has to get them as contraband from Viet Minh

territory. Catholics make up one-quarter of the people under his authority, but they are quite ignorant of religious persecution in China or in Europe.

Flying into Phat Diem creates some very curious impressions. One leaves the land of pagodas and suddenly one seems to have arrived in Europe over the Netherlands. In the distance, the straight canals run off towards the sea: at regular intervals of some 100 metres they intersect villages; and in every village there rises up a church as big as a cathedral. From the plane you can count more than twenty of these big churches at the same time. In the flat landscapes they take the place of windmills, and in this climate they all seem very old, even though some were built less than ten years ago.

But Phat Diem is in the very centre of the Orient, and sometimes one might imagine oneself in Europe seven centuries ago: the cathedral erected by Père Six, with its huge columns formed out of single tree trunks; the straight, endless road running from one village to another and crossing over the canals, forming a single city. It was a city noisy and dirty and full of life when I first saw it in November, but under their mushroom-shaped hats the faces were gayer than in Hanoi. There was no electricity, no public transport, no cinema, and only one rudimentary hospital, but sometimes one saw the Prince-Bishop passing through the streets on his way to the seminary, or a procession with lights and censers flowing out of the cathedral precincts, and every now and then a performance would be given in the Bishop's fantastic theatre, with its Swiss statues at the entrance, its religious symbols on the pediment, and under the stage a low, dirty dungeon where Viet Minh prisoners were locked up last summer. Life there was curiously free of monotony, and until June 1951 no one thought much about the war. The June attack itself only involved the forward positions.

"How happy we are to have such a Bishop," an old man said to me. "His prayers have saved Phat Diem!"

But in December, while the French were preparing to face

the first important Viet Minh counter-attack on Phat Diem,
the Bishop's prayers proved to be without effect.

Since the Bishop's visit to Portugal, Our Lady of Fátima
was the object of a special devotion at Phat Diem, and on 9 December, as a gesture of amity towards the Bishop, the French
commandant announced his wish to take part in the ritual procession of Fátima. He acted from the best of intentions, but
while he marched at the head of the procession, the Viet Minh
vanguard entered the village at its rear. No one reported their
arrival until the Colonel was awakened at 4:30 in the morning
by the explosion of a bazooka shell which blew out the façade
of the house where the officers were billeted. His radio post,
set up in a room opening on to the courtyard, was destroyed
and a field gun was put out of action in the courtyard itself.
The house was attacked on three sides by small advance units
of the battalion that were making their way into the city. All
the nearby French posts were cut off and when the officers did
succeed in driving the enemy from their own house, the Viet
Minh were installed opposite it. Clearing the main street took
twelve hours, and when I arrived in the city five hours later,
the Viet Minh forces had only been driven back 600 metres,
leaving small French outposts still isolated.

Under such circumstances, the French considered themselves lucky to have lost only one officer and twenty-five men
killed in the course of the first attack. It is hard to assess the
losses of the Viet Minh: here and there the canal was filled with
a thick gruel, heads floating above the accumulation of bodies
below. But my most striking memories were still of that long
empty street leading to the cathedral, so recently noisy and
animated, where now only a few soldiers on patrol in front of
the deserted houses were finishing mopping-up operations; of
the interior of the cathedral where the population of Phat Diem
had assembled in the cold night with their furniture, their stat-
uettes, their portable stoves—an enormous, sad fairground
where not a face was smiling; of some cheap religious pictures
hanging on the wall of an abandoned farm; and of the bodies

of a woman and her small boy caught in a crossfire between the parachutists and the enemy. This mother and child suddenly lost their anonymity when I realized that their faith and mine were the same.

All that already belongs to the past, a past without importance, without urgency, beyond remedy: the names of a few more officers among those I knew added to the list of the thousand officers killed; that pleasant and cultivated administrative officer, who came to see me at Phat Diem on a calm November day to talk about old books and theology, dead of his wounds; Vandenburg, with his long, dangling arms, leader of a famous commando unit composed of Viet Minh prisoners, assassinated by his own men and his unit broken up. Hoa-Binh has been evacuated. The French have returned to exactly where they were last year: the delta still holds.

While General de Lattre was alive, predictions were based on the possibility of a Chinese intervention. Most of the rumours concerning Chinese troop movements came from the Formosan intelligence service, the most suspect of all services of this type and one which, unfortunately, is too often taken seriously by—amongst others—American authorities. To break the French line in the Red River delta there is no need of Chinese volunteers, and they would be very badly received, for the traditional hostility of the Tongkinese towards China has been reinforced since 1945 by the behaviour of Chinese nationalist troops who occupied Tongking between the departure of the Japanese and the return of the French. All the Viet Minh needs is more aircraft and a better anti-aircraft system.

People speak less now of Chinese intervention than of the possibility of an armistice. Would it be possible, one speculates, to stabilize the front as in Korea, and even to recognize Ho Chi Minh's government, and also to secure the progressive withdrawal of French troops (as in the old Hanoi Convention of April 1946), and finally to protect the frontier with China under a UN guarantee?

France, with a population one-third of the United States,

has for almost seven years, in addition to the enormous financial burden, sustained a war as costly in human lives as the war in Korea. Who could blame her for wanting someone else to take over?

In the beginning the war may very well have been a colonial war (even if the Viet Minh fired the first shots), but the young men who, with stubborn and ferocious determination, are doing the actual fighting in a hard climate against a savage and fanatical enemy, care little for the rubber plantations of Cochin China and Cambodia. They are fighting because France itself is at war and firmly determined not to let its allies down *as long as humanly possible*. If we have criticized certain aspects of French administration in Vietnam we have not criticized France itself. France is the young pilot in his little B26 bomber probing his way between a hostile mountain and a hostile jungle into a valley too narrow to permit him to alter course. France is the soldier up to his chest in a rice paddy, the nurse parachuted into an isolated post, and even the police superintendent knifed in his bed by his trusted native servant. As for the future, England and America ought to remember that every human possibility has its limits.

Once this important reservation has been made, there is no doubt that the French are firmly determined to hold on. One could even observe a kind of recovery of optimism after the retreat from Hoa-Binh (carried out brilliantly and with complete success, this was a much more difficult operation than the one at Vinh-Yen, whose victorious outcome caused so much boasting).

Europe has the most urgent need of the troops the French are maintaining in Indo-China; but their return depends in large part on the realization of a single hope: the Vietnamese army. The high command calculates that in a year's time French non-commissioned officers can be withdrawn (it is said that General Salan counts on repatriating 15,000 men between now and the end of the year), officers up to the rank of captain within two years perhaps, and in three years . . .

It is a stern and sad outlook and, when everything is considered, it represents for France the end of an empire. The United States is exaggeratedly distrustful of empires, but we Europeans retain the memory of what we owe to Rome, just as Latin America knows what it owes to Spain. When the hour of evacuation sounds there will be many Vietnamese who will regret the loss of the language which put them in contact with the art and faith of the West. The injustices committed by men who were harassed, exhausted, and ignorant will be forgotten and the names of a good number of Frenchmen, priests, soldiers, and administrators, will remain engraved in the memory of the Vietnamese: a fort, a road intersection, a dilapidated church.

"Do you remember," someone will say, "the days before the Legions left?"

# Graham Greene

*Also from* Reflections, *this memoir (noted in Wobbe, C457) was published in* The Listener, *15 September 1955. One should compare what Greene writes here with the almost identical passage in* The Quiet American, *pp. 147–50. Also, Greene was not in Vietnam during December 1952. The date should be 15 November 1951 (Sherry, vol. II, p. 387).*

## A MEMORY OF INDO-CHINA

It was December 1952. For hours I had played at iron bowls in the airport at Haiphong, waiting for a mission. The weather was overcast and the planes stood about and nobody had anything to do. At last I went into town and drank brandy and soda in the mess of the Gascogne Squadron. Officially, I suppose, I was at the front, but it was hardly enough: if one is writing about war, self-respect demands that occasionally one shares a very small portion of the risk.

That was not so easy since orders had come down from the État Major in Hanoi that I was to be allowed only on a horizontal raid. In this Indo-China war horizontal raids were as safe as a journey by bus. One flew above the range of the enemy's heavy machine-guns; one was safe from anything but a pilot's error or a fault in the engine. One went out by timetable and came home by timetable: the cargoes of bombs sailed diagonally down and a spatter of smoke blew up from the road junction or the bridge and then one cruised back for the hour of the *apéritif* and drove the iron bowls across the gravel.

### VERTICAL RAID

But that afternoon, as I drank brandy and soda in the mess, orders for a mission came in. "Like to come?" I said yes. Even a horizontal raid would be a way of killing time. Driving out to the airport the officer remarked: "This is a vertical raid." I said, "I thought you were forbidden. . . ." "So long as you write nothing about it," he said. "It will show you a piece of country near the Chinese border you will not have seen before. Near Lai Chau."

"But I thought all was quiet there and in French hands."

"It was. They captured this place two days ago. Our parachutists are only a few hours away. We want to keep the Viets head down in their holes until we have recaptured the post. It means low diving, and machine-gunning. We can only spare two planes—one's on the job now. Ever dive-bombed before?"

"No."

"It is a little uncomfortable when you are not used to it."

The Gascogne Squadron possessed only small B26 bombers, prostitutes the French call them, because with their small wingspan they have no visible means of support. I was crammed onto a little metal pad the size of a bicycle seat with my knees against the navigator's back. We came up the Red River, slowly climbing, and the Red River at this hour was actually red. It was as though one had gone far back in time, and saw it with the old geographer's eyes who had named it first, at just such an hour, when the late sun filled it from bank to bank. Then we turned away at 9,000 feet towards the Black River, and it was really black, full of shadows, missing the angle of the light:

and the huge, majestic scenery of gorge and cliff and jungle wheeled round and stood upright below us. You could have dropped a squadron into those fields of green and grey and left no more trace than a few coins in a harvest field. Far ahead of us a small plane moved like a midge. We were taking over.

We circled twice above the tower and the green-encircled village, then corkscrewed up into the dazzling air. The pilot turned to me and winked: on his wheel were the studs that controlled the gun and the bomb chamber: I had that loosening of the bowels as we came into position for the dive that accompanies any new experience—the first dance, the first dinner-party, the first love. I was reminded of the Great Racer in the Festival Gardens when it comes to the top of the rise—there is no way to get out: you are trapped with your experience. On the dial I had just time to read 3,000 metres when we drove down.

Now all was feeling, nothing was sight. I was forced up against the navigator's back: it was as though something of enormous weight were pressing on my chest. I was not aware of the moment when the bombs were released; then the gun chattered and the cockpit was full of the smell of cordite, and the weight was off my chest as we rose. And it was the stomach that fell away, spiralling down like a suicide to the ground we had left. For forty seconds no worries had existed: even loneliness hadn't existed. As we climbed in a great arc I could see the smoke through the side window pointing at me. Before the second dive I felt fear—fear of humiliation, fear of vomiting over the navigator's back, fear that middle-aged lungs would not stand the pressure. After the tenth dive I was aware only of irritation—the affair had gone on too long, it was time to go home. And again we shot steeply up out of machine-gun range and swerved away and the smoke pointed. The village was surrounded on all sides but one by mountains. Every time we had to make the same approach, through the same gap. There was no way to vary our attack. As we dived for the four-teenth time I thought, now that I was free from the fear of physical humiliation, "they have only to fix one machine-gun in position." We lifted our nose again into the safe air—perhaps they didn't even have a gun. The forty minutes of the patrol had seemed interminable, but it had been free from the discomfort of personal thought. The sun was sinking as we turned for home: the geographer's moment had passed: the Black River was no longer black, and the Red River was only gold.

Down we went again, away from the gnarled and fissured forest towards the river, flattening out over the neglected rice fields, aimed like a bullet at one small sampan on the yellow stream. The gun gave a single burst of tracer, and the sampan blew apart in a shower of sparks; we didn't even wait to see our victims struggling to survive, but climbed and made for home. I thought again, as I had thought when I saw a dead child in a ditch at Phat Diem, "I hate war." There had been something so shocking in our fortuitous choice of a prey—we had just happened to be passing, one burst only was required, there was no one to return our fire, we were gone again, adding our little quota to the world's dead.

I put on my earphones for the pilot to speak to me. He said, "We will make a little detour. The sunset is wonderful on the Calcaire. You must not miss it," he added kindly, like a host who is showing the beauty of his estate; and for a hundred miles we trailed the sunset over the Baie d'Along. The helmeted Martian face looked wistfully down on the golden groves, among the huge humps and arches of porous stone, and the wound of murder ceased to bleed.

# Graham Greene

*Greene returned to Vietnam in December of 1953, and this essay from* Reflections, *originally published in* The Times *(London) in March 1954, indicates his feeling of despair that created one of the major political themes of* The Quiet American. *This selection is not noted in Wobbe.*

## RETURN TO INDO-CHINA

For the third time, and after two years, one was back. There seemed at first so little that had changed: in Saigon there were new traffic lights in the rue Catinat and rather more beer-bottle tops trodden into the asphalt outside the Continental Hotel and the Imperial Bar. *Le Journal d'Extrême Orient* reported the same operations in the north, around Nam Dinh and Thai-Binh, the same account of enemy losses, the same reticence about French Union losses.

In Hong Kong one had read the alarmist reports—the fall of Thakhek, the cutting in two of Annam and Laos, "thousands of columns pouring south on the route to Saigon." One knew then these reports were unreal—this grim shadow-boxing war will never end spectacularly for either side, and in Saigon I

From *Reflections* by Graham Greene, edited by Judith Adamson. New York: Penguin, 1990, 160–66. Copyright © by Graham Greene. Used by permission of Viking Penguin, a division of Penguin USA Inc.

knew there would be little sign of war except the soldiers in the cafés, the landing-craft tied up outside the Majestic for repairs as noisy as road drills in a London summer—less now than ever for two years ago there still remained the evening hand-grenades, flung into cinemas and cafés, spreading a little local destruction and listed in a back-page column of the *Journal*. They had ceased with the shooting of some prisoners, and who could blame the executioners? Is it worse to shoot a prisoner than to maim a child?

The only people in Saigon who were thoroughly aware of war were the doctors, and they were aware of something the French were most of them inclined to forget. "Until I became a doctor in a military hospital," one said to me, "I had not realized that nine out of every ten wounded were Vietnamese."

And yes, there was another change. I noted that first evening in my journal, *"Is there any solution here the West can offer? But the bar tonight was loud with innocent American voices and that was the worst disquiet. There weren't so many Americans in 1951 and 1952."* They were there, one couldn't help being aware, to protect an investment, but couldn't the investment have been avoided?

In 1945, after the fall of Japan, they had done their best to eliminate French influence in Tongking. M. Sainteny, the first post-war Commissioner in Hanoi, has told the sad ignoble story in his recent book, *Histoire d'une paix manquée*—aeroplanes forbidden to take off with their French passengers from China, couriers who never arrived, help withheld at moments of crisis. Now they had been forced to invest in a French victory.

I suggested to a member of the American Economic Mission that French participation in the war might be drawing to an end. "Oh, no," he said, "they can't do that. They'd have to pay us back"—I cannot remember how many thousand million dollars.

It is possible, of course, to argue that America had reason in 1945; but, if their policy was right then, it should have been followed to the end—and the end could not have been more

bitter than today's. The policy of our own representative in
Hanoi, to whom M. Sainteny pays tribute, was to combine a
wise sympathy for the new nationalism of Vietnam with a recognition that France was our ally who had special responsibilities and, more important perhaps, a special emotion after the
years of defeat and occupation.

American hostility, humiliation at the hands of the defeated Japanese and the Chinese occupying forces, exposed
French weakness and saw to it that Vietnamese intransigence
should grow until in 1946 France could hardly have bought
peace with less than total surrender.

I suppose in a war the safe areas are always the most de-
pressing because there is time to brood not only on dead hopes,
dead policies, but even on dead jokes. What on my first two
visits had seemed gay and bizarre was now like a game that has
gone on too long—I am thinking particularly of the religious
sects of the south, the local armies and their barons to whom
much of the defence of the Saigon delta is entrusted: the Buddhist Hoa Haos for instance.

Their general's wife has formed an Amazon army which is
popularly believed to have eliminated some of the general's
concubines. The French had originally appointed the Hoa Hao
leader a "one star" general, but when he came to the city to
order his uniform he learned from the tailor that there was no
such rank in the French army. Only a quick promotion to two
stars prevented the general from leading his troops over to the
Viet Minh.

The Caodaists, too, began by amusing—this new religious
sect founded by a Cochin civil servant in the 1920s, with its
amalgam of Confucianism, Buddhism, and Christianity, its
"Pope," its Holy See, its female cardinals, its canonization of
Victor Hugo, its prophecies by a kind of planchette. But that
joke had palled, too; the Caodaist cathedral in the Walt Disney
manner, full of snakes and dragons and staring eyes of God,
seemed no longer naïve and charming but cunning and unreliable like a smart advertisement.

You cannot fight a war satisfactorily with allies like this. The Caodaists, by the military absorption of the surrounding country, number 2 million and have an army of 20,000. They have had to be courted, and the moment the courtship loses warmth the threat appears. They have been given no Ministerial appointment in the new Government of Prince Buu Loc, and no Minister went down to their great feast day last month that was supposed to commemorate the seventh anniversary of the Caodaist fight against Communism. Though messages were read from General Navarre and the Emperor Bao Dai, there were none from the Government. [Nor] the money or the influence to ensure their stay in the south.

One flies from the bizarre and complicated Cochin to the sadder and simpler north. In the plane to Hanoi I thought of what the doctor had told me; for in the plane were many crippled Tongkinese returning home after being patched in the south. One had seen just such faces, patient, gentle, expecting nothing, behind the water buffaloes ploughing the drowned paddy fields: it seemed wrong that war should have picked on them and lopped off a leg or an arm—war should belong to the brazen battalions, the ribboned commanders, the goose-step and the Guards' march.

Outside the air terminus at Hanoi the trishaw drivers waited for fares, and not one driver would lend a hand to help his crippled countrymen alight. A French officer shouted at them furiously to help, but they watched without interest or pity the shambling descent of the wounded. There, by the dusty rim of the street, lay the great problem—those men were not cruel, they were indifferent. This was not their war, and the men on the crutches were unhurt by their silence. They had not come home, like Europeans, as heroes, but as victims —this was not their war either.

One cannot escape the problem anywhere, in the office of a general, the hut of a priest, at an Annamite tea party. Vietnam cannot be held without the Vietnamese, and the Vietnamese army, not yet two years old, cannot, except here and there stiffened by French officers, stand up against their fellow countrymen trained by Giap since 1945.

Last year General Cogny made the brave experiment inside the delta defences of entrusting the region of Bui-Chu purely to Vietnamese troops. It seemed a favourable place for the experiment since the region is almost entirely Catholic, and the Catholics, however nationalist, are absolute opponents of Viet Minh. But Giap's intelligence was good: he loosed on these troops one of his crack regiments and two battalions deserted with their arms. A third of Bui-Chu with its villages and rice fields passed under Viet Minh control. One could match this, of course, in European armies—inexperience can look like cowardice—but perhaps the cause in this case was neither.

The repeated argument of the Vietnamese is: "How can we fight until we have real independence—we have nothing to fight for?" They recognize that their present army without the French could not stand up against the revolutionary regiments of Giap's for a fortnight. They cannot expect full independence until their army is capable of resistance, and their army cannot fight with proper heart until they have achieved it. The result is frustration and bewilderment.

The frustration and repetitiveness of this war—running hard like Alice to remain on the same square—lead inevitably to day-dreams. In time of despair people await a miracle, hopes become irrational.

One propaganda offensive is matched by another. Both sides perform before a European audience and gain inexpensive tactical successes. Giap seizes for a while Thakhek and the world's Press takes note—its recapture, like the denial of a newspaper report, figures very small. The French stage "Operation Atlante" on the coast of Annam, reclaiming an area of impressive size that had been administered by the Viet Minh since 1946—an easy offensive, for there were hardly more soldiers in the area than administrators. But troops were needed to guard the new territory, so that Giap was enabled to attack on the high plateau above and the fall of Kontum stole the news value.

So the war goes drearily on its way. Dien Bien Phu takes the place of Na-Sam in the news: the 1953 attack on Luang Prabang is repeated in 1954 and stops again within a few miles of the Laotian capital. Lunching at Nam Dinh, I was asked by the general commanding whether I had ever had so good a *soufflé* before to the sound of gunfire. I could have replied that I had—two years before, at the same table, to the sound of the same guns.

Everybody knows now on both sides that the fate of Vietnam does not rest with the armies. It would be hard for either army to lose the war, and certainly neither can win it. However much material the Americans and Chinese pour in they can only keep the pot hot, they will never make it boil.

Two years ago men believed in the possibility of military defeat or victory: now they know the war will be decided elsewhere by men who have never waded waist-deep in fields of paddy, struggled up mountain sides, been involved in the muddle of attack or the long boredom of waiting.

# III

# Analogies and Perspectives

# Robert F. Futrell

*Dr. Robert F. Futrell served for many years in the Office of Air Force History, Bolling Air Force Base, Washington. He has written histories of Air Force operations from World War II to Vietnam, including* The United States Air Force in Korea, 1950–53, *and* Ideas, Concepts, Doctrine, *a discussion of military airpower doctrine from 1907 to 1964. He completed the manuscript of this book on the advisory years in Vietnam just prior to his retirement in 1974. This selection is a concise, accurate summary of the early American involvement in Vietnam to 1951.*

## ORIGINS OF THE AMERICAN COMMITMENT TO VIETNAM

About 700 miles west of the Philippine Islands, across the China Sea, lies the great Indochinese peninsula. China is to the north, Burma to the west, and Malaysia to the south. The western part of the peninsula holds Thailand (ancient Siam) while the eastern portion contains Laos, Cambodia, and Vietnam (formerly elements of French Indochina). This area of Southeast Asia (SEA) attracted little American interest and attention until the closing months of World War II.

Reprinted from Robert F. Futrell, *The Advisory Years to 1965*, volume I in the series *The United States Air Force in Southeast Asia*. Office of Air Force History, Washington, D.C., 1981, 3–10.

American policymakers who shared President Franklin D. Roosevelt's anticolonial sentiments expected Indochina to be freed from French hegemony. Yet France reestablished control over Laos, Cambodia, and Vietnam, which had been part of the French Empire since the nineteenth century. To some extent this occurred because the British government wished to resuscitate France as a European power to help Britain balance somewhat the growing strength of the Soviet Union. The United States acquiesced in this aim, and increasingly so as the confrontation of the postwar superpowers evolved into the cold war. It was the cold war that drew the United States into this region.[1]

Japan had virtually occupied Laos, Cambodia, and Vietnam after the fall of France in 1940. While allowing the French to maintain a presence and a measure of control, the Japanese incorporated the Indochinese economic resources into their system. In March 1945, with Metropolitan France liberated and a full-fledged member of the Allied coalition, the Japanese interned French civilian and military officials and removed the pretense of a combined occupation.[2]

French police agencies and other offices of internal control having been eliminated, indigenous groups seeking Vietnamese independence began to expand their activities. The most vigorous organization was the Viet Minh. Dominated by the Indochinese communist party and directed by Ho Chi Minh, the Viet Minh launched guerrilla operations against the Japanese and soon claimed to control much of northern Vietnam, the Tonkin provinces. To help harass the Japanese and also to gather intelligence, the U.S. Office of Strategic Services sent several small teams to Vietnam.

By the time of the Japanese surrender in August 1945, the Viet Minh had emerged as the leading nationalist group in Vietnam. Viet Minh soldiers on August 19 arrived in Hanoi, capital of Tonkin, and assumed de facto control. In Hue, capital of Annam, the central provinces, Emperor Bao Dai, last of the Vietnamese royal family and a puppet of both France and

Japan, abdicated. In Saigon, capital of Cochin China in the south, a committee took power while recognizing the overall authority of the Hanoi regime. On December 2 in Hanoi, Ho Chi Minh proclaimed the independence of the Democratic Republic of Vietnam.

Meanwhile, the war in Europe had closed and in July 1945 the Potsdam Conference convened. The American, British, and Russian representatives agreed to include French military forces in operations being planned in Asia, chiefly to liberate Indochina. The conferees also acted to regularize operational boundaries. The China theater under Generalissimo Chiang Kai-shek was extended southward to the 16th parallel, just below Tourane (Da Nang). The territory south of that line came under the Southeast Asia Command headed by Admiral Lord Louis Mountbatten. This division determined who was to exercise control after the Japanese capitulation.[3]

In August 1945, Chinese nationalist troops moved into Tonkin and part of Annam, while British troops occupied the rest of Annam and all of Cochin China. The British restored French authority in the south, and the French brought military forces into the country and ruthlessly suppressed Vietnamese aspirations for independence. Despite some continuing guerrilla activity, the French had regained their former colonial status and were well established in Saigon by the end of the year.

In the north the Chinese refused to intervene in a contest between the well-organized Viet Minh and the small numbers of French. Concerned by the threat of the Chinese communists under Mao Tse-tung, the Chinese nationalists were reluctant to see the triumph of Ho Chi Minh in Vietnam. They preferred the return of the French if France would abandon territorial and economic rights formerly granted as concessions in China. This generally neutral stance fueled the struggle for power between the Viet Minh and the French. A guerrilla war of low intensity soon developed.

When the French agreed to renounce their concessions

early in 1946, Nationalist China recognized French sovereignty in Indochina and moved Chinese troops out of Vietnam. By the end of March, they were being replaced by French military forces.

Ho Chi Minh had been negotiating with the French authorities for recognition of his new government and ultimate independence. The exchanges were futile and incidents of violence multiplied. The climax came in November 1946 after a French patrol boat in Haiphong harbor clashed with Vietnamese militia. The French responded by brutally bombarding the city and killing an estimated 6,000 civilians, whereupon Ho broke off the talks. In December he moved his government into the mountains of Tonkin and opened full-scale guerrilla war by attacking the French in Hanoi.

American policymakers had conflicting feelings. Their sympathy for the Vietnamese nationalists left them reluctant to see France restore control by force—they wanted French authority to enjoy the support of the Vietnamese people. On the other hand, Americans were uneasy because Vietnamese independence might produce a communist state.[4]

Hoping that the Vietnamese were more nationalistic than communistic, U.S. government officials urged the French to end the guerrilla warfare and to find a political solution acceptable to both parties. If France made a bona fide accommodation to ultimate Vietnamese sovereignty, Ho's strength might collapse. Continually advocating an equitable solution to the problem of conflicting claims to power, the United States prohibited the export of war materials to the French in Vietnam, although munitions sent to Metropolitan France could, of course, be reshipped to Southeast Asia.[5]

While combating Ho's guerrilla activities, France entered into negotiations with anti-Ho Vietnamese parties. To give these elements a native leader, the French in the spring of 1949 installed Bao Dai, the former emperor, as the chief of state of an entity formed by the union of Tonkin, Annam, and Cochin China. But this was hardly more than a show of sovereignty, for the French retained control of Vietnamese foreign and military affairs.[6]

Troubled American officials began to accept this arrangement as the cold war intensified everywhere. The Greek civil war, the Berlin blockade, the coup d'état in Czechoslovakia, as well as the successes of the Chinese communists against the nationalists, led to a heightened concern with worldwide communism that appeared to be monolithic. Surely, Ho Chi Minh's communist affiliation was part of a growing global menace. To cope with this and to rehabilitate Western Europe as a force against communist encroachment, the United States early in 1949 helped to form and joined the North Atlantic Treaty Organization (NATO) for mutual defense.

The final triumph of the Chinese communists in October 1949 seemed to confirm the worst American fears. It spurred the Congress to pass the Mutual Defense Assistance Act designed to deal with the cold war. The President was empowered to dispense funds to various nations, including "the general area of China" which was extended to cover Southeast Asia and specifically Vietnam.[7]

The ongoing guerrilla war in Vietnam that weakened French support of NATO and the defense of Western Europe, the arrival of Chinese communist troops at the northern frontier of Vietnam at the beginning of 1950, the formal recognition of Ho Chi Minh's Democratic Republic of Vietnam by Communist China and the Soviet Union in January 1950—all persuaded the United States government to adopt the Bao Dai solution. On February 7, 1950, the United States extended diplomatic recognition to the State of Vietnam as well as to the Kingdoms of Cambodia and Laos.

Nine days later, France requested American economic and military assistance for prosecution of the war in Indochina. Unable to bear the burden without American aid, France was thinking of withdrawing from the region if Ho Chi Minh received increasing resources from China and the Soviet Union.[8]

What the French needed immediately were ammunition,

napalm, and barbed wire to help defend perimeters around Hanoi and Haiphong against Viet Minh attacks. Their air units in the Far East possessed only obsolete and miscellaneous aircraft.* Few fully trained military maintenance technicians were on hand because of a general shortage in Metropolitan France, where the French Air Force depended in large part on contract aircraft maintenance.[9]

President Harry S Truman regarded the emergence of Communist China as an extension of Soviet power and saw the growth of communist influence over Asia as a threat to American interests. He instructed the National Security Council to formulate a policy for strengthening non-communist Asian nations. The result was a resolve to block communist expansion by collective and bilateral security treaties. Since the Joint Chiefs of Staff (JCS) had already recommended spending funds to support anti-communist forces in Indochina, $75 million allocated in the Mutual Defense Assistance Act for "the general area of China" was appropriately at hand.

The French wanted a substantial and long-term American commitment. And in the spring of 1950, American decision-makers all opposed what was called losing Southeast Asia to communism. Consequently, the United States Government during fiscal year 1951 decided to provide $164 million in military aid to France for use in Indochina.[10]

Whatever doubts some American officials may have had that French military success, predicated on American military assistance, would necessarily lead to a strengthened non-communist government in Vietnam vanished in the face of two

---

*French Air Force Indochina consisted of two squadrons totaling forty-six British MK-IX Spitfires, three squadrons of sixty-three American F-63 Kingcobras, two squadrons of thirty-five German JU-52 transports, and one squadron of twenty American C-47s, plus some light liaison planes. The French Navy had a patrol squadron of eight American PBY-5A Catalinas and a reconnaissance squadron of nine British Supermarine-1 Sea Otters. A lack of specialized aircraft required the use of fighters for reconnaissance, strafing, and bombing missions. In general, however, bombardment was conducted by PBY patrol planes and by JU-52 transports under contract.

events. The first was intelligence confirmation of increasing aid to the Viet Minh by the People's Republic of China. The second was the invasion of the Republic of Korea on June 25, 1950, by the communist forces of the Democratic People's Republic of Korea.

Now the struggle seemed absolutely clear. As President Truman told Americans on June 27, the communists had "passed beyond the use of subversion to conquer independent nations and will now use armed invasion and war." The United States, he promised, would resist aggression in Korea and at the same time accelerate military assistance to France and the Associated States in Indochina (Vietnam, Laos, and Cambodia).[11] Even as he spoke, eight C-47 transports were being prepared for delivery to Metropolitan France. Because the situation was critical in Southeast Asia, American pilots flew these planes direct to Saigon and turned them over even before formal U.S. agencies were in the country to coordinate shipments of assistance materials. These eight aircraft were the first aviation aid furnished by the United States to the French in Vietnam.

As American forces entered the war in Korea and as the French resisted Viet Minh attacks in Tonkin, Donald R. Heath became the U.S. Minister to the Associated States on July 6, 1950. The initial elements of the U.S. Military Assistance Advisory Group (MAAG) entered Saigon on August 3. Brig. Gen. Francis G. Brink, USA, assumed command on October 10, and Lt. Col. Edmund F. Freeman, the Air Attaché in Saigon, handled air assistance duties until the Air Force Section of MAAG-Indochina came into being on November 8 under Col. Joseph B. Wells.[12]

Mr. Heath was the Chief of Mission and the senior U.S. representative in Saigon. General Brink, the MAAG chief, was his military advisor. MAAG received and reviewed requests for American aid to the ground, naval, and air forces, established requirements and, after coordinating with Heath, submitted them to the Department of Defense (DOD).[13]

Although Americans hoped to work directly with the Viet-

namese as well as with the French, the French termed the Bao
Dai government and its military forces incapable of dealing
with assistance matters. French troops were carrying the burden
of the war, and the few Vietnamese units in existence had limited capacities except as auxiliaries.

As a consequence, MAAG received requests from the
French, transferred title of military assistance program materials to them, and tried to insure the proper use of the items
supplied. On December 23, 1950, the United States, France,
Vietnam, Cambodia, and Laos signed the Mutual Defense
Assistance Agreement. A provision stipulated that American
goods destined for Indochina would pass through French
hands.[14]

The military assistance effort had three priorities. The first
was responding to emergency requests to enable French forces
to meet immediate threats. The second was improving French
military capabilities. The third and least important was devel-
oping indigenous Vietnamese armed forces.

With respect to aviation requirements, not until October
1950, when forty U.S. Navy F-6F Hellcats arrived in Saigon
aboard a French carrier, could the United States make available
fighter aircraft to replace the old MK-IX Spitfires.

While the French requested F-63 Kingcobras primarily be-
cause of their 37-mm cannon, the United States Air Force
(USAF) had no spare parts or ammunition for these obsolete
aircraft and instead furnished ninety F-8F Bearcat fighters,
which were ferried to Vietnam in February and March 1951.
Delays in installing ground equipment postponed the arrival in
Vietnam of five RB-26 reconnaissance planes until July.
Twenty-four B-26 bombers were renovated and transported to
Hawaii by carrier in December, then flown to Tourane. Nine
others flew from Sacramento to Hawaii and on to Vietnam at
the end of the year.

These deliveries completed the initial aviation schedules
under the Mutual Defense Assistance Program. The planes enabled the French to expand sortie rates from an average of 450

a week in the summer of 1950 to 930 in the spring of 1951.[15]

Despite higher American priorities in Korea, U.S. materiel dispatched to Vietnam helped the campaigning. High Commissioner and Commander in Chief Gen. Jean de Lattre de Tassigny said in January 1951 that U.S. air resources, "especially napalm bombs, arrived in the nick of time." Mr. Heath believed that "French superiority in aviation and artillery was responsible for turning back a Viet Minh offensive. In particular, the use of napalm . . . was a decisive factor in the French holding operations."[16]

Further French victories in May 1951 compelled the Viet Minh to abandon battles of confrontation and to retreat to lower-key guerrilla operations of harassment and ambush. The war assumed the characteristics of a stalemate.[17]

## NOTES

1. Grateful acknowledgement is made of the help furnished by Mr. Charles B. MacDonald of the Army's Center of Military History on the background of the American involvement in Vietnam. The literature on the roots of the American commitment to Southeast Asia is extensive, but see especially Cordell Hull. *The Memoirs of Cordell Hull* (New York, 1948), II, 1596–77; *The Public Papers and Addresses of Franklin D. Roosevelt: Victory and the Threshold of Peace* (New York, 1950), pp. 562–63; Hearings before the Committee on Foreign Relations, U.S. Senate, *Military Situation in the Far East*, 82d Cong. 1st sess (Washington, 1951), pt. 4, pp. 1890–92; U.S. Dept. of State, *The Conference at Malta and Yalta* (Washington, 1955), p. 770. See also John L. Gaddis, *The United States and the Origins of the Cold War, 1941–45* (New York, 1972).

2. Ellen Hammer, *The Struggle for Indochina* (Stanford, 1954), and Joseph Buttinger, *Vietnam: A Dragon Embattled* (New York, 1967), are especially helpful on the events in Southeast Asia during World War II and after.

3. Hull, *Memoirs*, II, 1598; Terminal Conf. Papers and Minutes of Meetings, July 1945, pp. 217–26, 252–53, and 305; Marcel Vigneras, *Rearming the French-U.S. Army in World War II* (Washington, 1957), pp. 396–99; Supreme Allied Commander Southeast

Asia, *Dispatch*, pt. IV-A. pp. 520–28; Charles de Gaulle, *The War Memoirs of Charles de Gaulle* (New York, 1960), III, 242–43.

4. See msg. Dean Acheson to chargé in China, October 5, 1947, in *Department of Defense (The Pentagon Papers), United States-Vietnam Relations, 1945–1967* (Washington, 1971), Bk 8:49 [hereafter cited as *DOD Pentagon Papers*].

5. *Ibid.*, pp. 144–49; William C. Bullitt, "The Saddest War," *Life*, Dec. 29, 1947, pp. 64–69; Allan B. Cole, ed. *Conflict in Indo-China and International Repercussions: A Documentary History, 1945–1955* (Ithaca, 1956), pp. 83–84.

6. Military Assistance Command Vietnam Historical Monograph, *Military Assistance to the Republic of South Vietnam, 1960–1963*, p. 2.

7. 63 Statutes 714, Oct 6, 1949; Hearings Held in Executive Session before the Committee on Foreign Relations, U.S. Senate, *Economic Assistance to China and Korea: 1949–50* (Washington, 1974), p. 194.

8. U.S. Dept. of State, *American Foreign Policy, 1950–1955* (Washington, 1957), pp. 2364–65; *DOD Pentagon Papers*, Bk. 1: II, A-17, A-35, A-36; see also Dean Acheson, *Present at the Creation: My Years in the State Department* (New York, 1967), pp. 671–78.

9. HQ USAF, Air Order of Battle, Apr 1, 1950, *USAF Air Intelligence Digest*, Apr 52, p. 4.

10. Memo, Gen. Omar N. Bradley to SEC-DEF, Apr 10, 1950; msg. Acheson to AmEmb London, May 3, 1950; Dept. of State Press Release 485, Aid to Southeast Asia, May 11, 1950; all in *DOD Pentagon Papers*, Bk 8: 308–13, 321, and 327.

11. *Public Papers of the Presidents: Harry S Truman, 1950* (Washington, 1965), p. 492.

12. Hearings before the Committee on Foreign Relations and the Committee on Armed Services, U.S. Senate, *Mutual Security Act of 1951*, 82d Cong. 1st sess. (Washington, 1951), pp. 563–64; Edgar O'Ballance, *The Indochina War, 1945–1954: A Study in Guerrilla Warfare* (London, 1964), p. 114; hist. 1020th USAF Special Activities Wg. Apr–Jun 52.

13. Study submitted by the Subcommittee on National Security Staffing and Operations, *The Ambassador and the Problem of Coordination*, 88th Cong. 1st sess. (Senate Document 36) (Washington, 1963), pp. 12, 14–15, and 53–58.

14. U.S. Dept. of State, *U.S. Treaties and Other International Agreements* (Washington, 1952), III, pt. 2, pp. 2756–99.

15. *USAF Air Intelligence Digest*, Apr 52, pp. 6–7, Maurer Maurer,

*History of USAF Activities in Support of the Mutual Defense Assistance Program* (Wright-Patterson AFB: AMC Hist Office, 1951), pt. 1, pp. 52–53; pt. 2, pp. 64–65 and 80–81; and pt. 3, pp. 138–39.

16. *Ibid.*, pt. 3, p. 261: U.S. Senate, *Mutual Security Act of 1951*, 82d Cong. 1st sess. p. 564.

17. *Public Papers of the Presidents: Harry S Truman, 1951* (Washington, 1965), p. 267.

# Maj. Gen. Nguyen Duy Hinh and Brig. Gen. Tran Dinh Tho

*From the viewpoint of quite a few middle-class Vietnamese, so many of whose officials and military men had been trained and educated in France, the Viet Minh at first represented a truly nationalistic movement. This summary by two South Vietnamese Army generals, however, shows some of the reasons that significant numbers of Vietnamese eventually welcomed the American presence. Major General Hinh and Brigadier General Tho served with the Army of the Republic of Vietnam (South Vietnam) until the end of the war in 1975.*

## A SOCIETY IN TRANSITION

During her domination of Vietnam, France was involved in two world wars. World War I had compelled France to obtain resources from her colonies to satisfy the requirements of the war in Europe. In terms of human resources, France had impressed a total of 43,000 troops and 49,000 workers from Vietnam to serve in the French Army. To help finance the war effort, the French government also obtained funds from Vietnam by issuing treasury bonds under a program attractively called "the Vietnamese dragon spits money to help defeat Germany."

Reprinted from *The South Vietnamese Society*, one of a series of Indochina monographs published by the U.S. Army Center of Military History, Washington, D.C., 1980, 13–19.

To exploit indigenous resources, the French operated rubber plantations in the South and coal mines in the North. The dearth of labor in Cochinchina prompted the French to recruit a work force from Tonkin, which was always overpopulated. French exploitation of workers and efforts to recruit workers in Tonkin to meet labor demands in Cochinchina and French possessions in the Pacific by impressing tax delinquents finally led to the assassination of Bazin, a French recruiter, in a Hanoi park in February 1929, touching off a series of arrests and repressive measures from French authorities.

To generate more revenue, the French legalized drinking and opium smoking. The sale of alcoholic beverages and opium, however, was a monopoly of the colonial government. Customs personnel, therefore, clamped down on moonshiners and those who dealt in alcohol and opium without a license. Though not prohibited, gambling during that period was not as widespread and open as it was in 1953–54, partly because of general poverty and partly because Vietnamese society was rather conservative.

Social stratification and class discrimination, once benign, now became accentuated. This was because the French had always wanted Vietnamese society to be deeply class-conscious. The old social hierarchy of "scholars-farmers-craftsmen-merchants" underwent some change which found the merchants prevailing over the farmers. A new class, the soldiers, had been added to the bottom rung of the social ladder; since they came mostly from the ranks of the illiterate peasantry, the soldiers were the most spurned by society. Men of letters still retained their preeminent rank although true scholars were becoming rare. During this transitional period, people with an elementary or junior high education were all called educated. That was the educational level required to qualify for a low- or middle-level civil servant job, which was socially quite prestigious. Therefore, academic degrees, especially those conferred by French schools in the country or in France, were the criteria by which a person's worth was evaluated, the crown of social success. Vietnamese were conscious of the prestige and distinction of French schools with French teachers and an all-French curriculum. In time, they assumed that there was a difference in value between the diplomas earned in French schools and those conferred by Vietnamese institutions, although both curricula were practically the same. This prejudice pushed the snobbish and the well-to-do to send their children abroad, especially to France, or at least to local French schools, to complete their education.

As for religion, Christianity gradually gained ascendency from the support of French authorities as well as from its own organizational success. Though much less numerous than Buddhists, the Roman Catholics constituted the most powerful community in Vietnam, especially in the North. For their part, the more numerous Buddhists were losing ground because of their inability to unite into a national religious organization and the fact that Buddhism became increasingly riddled by heresy and superstition.

In late 1944 and early 1945, a terrible famine struck North Vietnam causing more than a million deaths. This came as a result of floods and the fact that the peasants had been ordered by the French government to reduce their rice crop in order to plant jute which was being sought by the Japanese. Though causing the worst misery, the famine instigated no popular revolt, a fact that testified to the French success in paralyzing Vietnamese society in a systematic way. French authorities took no action to organize or encourage relief. Meanwhile, of the huge rice surplus available in the South, the French redistributed only a tiny portion, more for propaganda than for humanitarian purposes.

In short, Vietnamese society at the end of World War II, after French rule had been suddenly terminated by the Japanese, displayed all the signs of stagnancy and backwardness. Still laboring under traditionalism and the vestiges of Chinese influence, this society was suffering from the half-hearted reforms and colonial policies of French rule. The process of eradicating ancient Chinese influence and reforming society on a

modern pattern had just begun and resulted in many disloca-
tions. This was a transitional period during which the old evil
was yet to be replaced by the new good and the new evil had
already arrived to add to the old one.

Nationalists who were fighting against the French were all
patriotic, but they lacked political shrewdness and experience.
Premature emergence from the underground also doomed their
activities to failure. They were even betrayed by Vietnamese
who shared their anti-colonialist stance but not their political
ideas, then also by the Communists who sold them out to the
French. Finally, those who had allied themselves with the Japanese against the French ended up being betrayed, too. This
hopeless situation lasted until the Japanese defeat. By that
time, nationalist parties had been so depleted of talent and
leadership that they were unable to take advantage of the
political vacuum and seize power. Their inaction gave the
Communist Viet Minh a chance to prevail on the people's patriotism and win national independence. Cunningly concealing
their true nature and posing as nationalists, the Communists
had managed to win the prime sympathy of the people.

## CONTACT WITH COMMUNISM

The Indochinese Communist party (ICP) was founded in 1930.
When the Viet Minh, its frontal organization, seized power on
19 August 1945, the overwhelming majority of Vietnamese had
only a vague idea of communism. Of particular significance at
this juncture, most Vietnamese at heart seemed to consider the
Viet Minh as just another nationalist group with a different
organization and policy.

The psychology of the Vietnamese people at that time was
one of yearning for national independence. At any price, Vietnam had to be returned to Vietnamese rule; political persuasion
only came second. Ho Chi Minh's skill was in his ability to
exploit popular hatred of French colonialism and his manipu-
lation of nationalists. In late 1945, therefore, he disbanded the

Indochinese Communist party to the confusion of domestic
and world opinion. In fact, he had shrewdly prepared for an
eventual showdown with the French that required total popular
support for success.

In the rush of events that preceded the eruption of the
resistance war against the French on 19 December 1946, the
Viet Minh also astutely instituted some long due social reforms.
They advanced a program of anti-feudalism and anti-colonialism. Feudalism, they maintained, was at the source of all social
evils and had to be destroyed first; then came the fight against
colonialism. The anti-feudalism campaign sought primarily to
demolish all monarchical vestiges in Vietnam and eliminate the
old ruling class.* Popular sentiment, however, was only lukewarm toward this effort. The majority of the Vietnamese people
only saw the French as the main enemy to eliminate. Their
spirit and courage were evident at the outbreak of the war,
when the people of Hanoi organized themselves into self-
defense groups and battled the French from house to house for
one month. The Viet Minh government and army, meanwhile,
had withdrawn from the capital city before fighting broke out
to establish a defense line in the highlands.

The call to join the Viet Minh army and fight for national
salvation during 1947–50 was enthusiastically supported by
many men from the middle class. Many of them had risen to
the positions of battalion and regimental commanders in Vo
Nguyen Giap's army. But most of these people were subse-
quently purged when the Viet Minh, in a move toward socialism, began to systematically eliminate the rich, the large
landowners, and the petty bourgeoisie through the device of
class struggle and land reform.

Vietnamese from all walks of life, with the exception of
destitute peasants and workers, were greatly disappointed. They

---

*Pham Quynh, a prominent scholar, and Ngo Dinh Khoi were both assassinated
during the process.

felt that the Viet Minh had betrayed them after enticing them to join the resistance. Driven by patriotic ardor and zeal, they had never thought of themselves as belonging to the classes destined to be eliminated.

From the very beginning of this watershed event, the poor farm workers had gained ascendency as they were entrusted with leadership positions in villages, districts, and provinces against the will of members of other classes. But as the new leaders exercised power under the aegis of the Lao Dong (Communist) party, opposition and criticism began to evaporate. This change in the power structure of society entailed drastic change in the role of the Vietnamese women. Heretofore, utterly dependent in a traditional way, they had now emerged as men's equal partners in all aspects of social endeavor.

Living under Viet Minh control, Vietnamese from disfavored classes suffered from a radical change in social values. Being mostly city dwellers, they had been brought to the countryside by the war. The Viet Minh's scorched-earth policy had deprived them of economic advantages, and in a sense, this had the good effect of bridging the gap between city and countryside.

However, beginning in 1950, and especially during 1951, when the Viet Minh launched a forceful campaign of class struggle under the land rent reduction program, the illusion of class harmony was quickly fading away and yielded to the stark fact that only one class, the class of landless peasants and workers, was to remain and that all others were to vanish regardless of their contributions to the resistance. For this reason, a number of nationalists began to leave the Viet Minh zone for the cities, especially after the political reincarnation of ex-emperor Bao Dai who was being used as a rallying point for those disillusioned with the Viet Minh. Except for Central Vietnam where royalist sentiments were still strong, Bao Dai failed to attract enough ralliers elsewhere because of his pro-French stance. Nevertheless, he was the only straw for all nationalists to cling to while they waited for a chance to revive their cause. The only alternative would have been capitulation and complete subservience to the French.

The socialist transformation carried out by the Viet Minh was forceful and rigid in North and Central Vietnam. But in the South, it had been so mild that in 1954 when the Geneva Agreements were concluded there were no significant popular grievances against Communist policy except for a few die-hard nationalists and members of the Cao Dai, Hoa Hao and Binh Xuyen, who had been frustrated with the treachery of the Communist Viet Minh.

The French defeat at Dien Bien Phu in May 1954 led rapidly to the signing of the Geneva Cease-Fire Agreement in late July 1954. Vietnam was temporarily divided at the 17th parallel into two zones, North and South, pending the holding of general elections to reunify the country. The North was under a Communist government led by Ho Chi Minh while the South, nominally under the leadership of ex-emperor Bao Dai and a nationalist government headed by Prime Minister Ngo Dinh Diem, still labored under French political and military control.

In its first steps toward regaining full sovereignty, South Vietnam had become an arena for the infighting of several opposing forces. First there was the French influence, which was exerted by the presence of the French High Commissioner and the French Expeditionary Corps. Then there were pro-French groups who worked with the French to promote their material interests as well as dubious political aims. In direct opposition to the French, there were the Communist Viet Minh who, despite their regrouping to the North, still enjoyed tremendous popular sympathy; their infrastructure and capability to return constituted perhaps the most obvious threat. All forces of nationalist persuasion wanted to take advantage of the temporary partition and the impending withdrawal of French forces to forge an independent course for the building of a non-Communist nation. To achieve this, they, who had never lived in harmony with each other, had to find a common rallying point.

In the midst of these searing conflicts, the stabilization of South Vietnam required immediate solutions in several areas. There were social differences to patch up; there was the shaky old order to unravel while a foundation for new values had yet to become firm; there was the need for rehabilitating a countryside torn up by war in addition to satisfying a Westernized pluralistic city population which was forever clamoring for more benefits; finally, there were the smoldering embers of discrimination to be mitigated, and this encompassed almost the entire fabric of society. Even though the American involvement was most opportune, the initial stages of South Vietnam's struggle to stand on its own feet were beset with obstacles.

# National Security Council
# Position Paper

*The National Security Council is one of the primary advisory and policy-making bodies in the U.S. Government. This report, written for President Truman during the time when anti-Communist fervor was beginning to surge in the United States, shows the growing concern over the inability of the French to achieve victory, and it also contains an early statement of "The Domino Theory" (see* The Quiet American, *p. 95).*

## REPORT BY THE NATIONAL SECURITY COUNCIL ON THE POSITION OF THE UNITED STATES WITH RESPECT TO INDOCHINA

*27 February 1950*

THE PROBLEM

1. To undertake a determination of all practicable United States measures to protect its security in Indochina and to prevent the expansion of communist aggression in that area.

ANALYSIS

2. It is recognized that the threat of communist aggression against Indochina is only one phase of anticipated communist

From *The Pentagon Papers*, quoted in John Clark Pratt, *Vietnam Voices*. New York: Viking Penguin, 1983, 6–8.

plans to seize all of Southeast Asia. It is understood that Burma is weak internally and could be invaded without strong opposition or even that the Government of Burma could be subverted. However, Indochina is the area most immediately threatened. It is also the only area adjacent to communist China which contains a large European army, which along with native troops is now in armed conflict with the forces of communist aggression. A decision to contain Communist expansion at the border of Indochina must be considered as a part of a wider study to prevent communist aggression into other parts of Southeast Asia.

3. A large segment of the Indochinese nationalist movement was seized in 1945 by Ho Chi Minh, a Vietnamese who under various aliases has served as a communist agent for thirty years. He has attracted non-communist as well as communist elements to his support. In 1946, he attempted, but failed to secure French agreement to his recognition as the head of a government of Vietnam. Since then he has directed a guerrilla army in raids against French installations and lines of communication. French forces which have been attempting to restore law and order found themselves pitted against a determined adversary who manufactures effective arms locally, who received supplies of arms from outside sources, who maintained no capital or permanent headquarters and who was, and is able, to disrupt and harass almost any area within Vietnam (Tonkin, Annam and Cochinchina) at will.

4. The United States has, since the Japanese surrender, pointed out to the French Government that the legitimate nationalist aspirations of the people of Indochina must be satisfied, and that a return to the prewar colonial rule is not possible. The Department of State has pointed out to the French Government that it was and is necessary to establish and support governments in Indochina particularly in Vietnam, under leaders who are capable of attracting to their causes the non-communist nationalist followers who had drifted to the Ho Chi Minh communist movement in the absence of any non-

communist nationalist movement around which to plan their aspirations. . . .

7. The newly formed States of Vietnam, Laos and Cambodia do not as yet have sufficient political stability nor military power to prevent the infiltration into their areas of Ho Chi Minh's forces. The French Armed Forces, while apparently effectively utilized at the present time, can do little more than to maintain the status quo. Their strength of some 140,000 does, however, represent an army in being and the only military bulwark in that area against the further expansion of communist aggression from either internal or external forces.

8. The presence of Chinese Communist troops along the border of Indochina makes it possible for arms, material and troops to move freely from Communist China to the northern Tonkin area now controlled by Ho Chi Minh. There is already evidence of movement of arms.

9. In the present state of affairs, it is doubtful that the combined native Indochinese and French troops can successfully contain Ho's forces should they be strengthened by either Chinese Communist troops crossing the border, or Communist-supplied arms and material in quantity from outside Indochina strengthening Ho's forces.

CONCLUSIONS

10. It is important to United States security interests that all practicable measures be taken to prevent further communist expansion in Southeast Asia. Indochina is a key area of Southeast Asia and is under immediate threat.

11. The neighboring countries of Thailand and Burma could be expected to fall under Communist domination if Indochina were controlled by a Communist-dominated government. The balance of Southeast Asia would then be in grave hazard.

12. Accordingly, the Departments of State and Defense should prepare as a matter of priority a program of all practicable measures designed to protect United States Security interests.

# Ho Chi Minh

*No doubt hurt by the refusal of President Truman even to reply to his letters requesting the kind of support he has received when fighting the Japanese, Ho (who has intentionally modelled his new constitution on that of the United States) begins to comment publicly on the growing American presence in Vietnam.*

## PRESS CONFERENCE, 25 JULY 1950

*Question:* What is, Mr. President, the present situation of the U.S. imperialists' interventionist policy in Indochina?

*Answer:* The U.S. imperialists have of late openly interfered in Indochina's affairs. It is with their money and weapons and their instructions that the French colonialists have been waging war in Viet-Nam, Cambodia, and Laos.

However, the U.S. imperialists are intensifying their plot to discard the French colonialists so as to gain complete control over Indochina. That is why they do their utmost to redouble their direct intervention in every field—military, political, and economic. It is also for this reason that the contradictions between them and the French colonialists become sharper and sharper.

———

From *The Selected Works of Ho Chi Minh.* Hanoi: Foreign Languages Publishing House, 1960, 1961, 1962.

*Question:* What influence does this intervention exert on the Indochinese people?

*Answer:* The U.S. imperialists supply their henchmen with armaments to massacre the Indochinese people. They dump their goods in Indochina to prevent the development of local handicrafts. Their pornographic culture contaminates the youth in areas placed under their control. They follow the policy of buying up, deluding, and dividing our people. They drag some bad elements into becoming their tools and use them to invade our country.

*Question:* What measure shall we take against them?

*Answer:* To gain independence, we, the Indochinese people, must defeat the French colonialists, our number one enemy. At the same time, we will struggle against the U.S. interventionists. The deeper their interference, the more powerful are our solidarity and our struggle. We will expose their maneuvers before all our people, especially those living in areas under their control. We will expose all those who serve as lackeys for the U.S. imperialists to coerce, deceive, and divide our people.

The close solidarity between the peoples of Viet-Nam, Cambodia, and Laos constitutes a force capable of defeating the French colonialists and the U.S. interventionists. The U.S. imperialists failed in China, they will fail in Indochina.

We are still laboring under great difficulties but victory will certainly be ours.

# Doris M. Condit

*Doris Condit holds two degrees from George Washington University and has worked with Johns Hopkins University, American University, and the American Institutes for Research. She is the author of numerous publications, including the three-volume* Case Study in Guerrilla War: Greece During World War II *and* Modern Revolutionary Warfare: An Analytical Overview. *This excerpt from her book about the early days of the Vietnam War provides a general overview of how American officials and policy makers see the history and politics of the period.*

## INDOCHINA: THE THREAT IN SOUTHEAST ASIA

Just as the outbreak of the Korean War changed U.S. policy on Formosa and facilitated a peace treaty with Japan, it also affected U.S. policy on Indochina, where the French were in the fourth year of a bitter struggle against the Communist Viet Minh movement led by Ho Chi Minh and supported by Communist China. Although the French in early 1950 granted Cambodia, Laos, and Vietnam a measure of independent status as Associated States of the French Union, most of the Indochinese people believed the French intended to retain control

Reprinted from Doris M. Condit, *The Test of War.* Historical Office: Office of the Secretary of Defense, Washington, D.C., 1988, 205–21.

over their entire country, and few in Vietnam supported the
French wholeheartedly in the ongoing battle to save the northern Vietnamese area of Tonkin from the Viet Minh.

The United States viewed Indochina as the "most strate-
gically important area" of Southeast Asia and "subject to the
most immediate danger." Arguments advanced in support of
these assumptions, which quickly became generally accepted as
conclusions, centered about the need to contain the advance
of communism in Asia by the Chinese and the Russians. Indochina constituted an indispensable part of the line of containment against communism in the Pacific that stretched from
Japan through Formosa and the Philippines. It was the strategic
key to Southeast Asia, where Thailand, Malaya, Burma, and
Indonesia would be ripe targets for Communist expansion if
the Viet Minh triumphed. This chain reaction, according to the
"domino theory," could have a powerful psychological impact
on India, Pakistan, and the Philippines, adversely affecting U.S.
security interests in those areas. And finally, Indochina had
great strategic and economic importance because of its location
astride one of the great sea crossroads of the world.[1]

Both the State and Defense departments fully understood
that political and racial factors complicated the French role in
Indochina and had to be taken into account in formulating U.S.
policy. These factors derived largely from the colonialism whose
demise in Asia and Africa the United States had been encour-
aging since the end of World War II. The Indochinese people
wanted independence and an end to French domination. These
nationalist, racial, and colonial elements had to be given heavy
weight in any calculations of U.S. policy toward Indochina. It
followed logically that the United States, while supporting the
French in the struggle against the Viet Minh, would favor independence for the Indochinese states, eventual French withdrawal, and establishment of effective local defenses against
Viet Minh aggression.

The Joint Chiefs of Staff agreed with State's assessment of
the strategic importance of the Southeast Asian mainland to

the United States and that Indochina's fall would undoubtedly lead to the fall of neighboring countries. They recommended quick implementation of military aid programs for the area but urged, in view of the earlier U.S. experience with the Chinese Nationalists, that aid be carefully controlled and integrated with political and economic programs. Because the French military needs were acute, the JCS proposed sending interim assistance to Indochina and establishing a small U.S. military aid group there immediately.[2] These views and those of the State Department came under consideration by the NSC in the spring of 1950. Approving Southeast Asia policy in NSC 64 on 24 April 1950, President Truman directed State and Defense to prepare a program to protect U.S. security interests in Indochina.[3]

The Joint Chiefs soon urged an even more forceful U.S. position, including U.S. assumption of Western leadership in helping the Southeast Asia area, and they again affirmed the pressing need for early U.S. military aid to Indochina. Only a few steps were taken toward implementing NSC 64, however, before the Korean War started.[4] Despite recommendation for a $23.5 million economic program and a $17 million military assistance program, the president in May 1950 authorized only $750,000 in economic and $10 million in military assistance. First deliveries began in June 1950.[5]

## EFFECT OF THE KOREAN WAR

The Korean War had immediate impact on U.S. assistance to Indochina. On 27 June 1950 Truman announced acceleration of military aid to the area and allocated an additional $5 million. On 8 July he raised the total amount to $31 million. The U.S. program was to supplement rather than replace French assistance, help the three Associated States achieve internal security, and strengthen the French Union Army's resistance to Communist subversion and aggression. Acknowledging that future events, in Korea or elsewhere, might make it necessary to divert U.S. aid from Indochina, Secretary of State Acheson declared that the United States would meanwhile give the "strongest support possible." A U.S. Military Assistance Advisory Group (MAAG) under Brig. Gen. Francis G. Brink began arriving in Saigon in late July.[6]

U.S. officials also took a sharper look at the activities of the Chinese Communists, who began a major program in April 1950 to equip and train the Viet Minh and appeared ready to intervene openly. Early in July the Joint Chiefs suggested that, if the PRC gave overt military assistance to the Viet Minh, the United States should increase its military aid to the French, consider providing air and naval assistance, and ask the United Nations to make forces available to resist the Chinese aggression. A joint State–Defense survey mission, headed by John F. Melby of the State Department and including a military group under Maj. Gen. Graves B. Erskine (USMC), recommended on 6 August an increase in U.S. military assistance, citing the threat of the Chinese Communists and the Viet Minh and the apparent inability of the French to control the situation. Donald R. Heath, who became minister to Vietnam, Laos, and Cambodia in late June, strongly supported the recommendation of the survey mission.[7]

By mid-August 1950 the situation had grown increasingly serious, and State considered possible political concessions by the French, including a date for independence of the Associated States, that might gain the "spontaneous cooperation" of the Indochinese peoples.[8] Nonetheless, Indochina was still viewed as primarily a French problem. NSC 73/4, approved by Truman on 24 August, recommended, in the event of an overt Chinese attack in Indochina, that the United States join with the British in supporting France and the Associated States and accelerate and increase U.S. military assistance, but avoid a general war with the Chinese.[9]

Although U.S. plans called for a total of $133 million for Indochina in the regular and first supplemental FY 1951 military assistance appropriations, the Joint Chiefs noted that U.S.

aid would increase the military capabilities of the French Union Forces but would not enable them to defeat the Viet Minh. Alarmed that a French loss could jeopardize the U.S. military position in Asia, the JCS recommended taking bolder political measures and expediting additional military aid. Moreover, the French should plan for operations acceptable to the United States and within U.S. aid capabilities, form separate national armies in the Associated States, and hold military talks with British and U.S. commanders in the Far East regarding coordination of operations. The JCS also wanted the French informed that under existing circumstances no U.S. armed forces would be committed in Indochina.[10] Concurring "generally," Defense Secretary Johnson forwarded the JCS views to Acheson. In early September Acheson warned the French of limits on U.S. military assistance and of the need for a coordinated plan; he proposed tripartite military talks.[11]

In September and October the French suffered serious reverses along the Chinese border. Lacking manpower, leadership, and adequate military intelligence, they were overextended and unable to counterattack, reinforcing doubt about their ability to remain in the northern area. Claiming that they could no longer meet their military commitments to both NATO and Indochina, the French told the Americans of their need for more U.S. military equipment—but no U.S. divisions "for the moment."[12]

With some Pentagon officials worried that the French might "quit cold," the Americans sought to keep the French and Indochinese forces viable long enough to allow them to catch up with the Viet Minh in strength.[13] During conversations in Washington in October, Defense Secretary Marshall told French Defense Minister Jules Moch that Indochina would have top priority on all military assistance shipments, and in fact a priority equal to that for Formosa was granted on 23 October. Over JCS opposition and even at the "expense of the Korean pipeline," Marshall decided to send 30 much-wanted B-26 aircraft.[14] The JCS received approval for a FY 1951 military assistance program of $133 million for the French and the Associated States on 23 October, and shipments began almost immediately. The United States also indicated willingness to make funds available to increase military production in France. By the end of January 1951 about $50 million in U.S. military equipment had been shipped to Indochina, and some Americans considered the aid as possibly decisive in enabling the French to hold on.[15]

Seeking a greater voice in the employment of its military assistance in Indochina, the United States became steadily more involved in Vietnam. State and Defense agreed that the French should signal the waning of colonialism in Indochina by making political and economic concessions and creating national armies.[16] The trend toward greater U.S. involvement was such that John Ohly, the State Department's deputy director of military assistance, wrote Acheson that the United States seemed to be supplanting the French in Indochina and that failures were beginning to be attributed to the Americans. Not only might the United States be "on the road to being a scapegoat," but he felt it was dangerously close to direct intervention.[17]

Shortly after the Chinese Communists attacked in Korea in late November 1950, the Joint Chiefs recommended to Marshall that for the long term the United States should try to establish conditions in Indochina requiring no foreign armed forces, press the French to provide eventual self-government "either within or outside of the French Union," support UN membership for the Associated States, and encourage a regional security arrangement for Southeast Asia. For the short term, the United States should ensure that the French retained primary responsibility in Indochina. U.S. military assistance was to be limited to logistical support and tied to an "overall military plan prepared by the French, concurred in by the Associated States of Indochina, and acceptable to the United States." Further increases in military assistance were to depend on French moves to create greater popular support.[18]

If the Chinese Communists should attack in Indochina, the JCS recommended that the United States support France and the Associated States by all means short of using American military forces or becoming involved in a general war with Peking. If the French appeared ready to abandon the war in Indochina, the United States would have to reconsider its policy. Some U.S. officials doubted, however, that the United States would intervene militarily even in that event. On 20 December Marshall sent the JCS paper to the National Security Council, which considered it later during work on NSC 124.[19]

## MOVES TO STEM THE TIDE

The French were willing to grant greater independence to the Indochinese states as long as they remained within the framework of the French Union. In November 1950 the French increased the Associated States' responsibilities while continuing financial aid. They retained their base rights in Indochina, continued to maintain a number of their own administrators, and restricted the three states' freedom in foreign affairs. Even the French agreement to establish in 1951 a national Vietnamese army under the supreme command of Emperor Bao Dai seemed suspect to the Vietnamese since it would be responsible to the French High Command. The French also increased their 1951 budget for Indochina and considered sending more troops from home.[20]

Hoping to achieve greater cohesion and unity, the French on 7 December 1950 named General Jean de Lattre de Tassigny to two posts—commander in chief of the French Union Forces and high commissioner in Indochina. Despite French concessions, Asians still saw Indochina as under tight French control. Bao Dai was not an effective ruler, there were rivalries within his government, and some friction between it and de Lattre.[21] Finding a local leader around whom public support would rally proved extremely difficult. Almost despairingly, U.S. Minister Heath told Washington in early 1951 that the enemy leader,

Ho Chi Minh, was the "only Viet who enjoys any measure of national prestige."[22]

Both French and Indochinese officials felt that U.S. aid held the key to containment of the Viet Minh. When he visited Washington in late January 1951, French Premier René Pleven proposed to Truman, Acheson, and Marshall that permanent procedures be established for coordination and cooperation in the Far East among the United States, Britain, and France. Before responding to de Lattre's current demands for French reinforcements, the French government needed to know what the United States could supply. Plans for a four-division Indochinese national army were dependent on U.S. funding of about $70 million, almost half the cost. The French wanted to obtain the use of a U.S. aircraft carrier and asked whether the United States would send men and materiel to help them to fight, or, if the Chinese attacked, to get out of Indochina. Truman told Pleven that, "barring unforeseen developments," the United States would expedite deliveries on currently planned aid programs. Marshall ruled out a new carrier, but he promised that restrictions limiting use of the *Langley* (recently transferred to France) to the Mediterranean area would be lifted, allowing its employment in Asian waters. Truman refused to provide an additional $70 million for the national army and said that no U.S. forces would be committed to Indochina, but he declared that the United States would, if possible, assist in evacuating the French if the Chinese invaded.[23]

Meanwhile, U.S. military assistance programs for Indochina mushroomed, reaching more than $210 million for FY 1951 by the end of March 1951, with plans for a $170 million program in FY 1952. Having given Indochina priority over all other military assistance countries at the end of 1950, the United States had shipped or was ready to load by 31 March 1951 more than $79 million in equipment. In March the French government decided to send de Lattre the troops he requested. But the Viet Minh, having developed large-size regular military units and relying on strong Chinese logistical support, presented a growing military threat that the French feared they might not be able to contain even with reinforcements.[24]

Preparing in May for military talks with the British and French later in the month in Singapore, the JCS thought that, despite U.S. aid, the Viet Minh would conquer most of Tonkin if Chinese logistical aid continued and French strength was not augmented further. They suggested accelerating U.S. military assistance deliveries, helping to train the national armies, and planning for emergency evacuation aid, but again underlined the primary French responsibility in Indochina. Approved by the president on 17 May, NSC 48/5 reemphasized U.S. determination not to commit troops to Indochina but to provide military assistance, encourage internal autonomy and social and economic reforms, and promote international support for the Associated States. The Singapore talks developed no concrete tripartite arrangements for operations in Indochina. If Tonkin was the key to Southeast Asian security, the French alone remained responsible for its defense.[25]

The administration of U.S. economic aid in Indochina in this period further complicated Franco–American relations. The Economic Cooperation Administration (ECA), which managed this effort to strengthen the fragile Indochinese governments, bypassed the French and dealt directly with the Associated States. The French resented the publicity for American programs and disregard of their own efforts. Objecting specifically to large-scale U.S. classes in the English language and the size of the U.S. mission in Saigon, the French feared Indochina might become a U.S. zone of influence. Heath reported that these views, held by a majority of French civil officials, and probably by de Lattre also, were potentially harmful to future efforts. Heath told Washington in mid-June 1951 that the general remained determined to let nothing "interfere with his formula for Franco–Vietnamese solidarity" or Vietnam's retention in the French Union.[26]

By the end of June Heath himself pointedly reiterated that U.S. policy should still be to "supplement but not to supplant" the French in Indochina. Noting that only French arms and resources were keeping Indochina from collapsing, Heath made a number of suggestions for improving Franco–American relations. He was instructed to reassure de Lattre and did so with apparently good results.[27] The Truman administration considered this an opportune time for the general to visit the United States, an invitation he had long sought. When de Lattre came to Washington in September, he emphasized that, rather than limiting Indochinese independence, as many Americans seemed to assume, the French were trying hard to promote the independence of the Associated States, at huge expense spending a billion dollars a year for a war in which French losses already amounted to 98,000 men, including 30,000 killed.[28]

Pointing out that the same Vietnamese who made a "Grade A parachutist in the governmental forces would make a fanatical communist guerrilla if Ho Chi Minh had reached him first," de Lattre hoped for increased and speedier deliveries of promised U.S. military equipment. Conferring with Lovett on 20 September, de Lattre emphasized Indochina's importance in the fight to save Asia from communism and the U.S. responsibility to supply Indochina as well as Korea: "I am your man just as General Ridgway is your own man. Your own spirit should lead you to send me these things without my asking." Assuring de Lattre that the United States regarded him as a "comrade in arms," Lovett pushed the military services to accommodate French requests and got their promise to ship most of the critical items by the end of the year. Although de Lattre later upset the State Department by publicly claiming that his visit had changed U.S. policy toward Indochina, his major success lay in getting the Pentagon to try to accelerate already programmed aid.[29]

In Vietnam the situation seemed to be getting worse at the end of 1951. Under Bao Dai and Prime Minister Tan Van Huu the Vietnamese government remained internally divided, unrepresentative of most Vietnamese, and unable to attract new leaders.[30] In October 1951 the Viet Minh attacked in the north-west, weathered a counterattack, pinned French forces down at Hoa Binh, and reinfiltrated the recently cleared Tonkin Delta area. The French public, for its part, keenly resented the costs and casualties sustained in Indochina. In December Ambassador David Bruce cabled from Paris that the French might greet a proposal to quit Indochina "with a sense of emotional relief."[31] By this time too, General de Lattre, sick and reportedly despairing of victory, had left Indochina, a loss that to Americans had appalling political and military implications.[32]

De Lattre died in January 1952, and in April Jean Letourneau became high commissioner while simultaneously continuing in Paris as minister of state in charge of relations with the Associated States. The new military commander, General Raoul Salan, believed the French could hold out provided the Chinese did not enter in force. In February the French skillfully retreated from Hoa Binh but were humiliated by their failure to hold the base after high-cost battles.[33]

In the face of continuing setbacks, the French in December 1951 requested immediate military conversations with the British and Americans on concerted action to be taken if the Chinese entered Indochina in force. Agreeing to the meeting, the JCS recommended to Lovett that in the event of overt or major "volunteer" Chinese intervention the United Nations should act and the United States should consider air or naval action but commit no ground forces. In the event of either UN or U.S. action, operations might have to include an air and naval blockade of the China coast, concurrent action against selected Chinese targets, and the use of Chinese Nationalist forces.[34]

With representatives of Canada, Australia, and New Zealand present as observers at the Washington tripartite meeting in January 1952, the French, British, and American delegates recommended that their governments warn Peking that any aggression in Southeast Asia would bring three-power retaliation not necessarily confined to the area of aggression. Unable to agree on specific retaliatory steps, they turned the question over to a five-power ad hoc committee including the Australians and

New Zealanders. The talks left the French without any firm
assurances as to what would be done if the Chinese entered
Indochina before issuance of a warning.[35]

The ad hoc committee's deliberations were also inconclusive. The British believed that a coastal blockade of China or
attacks on mainland military targets would invite Chinese
Communist action against Hong Kong, while the French
thought such actions would divert forces from Indochina; both
wanted retaliation confined to the immediate area of the attack
in Indochina or along the China border. The British and French
also wanted a combined Allied command. Apparently, the conferees did not discuss the possible use of atomic weapons. They
agreed on only one point—the inadvisability of using Nationalist forces from Formosa on the Asian mainland. Since the
British and French representatives seemed to be speaking from
firm governmental positions, it was clear that U.S. policy would
have to be reconsidered.[36] The three nations had agreed to a
warning but not on any steps to take if the warning was dis-
regarded. . . .

The U.S. commitment in Indochina grew prodigiously during the Korean War, with most of the burden of support falling
on the Department of Defense. The bold onslaught of the Chinese Communists in Korea and their backing of the Viet Minh
in Indochina confirmed U.S. perception of the PRC as an ag-
gressive and expansionist power bent on dominating East Asia.
Fear that the fall of Indochina would lead to the loss of all
Southeast Asia to communism provided much of the motivation for the growing U.S. involvement in Indochina. The determination to deny Indochina to the Communists would
require ever greater U.S. engagement in the peninsula, and
eventually, more than a decade later, the ultimate step of committing American troops to battle in Vietnam. Beginning in
1953 the new administration would have to make further decisions about the U.S. role in the struggle for Indochina, for,
while Acheson and Lovett had increased the U.S. stake in that
country, they had also apparently kept U.S. options open. Al-

though it appeared that the United States could still disengage itself from Vietnam, each successive commitment would draw it closer to the vortex in which it would eventually be engulfed.

## NOTES

1. Rept. State to NSC, 27 Feb 50, w/draft rept. NSC 64, 27 Feb 50, US Dept State, *Foreign Relations of the United States, 1950* (hereafter cited as *FRUS* with year and volume number), VI:744–47; memo ActingASecState(FE) for SecState, 7 Mar 50, w/memo DepASecState(FE) for ASecState(FE), 7 Mar 50, ibid, 749–51; ltr DepUSecState to ATSD(FMA&MA), 7 Mar 50, ibid, 752. The Indochina war is variously dated from the French bombardment of Haiphong, which left 6,000 dead on 23 November 1946, or from 19 December 1946, when Ho made a surprise attack on the French.

2. Memo JCS for SecDef, 10 [5?] Apr 50, Dept Defense, comp, *United States–Vietnam Relations, 1945–1967* (hereafter cited as *US–Vietnam Relations* with volume number), H Cte print (1971), VIII:308–13.

3. Briefing paper [DefRepSrNSCStf], "Item 1, Current Situation in the Far East," 28 Jun 50, RG 218, CCS 334 NSC (9-25-47).

4. Memo JCS for SecDef, 2 May 50, *US–Vietnam Relations*, VIII: 315–17; briefing paper JCS for SecDef, 2 May 50, ibid, 318–20; briefing paper [DefRepSrNSCStf], "Item 1, Current Situation in the Far East," 28 Jun 50, RG 218, CCS 334 NSC (9-25-47).

5. Memo SecState for Pres, 17 Apr 50, *FRUS 1950*, VI:785–86; memo DirOMA OSD for DirMDAP State, 19 Apr 50, ibid, 787–89; ltr Pres to SecState, 1 May 50, ibid, 791; msg SecState for USEmb UK, 3 May 50, ibid, 792; rept USecState to ExecSecNSC, 15 Mar 51, *FRUS 1951*, VI, pt 1:397–400.

6. Memo SecState for Pres, 3 Jul 50, *FRUS 1950*, VI:835–36, 835nn1,2; ltr Pres to SecDef, 8 Jul 50, RG 330, CD 091.3 (MDAP Indochina); memo R.E. O'Hara (OASD(C)) for DirOMA OSD, 14 Jul 50, ibid; msg SecState for USLegn Saigon, 1 Jul 50, *FRUS 1950*, VI:833–34; JCS Hist Div, *History of the Indochina Incident, 1940–1954* (hereafter cited as *History of Indochina Incident*) in *The History of the Joint Chiefs of Staff: The Joint Chiefs and the War in Vietnam*, 186.

7. Notes on consultants' mtg, 25 Jul 50, *US–Vietnam Relations*, VIII: 341–42; prog rept [NSC 64] USecState for ExecSecNSC, 15 Mar

51, *FRUS 1951*, VI, pt 1:397–400; ltr Jt State–Def MDAP Survey Mission SEA to FMACC, 6 Aug 50, *FRUS 1950*, VI:840–44; ibid, 821n1; msg USMin Saigon for SecState, 9 Aug 50, ibid, 849–51.

8. Memo ATSD(FMA&MA) for DirNavalIntel, 31 Jul 50, RG 330, CD 092 (Indochina); msg USMin Saigon for SecState, 7 Aug 50, *FRUS 1950*, VI:845–48; briefing paper [DefRepSrNSCStf], "Item 3, Situation in the Far East," 10 Aug 50, RG 218, CCS 334 NSC (9-25-47); memo PPS State, 16 Aug 50, *FRUS 1950*, VI:857–58.

9. Note ExecSecNSC to NSC, 25 Aug 50, w/rept NSC, *FRUS 1950*, I:375–89.

10. Memo JCS for SecDef, 7 Sep 50, RG 330, CD 092.3 (NATO Council of Ministers).

11. Ltr SecDef to SecState, 11 Sep 50, ibid; SFM Min–4 US Deleg, [14 Sep 50], *FRUS 1950*, III:1224–28; msg ActingSecState for US-Legn Saigon, 16 Sep 50, *FRUS 1950*, VI:880–81.

12. Memo info DirNavalIntel, 17 Oct 50, RG 330, CD 091.3 (SE Asia); msg USMin Saigon for SecState, 15 Oct 50, *FRUS 1950*, VI:894–96; msg USMin Saigon for SecState, 24 Oct 50, ibid, 906–09 (908, quote); memo ATSD(FMA&MA) for SecDef, 28 Oct 50, RG 330, CD 092 (France).

13. Memo K.T. Young (OFMA OSD) for [MajGen Harry J.] Malony (DefMbr SEAAidPolCte), 13 Oct 50, *US–Vietnam Relations*, VIII:369–70; msg USMin Saigon for SecState, 15 Oct 50, *FRUS 1950*, VI:894–96; memrcd Young, [ca 17 Oct 50], *US–Vietnam Relations*, VIII:373–76; memo SPS [MajGen Sidney P. Spalding] for SecAF, 19 Oct 50, ibid, 391–92.

14. Memcon DirOMA OSD, 13 Oct 50, RG 330, CD 300-1-1; memcon DirOMA OSD, 16 Oct 50, ibid; draft memo JCS for SecDef, [14 Sep 50], enc A w/JCS Decision 1966/46, 14 Sep 50, RG 330, CD 104-1 (1950); draft memo JCS for SecDef, [18 Oct 50], enc A w/JCS Decision 1992/32, 18 Oct 50, ibid; memcon A.C. Murdaugh (OFMA OSD), 5 Jan 51, RG 330, CD 300-1-1; *History of Indochina Incident*, 176, 178.

15. *History of Indochina Incident*, 177–78; draft memo JCS for SecDef, [18 Oct 50], enc A w/JCS Decision 1992/32, 18 Oct 50, RG 330, CD 104-1 (1950); PR 1066 Dept State, 17 Oct 50, *US–Vietnam Relations*, VIII:371–72; prog rept USecState to ExecSecNSC, 15 Mar 51, *FRUS 1951*, VI, pt 1:397–400.

16. Memo SEAAidPolCte for SecState and SecDef, 11 Oct 50, w/draft statement (SEAC D-21 Rev 1), 11 Oct 50, *FRUS 1950*, VI:886–90; msg USMin Saigon for SecState, 13 Oct 50, ibid, 890–93; memo Young for Malony, 13 Oct 50, *US–Vietnam Relations*, VIII:

369–70; memo SPS [Spalding] OSD for SecAF, 19 Oct 50, ibid, 391–92; msg SecState for USLegn Saigon, 25 Oct 50, *FRUS 1950*, VI:909–10; memo JCS for SecDef, 27 Oct 50, RG 330, CD 091.3 (SEAsia); msg USMin Saigon for SecState, 15 Nov 50, *FRUS 1950*, VI:921–23; memo ExecSecNSC for NSC, 21 Dec 50, w/ memo JCS for SecDef, 29 [dated 28 in error] Nov 50, ibid, 945–53.

17. Msg SecState for USLegn Saigon, 18 Oct 50, *FRUS 1950*, VI:898–99; msg USMin Saigon for SecState, 23 Oct 50, ibid, 902–05; memo DepDirMDAP State for SecState, 20 Nov 50, w/memo Ohly for SecState, 20 Nov 50, ibid, 925–30. Dean Acheson acknowledged Ohly's "perceptive warning" in *Present at the Creation: My Years at the State Department*, 674.

18. Memo ExecSecNSC for NSC, 21 Dec 50, w/memo JCS for SecDef, 29 [dated 28 in error] Nov 50, w/enc, *FRUS 1950*, VI: 945–53.

19. Ibid; mins [extract] Truman–Attlee convs, 4 Dec 50, *FRUS 1950*, VII:1367; memo SecDef for ExecSecNSC, 20 Dec 50, RG 330, CD 092 (Indo-China).

20. PR 1187 Dept State, 27 Nov 50, *US–Vietnam Relations*, VIII:397; msg USAmb France for SecState, 21 Nov 50, *FRUS 1950*, VI:930–32; msg USAmb France for SecState, 24 Nov 50, ibid, 936–37; msg SecState for Certain Dipl Offs, 27 Nov 50, ibid, 938; msg USAmb France for SecState, 6 Dec 50, ibid, 941–43; memo Robert E. Hoey (PSA State) for Amb at Lge, 27 Dec 50, ibid, 955–58; memo ATSD(FMA&MA) for SecDef, 5 Jan 51, w/enc, RG 330, "Briefings" binder; mins SEAC M-13 SEAAidPolCte, [ca 7 Feb 51], *FRUS 1951*, VI, pt 1:376–78; memo USecState for ExecSecNSC, 15 Mar 51, ibid, 397–400; *History of Indochina Incident*, 181–84.

21. Msg USAmb France for SecState, 6 Dec 50, *FRUS 1950*, VI:941–43; mins SEAC M-13, [ca 7 Feb 51], *FRUS 1951*, VI, pt 1:376–78; msg USMin Saigon for SecState, 23 Oct 50, *FRUS 1950*, VI: 902–05; msg USMin Saigon for SecState, 20 Jan 51, *FRUS 1951*, VI, pt 1:350–52; memcon Chf USSplTech&EconMission Saigon, 19 Mar 51, ibid, 406–07; msg USMin Saigon for SecState, 9 Jul 51, ibid, 444–45; msg USMin Saigon for SecState, 30 Jul 51, ibid, 466–68.

22. Msg USMin Saigon for SecState, 24 Feb 51, *FRUS 1951*, VI, pt 1:384–85.

23. Editorial note, ibid, 366–67; msg SecState for USLegn Saigon, 30 Jan 51, ibid, 368–69; *History of Indochina Incident*, 215–17.

24. OMA OSD, MDAP *(Mutual Defense Assistance Program): De-partment of Defense Operations* (hereafter cited as MDAP: DoD Opns), Apr 51, 26; prog rept USecState to NSC, 15 Mar 51, *FRUS 1951*, VI, pt 1:397–400; memo JCS for SecDef, 29 Dec 50, RG 330, CD 091.3 (MDAP China); msg Bohlen (chgé in France) for SecState, 21 Mar 51, *FRUS 1951*, VI, pt 1:408–09, 409n2; msg USMin Saigon for SecState, 23 Mar 51, ibid, 409–10; msg USMin Saigon for SecState, 24 Mar 51, ibid, 410–12.

25. Memo JCS for SecDef, 11 May 51, w/apps, RG 330, CD 092 (Indo-China); *History of Indochina Incident*, 211–12; rept Exec-SecNSC to NSC, 17 May 51, w/enc NSC 48/5, *FRUS 1951*, VI, pt 1:33–63; ltr ATSD(ISA) to SecState, 17 Sep 51, RG 330, CD 337; conf rept Tripartite Mil Talks on SEAsia, Singapore, 15–18 May 51, *FRUS 1951*, VI, pt 1:64–71.

26. Msg Heath (USMin Saigon) for SecState, 29 Jun 51, *FRUS 1951*, VI, pt 1:432–39, 436n2; msg Heath for SecState, 14 Jun 51, ibid, 425–28 (428, quote); msg Heath for SecState, 30 Jun 51, ibid, 439–41; msg Chf SplTech&EconMission Saigon for ECA Admr, 12 Jul 51, ibid, 450–52; mins mtg with de Lattre, 17 Sep 51, ibid, 511–15.

27. Msg USMin Saigon for SecState, 29 Jun 51, ibid, 432–39, 439n3; memo ADir Non-EuropeanAffs OISA State for ASecState(FE), 12 Jul 51, ibid, 447–49; msg USMin Saigon for SecState, 18 Jul 51, ibid, 454–56; msg USMin Saigon for SecState, 20 Jul 51, ibid, 457–59.

28. Msg USMin Saigon for SecState, 17 Mar 51, ibid, 402–04; msg USChgé Saigon for SecState, 18 Aug 51, ibid, 480–84, 480n3; mins [State] mtg with de Lattre, 17 Sep 51, ibid, 506–11.

29. Memcon Gibson (PSA State), 14 Sep 51, ibid, 502–04; mins [State] mtgs 1 and 2 with de Lattre, 17 Sep 51, ibid, 506–11, 511–15; mins mtg with de Lattre, 20 Sep 51, ibid, 517–21; msg SecState for USLegn Saigon, 26 Sep 51, ibid, 524–25; ltr SecDef to SecState, 1 Oct 51, ibid, 525–26; memcon William W. Gibson (PSA), 12 Oct 51, ibid, 530–32; msg SecState for USLegn Saigon, 15 Oct 51, ibid, 532.

30. Msg USMin Saigon for SecState, 30 Nov 51, ibid, 547–48; msg USConsul Singapore for SecState, 30 Nov 51, ibid, 548–50; msg USMin Saigon for SecState, 9 Dec 51, ibid, 558–59; msg ActingSecState for USLegn Saigon, 12 Dec 51, ibid, 560–61; msg USMin Saigon for SecState, 27 Dec 51, ibid, 578–79.

31. Memo ActingASecState(FE) for SecState, 19 Dec 51, ibid, 562–63; msg SecState for USEmb France, 20 Dec 51, ibid, 563–64;

notes [State] State–JCS mtg, 21 Dec 51, ibid, 568–70; msg USAmb France for SecState, 22 Dec 51, ibid, 571–72; msg USMin Saigon for SecState, 22 Dec 51, ibid, 572–73; msg USAmb France for SecState, 26 Dec 51, ibid, 573–78; paper [DoD], "Brief Estimate of Situation in Indochina . . . ," [ca Feb 53], RG 330, ISA files, Nash papers, "French Talks" folder.

32. Msg USMin Saigon for SecState, 5 Dec 51, *FRUS 1951*, VI, pt 1: 556–57; notes [State] State–JCS mtg, 21 Dec 51, ibid, 568–70; msg USMin Saigon for State, 17 Jan 52, *FRUS 1952–1954*, XIII, pt 1:18–21; NIE 35/1 CIA–IAC, 3 Mar 52, ibid, 53–60; Bernard B. Fall, *Street Without Joy: Indochina at War, 1946–54*, 42–54.

33. Msg USMin Saigon for State, 17 Jan 52, *FRUS 1952–1954*, XIII, pt 1:18–21; msg ActingSecState for USEmb France, 2 Feb 52, ibid, 39; msg USMin Saigon for State, 26 Feb 52, ibid, 40–42; memo ASecState(FE) for DepUSecState(PolAffs), 28 Feb 52, ibid, 42–43; msg USMin Saigon for State, 29 Feb 52, ibid, 46–48; msg USMin Saigon for State, 6 Mar 52, ibid, 62–63; msg USAmb France for State, 22 Apr 52, ibid, 104n7; Fall, *Street Without Joy*, 54–55 (quote).

34. Msg USEmb France for SecState, 22 Dec 51, *FRUS 1951*, VI, pt 1:571–72; memo SecState for Pres, 29 Dec 51, ibid, 579–80; memrcd ATSD(ISA), [ca 26 Nov 51], RG 330, CD 334 (State–JCS); ltr SecDef to SecState, 6 Jan 52, w/memo JCS for SecDef, "Indochina . . . , 28 Dec 51," *FRUS 1952–1954*, XII, pt 1:3–5; memo JCS for SecDef, "Defense of Southeast Asia . . . ," 28 Dec 51, ibid, 6–7.

35. Notes SJCS and DepSJCS, 11 Jan 52, *FRUS 1952–1954*, XII, pt 1:8–22; msg SecState for USLegn Saigon, 15 Jan 52, ibid, 14–16; *History of Indochina Incident*, 240–42.

36. Memo VAdm A.C. Davis for JCS, 5 Feb 52, with encs, *FRUS 1952–1954*, XII, pt 1:36–44; *History of Indochina Incident*, 243–46.

# Ho Chi Minh

*In January 1952, while Graham Greene is completing his second visit to Vietnam and* The Quiet American's *Alden Pyle is approaching his fate, Ho writes the following analysis of the past year's military and political events.*

## THE IMPERIALIST AGGRESSORS CAN NEVER ENSLAVE THE HEROIC VIETNAMESE PEOPLE

I avail myself of the short New Year's holiday to write these lines.

More fortunate than other peoples, we, the Vietnamese people, like our friends the Chinese and the Korean peoples, enjoy two New Year's festivals every year. One New Year's Day is celebrated according to the Gregorian calendar and falls on the first of January. On that day, which is the official New Year's Day, only government offices send greetings to one another. Another New Year's Day, the Tet, is observed according to the lunar calendar, and this year falls on a day of the closing week of January. This traditional New Year's Day, celebrated by the people, usually lasts from three to seven days in peacetime.

From *For a Lasting Peace, for a People's Democracy*, 4 April 1952. Ho used the pseudonym Din. Published in Ho Chi Minh, *The Selected Works of Ho Chi Minh.* Hanoi: Foreign Languages Publishing House, 1960, 1961, 1962.

In our country, spring begins in the first days of January. At present, a splendid springtime prevails everywhere. The radiant sunbeams bring with them a merry and healthy life. Like an immense green carpet, the young rice plants cover the fields, heralding a coming bumper harvest. The birds warble merrily in evergreen bushes. Here winter lasts only a few days and the thermometer rarely falls to 10 degrees above zero. As far as snow is concerned, generally speaking it is unknown to our people.

## REVOLUTION AND LIBERATION WAR (1930–54)

Before, during the Tet festival, pictures and greetings written on red paper could be seen stuck at entrance doors of palaces as well as tiny thatched huts. Today these greetings and pictures are replaced by slogans urging struggle and labor, such as: "Intensify the Emulation Movement for Armed Struggle, Production, and Economic Development!" "The War of Resistance Will Win!" "Combat Bureaucracy, Corruption, and Waste!" "The National Construction Will Certainly Be Crowned with Success!"

During the Tet festival, people are clad in their most beautiful garments. In every family the most delicious foods are prepared. Religious services are performed in front of the ancestral altars. Visits are paid between kith and kin to exchange greetings. Grown-ups give gifts to children; civilians send presents to soldiers. In short, it can be said that this is a spring festival.

Before telling you the situation of Viet-Nam, may I send you and all your comrades my warmest greetings!

*Collusion Between the Aggressors*
Let us review Viet-Nam's situation in 1951.

After their defeat in the China–Viet-Nam border campaign in October 1950—the greatest reverse they had suffered in the whole history of their colonial wars, which involved for them the loss of five provinces at one time (Cao Bang, Lang Son, Lao Cai, Thai Nguyen, and Hoa Binh)—the French colonialists began the year 1951 with the dispatch of General de Lattre de Tassigny to Viet-Nam.

They resorted to total war. Their maneuver was to consolidate the Bao Dai puppet government, organize puppet troops, and redouble spying activities. They set up no man's lands of from 5 to 10 kilometers wide around areas under their control and strengthened the Red River delta by a network of 2,300 bunkers. They stepped up mopping-up operations in our rear, applied the policy of annihilation and wholesale destruction of our manpower and potential resources by killing our compatriots, devastating our countryside, burning our rice fields, etc. In a word, they followed the policy of "using Vietnamese to fight Vietnamese and nursing the war by means of warfare."

It is on orders and with the assistance of their masters, the American interventionists, that the French colonialists performed the above-mentioned deeds.

Among the first Americans now living in Viet-Nam (of course, in areas under French control) there are a fairly noteworthy spy, Donald Heath, ambassador accredited to the puppet government, and a general, head of the U.S. military mission.

In September 1951, de Lattre de Tassigny went to Washington to make his report and beg for aid. In October, General Collins, Chief of Staff of the U.S. Army, came to Viet-Nam to inspect the French Expeditionary Corps and puppet troops.

In order to show their American masters that U.S. aid is used in a worthwhile manner at present as well as in the future, in November, de Lattre de Tassigny attacked the chief town of Hoa Binh province. The result of this "shooting offensive," which the reactionary press in France and in the world commented on uproariously, was that the Viet-Nam People's Army held the overwhelming majority of enemy troops tightly between two prongs and annihilated them. But this did not

prevent de Lattre de Tassigny and his henchmen from hulla-
balooing that they had carried the day!

At the very beginning of the war, the Americans supplied
France with money and armaments. To take an example, 85
per cent of weapons, war materials, and even canned food captured by our troops were labeled "Made in U.S.A." This aid
had been stepped up all the more rapidly since June, 1950,
when the United States began interfering in Korea. American
aid to the French invaders consisted of airplanes, boats, trucks,
military outfits, napalm bombs, etc.

Meanwhile, the Americans compelled the French colonialists to step up the organization of four divisions of puppet
troops, with each party footing half the bill. Of course, this
collusion between the French and American aggressors and the
puppet clique was fraught with contradictions and contentions.

The French colonialists are now landed in a dilemma: either
they receive U.S. aid and be then replaced by their American
"allies," or they receive nothing and be then defeated by the
Vietnamese people. To organize the puppet army by means of
press-ganging the youth in areas under their control would be
tantamount to swallowing a bomb when one is hungry: A day
will come when at last the bomb bursts inside. However, not
to organize the army on this basis would mean instantaneous
death for the enemy because even the French strategists have
to admit that the French Expeditionary Corps grows thinner
and thinner and is on the verge of collapse.

Furthermore, U.S. aid is paid for at a very high price. In
the enemy-held areas, French capitalism is swept aside by
American capitalism. American concerns like the Petroleum Oil
Corporation, the Caltex Oil Corporation, the Bethlehem Steel
Corporation, the Florida Phosphate Corporation, and others
monopolize rubber, ores, and other natural resources of our
country. U.S. goods swamp the market. The French reactionary
press, especially Le Monde, is compelled to acknowledge sadly
that French capitalism is now giving way to U.S. capitalism.

The U.S. interventionists have nurtured the French aggressors and the Vietnamese puppets, but the Vietnamese people do not let anybody delude and enslave them.

People's China is our close neighbor. Her brilliant example gives us a great impetus. Not long ago the Chinese people defeated the U.S. imperialists and won a historical victory. The execrated Chiang Kai-shek was swept from the Chinese mainland, though he is more cunning than the placeman Bao Dai. Can the U.S. interventionists, who were drummed out of China and are now suffering heavy defeats in Korea, conquer Viet-Nam? Of course not!

*Atrocious Crimes of the U.S. Interventionists*
Defeated on the battlefield, the French colonialists retaliated upon unarmed people and committed abominable crimes. The following are a few examples:

As everywhere in the enemy-controlled areas, on October 15, 1951, at Ha Dong, the French soldiers raided the youths even in the streets and press-ganged them into the puppet army. And there as everywhere, the people protested against such acts. Three young girls stood in a line across the street in front of the trucks packed with the captured youngsters to prevent them from being sent to concentration camps. . . . The French colonialists revved the engines and, in a split second, our three young patriots were run over.

In October 1951, the invaders staged a large-scale raid in Thai Binh province. They captured more than 16,000 people— most of whom were old people, women, and children—and penned them in a football field surrounded by barbed wire and guarded by soldiers and dogs. For four days, the captives were exposed in the sun and rain, ankle-deep in mud. They received no food and no drinking water. Over 300 of them died of exhaustion and disease.

The relatives and friends who brought food to the captives were roughly manhandled, and the food was thrown into the mud and trampled under foot. M. Phac, a surgeon of seventy who tried to save the victims' lives, was shot dead on the spot, as were a number of pregnant women.

Incensed by these barbarous acts, the townsfolk staged a strike and sought ways and means to help the internees. The determination of the population compelled the French colonialists to let the food in, but on order of Colonel Charton of the French Expeditionary Corps, it was declared a donation from the United States.

On October 28, 1951, Le Van Lam, twenty-seven, from Ha Coi, a puppet soldier who had been saved from drowning by an old fisherman at Do Son, said after he had recovered consciousness: "On October 27, the French embarked me, as well as 100 other wounded men, on board a steamer, saying they would send us to Saigon for medical attention. In the night, when the ship was in the offing, they threw us one by one into the water. Fortunately, I managed to snatch at a piece of floating wood and swam landward. I was unconscious when I was saved."

The following is the confession of Chaubert, a French captain captured at Tu Ky on November 25, 1951: "The French High Command gave us an order to destroy everything in order to transform this region into a desert. This order was observed to the letter. Houses were burned down. Animals and poultry were killed. Havoc was wrought to gardens and plants and trees hewn down. Rice fields and crops were set afire. Many days on end, black smoke covered the sky and there was not a single soul alive, except the French soldiers. The conflagration lasted until November 25, when the People's Army unexpectedly attacked and annihilated our unit."

The examples quoted above can be counted by the thousands and are sufficient proof to substantiate the essence of the French colonialists' and U.S. interventionists' "civilization."

*Achievements Recorded by the Democratic Republic of Viet-Nam*
In 1951, the Vietnamese people made a big stride forward. In
the political field, the founding of the Viet-Nam Workers'
Party, the amalgamation of the Viet Minh and Lien Viet, and
the setting up of the Committee of Action for Viet-Nam, Cambodia, and Laos greatly consolidated the unity and enhanced
the confidence of the Vietnamese people. They strengthened
the alliance between the three brother countries in their struggle against the common enemies—the French colonialists and
the U.S. interventionists—in order to realize their common
goal, i.e., national independence.

So we were able to frustrate the enemy's policy of divide
and rule.

In the economic field, the National Bank of Viet-Nam
has been established, our finance is placed under centralized
and unified supervision, and communications have been
reorganized.

Formerly, we demolished roads to check the enemy's advance; at present, we repair them to drive the enemy to an
early defeat. Formerly, we did our utmost to sabotage roads;
now we encounter great difficulties in mending them, but have
managed to complete our work quite rapidly. This is a hard job,
especially when we lack machines. However, thanks to the enthusiasm and sacrificing spirit of our people, this work was carried through. To avoid enemy air raids, it was done at night by
workers often knee-deep in water. In the bright torchlight, hundreds of men, women, and young people dug the earth to fill
the gaps in the roads, broke stones, felled trees, and built
bridges. As in any other work, the workers' enthusiasm was
roused by emulation drives. I am sure that you would be astonished to see teams of old volunteers of from sixty to eighty
years competing with teams of young workers.

Here it must be pointed out that in the free zone, most of
the work is done at night—children go to school, housewives
go to market, and guerrillas go to attack the enemy.

Great successes have been achieved in the elaboration of

the agricultural tax. Formerly, the peasants were compelled to pay taxes of various kinds and make many other contributions; nowadays, they have only to pay a uniform tax in kind. Households whose production does not exceed 60 kilograms of paddy per year are exempt from the tax. Households who harvest greater quantities have to pay a graduated tax. Generally speaking, the taxes to be paid do not exceed 20 per cent of the total value of the annual production. To collect taxes in time, the Party, the National United Front, and the Government have mobilized a great number of cadres to examine the new tax from the political and technical points of view. After their study, these cadres go to the countryside and hold talks and meetings to exchange views with the peasants and explain to them the new taxation policy.

After this preparatory period, the peasants of both sexes appoint a committee composed of representatives of the administration and various people's organizations, whose duty it is to estimate the production of each household and fix the rate to be paid after approval by a Congress in which all the peasants take part.

This reform was welcomed by the population, which enthusiastically took part in this tax collection.

The agricultural tax has been established simultaneously with the movement for increased production. At present, the Government possesses adequate stocks of foodstuffs to cater for the soldiers and workers. So we have thwarted the enemy's cunning plot of blockading us to reduce us to starvation.

As far as mass education is concerned, in 1951 we scored worthwhile results. Though great difficulties were created by the war, such as frequent changes of school site, schooling at night time, lack of school requisites, the number of schools rose from 2,712 in 1950 to 3,591 in 1951, with an attendance of 293,256 and 411,038 pupils, respectively.

In South Viet-Nam, the situation is all the more ticklish. There, the free zones exist everywhere, but they are not safe. Children go to their classrooms—in fact, there are only single

classrooms and not schools in the strict meaning of the word
—with the same vigilance that their fathers and brothers
display in guerrilla fighting. At present, there are in South Viet-
Nam 3,332 classrooms, with an attendance of 111,700 pupils.

The liquidation of illiteracy is actively undertaken. In the
first half of 1951, there were in Zone III, Zone V, and Viet Bac
Zone 324,000 people who were freed from illiteracy and
350,000 others who began learning. During the same period,
illiteracy was wiped out in 53 villages and 3 districts (one district is composed of from 5 to 10 villages). People's organizations opened 837 classes attended by 9,800 public employees.
The Party, National United Front, Government, the General
Confederation of Labor, and the Army have periodically opened
short-term (about one week) political training courses.

In short, great efforts are being made in mass education.

*Development and Strengthening of International Relations*
In 1951, the relations between the Vietnamese people and foreign countries were developed and strengthened.

For the first time, in 1951, various delegations of the Vietnamese people visited great People's China and heroic Korea.
Through these visits, the age-old friendship between our three
countries has been strengthened.

The delegation of Vietnamese youth to the Youth Festival
in Berlin, the delegation of the Viet-Nam General Confederation of Labor to the Congress of the World Federation of Trade
Unions in Warsaw, and the delegation to the World Peace
Conference in Vienna have returned to Viet-Nam filled with
confidence and enthusiasm. At various meetings and in the
press, members of these delegations told the Vietnamese people
of the tremendous progress they had witnessed in the people's
democracies and the warm friendship shown by the brother
countries to the Vietnamese people who are struggling for national independence and freedom.

Those delegates who had the chance of visiting the Soviet
Union are overjoyed because they can tell us of the great tri-

umph of socialism and the ever-growing happiness enjoyed by the Soviet people. Upon returning from the Youth Festival, Truong Thi Xin, a young woman worker, said, "The youth in the Soviet Union received us most affectionately during our stay in their great country."

The talks held by these delegates are living lessons most useful for the inculcation of internationalism.

"Peace in Viet-Nam!" and "Withdraw Foreign Troops from Viet-Nam!" were the claims formulated in a resolution passed by the plenary session of the World Peace Council held in Vienna, claims which have given great enthusiasm to the Vietnamese people.

## The Interventionists Suffer Defeat After Defeat

Last year was a year of brilliant victories for our People's Army, and a year of heavy defeats and losses in men and materials for the invaders. According to incomplete figures and excluding the China–Viet-Nam border campaign in October 1950, during which the French Army lost more than 7,000 men (annihilated and captured), in 1951 the enemy lost 37,700 officers and men (P.O.W.'s included). He will never forget the Vinh Yen–Phuc Yen campaign (North Viet-Nam) in January last year, during which he received a deadly blow from the Viet-Nam People's Army. He will not forget the strategic points of Quang Yen (Road Number 18), Ninh Binh, Phu Ly, and Nghia Lo in North Viet-Nam, where our valiant fighters crushed him to pieces in March, May, June, and September. But the most striking battle was waged in December in the Hoa Binh region, which left to the enemy no more than 8,000 men alive. Our heroic militiamen and guerrillas who operate in the north, center, and south of Viet-Nam have caused heavy losses to the enemy. From the outbreak of the war of aggression unleashed by the French, their Expeditionary Corps has lost 170,000 men (killed, wounded, and captured), while the Vietnamese regular army and guerrilla units have grown stronger and stronger.

Guerrilla warfare is now being intensified and expanded in

the enemy-controlled areas, especially in the Red River delta. Our guerrillas are particularly active in the provinces of Bac Giang, Bac Ninh, Ha Nam, Ninh Binh, Ha Dong, Hung Yen, and Thai Binh.

Early in October, 1951, fourteen enemy regiments carried out a large-scale raid in the districts of Duyen Ha, Hung Nhan, and Tien Hung. From October 1 to October 4, our guerrillas waged violent battles. In three points (Cong Ho, An My, and An Binh), 500 French soldiers were annihilated. All these victories were due to the heroism of our soldiers and guerrillas and to the sacrifice of the entire Vietnamese people. In each campaign, tens of thousands of voluntary workers of both sexes helped the armymen. As a rule, they worked in very hard conditions, in pelting rain, on muddy and steep mountain tracks, etc.

Thousands of patriots have left the enemy-controlled areas to take part in the above-mentioned task. It is worth mentioning here that the youth have set up many shock units.

The following example will illustrate the great patriotism and initiative of our people:

In the Hoa Binh campaign, our army had to cross the Lo River. French troops were stationed along the right bank, while their boats continually patrolled the river. In these conditions how could the crossing be made without the enemy's noticing it?

But the local population managed to find a way. In a locality some dozen kilometers from the Lo River, they called in a great number of craft and, through roundabout paths, carried them to the spot assigned at scheduled time. As soon as our troops had crossed the river, the inhabitants carried their craft back so as to keep secrecy and avoid enemy air raids.

Here I wish to speak of the women who support the soldiers. Most of them are old peasants; many have grandchildren. They help our officers and men and nurse the wounded as if they were their own sons. Like "goddesses protecting our lives," they take care of those of our fighters who work in enemy-controlled areas. Their deeds are highly esteemed and appreciated.

As is said above, the French colonialists are compelled to set up puppet troops in order to offset the losses suffered by the French Expeditionary Corps. But this is a dangerous method for the enemy.

First, everywhere in the enemy-held areas, the population struggles against the enemy's raiding and coercing the youth into their army. Second, the people so mobilized have resorted to actions of sabotage. Take an example: Once, the Quisling governor of Tonkin, styling himself "elder of the youth," paid a visit to the officers' training school of second degree at Nam Dinh. On hearing this news, the cadets prepared in his honor a "dignified" reception by writing on the school wall the slogans "Down with Bao Dai!" and "Down with the Puppet Clique!" while Bao Dai's name was given to the lavatory.

During this visit, the cadets made so much noise that the governor was unable to speak. They put to him such a question as, "Dear elder! Why do you want to use us as cannon fodder for the French colonialists?" A group of cadets contemplated giving him a thrashing, but he managed to take French leave like a piteous dog.

Many units of the puppet army secretly sent letters to President Ho Chi Minh, saying that they were waiting for a propitious occasion to "pass over to the side of the Fatherland" and that they were ready to "carry out any orders issued by the Resistance, despite the danger they might encounter."

*Complete Failure of the French Colonialists*
As soon as de Lattre de Tassigny set foot in Viet-Nam early in 1951, he boasted of the eventual victories of the French troops.

After his defeat and disillusion at the beginning of 1952, he realized that he would soon meet with complete failure.

The fate of the French colonialists' policy brought misgivings to the most reactionary circles in France.

In the October 22, 1951, issue of *Information* Daladier, one of the "criminals" in the Munich affair, wrote:

> Delving into the real reason of our desperate financial situation, we shall see that one of the underlying causes was lack of ripe consideration of our policy over Indo-china. . . . In 1951, an expenditure of as much as 330,000 million francs was officially reserved for the Indochinese budget. Due to the constant rise in the prices of commodities and increase in the establishments of the French Expeditionary Corps, which number 180,000 at present, it should be expected that in 1952 this expenditure will increase by 100,000 million francs. We have the impression that the war in Indo-china has caused exceedingly grave danger to our financial as well as military situation. . . . It is impossible to foresee a rapid victory in a war which has lasted five years and is in many ways reminiscent of the war unleashed by Napoleon against Spain and the expedition against Mexico during the Second Empire.

In its issue of December 13, 1951, the paper *Intransigeant* wrote:

> France is paralyzed by the war in Indochina. We have gradually lost the initiative of operation because our main forces are now pinned down in the plains of North Viet-Nam. . . . In 1951, 330,000 million francs were earmarked for the military budget of Indochina, while according to the official figures, our expenditure amounted to over 350,000 million. A credit of 380,000 million francs will be allotted to the 1952 budget, but in all probability the mark of 500,000 million will be reached. Such is the truth. . . . Whenever France tried to take some action, well, she immediately realized that she was paralyzed by the war in Indochina.

In its issue of December 16, 1951, *France Tireur* wrote:

> General Vo Nguyen Giap's battalions, which are said to
> have been annihilated and to have a shattered morale,
> are now launching counter-offensives in the Hanoi re-
> gion. . . . It is more and more obvious that the policy
> we have followed up to the present time has failed. To-
> day it is clear that it has met with complete failure.

The following excerpt is from a letter sent to his colleagues
by Captain Gazignoff of the French Expeditionary Corps, captured by us on January 7, 1952, in the Hoa Binh battle:

> Taken prisoner a few days ago, I am very astonished at
> the kind and correct attitude of the Viet-Nam People's
> armymen toward me. . . . The Vietnamese troops will
> certainly win final victory, because they struggle for a
> noble ideal, a common cause, and are swayed by a
> self-imposed discipline. It is as clear as daylight that the
> Viet-Nam People's Army will crush the French Expe-
> ditionary Corps, but it is ready to receive any of us who
> will pass over to its side.
>
> French officers, noncommissioned officers, and men
> who want to go over to the Viet-Nam People's Army
> will be considered as friends and will be set free.

*The Vietnamese People Will Win*

In 1952, Viet-Nam will embark on a program which includes
the following points: to buckle down to production work and
consolidate the national economy; to struggle and annihilate
the enemy's forces; to intensify guerrilla warfare; to expose by
all means the enemy's policy of "using the Vietnamese to fight
the Vietnamese, and nursing the war by means of warfare"; to
closely link patriotism to internationalism; energetically to combat bureaucracy, corruption, and waste.

The patriotism and heroism of the Vietnamese people allow us to have firm confidence in final victory.

The Vietnamese people's future is as bright as the sun in spring. Overjoyed at the radiance of the sun in spring, we shall struggle for the splendid future of Viet-Nam, for the future of democracy, world peace, and socialism. We triumph at the present time, we shall triumph in the future, because our path is enlightened by the great Marxist–Leninist doctrine.

# Edward Geary Lansdale

*Assigned as Chief of the CIA's Saigon Military Mission with the task of assisting the South Vietnamese in their struggle against the Viet Minh, Colonel Lansdale uses the cover of the Military Assistance Advisory Group. When Hollywood producer Joseph Mankiewicz seeks background information for his version of* The Quiet American, *Lansdale writes this letter. It is obvious that Colonel Lansdale has a noticeable effect on the final version of the movie.*

## LETTER TO JOSEPH MANKIEWICZ

*Headquarters*
*Military Assistance Advisory Group*
*Saigon, Vietnam*

17 March 1956

Mr. Joseph L. Mankiewicz
Figaro Incorporated
1270 Sixth Avenue
New York, New York

Dear Mr. Mankiewicz,
   During your visit to Saigon, I promised to send you answers to some of your questions about "The Quiet American." Some

The editor is indebted to Professor George C. Herring for this and the following Lansdale letters. This letter is located in Box 35, the Edward G. Lansdale Collection, Hoover Institution Archives, Stanford University, California.

of the answers are given below, and I think I've figured out a helpful way for you to get answers to any other questions that come to you.

"The Quiet American" became a much sought after book in Saigon, so it took a little quiet larceny to obtain a copy long enough to read it. I have, and can see how it begs to be put on film. Also, I can see how your handling of the plot is thoroughly justified.

First of all, a few facts for you.

Trinh Minh Thé changed from Chief of Staff of the Cao Dai Army to Chief of the Quoc Gia Lien Minh, his "National Resistance Front," on 7 June 1951; as Cao Dai Chief of Staff, he commanded forces known as "suppletifs" of the French Expeditionary Corps, which received pay, arms, and other munitions from the French for the fight against the Vietminh. He made his Lien Minh headquarters at Nui Ba Den, or "Black Lady Mountain" (the heavily wooded mountain that sticks up all alone on the plain right next to the seat of the Cao Dai at Tayninh). His Lien Minh platform was pro an independent Vietnam and both anti-Vietminh and anti-French colonialism; these Lien Minh ideas strike a chord of memory of our own days prior to 1776, particularly of some of the ideas of our Committees of Correspondence.

The explosion in front of the Continental Hotel took place on 9 January 1952. One account of the incident states that the explosion was believed to be caused by a charge of approximately 20 kilos of French melenite (this explosive is commonly called "plastic" due to its plasticity), wrapped in prima cord, placed in the trunk of a Citroen "15CV" and detonated by some type of time device, possibly an ordinary time pencil. Six to nine people were killed by the explosion and about eighteen were injured. Although the exact source of the "plastic" is not known, it seems probable that General Thé obtained it from the French Expeditionary Corps originally, since the French handled the supply of all munitions to our side. U.S. military supplies were handled by the French entirely in Vietnam.

General Thé claimed credit for this explosion via a broadcast over the National Resistance Front radio. I never discussed this particular incident with him, so I don't know for certain sure whether this claim was fact or not, although he readily admitted to other guerrilla-type actions, as I told you, which make this claim probably true. However, I doubt if more than one or two Vietnamese now alive know the real truth of the matter, and they certainly aren't going to tell it to anyone, even a "quiet" American. The French and others have put reports together and have concluded that Thé did it.

Since General Thé is quite a national hero for his fight against the Binh Xuyen in 1955, and in keeping with your treatment of this actually having been a Communist action, I'd suggest that you just go right ahead and let it be finally revealed that the Communists did it after all, even to faking the radio broadcast (which would have been easy to do). As a statement obtained as an admission by one of the Vietminh involved, I doubt that even French Sûreté or military intelligence personnel who were here at the time would do more than take another look at their old reports and wonder if maybe that might not be the way it happened after all.

So far, John Gates and the others have been unable to confirm the existence of "diolacton." All of us are convinced that this is a literary invention.

I noticed in the book that Greene kept mentioning "tri-shaws" and cannot recall if this came up in our conversation. As you no doubt found out quickly in Saigon, these are not called "tri-shaws" but are known as "pousse-pousse" or "cyclo-pousse," In some French writing about modern Saigon, this wondrous vehicle is also called "moto-pousse," although I've never heard them spoken of as such in Saigon itself.

We discussed what sort of a job Pyle might have had out here. If he were out here on a foundation grant from some U.S. foundation, he could easily be doing a study of the government administrative system. At that time, the Vietnamese government was administering all territory not actively in the hands of the Vietminh, right up to the Chinese border in Tonkin. This government, of course, was subject to Vietminh action against it and, if a person such as Pyle should stumble into a Vietminh plot against it, it would be logical that he would be eliminated for endangering the plot or for knowing too much or even for revenge.

Now, about some help for you in answering other questions. Mr. Arthur Arundel, who served with me in Vietnam in 1954–55 while he was on active duty as a captain in the U.S. Marine Corps, is now in the U.S. and visits New York from time to time. I've written him, asking him to look you up for me, and to give you any help he can. He's bright and has done a lot of study on Vietnam. I feel sure you will take to Nick (Mr. Arundel's nickname). He may have called upon you by the time you receive this.

If there's anything else that we can do to help from here, please let me know. We all enjoyed the opportunity to become acquainted with you, and wish you all success in your work.

Sincerely,

EDWARD G. LANSDALE
Colonel               USAF

P.S.: Since writing the above, I happened to have a chat with a Vietnamese friend who was in Saigon at the time of the explosion and was in a position to know the facts. He tells a slightly different version of the story. According to him, General Thé used two bombs (duds) which the French had dropped on his forces during air attacks on Nui Ba Den (near Tayninh). He rigged each one up with a timing device and installed them in a sealed compartment in the gas tanks of two stolen cars, which were left parked in front of the Continental and the Prefecture. They blew up within seconds of each other.

# Renny Christopher

*Renny Christopher's Ph.D. dissertation was on the Vietnam War. She reviews films for* Matrix Women's News Magazine *and has published numerous articles on the war. The plot summary of and commentary about the film version of the novel is one of hundreds of entries in the massive and remarkable book* Vietnam War Films. *Unfortunately, the film version of* The Quiet American *is not yet available on videotape.*

## THE QUIET AMERICAN

1958, U.S.A. United Artists. Black and White, 120 mins.

Director: Joseph L. Mankiewicz; Producer: Joseph L. Mankiewicz; Screenplay: Joseph L. Mankiewicz, based on the novel by Graham Greene; Director of Photography: Robert Krasker; Editor: William Hornbeck; Music: Mario Nascimbene; Cast: Michael Redgrave (Thomas Fowler), Audie Murphy (Alden Pyle), Giorgia Moll (Phuong), Claude Dauphin (Insp. Vigot), Richard Loo (Mr. Heng), Bruce Cabot (Bill Granger), Kerima (Miss Hei).

From *Vietnam War Films: Over 600 Feature, Made-for-TV, Pilot and Short Movies, 1939–92, From the United States, Vietnam, France, Belgium, Australia, Hong Kong, South Africa, Great Britain and Other Countries*, copyright ©1994 by Jean-Jacques Malo and Tony Williams. Jefferson, N.C.: McFarland & Company, Inc., Publishers. Reprinted by permission of the publisher.

*Themes and key words:*
French Indochina war; C.I.A.; reporter; flashback.

*Synopsis:*
The body of Alden Pyle, an American, is found floating in a river in Saigon. Fowler, an English journalist, is questioned regarding Pyle's death along with Phuong, Pyle's fiancée. Flashback to Fowler and Pyle first meeting. Pyle works for an organization that is a C.I.A. cover. He's looking for a "third force" between the communists and the colonialists for the U.S. to back. Pyle, Fowler and others visit a Cao Dai festival at a temple outside Saigon; due to a problem with a car, Fowler and Pyle ride back together. They run out of gas and are stranded in a guard post along the road. When they are attacked by the Viet Minh, Pyle saves Fowler's life. Fowler is tipped off that Pyle is involved in importing plastic; he finds evidence at the shop of a Mr. Heng. A bomb in the shape of a bicycle pump goes off in a square, killing many civilians. Phuong leaves Fowler, who is married, for Pyle, who will marry her. Pyle travels into the combat zone, where Fowler is reporting on the war, to tell Fowler that he intends to propose to Phuong. Heng, a communist, convinces Fowler to betray Pyle so they can kill him. After Pyle's death Insp. Vigot, a French policeman, proves to Fowler that Pyle was innocent of the bombings—he has been framed by Heng, a communist, with plastic for New Year's toys.

*Comments:*
Graham Greene's novel indicts the American presence in Vietnam, because of the Americans' ignorance of the country's history and politics, and their propensity, symbolized by Pyle, to get innocent people killed. Joseph Mankiewicz's film changes all that. By making several alterations in key details, the story is transformed from being anti-American to being anti-communist.

In the novel, Pyle works for the Economic Mission—a clear C.I.A. cover, and not a benign one. Under its cover, he is importing plastic into Vietnam and supplying it to Gen. Thé, a Cao Daist with a private army which Pyle hopes to make into his "third force." He quite indiscriminately uses it to bomb civilians. In the film, Pyle works for "Friends for Free Asia"— a much more noble-sounding fictitious organization. From the book's upper-class New England Harvard boy, Pyle is transformed into Audie Murphy, an aw-shucks, crew-cut type from Texas. In the novel, Granger is a loud, obnoxious journalist, the noisy and unpleasant American contrast to the quiet Pyle; in the film, he is politically engaged, a critic of inhumane French military tactics, and he is not a drunk. In the novel, Fowler writes his Catholic wife asking for a divorce, and his paper, asking to stay on in Vietnam, in order to keep Phuong. In the film, he lies to Phuong about having done so. In one of the novel's most devastating scenes, Pyle and Fowler meet in the square after the bombing; this is the incident that convinces Fowler to betray Pyle. In the book, Pyle gets blood on his shoe, and wanders off ineffectually; in the film, Pyle cuts off Fowler's lecture with the line, "Why don't you shut up and help someone?" rushing off with a medical bag in his hand. The police believe that Heng, the communist, and not the "third force," is responsible for the bombing. The film, made several years after the book was published, makes a bow to history—Pyle has met an "independent Vietnamese" living in New Jersey while he was at Princeton (not Harvard!). Pyle is scouting out Gen. Thé as an advance man for the New Jersey Vietnamese, clearly meant to represent Ngo Dinh Diem. In the novel, Fowler betrays Pyle by reading a passage of Kipling—"I can pay for the damage if ever so bad./ So pleasant it is to have money, heigh ho!" In the film, Fowler reads a passage about jealousy from Othello, thus suggesting that his motive for betraying Pyle is jealousy over Phuong, which, in the novel, it expressly is not. Aside from its political transformation of Greene's novel, the film is visually interesting, because it was filmed on location in Saigon, one of very few American films to be made in Vietnam. Although its style has become outdated, it's still quite watchable.

# Edward Geary Lansdale

*When the movie version of* The Quiet American *comes out, Colonel Lansdale is one of its strongest supporters, as shown in these two letters written on the same day. Ngo Dinh Diem is President of South Vietnam and a good friend of Lansdale's; General O'Daniel has recently returned from his duties as Chief of the Military Assistance Advisory Group (MAAG), Vietnam.*

## TWO LETTERS

28 October 1957

Dear President Ngo Dinh Diem:

Just a little note to tell you that I have seen the motion picture, "The Quiet American," and that I feel it will help win more friends for you and Vietnam in many places in the world where it is shown. When I first mentioned this motion picture to you last year, I had read Mr. Mankiewicz's "treatment" of the story and had thought it an excellent change from Mr. Greene's novel of despair. Mr. Mankiewicz had done much more with the picture itself, and I now feel that you will be very pleased with the reactions of those who see it.

Courtesy of Professor George C. Herring. Located in Box 39, the Edward G. Lansdale Collection, Hoover Institution Archives, Stanford University, California.

From what I see in the newspapers, you continue to be a very busy man. Please do not forget to take a rest now and then. I hope you are using the cottage at Long Hai when you can; it's good for you. I look back to its restfulness with considerable longing from Washington!

With warmest personal wishes for you, as always,

                                        Sincerely,

                                        EDWARD G. LANSDALE
                                        Colonel                    USAF

President Ngo Dinh Diem
Freedom Palace
Saigon, Vietnam

                                                    28 October 1957

Dear General O'Daniel:

Thanks to you, I attended the screening of "The Quiet American" in Washington last Thursday. It was quite an experience to see and listen to a mature approach to such recent events in Vietnam, and one so understanding of the things free men believe in.

I'm happy that you have been planning sponsorship of this picture by the American Friends of Vietnam. It's a natural association of ideas, with the way Mankiewicz treated the story —one that the American Friends can feel some pride in doing.

I understand, from your charming friend Mrs. Marx, that some of the American gals who were out in Vietnam when we were, had expressed some concern about getting some sort of government clearance on this. I feel that this is nonsense. However, I took the liberty of inviting a number of folks from practically all departments, agencies, and services concerned with psychological, political and security affairs to attend the screening—and they all seemed to enjoy it as much as I did.

Suggest that you don't let the question of security raise its head again.

Hope to see you on your next visit back this way, whether it's for the premiere or not. Sorry that the trip I was trying to use some influence to arrange just didn't get arranged—but you know that we dog-faced kiwis just don't give up ever.

Warmest and best regards to both you and Mrs. O'Daniel,

Sincerely,

EDWARD G. LANSDALE
Colonel                    USAF

General John W. O'Daniel
3443 Custis Street
San Diego 6, California

# Christopher Hawtree

*In addition to publishing numerous articles in periodicals, Christopher Hawtree has written a novel,* Lying Down, *has edited an anthology of pieces from the magazine* Night and Day, *and (with Charles Moore) has compiled* 1936, *a collection of essays from that year's* Spectator. *Here he supplies context and commentary for Greene's letter to* The Times *(London) about the movie, which is quoted below. Greene also referred to the film as "the later treachery of Joseph Mankiewicz" (Ways of Escape, p. 17).*

## CASE OF *THE QUIET AMERICAN*

To *The Times* / 29 January 1957

—Your report of 9 January from Saigon has only just overtaken me [at the Hotel Algonquin, New York]. It is certainly true that if a story is sold to Hollywood the author retains no control over the adaptation. But perhaps a Machiavellian policy is justified—one can trust Hollywood to overbid its hand. If such changes as your Correspondent describes have been made in the film of *The Quiet American* they will make only the more obvious the discrepancy between what the State Department would like the world to believe and what in fact happened in Vietnam. In that case, I can imagine some happy evenings of laughter not only in Paris but in the cinemas of Saigon.

"Hollywood's version will be a safe one—that of the triumphant emergence of the democratic forces in the young and independent state of Vietnam backed by the United States, accompanied by the downfall of British and French imperialists," *The Times*'s correspondent had written. "Though some commentators here [Saigon] are mildly shocked that Mr. Greene should permit this travesty of his work, others are saying 'it serves him right for writing such an anti-American book.' There is quite a controversy about it."

"I try to explain to my friends," Greene had told Alan Brien (*Evening Standard*, 25 January 1957), "that once you sell a book to a company, it's out of your control. You can't spend all your life in film studios trying to keep your work intact." And, in an interview with Thomas Wiseman (*Evening Standard*, 24 August 1956), he said: "I don't suppose they can film it in the way it is written. They'll probably make it so that it looks as if the American was being bamboozled all the time by the Communists or somebody." Wasn't it unfair to Americans? "Oh, I don't know. Some of those bombs that went off in Vietnam, it was generally thought that the Americans were behind that. It's very dangerous writing in the first-person. Everybody thinks I am Fowler—well, I share some of his views about the Americans. But I'm not as bitter about them as he is. I didn't have my girl stolen by an American."

One of the film's cast, Michael Redgrave, wrote to *The Times*; his letter was printed below the author's, and said that the report was speculation: "Most of these differences can safely be left, so far as I am concerned, to other arbiters, when the film is completed and released, which is after all the normal time for such assessment; but as the only English member of the cast I would like to assure the many admirers of the novel, and a great many more people as well, that in no way is the 'downfall of French and British imperialists' injected into the film-translation of Mr. Greene's novel.

"People may travel half-way round the world and still get things wrong, but a film-unit and cast which do so are not content merely to 'take views of Saigon and the surrounding countryside,' as your Correspondent condescendingly puts it, and move on 'when sufficient local colour has been gathered.' They may surely be credited, at least for the time being, with a desire to get things right. It does not ease a difficult task to know that before the start so many people have been assured by 'the man on the spot' that the whole conception is a 'travesty.'"

Greene would later regard the film, adapted, produced and directed by Joseph Mankiewicz, as "a complete travesty" and "that film was a real piece of political dishonesty. The film makes the American very wise and the Englishman completely the fool of the Communists. And the casting was appalling. The Vietnamese girl Phuong was played by an Italian." In an essay the following year, he wrote: "One could believe that the film was made deliberately to attack the book and its author. But the book was based on a closer knowledge of the Indo-China war than the American possessed and I am vain enough to believe that the book will survive a few years longer than Mr. Mankiewicz's incoherent picture."

# Jonathan Nashel

*Jonathan Nashel received his Ph.D. in history from Rutgers University in 1994. His dissertation is entitled "Edward Lansdale and the American Attempt to Remake Southeast Asia, 1945–1965." The excerpt that follows comes from the dissertation, an expanded version of which was read at the American Studies Association meeting in Nashville, Tennessee, in October 1994.*

## LANSDALE AND GREENE

Greene's responses to the growing American intervention in Vietnam become apparent in his characterization of Alden Pyle, and led to his battles with Edward Lansdale, a real-life representative of American interests in Southeast Asia. Lansdale was arguably the most infamous CIA agent of our time. His exploits in the Philippines and Vietnam after World War II have provided not only historians but also journalists, novelists, and filmmakers with material for their countless stories and myths. Throughout the cold war era and into the present they have responded to Lansdale's renown in managing third world revolutions and have helped to create his celebrity at home and abroad—that he became Oliver North's hero is indicative of the effect he had upon others. Central to the glamour that came to be associated with his name were his actions in first defeating the nationalist/revolutionary movement in the Philippines, the Hukbalahap (the People's Anti-Japanese Army), or "Huks," from 1950 to 1953. He not only worked closely with Ramon Magsaysay, the Philippine presidential leader, but assiduously promoted his leadership in both his home country and in Washington. By 1954 Lansdale's successes convinced the Dulles brothers—John Foster and Allen—to transfer him to the newly created country, South Vietnam. There, Lansdale's activities ranged from clandestine operations waged against Ho Chi Minh's Communist government in North Vietnam, to solidifying Ngo Dinh Diem's anti-communist rule in South Vietnam.[1]

The question of Greene's characterization of "Lansdale" in the novel revolves around the youthful, idealistic character, Alden Pyle.[2] While Greene consistently denied that he modeled Pyle after Lansdale, most commentators on the novel have assumed otherwise, given the number of similarities between the two characters. Even if we accept Greene's repudiation of any links between the two men, one cannot help but draw obvious parallels: Pyle is introduced in the novel as having "an unmistakably young and unused face"; he had a genuine desire to graft American institutions onto Vietnam ("he was determined . . . to do good, not to any individual person but to a country, a continent, a world . . . he was in his element now with the whole universe to improve"); and he was a true believer in the future of the American Century ("you two," Pyle informs Fowler about the British and French, "couldn't expect to win the confidence of the Asiatics. That was where America came in now with clean hands"). Finally, Pyle had an unshakable belief in and support of a "Third Force" within Vietnam.[3]

Each of these descriptions aptly describes Lansdale. Of these parallels it is third force that most closely links the two. The third force is in many ways the crux of the novel and illuminates why Greene spent a lifetime condemning U.S. foreign policy and why Lansdale became a "real" foe in Greene's political world. Greene did not invent the term "third force," but it became a catch-all phrase for any real or imagined independent political force wedded to neither communism nor colonialism, one that was pro-American in the optimistic self-projections of Americans like Lansdale. In Vietnam the term was used to distinguish such political/religious organizations as the Cao Dai movement (headed by General Thé), from the Ngo Dinh Diem's Can Lao party, and from Ho Chi Minh's communist party as well.

Furthermore, Pyle's championing of the third force, both publicly in conversations with Fowler, and covertly (Pyle supplies *plastique*—an explosive—to General Thé who uses it outside a Saigon hotel) parallels Lansdale's attempts to strengthen Thé's political and military power base. Fiction becomes fact in this case, for recently declassified documents disclose that Lansdale championed the idea of the third force at the same time Greene was writing the novel. In this case, Lansdale was involved in top-secret discussions within the American Joint Chiefs of Staff on the Cao Dai movement and the possibilities that this organization could be used as a psychological weapon against communism. In this particular memorandum, Thé's charisma, political strength, and ability to sustain a third force within Vietnam were not only assessed but deemed crucial to achieving victory in Vietnam. It is worth keeping in mind that even after Thé's death in 1955, Lansdale continued to attempt to remake Vietnam along "third force" lines.[4]

To Greene the propagation of a third force by Americans had a horribly corrosive impact upon the Vietnamese people; it weakened and corrupted the Vietnamese political system, and made it increasingly beholden to American largesse. The anti-communist element of the third force was linked to the ideology of modernization, an influential social science theory promulgated in American universities like Harvard, Princeton, and Michigan State, and acted upon in Southeast Asia by a host of U.S. government agencies after World War II. A close friend of both Lansdale's and Diem's was Wesley Fishel, a professor of political science at Michigan State University. He was a firm believer in modernization and wrote about it in numerous American periodicals—he titled one article "Vietnam's Democratic One Man Rule"—and continually tried to implement its core ideas in Vietnam.[5] Briefly, modernization theory described a series of economic and political strategies to combat communism in the third world which were widely discussed in both academic and popular journals. These became the type of popular "serious talk" favored by Americans when lecturing about the problems facing the world. In the hands of Greene, this American social science theory spoke universal truths to Pyle, and his propagation of it in support of the third force was one of the reasons why he was killed.[6]

Greene's most explicit critique of the third force takes place in a scene between Fowler and the French inspector Vigot immediately following the death of Pyle:

> "There it is on your shelf. *The Rôle of the West.* Who is this York Harding?"
> "He's the man you are looking for, Vigot. He killed Pyle—at long range."
> "I don't understand."
> "He's a superior sort of journalist—they call them diplomatic correspondents. He gets hold of an idea and then alters every situation to fit the idea. Pyle came out here full of York Harding's idea."[7]

Implied in this passage is a sense of Greene meting out the form of justice most appropriate to those who preach the virtues of a third force/modernization theory, since Pyle is actually killed by the Communists. Of interest to this discussion is that while historians and journalists have spent a great deal of time trying to definitively establish if Pyle was modeled on Lansdale, little has been done on the York Harding character. Like Pyle, he could easily be based upon an American figure of the time like Fishel or even Walt Rostow, the American economist from

Harvard who shared Lansdale's faith in the concept of the third force.

Rostow sought to write an antidote to Marx's *Communist Manifesto,* and that offered a creed by which modern societies could be built upon counter-revolution and market economies.[8] These theories were precisely those mouthed by Pyle's hero, York Harding. Lansdale had his differences with this "real" York Harding. While both remained convinced that American efforts to defeat the Communists in Vietnam would not be simple, Rostow always favored technological and military solutions, while Lansdale endorsed "people" solutions.[9] They both believed that a U.S. victory was possible in Vietnam if enough will was put into the matter, with "will" being the key component.[10]

As Fowler tells Pyle, "this Third Force—it comes out of a book, that's all," a moment that indicates Greene's own realism (or cynicism) about the applicability of the theory to the practice.[11] Later, an exchange between Pyle and Fowler allows Greene to explore the essence of America's mission in Vietnam, its illusions, and why it would inevitably be a disaster for all concerned. Fowler tells Pyle:

> "Sometimes the Viets have a better success with a megaphone than a bazooka. I don't blame them. They don't believe in anything either. You and your like are trying to make a war with the help of people who just aren't interested."
>
> "They don't want Communism."
>
> "They want enough rice," I [Fowler] said. "They don't want to be shot at. They want one day to be much the same as another. They don't want our white skins around telling them what they want."
>
> "If Indo-China goes . . ."
>
> "I know the record. Siam goes. Malaya goes. Indonesia goes. What does 'go' mean? If I believed in your God and another life, I'd bet my future harp against

your golden crown that in five hundred years there may
be no New York or London, but they'll be growing
paddy in these fields, they'll be carrying their produce
to market on long poles, wearing their pointed hats . . ."

"They'll be forced to believe what they are told, they
won't be allowed to think for themselves."

"That's a luxury. Do you think the peasant sits and
thinks of God and Democracy when he gets inside his
mud hut at night?"[12]

Fowler's last sentence sums up precisely what Pyle and many
Americans believed after World War II—that peasants did sit
in their huts and dream American dreams.[13] Based on these
assumptions, Pyle is able to remake complex peasant societies
into primitive reflections of American ideology in 1954; they
appear to him as the fertile yet still unformed foundations for
a country based upon American principles. In this passage
Greene is at his best in depicting the dangers of Americans
practicing cold war theory upon another people, and why the
assumptions of Pyle (a.k.a. "Lansdale") are not only faulty but
pervasively malignant.

Parallels between Pyle and Lansdale become even starker
when one takes into account Lansdale's 1961 memo about Vietnam and its eery mimicry of Pyle's lecturing style:

If Free Vietnam is won by the Communists, the remainder of Southeast Asia will be easy pickings for our
enemy. . . . A Communist victory also would be a major
blow to U.S. prestige and influence, not only in Asia
but throughout the world, since the world believes that
Vietnam has remained free only through U.S. help.
Such a victory would tell leaders of other governments
that it doesn't pay to be a friend of the U.S. . . .[14]

In this respect Pyle is Lansdale to the extent that both sought
to enact various "nation-building" efforts in Southeast Asia,

even if these realities resulted in having whole societies refashioned into American proxies. And Lansdale can easily be critiqued for not only acting imperially but for continuing to deny that he was doing so. In his mind his actions were benevolent, and the carnage caused by *plastique* or the perils of backing Diem against insurmountable odds were simply not considered relevant to the ends he sought to achieve. Greene's "real fiction" is evident here as well: both Lansdale and Pyle pursued their conception of American idealism and the nature of American modernity, regardless of its fatal consequences for so many of the Vietnamese people. It is these concrete policies that propelled Greene to expose such acts of American "benevolence," as well as to explore their roots.

Yet even with all of this background the question remains: was Pyle really modeled after Lansdale? Almost all writers about Lansdale have thought so, and then depending upon the author's politics, the novel was either praised or panned. Over time, efforts to definitely settle this question developed into something of a cottage industry. Greene and Lansdale were drawn into the dispute with each trying to outdo the other in their rejections and denunciations. In a 1966 letter to the *British Sunday Telegraph*, Greene declared:

> Just for the record, your correspondent . . . is completely wrong in thinking that I took General Lansdale as the model for *The Quiet American*. Pyle was a younger, more innocent and more idealistic member of the CIA. I would never have chosen Colonel Lansdale, as he then was, to represent the danger of innocence.[15]

As the vehemence of this letter makes clear, Greene's goal was to literally bury Lansdale and his beliefs; he certainly wanted no part in creating a legend of a man who he detested. And the fact that this mistaken identity persisted only increased Greene's anger. In 1975 Greene again returned to this question and wrote a letter to the same newspaper:

I grow tired of denying that there is any connection between my character Pyle in *The Quiet American* and General Lansdale, the American counter-insurgency expert whom I have never had the misfortune to meet. Pyle was an innocent and an idealist. I doubt whether your correspondent Mr. Beeston would so describe General Lansdale. He should not refer in this way to a book which he has obviously never read, but I hope at least he will read this letter. Other journalists please note.[16]

Greene's adamant denials can be taken at face value. Yet they did know one another, and curiously, a bit more than Greene let on. Years later Lansdale recounted the time he encountered Greene while meeting some of his friends:

The only time I ever saw Graham Greene, he was sitting on a hotel terrace with some French, in 1954, I guess it was. He was very close to the French. Peg and Tilman Durdin were a husband and wife writing team with *The New York Times.* . . . They were staying at the Continental Hotel. When I drove in there, some French officers were sitting out on the sidewalk terrace and Graham Greene was with them. There was a sizeable group—30 to 50—and they started booing me. I wasn't very popular with the French. Graham Greene said something . . . and Peg stuck out her tongue at him and said to him, "but we love him." Then she turned around and gave me a big hug and kiss. I said, "Well, I'm going to get written up someplace as a dirty dog." So I guess I made his book. I had a french poodle at the time and he was with me, in the car with me, and they commented about the dog.[17]

This recollection fits nicely with how one literary critic has judged Greene's method of writing: Judith Adamson argues that Greene "concentrated on particular incidents that caught his eye, adding to them by juxtaposing other points of view until the episode became visual metaphors for the history playing itself out before him."[18] If Adamson's "narrative of a narrative" is appropriate in this case, an argument can be made only for the metaphorical linking the two characters, especially when one considers how Greene later recalled how he came to write the novel:

> . . . the moment for The Quiet American struck as I was driving back to Saigon after spending the night with Colonel Leroy. . . . I shared a room that night with an American attached to an economic aid mission—the members were assumed by the French, probably correctly, to belong to the C.I.A. My companion bore no resemblance at all to Pyle, the quiet American of my story—he was a man of greater intelligence and less innocence, but he lectured me all the long drive back to Saigon on the necessity of finding a "third force" in Vietnam. I had never before come so close to the great American dream which was to bedevil affairs in the East as it was to do in Algeria.[19]

Greene's penchant for answering every real or imaginary slight against him (he wrote hundreds of "letter to the editor") only complicates matters; his denials take on the quality of "he doth protest too much." Added to this puzzle is the question of Lansdale and Thé: Lansdale freely admits that they worked closely together, and one historian has written of the period that there were "rumors that Thé had acquired his 'know-how' from agents of the American Central Intelligence Bureau [sic] who, in their desire to promote a third force, had provided the Cao Dai Colonel with some technical assistance in addition to moral support."[20] In any case, journalistic responses to the novel and to Lansdale's celebrity gradually built upon one another so that even if Greene did not use Lansdale to create the character of Pyle, it became a "fact" buried in the layers of his fame nonetheless. In the end it becomes virtually impossible to untangle the myths from the facts surrounding these events.

Although Lansdale never took part in this game of "Pyle as Lansdale," he seemed intrigued by the comparisons however unflattering they may have been. One journalist summarized Lansdale's response to this question in the following manner:

> "I felt that Greene was anti-American. . . . Greene knocked him [Pyle] off in the first chapter," General Lansdale laughed.[21]

Lansdale knew that his fame was partially linked to his association as the quintessential "quiet American," so his attempts to capitalize on this phenomenon whenever possible seem only natural for a man who so avidly sought access to power.

In other ways too Lansdale marketed his notoriety to good effect. Typical here was his address entitled "The True American"—a not too subtle play upon his reputation as the "quiet American." In this private session with both Philippine and American policy makers, Lansdale outlined why a series of problems that had recently developed between the two countries were not fatal to their "special relationship." Lansdale spoke reassuringly of the ties that bound the two countries, and spoke with passion on the need for Americans to understand the Filipino perspective; he knew the Filipino mind, he noted, for he had lived in the Philippines for years and was certainly no tourist. Typical of the Lansdale touch this relationship needed to be implemented by a special type of person, a "true" American, who:

> emerges as a larger-than-life image: a person of integrity, with the courage of his convictions, with competence in some technical field, with devotion to getting things done, and with Christian affection for his fellow man.[22]

JONATHAN NASHEL ·

Even Lansdale's rhetoric does not mask the imperialist tone. One might even add that a Nietzschean *übermensch* lurks not far under this idealist conception, especially when he concludes "the whole climate of relationships can brighten to permit us to have a teamwork with Filipinos really consonant with a United States which is the leading nation in the world."[23] In other words, this teamwork involved the continuation of the American presence in and power over the Philippines.

Years later when Lansdale returned to the question of Lansdale as Pyle, weariness of the entire affair had clearly set in and he answered a writer in the following manner: "I guess the most honest way to answer you is to say that I no longer care whether or not folks identify me with fictional characters. . . ." Yet in this very same letter, Lansdale once again writes about the entire ordeal in a way that raises more questions than it answers:

> Graham Greene once told someone, who later mentioned it to me, that he definitely did not have me in mind when he created the character, Alden Pyle. I sure hope not, since Pyle apparently unsexed himself by hanging around air-conditioned bathrooms.[24]

Of course, nowhere in the novel did Pyle "unsex" himself, so the question becomes then not one of a faulty memory— though this could play a part here—but one last swipe at Greene by Lansdale. Lansdale never forgot or forgave the man who so unsparingly attacked all that Lansdale believed in. And, perhaps the best way to answer this attack was to question Greene's manliness, his penchant for having homosexuals in his novels. For a man's man, Lansdale could probably think of no better retort.

To be sure, Lansdale was not alone in dismissing Greene's views of Vietnam and of America. The *Saturday Evening Post* found the British novelist's writings less than helpful in waging the cold war. In one editorial, entitled "To Get Rave Reviews Write an Anti-U.S.A. Novel," they condemned Greene's "neutralist" politics, and the *San Francisco Chronicle* hailed Lansdale in an article entitled the "Savvy American."[25] More importantly, underlying each of these attacks on Greene's reading of the cold war was the enthusiastic acceptance by all "proper" American publications that John Foster Dulles's famous dictum on the immoral quality to neutralism in waging the Cold War was correct—"us" or "them" permeates almost all of Washington's actions during this period.[26] And given the tenor of these times, Greene was clearly marked one of them, with the result that the American Government amassed a forty-five-page security file on him.[27]

Whether there were winners or losers in this entire affair really depends on how one keeps score; almost every single book that mentions Lansdale prefaces his actions abroad by declaring that he was the "quiet American." Greene's denials are hardly ever noted, even as Lansdale was forever encapsulated by the novelist as the American who got killed in Vietnam in the 1950s for meddling in other people's affairs.

## NOTES

1. Recent academic works on Lansdale include a flattering biography by Cecil Currey, *Edward Lansdale: The Unquiet American* (Boston, 1988), and a damning portrayal by Richard Drinnon, whose *Facing West: The Metaphysics of Indian-Hating and Empire Building* (New York, 1980) made Lansdale a central villain in American imperialism. Other renditions of Lansdale seem to multiply by the hour. See for instance, Zalin Grant's *Facing the Phoenix* (New York: Norton, 1991) or even the movies made by Prince Norodom Sihanouk in the 1960s where Sihanouk cast himself as the hero and triumphs over an American CIA agent called "Lansdale." Oliver Stone also has his "Lansdale" (the "General Y" character) in his recent film *JFK*. For a brief discussion of "General Y" as Lansdale, see Oliver Stone and Zachary Sklar, *JFK: The Book of the Film* (New York, 1992), 182–83.

    The question of the relationship between North and Lansdale is in Raymond Bonner, *Waltzing with a Dictator: The Marcoses and the Making of American Policy* (New York: Vintage, 1988), 34;

and "The Road from Laos to Nicaragua," *The Economist*, 3/7/87, 35. See Jonathan Nashel, "Edward Lansdale and the American Attempt to Remake Southeast Asia, 1945–1965" (Dissertation, Rutgers University, 1994) for a fuller discussion of these events.

2. The fact that Greene called his American character "Pyle" is of interest. It may be an allusion to one of the first Puritans in the New World, John Alden, who was one of the youngest males on the *Mayflower* and supposedly the first person to set foot on Plymouth Rock. Others believe that Pyle was simply shorthand for "pain in the ass." Cited in Kenneth Geist, *Pictures Will Talk: The Life and Films of Joseph L. Mankiewicz* (New York: Scribners, 1978), 268, n. 9.

3. Graham Greene, *The Quiet American* (New York: Viking Penguin, 1996), 25. A particularly good reading of Pyle is by William Chace: "He [Pyle] is not so much a 'child' as a 'liberal,' which to Greene is a person with a willed ignorance of the world. Pyle's innocence is dangerous. . . ." William Chace, "Spies and God's Spies: Greene's Espionage Fiction," in *Graham Greene: A Revaluation, New Essays,* Jeffrey Meyers, editor (New York: St. Martin's, 1990), 167. One must keep in mind that Greene was also an extremely well read and allusive writer. His description of Pyle as having an "unused" face may have been based on Herman Melville's description of the Devil in *The Confidence-Man: His Masquerade*: "His cheek was fair, his chin downy, his hair flaxen. . . ." (New York: Norton, 1971), 1.

4. Lansdale Papers, Hoover Institution, 4/4/52, 1990 declassified box. Later, Lansdale wrote a memo to the American Ambassador to Vietnam, Elsworth Bunker, 7/13/67, on the merits of a "third force." Here, Lansdale related a conversation he had with a longstanding Vietnamese political friend, Nguyen Ngoc Tho:

> Tho switched subjects abruptly by asking me about "a third party or force." I asked him in turn what he was talking about. He grinned and said the local press was publishing hints that I was engineering the forming of a "third party or third force," but was quite mysterious about the names of Vietnamese involved. I told Tho that this was the first I'd ever heard of it and couldn't help but wonder what the first two forces might be. [Lansdale Papers, Hoover Institution, 1991 declassified box.]

5. Wesley Fishel, "Vietnam's Democratic One-Man Rule," *New Leader*, 11/2/59.

6. Greene wrote on the absurdity (and costs) of bringing Americana to Vietnamese peasants whenever possible. In the following section Greene combines these in a way that also allows him to critique modernization theory:

> It is difficult to feel so grateful when a gift is permanently stamped with the name of the donor. This is not the obtrusive spontaneous act of charity to which the poor are accustomed; the tents, the chicken coops, the packages of rations bearing the badge of American aid demand a kind of payment—co-operation in the Cold War. . . . The razors for hairless chins can be sold again perhaps (though to whom?) . . . and the white powder (that nobody tells them is milk and a few wily people may tell them is poison for their babies) can be spilt in the cracks of the ground and the tins scoured and used. [In Graham Greene, "Last Act in Indo-China," *The New Republic*, 5/9/55, 11.]

7. Greene, *The Quiet American*, 167–68.
8. Rostow's fullest description of modernization theory is in *The Stages of Economic Growth: A Non-Communist Manifesto* (New York: Cambridge University Press, 1972). David Halberstam's critique of Rostow and his enthusiasm for modernization theory remains the most insightful, *The Best and the Brightest* (New York: Random House, 1972), 156–62.
9. Roger Hilsman, for one, had a deep distrust of Rostow and later related how Kennedy referred to Rostow as the "air marshall" whenever problems developed in Vietnam—bombing was his immediate answer to all problems in this country. In Roger Hilsman, Jr., interview, 8/14/70, John F. Kennedy Library Oral History Program, 23.
10. Though different in approaches, two compelling critiques of modernization theory are James Scott, *The Moral Economy of the Peasant: Rebellion and Subsistence in Southeast Asia* (New Haven: Yale University Press, 1976), chap. 6; and Michael Adas, *Machines as the Measure of Men: Science, Technology, and Ideologies of Western Dominance* (Ithaca: Cornell University Press, 1989), 411–16.

    The irony here, to the extent that there can be any, is that modernization theory continues to have its champions—the devastation of Vietnam notwithstanding. See Lucian Pye, "Political Science and the Crisis of Authoritarianism," *American Political Science Review* 84 (March 1990): 3–19, especially the section en-

titled "The Vindication of Modernization Theory," 7–11. Thanks
to David Engerman for pointing out this article to me.

11. The question of Greene as Fowler is necessarily open. In an interview at the time of the publication of the novel Greene told a
journalist, "Everybody thinks I am Fowler—well, I share some of
his views about the Americans. But I'm not as bitter about them
as he is. I didn't have my girl stolen by an American." *The British
Evening Standard*, 8/24/56, cited in *Yours etc.*, 57.

Other clues exist that point to connections between the two,
such as the use of opium. Charlotte Loris, an American attached
to the American Embassy in Saigon during the mid-1950s, knew
Greene at this time and later discussed their encounter:

> So we got together a number of times and one evening
> we were discussing the ethnic background of Chinese and
> Asians and I said, I've always wanted to go to an opium
> den. . . . So we get in the cycle and the guy pedals us out
> to this opium den. Graham Greene was an habitue of
> opium dens and he knew Asia. . . . It was just like I
> expected it to be. Absolutely fascinating. I wouldn't have
> missed it for anything. I did want Graham Greene to buy
> me the silver opium pipe but he didn't. So he smoked
> nine pipes and I smoked three. But I didn't inhale be-
> cause I was scared shitless. But it was fun. [In *An Inter-
> view with Charlotte Loris*, 6/8/89, Foreign Affairs Oral
> History Program, Georgetown University.]

12. Greene, *The Quiet American*, 94–95.

13. Emily Rosenberg, *Spreading the American Dream: American Economic and Cultural Expansion, 1890–1945* (New York: Hill and
Wang, 1982), is particularly good on historicizing how Americans
believed the rest of the world sought to be American—materially,
culturally, even spiritually. See also the cover of *The Journal of
American History* for a view of Mr. Coca-Cola spanning the globe
in the much the same fashion that "international communism"
was portrayed. In *The Journal of American History* 79 (September
1992).

14. Lansdale to Secretary of Defense and Deputy Secretary of Defense, 1/17/61, Lansdale Papers, Hoover Institution, Box 49,
#1374.

15. Graham Greene, *Yours etc.: Letters to the Press*, (New York: Viking,
1989), 126.

16. Ibid., 127.

17. Lansdale interview with Cecil Currey, 5/16/84, Currey Papers, Lutz, Florida.

18. Judith Adamson, *Graham Greene and Cinema* (Norman, Okla.: Pilgrim Books, 1984), 79.

19. Graham Greene, *Ways of Escape* (New York: Simon and Schuster, 1980), 169–70.

20. Cited in Donald Lancaster, *The Emancipation of French Indochina* (New York: Oxford University Press, 1961), 234, n. 26.

21. Herbert Mitgang, "The Quiet American," *San Francisco Chronicle*, 8/21/66.

22. "The 'True American,' " paper by Lansdale, 6/3/60, Currey Papers, Lutz, Florida, 3.

23. Ibid., 6.

24. Lansdale to Peter McInerney, 9/4/80, Lansdale Papers, Hoover Institution, Box 79.

25. Herbert Mitgang, *San Francisco Chronicle* 8/21/65. Language, again, plays an important part in this discussion. The addition of an adjective in front of the word "American" was quite popular at the time, and began to take on aspects of parody with both supporters and critics of Lansdale and American actions abroad trying to attach ever more mindless words to describe him and his mission. Words such as "compelling," "splendid," and "smart" were the first way numerous writers familiarized Lansdale to their audience.

26. Dulles's actual words were "the principle of neutrality, which pretends that a nation can best gain safety for itself by being indifferent to the fate of others. This has increasingly become an obsolete conception, and, except under very exceptional circumstances, it is an immoral and shortsighted conception." *Department of State Bulletin* 34, 6/18/56, 999–1000.

27. Graham Greene, London *Times*, 7/19/88. Cited in *Yours etc.*, 249.

# Keith Honaker

*Lt. Col. Keith Honaker (U.S. Army, Ret.) lives in Knoxville, Tennessee. During World War II, he served in New Guinea and New Britain, and in 1951 was assigned to the MAAG (Military Assistance and Advisory Group), Saigon. Then a major, he arrived in Vietnam on 15 February 1952—about the time of the final scenes of* The Quiet American. *His autobiographical memoir accurately depicts the attitudes of many Americans in Vietnam at that time.*

## From VICTIMIZED BY THE FRENCH AND CHINESE

Easter Sunday, April 12, 1952, began many social functions among the Americans in Saigon. Mostly, these activities were to honor Americans whose tours of service had expired in Indochina and were to return to the "land of the round door knobs," as we affectionately called dear old USA. Among those departing was our Chief of Army Section, Colonel Saples, one of the officers who had met me and Major Harry Ellis at the Tan Son Nhut Airport in February. Also included in the group returning to the States were Colonel and Mrs. Freeman, the former Air Force Attaché at the American Legion.

From Keith Honaker, *The Eagle Weeps.* Knoxville, Tenn.: K&W Publishers, 1994, 211–22. By permission of the author.

One of the parties honoring the departing Americans was held at the Grand Monde in Cholon, one of the largest gambling casinos in the world at that time. Everyone gambled at the Grand Monde, from the richest to the poorest, be they French, American, German, Vietnamese, Chinese, or whatever. The bets could range from a few piasters to thousands. The dress ranged from black tie formals to the coolie in his black pajama-type clothing wearing his pinwheel hat; all jabbering in a language often not understood by the Americans. The party would progress from the gambling tables to a very elaborate dining room with tables placed on levels of different heights overlooking a dance floor often used as a stage for exotic dances. These shows and dances occurred concurrently as the patrons dined. The floor show was what the partying Americans wanted to see. However, there was a dance routine by very attractive French girls whose very brief attire was a short skirt and nothing from the waist up. This being 1952, almost stone age in present-day reckoning, it did not appeal to most American wives attending the party. They berated their husbands for bringing them to the Grand Monde. Their anger increased when the egotistic and mischievous Lieutenant Colonel Gennings, who often danced with the American ladies in more sedate surroundings, led a passel of males onto the dance floor to dance with the half-nude French girls. This act, acceptable to the French, was not appreciated by the American wives in the party that night. These ladies knew Gennings had a wife back home and considered his act, and that of those with him, cavorting on the dance floor with the half-nude French girls, revolting. One of the wives was heard to say, "Would Colonel Gennings permit his wife to carry on in such manner while he was away?" And the remainder concluded he would not. However, other American men, whose wives were home in the States, took to the dance floor to dance with the half-nude French girls, and this did not sit well with the American wives either. Gennings added to the embarrassing situation by coming over to ask one of the men for permission to dance with his wife. The husband agreed but the wife turned a cold shoulder to Gennings, not even recognizing his cavalier invitation. The other wives looked disgustedly at his efforts to be friendly. I don't think Gennings ever recovered from the embarrassment.

One of the going-away parties was hosted by the owners of the Grand Monde themselves. They were six very wealthy Chinese men having lumber holdings in the United States as well as other enterprises there. The Chinese never invited women to attend their parties and this one was no exception. Only American males were to attend. The party began with the floor show by the half-nude French girls while we sipped our free drinks and watched from the elevated tables above the dance floor. Gennings and the others refrained from dancing with the girls, perhaps still feeling the sting from the coolness of the American wives on their previous escapade. The philanderers decided it was time to improve their conduct, even though their performance on the dance floor a few nights before had been all in fun. Most all, except the goggled-eyed Americans, thought the show was a work of art. The girls' attire was brief but their dance was dignified and not suggestive or offensive to most.

The floor show finished, we were escorted by the wealthy Chinese men to several limousines lined up in convoy waiting for us. Our hosts leading the way, the caravan of luxury cars raced through the dark streets of Cholon, still teeming with Chinese coolies, to a spacious building surrounded by the usual high brick wall. The large building, reflecting Chinese architecture, sat behind a long circular driveway that passed under a large portico extending over the entrance. This was the home of one of the rich Chinese. The limousines stopped and parked on the driveway. Stepping from the cars, we were in awe of the structure and its well-kept lawn. We had never seen anything like it in Cholon. Entering the spacious and ornate mansion, we were impressed with the expensive works of art hanging on the high walls of the hallway. Coming to a double door, we entered into a most exquisite room with three large tables prepared to accommodate the large party of Americans and Chinese. The place settings included chopsticks for eating utensils and most of the Americans were not prepared to use them. My concern was relieved, however, when I found a porcelain spoon near my plate. The Chinese had been thoughtful.

Prior to the dinner, Colonel McDade, an old Chinese hand stemming from WWII days, informed me of their exotic dining habits. He said most Americans did not like Chinese food but since the Chinese were very sensitive people, we must be careful not to offend them and partake of the food whatever it was. Should something be served not palatable to us, we should at least taste it, and then set it aside. The servant would remove it and our host would not be offended. This bit of information was timely advice and would prepare me for the ordeal that followed.

The Chinese servant set a bowl of pigeon soup in front of each of us. The pigeon soup would not have been offensive had not the carcass of the pigeon been lying on its back in the soup, beak agape and black legs sticking above the liquid. It was repugnant. Wanting some kind of explanation, I looked at the other Americans. All, except McDade, were as astonished as I was, staring unbelievingly at the dead pigeons floating around in their soup. McDade, however, was consuming his pigeon soup with gusto, ignoring the painful expressions of his American brothers. Fortunately, I remembered McDade's instruction that I must take a portion of whatever I was served by the Chinese to avoid offending them. Quickly taking the porcelain spoon, closing my eyes, I scooped up a bit of the soup from around the dead pigeon, downing it. Shoving the bowl of dead pigeon soup away, I hoped no Chinese had been offended. Thankfully, the bowl containing the soup was removed from my sight; I was grateful. We continued the Chinese meal, having many courses, even one containing octopus and other unfamiliar food also offensive to the picky American army officers.

But the dead pigeon in the soup was a delicacy to a lover of Chinese food, McDade later informed me. The pigeon had been dressed and properly prepared for us. It was savored by all except us, the wacky Americans. "Food is food to the Chinese and they enjoy it in any form prepared," he said.

Shortly after the big affair at the Chinese mansion in Cholon, I was invited to another sumptuous dinner with still another group of Chinese businessmen. They were in real estate and we had just rented the WA Hotel from them. Wan, the agent in the transaction, represented the group proffering the invitation. Hedging, I delayed acceptance fearing what I had feared the most, an attempt to bribe me or even worse yet, getting involved in Grubbs's gun-running operations out of the Philippines. Grubbs could easily have been connected with this group and I did not want to face a set-up. Informing him that I would let him know in time, I immediately discussed the matter with McDade and the executive officer, both well experienced in Chinese customs. They suggested I accept the dinner engagement with the Chinese for it was their custom to entertain people with whom they dealt. It was a form of appreciation and such an invitation should be accepted. They added if I felt uneasy about attending, I should take a witness with me. Wan had assured me that business would not be discussed for it would be offensive in the views of Chinese custom. McDade further suggested that if we were to deal with the Chinese, we must learn more about them. Being grateful for the advice from the front office, I later informed Wan I would accept his invitation, and that another American officer would accompany me.

"Bring anyone you want, Majah," he said, and the date was set for another Chinese dinner in Cholon. Lieutenant Welling, MAAG Communications Section, was to accompany me.

On the evening of the dinner a black Chevrolet staff car from MAAG, driven by a Vietnamese driver, picked us up at the Continental Palace in Saigon at 6:30 PM. I gave the driver the address of the place and shortly we arrived in Cholon, its streets, as usual, filled with jabbering Chinese. The black sedan stood out like a sore thumb among the Chinese-filled streets.

We had to thread our way slowly through the people, the cyclos, and bicycles, who, like water, formed a stream of people closing the gap behind us as we continued down the street.

We were relieved when we found Wan waiting at the appointed place. He greeted us warmly as we got out of the sedan.

"Ah, Majah Honakah, so glad you and your friend could come. We feel honored that you visit our humble place, thank you," and he gave the driver instructions concerning parking and when to return for us.

The driver was now lost to our control as Wan led us down a dark, unlit side street. The black-clad people rushing by became darkened shadows as the late evening turned into nightfall. Wan continued his usual trite conversation, adding to our uneasiness. Why had he not let the driver bring us down the dark street? Our concern increased as we continued down the dirty, unlit narrow passageway among the Chinese who paid little attention to us.

Coming to a shabby, two-story stucco building, without a glimmer of light, we were led through a creaky door and headed up a flight of dark, noisy stairs and down a hallway lit by a single dim light bulb dangling from the ceiling. Silently, except for Wan's one-way conversation, we continued down the hallway. We felt like sheep being led to the slaughter and our steps thundered on the bare wooden floor of the ramshackle structure. Why were we having dinner in a place such as this, anyway? Or would there be dinner? The door at the far end of the hall slowly opened, permitting light to form the outline of a small man standing motionless in the doorway. Wan's one-way conversation stopped and he continued silently to lead us toward the shadow of the small man in the doorway. It became the focus of attention, and we approached with apprehension.

The little man came to life and gave way for us to enter into a large room prepared for several persons to sit. He extended his hand in welcome. What a relief! Welling grinned sheepishly from ear to ear. We felt we had been delivered from the sacrificial block.

The Chinese men, like the six at the Grande Monde a few nights earlier, were great hosts. As with the Grande Monde party, no females were at the dinner, but we were to be favored by their presence later. We were introduced by Wan to each of the Chinese and we had no difficulty feeling welcome. The Chinese are warm and gracious people once you understand them and their customs.

Then the drinking began. To my chagrin, cognac was served. It burned as it passed down my gullet to my stomach and continued to burn even there. I nursed my drink, sipping not too frequently, for I could not take another drink of the hot stuff. My barely sipping the cognac was obvious to Wan who complained that I was not doing my share of drinking, suggesting I catch up. He held an opened bottle of cognac poised to fill my glass once I had emptied it. I demurred by saying Welling was to do my drinking for the evening, only to be met by Welling's protest that he also was nursing his drink. Wan continued his insistence but we stood our ground for the time being.

The Chinese men were a friendly group well aware of the western way of life, so we talked about the United States and what a wonderful place it was. They talked of the wide open spaces in the Midwest, the Rocky Mountains, the industrial and agricultural might of the country, and its large cities. Judging from what had been said, all of the Chinese except Wan had been in the United States. They described the places they had visited and one had relatives living there. All of them spoke fluent English.

The drinking phase finished, we were invited to sit at the table already prepared for the dinner. I remembered the pigeon soup at the home of the rich Chinese and hoped and prayed that I would not have to go through a similar experience again. I had enough of that to last a lifetime. Hopefully, I would not have to offend my host by refusing such a course during the meal. I was spared the ordeal of eating pigeon soup but was served octopus and shark fin soup instead—both equally repulsive. Right then and there I added these two items to my rapidly growing list of unpalatable foods, with dead pigeon soup at the top.

The Chinese dinner, lasting two hours, had many courses, of which the two Americans ate very little. There was never a dull moment during the meal. The conversation, mixed with laughter and drink, never lagged, with the two Americans being the focus of attention. Finally, the Chinese pushed themselves back from the table. They smoked their American-made cigars and cigarettes with a glass of Cointreau in hand, enjoying the influence of the meal, wine, cognac, coffee, and whatever. Thinking it was about time for us to take leave of our hosts, I whispered to Welling to arrange for the car to take us back to our quarters.

Welling was about to ask Wan to arrange for our car when one of the Chinese clapped his hands, signaling seventeen beautifully dressed, bejewelled, and attractive Chinese young ladies to come into the room. My gosh! Here was the Madam Illoquet, the dragon lady of Haiphong, all over again, except there were seventeen beautiful dragon ladies. These beautiful young ladies took positions in front of us and I noticed the contrast of their beauty with the shabby surroundings. It was a clash one could not help but notice. But why were they present? They were a singing group and welcomed by the Chinese host. These beautiful girls, dressed in throat-choked, tight-fitting dresses split well up both thighs, sang to us, all seventeen in their native tongue, accompanied by some strange musical instrument. We were impressed by their soothing voices and gracious body movements, especially their hands, that illustrated a story they were singing.

The musical performance came to a conclusion, and we anxiously waited for what might be offered to us next. We didn't have to wait long.

"Now, Majah," Wan began, "the girls are to honor you as our guest of honor, see. They will now drink to your health."

"Good. Let them drink as much as they want if it concerns

my health," I ignorantly joked, not knowing what ordeal was waiting me in the dark recesses of the little Chinaman's mind.

"Majah, you don't understand, see," and he dropped the sledgehammer, so to speak, on my bone head. "As one of the girls drinks her tumbler of cognac toasting you, you must honor her by drinking yours also, emptying it completely." And the Chinese men laughed at my predicament. Wan, knowing I hated cognac, finally had me in a corner. The prankster stood with an opened bottle of cognac in hand, ready to fill my tumbler as I emptied it to each girl once she had toasted me.

"Hell, Wan, these girls won't be drinking to my health. Drinking this damn cognac will kill me and you know it," but he only grinned and waited for the torture to begin. "God, help me!" I pleaded.

Once again I looked at the seventeen beautiful Chinese girls who were eyeing me with some expectation or other. They seemed ready to pounce upon me like chickens on a June bug on a hot July afternoon.

"My God, Wan, I can't drink seventeen tumblers of cognac when I have trouble even drinking one." I pleaded for mercy.

"But Majah, don't disappoint them. They have looked forward to toasting the American majah." I even detected a plea in his scheming voice.

All seventeen girls, each with a thimble-sized tumbler full of cognac, lined up before me as Wan placed me in a chair in front of them. He called it a throne. Once in the chair, I was also given a thimble-sized tumbler filled with the hot stuff as the other Chinese men were watching with glee. However, Welling had both sympathy and happiness registering on his face. He was glad he was not sitting in the chair facing the seventeen blow-torches in the form of beautiful Chinese maidens with tumblers filled with cognac, ready and eagerly waiting.

Wan, with a sadistic smile, filled my tumbler to the brim. His smile looked like the rear end of a mule that I once saw being shod at Tom Dorsey's blacksmith shop down on Painter's Bethel Creek in Putnam County, West Virginia, when I was a small boy. Once again I was instructed in the rules of the game. As each of the girls honored me by sipping cognac from her thimble-sized tumbler, I was to acknowledge her by emptying mine, downing it in one gulp. This would be worse than the "prop blasting" I had received at my initiation into the 82nd Airborne Division, Fort Bragg, in 1948. There I had to drink a mixture of beer, whiskey, wine, or whatever from the "prop blast" cup that was kept under lock and key except for initiating new jumpers into the division. The prop blasting was almost a ritual ordeal never to be forgotten. The army brass brought it to an end, however, when a young officer died from an alcohol overdose. And now here I was about to go through a similar ordeal, perhaps even worse, forced upon me by this rat of a Chinese man who told me that it was all in my honor. Could I survive? Was I to drink seventeen tumblers of the hot stuff? Yes. If I didn't, the girls would be offended. I protested, good-naturedly, but I was encouraged by Wan, still smiling like the jackass he was. I looked at the beautiful Chinese maidens, all lined up front to rear before me. As the first girl sipped, I gulped, we touched glasses and she moved from the line only to have another as beautiful as she take her place. Again and again the slim and dainty hands of the beautiful Chinese young ladies were extended, touching tumblers followed by their sips and my gulps, and my esophagus burned as the cognac trickled down the gullet and into the holding pond called the stomach where it burned even worse. With twelve yet to go I was about to throw in the towel and cry for mercy, conceding defeat in favor of Wan. It was my darkest hour and my insides were aflame. But providence came to my rescue. A miracle occurred—or to me it was a miracle, anyway.

Without warning a terrible explosion took place, shaking the old ramshackle building from bottom to top and side to side. It was as if an earthquake had struck and the old building swayed back and forth. It recoiled from the awful tremor, slinging the china, silverware, and chopsticks crashing to the bare wooden floor, scattering from wall to wall. The young Chinese maidens scrambled to their feet and disappeared screaming, thank God, never to be seen again. Wan, with his companions, was cowering under one of the tables, leaving Welling and me standing alone as light from flames shooting high in the sky lit the darkened room. Broken glass from the window panes was scattered over the room, and a door hung on one hinge, demonstrating the force of the explosion. The darkened streets were filled with screaming Chinese as our hosts jumped to their feet and joined us, a bit shaken, inquiring what had happened. The direction of the fire several miles east of Cholon pointed to an ammunition dump that perhaps the Viet Minh had blown up, one on the outskirts of Saigon. We leaned on the paneless window sills and watched the fireworks that lasted for some time, the fingers of flame pointing high in the cloudless sky. Ironically, the party ended on a high note, even though the French had lost an ammunition dump stocked with American munitions.

"Well," I reasoned with Welling on our way back to quarters, "I hated to see the French lose all that ammunition but it came at a time of urgent need. It ended the cognac torture I was going through at the hand of Wan and the beautiful Chinese maidens."

"Yes, it was quite a party, complete with fireworks too," he added.

# Takeshi Kaiko

*Takeshi Kaiko, born in 1930, is an acclaimed Japanese novelist, essayist, and short-story writer who in 1964 was a correspondent in Vietnam. His novel based on his experiences,* Into a Black Sun, *won the Mainichi Cultural Prize. In the selection excerpted here, the novel's narrator, a Japanese newsman whose desire to remain unengaged is quite similar to that of Thomas Fowler's, is in search of a story for his Tokyo paper. The time is late 1964; the scene, Saigon.*

## From *INTO A BLACK SUN*

I left the card game at four o'clock and went in search of a small newspaper office behind the market. The office was the size of a printing shop in downtown Tokyo, the kind that might do name cards and advertising fliers. It was closed for the New Year, but a man was waiting there for me, the door latch left open. Tran had contacted him. He was a novelist who wrote for two or three papers under various pen names; his address was unknown. His manuscripts were usually delivered by some waif for a few coins. It would be a different face each time, and the boy would only say that some man, a passerby, had stopped him and asked him to deliver the package. The boy would take the money for the manuscript and disappear.

"He's not a bad writer," Tran had said.

I wandered down an alley littered with bits of vegetable refuse, fish entrails, and papaya rinds, looking for the address. A woman's voice, singing, came from somewhere behind the yellow plaster wall, probably a cheap bar. It was a Japanese song that had been popular when I was in grade school. Its turn had now come here.

> I'm a Manchurian, a girl just sixteen.
> March is here at last and the snow will melt,
> Flowers will bloom; it's spring again. . . .

The grooves of the record were worn and the woman's voice was peculiarly high-pitched, now fading, now panting; but the memories welled up like water in a hot spring. I lit a cigarette and listened until the song died away, then looked for the address again.

The cold fear of leprosy had receded to the back of my mind. I remembered the time my father took me to a department store. He was in an unusually expansive mood and offered to buy me a bicycle. Once in the store, however, I found the bicycle so magnificently shiny, so overwhelming, that I said I'd be happy to have *Treasure Island* instead. The book was also beautiful and came in a cloth-covered box, but when I got home I read it in one night, and in the morning thought that the bicycle would have been much better. My parents looked at me across the dining table and laughed, saying I was "easily bought." But they were wrong. The bicycle was so splendid and expensive that I'd thought my father must be making sacrifices for me; so I had chosen the book. The one who was fooled was my father. Being laughed at didn't appeal to me much, but I kept quiet. I remember grade schools still used to distribute red and white rice cakes on holidays then, and the song about the Manchurian girl was everywhere on the city streets.

I pushed open a door and went in. Inside a dark room full of scraps of paper, a middle-aged man was reading a newspaper.

He looked up and rose, apologizing in slow English.

"Unfortunately, I've only got thirty minutes," he said. For a Vietnamese, he was tall and muscular, and he had a bull's neck and shoulders.

He gestured at a sofa with protruding springs, and poured lukewarm tea from a chipped teapot. I offered him my cigarettes. Sipping tea, the man began to speak in a low voice, before I could ask any questions. In his youth, he said, he had studied in Paris and, enchanted by Proust, had decided to become a writer; but on returning home, he'd developed a greater interest in Russian literature, especially Chekhov and Gorki. Without any conscious decision, he had parted company with Proust at some point. When the first Indochina War broke out, he put his pen down and joined the Viet Minh; and as a guerrilla commander in a Delta district, he'd fought against the French and the Bao Dai Army. At present, he was writing a novel for serialization in a newspaper, based on his own experiences—not of famous officers and generals, but the nameless men who fought bravely and died. The government censored any anti-government material, and it was a constant struggle to escape the net.

"Have you read Graham Greene's *The Quiet American?*" the man asked me, sipping his tea.

"Yes, I have."

"What do you think of it?"

"Good. It's cynical, but it's a good book."

"The movie was bad, wasn't it."

"Terrible."

"I gave him the material for the novel. After it came out, I realized that Greene didn't really understand anything about this country. It's a novel written to please European readers. I was very disappointed with it. There's a young woman who smokes opium in the book. I know her, too. I hear she's in Paris now."

He looked up, narrowing his eyes nostalgically. He had piercing eyes, but they had softened, and a misty longing flickered in them. He went on talking. Greene had stayed at the Majestic Hotel and from there made periodic trips to the front, as well as to an opium den. He had contacted him in his Delta village, and my host had left his submachine gun and secretly gone to meet the novelist in Saigon. The defeat of the French had become inevitable, and "economic observers" and "medical aides" were the first signs of a growing American involvement. The man had told Greene all he could, on various subjects. One day, Greene had asked him what he thought of the Americans, so he'd told him a story that was popular at the time.

A young man who had studied Vietnamese history and language at Michigan State University came to Saigon "to defend freedom." He hailed a cyclo and in fluent Vietnamese ordered the driver to take him to the Majestic Hotel. On the way there the American said: "Listen. I did Vietnamese at Michigan State. I know the language—and just about everything else about this country. I know you people cheat foreigners sometimes, but you won't get far with me. So just take me straight to the Majestic."

The driver, shamefaced, replied: "Sir, you speak Vietnamese like one of us. I couldn't cheat you if I tried." In about thirty minutes, the young American arrived at his hotel and duly paid a hundred piastres for the ride. "You see," he said, "you can't fool me. It's a good school, Michigan." The next day, he went out for a walk and happened to pass the spot where he'd picked up the cyclo; it had taken him seven minutes from the hotel. As a test, he asked a cyclo driver in the area how much he would charge for a ride to the Majestic. The driver jumped up, clapping his hands, and said, "Sir, I'll take you there for five Ps."

The man smiled at me. "Isn't it a nice story?" I nodded in silence. They were a shrewd people. Even ten years ago, when there'd only been a handful of Americans here, this was the sort of comment that had been making the rounds. . . .

"Are they still like that?"

"Who?"

"The Americans here."

"Not as bad as they used to be," the man answered. "I must admit they try to learn, and they work hard at it. But they can sweat away at it for as long as they like, they're still too young. They're too young to understand people in old countries like Vietnam and Japan."

"But these old cultures don't necessarily understand themselves! It's not a question of old and new. Take me, I'm Japanese, but I don't understand the Japanese at all."

"That's a different matter."

The man suddenly peered at my watch, raised his head, and mumbled that he had to go. The sharp look had returned; alertness and a sense of danger had replaced the poise of that powerful body.

"Can we meet again?" I asked.

"Yes, sometime."

"What should I do?"

"Let me contact you. Please don't look for me. I'll choose the date. Wait until you hear from me."

His tone was modest and cautious, but a look of intense, ruthless energy flashed in his eyes. He rose nimbly from the sofa and shook hands with me. Even this brief contact left me aware of a strength that could have crushed my hand. There hadn't been a word to suggest it, but hadn't he perhaps kept his links with that Delta village?

# IV

## Literary Criticism

# A. J. Liebling

*Born in 1904, A. J. Liebling wrote for* The New Yorker *from 1935 until his death in 1963. Always provocative, he was known as "the gadfly of American journalism." Among his books are* Back Where I Came From *(1938) and* The Wayward Pressman *(1947). His third wife was author Jean Stafford.*

## A TALKATIVE SOMETHING-OR-OTHER

The traditional Englishman of Gallic fiction is a naïve chap who speaks bad French, eats tasteless food, and is only accidentally and episodically heterosexual. The sole tolerable qualities ever allowed him are to be earnest, in an obtuse way, and physically brave, through lack of imagination. When I began reading "The Quiet American," in its British edition, on a plane between London and New York last December (Viking has just now brought it out in this country), I discovered that Mr. Graham Greene, who is British, had contrived to make his Quiet American, Pyle, a perfect specimen of a French author's idea of an Englishman. I had bought "The Quiet American" at the waiting-room newsstand, on the assurance of the young lady attendant that it was good light reading. Pyle is as naïve as he

Originally published in *The New Yorker* (7 April 1956), 148–54, reprinted by permission of Russell and Volkening. Copyright © 1956 by *The New Yorker Magazine*; copyright renewed 1984 by Norma Liebling Stonehill.

can be and speaks French atrociously. He dotes on bland horrors in food: "A new sandwich mixture called Vit-Health. My mother sent it from the States." (In American, I think, a thing like that is called a sandwich *spread*.) Pyle's choice of idiom convinced me that he is a thinly disguised Englishman. But I was impressed by the *toupet* of Mr. Greene, sneering down at Pyle from the gastronomic eminence of a soggy crumpet. A British author snooting American food is like the blind twitting the one-eyed. Finally, Pyle says he has never had a woman, even though he is thirty-two. He is earnest, though, in an obtuse way, and physically brave, through lack of imagination.

This exercise in national projection made me realize that Mr. Greene, the celebrated whodunist, trapped on the moving staircase of history, was registering a classical reaction to a situation familiar to me and Spengler. When England, a French cultural colony, outstripped the homeland after Waterloo and the Industrial Revolution, all that remained for the French to say was "Nevertheless, you remain nasty, overgrown children." The Italians of the Renaissance said it to the French, and I suppose the Greeks said it to the Romans. It is part of the ritual of handing over.

When Greene undertook the composition of Pyle's sparring partner, he had more difficulty. He had already presented one basically English type as a Quiet American. Now he had to have somebody to contrast him with unfavorably—an Articulate Englishman. Such a person is a contradiction in popular-fiction terms, like a scrutable Oriental. To produce one, Greene had to defenestrate all the traits by which a whodunit reader identifies an Englishman—the tight upper lip, the understatement, the cheerful mask of unintelligence skillfully exploited to confuse the enemy. I needed a full thirty seconds in the company of the result—Fowler, the correspondent in Saigon of a London newspaper published in a grim Victorian building near Blackfriars Station—to see that Greene had run out at the turn.

Fowler is a sophisticated MacTavish. He knows French

writing from Pascal to Paul de Kock and speaks the language like a native, although not necessarily of France. He has brought with him from Bloomsbury, of all places, the gustatory savvy of a Prosper Montagné: "I sat hungerless over my apology for a chapon duc Charles." (He has, in fact, an edge on Montagné, who includes no such *plat* in his "Grand Livre de la Cuisine.") He is as active sexually as a North African jack and has a taste in women unaffected by the flicks, which glorify convex Marilyns and Ginas. Fowler prefers flat women with bones like birds, and he likes them to twitter on his pillow while he smokes opium. He associates informally with foreign-language-speaking people. None of these, especially the last, is a traditional British characteristic. Yet Fowler, from the moment I laid eyes on him, which was at about the time the takeoff sign flashed "FASTEN SAFETY BELTS—NO SMOKING," had a familiar air, like a stranger who resembles somebody whose name you can't remember.

Suddenly I made him. He was a mockup of a Hemingway hero—*donc* an American, *donc* One of Us. Fowler is not a Hemingway hero by Hemingway, of course. He is nearer the grade of Hemingway hero that occurs in unsolicited manuscripts. "What distant ancestors had given me this stupid conscience? Surely they were free of it when they raped and killed in their paleolithic world" is a fair example of Fowler in his jungle gym of prose. But he can also bring the beat down, quiet and sad, for contrast. Like "Ordinary life goes on—that has saved many a man's reason." Original but not gaudy. I hyphenated him Bogart-Fowler *sur le chung* (a bit of Indo-French I soaked up from Greene). There are aspects of Bogart-Fowler that lead me to think he may be an American by birth, although probably a naturalized British subject. His familiarity with the minutiae of American life that irritate him hint at a boyhood spent in a town like Barrington, Rhode Island. When he thinks that Phuong, his bird-boned baby doll, is about to marry Pyle, Fowler wonders, for example, "Would she like those bright, clean little New England grocery stores where even the celery was wrapped in cellophane?" Perhaps, when he was a child, he tried to eat the cellophane.

Maybe Fowler's father, a vicar, left Rhode Island because of a broken home, taking young Bogart with him, although he knew the boy was not his own son—a situation always rich in potential traumata. Back in Bloomsbury, he imparted to the little changeling an implacable hatred of milk shakes, deodorants, and everything else American. There—but this is again a hypothesis—Bogart-Fowler may have got a job writing readers' letters to a newspaper published in a grim Victorian building near Blackfriars Station, and then Fourth Leaders about the wiles of chaffinches, which have bones like birds.

"Good chap, that," the old Press Lord had said, with a wintry smile, as he spread Marmite on his fried beans Maison du Coin Lyonnaise and read the Fourth Leader. "Make a jolly good foreign correspondent." I had often wondered how some of my British newspaper friends got abroad.

I stopped there, though, because I have never been a man to let a hypothesis run away with me, and considered another possibility—that Fowler, born British, had merely been the Washington correspondent of the newspaper near Blackfriars long enough to take on a glaze of loquacity. If so, when had he got out of the Press Club bar in time to shop for celery for his wife? He had a wife; it says so in the book.

I found, as I read at Mr. Greene, that Fowler's pre-Saigon past interested me a lot more than what happened to him after he got there. Where, for instance, had he learned his distaste for reporters who asked questions at Army briefings? Had he perhaps been not a reporter at all but a press-relations officer with Montgomery? In Saigon, he gets his information from a sick Eurasian assistant who comes around to his digs every evening to share a pipe. Greene leaves the newspaper part of Fowler's past a mystery, such as where he had learned what was a proper chapon duc Charles and what was an apology for one. Had Fowler, during this obscure period, discovered that "good little French restaurant in Soho" that is as hard to verify as the Loch Ness monster? And where is it? Yes, Fowler's past is a blank, except in one department. He tells Pyle that before coming to Saigon he had forty-odd plus four women, of whom only the four were important to him, especially one in a red kimono. On Topic A he is a Talkative Englishman, native or naturalized.

At that point, I fell into one of those short, deep airplane sleeps, ten minutes long, that you hope have been longer, and, waking, found my hand where I had left it, around half a glass of Scotch-and-soda.

The book was open at the same place: Fowler telling the Quiet American about sex:

"One starts promiscuous and ends like one's grandfather," he says. (Dead, I thought, anticipating the next word, but it wasn't.) "One starts promiscuous and ends like one's grandfather, faithful to one woman" was the complete sentence. Fowler has *had* his fun; now he is a moralist. "We are fools," he concedes, "when we love." Still, he never leaves the Quiet American in any doubt about who of the two of them is the bigger fool. Poor old Q. A. Pyle, cold-decked by Mr. Greene, never suspects that Fowler is an American, too. Greene has fixed it so Pyle doesn't read fiction, except Thomas Wolfe, and Fowler is not in Wolfe. Pyle takes Fowler for a Legit Brit., the soul of honor. That is why he trusts him.

I wandered downstairs to the lounge bar, dragging "The Quiet American" with me. It was slow, but it was all I had, because I was making the trip on short notice and the other books on the stand had looked even less promising. I had a copy of the *British Racehorse*, but I had read through that early and lent it to one of the hostesses, who said she thought the Aly Khan was cute. Between drinks and dozes, I gnawed away at the novel, as though it were a gristly piece of apology for a chapon duc Charles, until at an unremembered point I began to wonder when Greene himself had realized that a possible second American had infiltrated his Eastern Western, and if that was the sort of thing that made him mad at us. Reading

a bad book is like watching a poor fight. Instead of being caught
up in it, you try to figure out what is the matter.

I signalled to the Aly Khan's fan for a fourth drink. The
book was written in imitation American, too—brutal, brusque
sentences tinkling with irony, not at all like Fourth Leaders
about chaffinches. Does Greene ever get homesick for Lewis
Carroll?

"They pulled him out like a tray of ice cubes, and I looked
at him." . . . "Death takes away vanity—even the vanity of the
cuckold who mustn't show his pain." . . . "I was a correspondent; I thought in headlines." . . . "She was the hiss of steam,
the clink of a cup, she was a certain hour of the night and the
promise of rest." The last quote is a switch to the poetic, but
it is an *American* style of poetry—simple, dynamic, full of
homely, monosyllabic comparisons. It reminded me of a lyric I
used to sing:

> *You're the cream in my coffee, you're the salt in my stew,*
> *You're the hiss of my and the bliss of my*
> *Steamy dreamy of you.*

Poor old Greene was in the position of the Javanese politician who told a correspondent he hated the Dutch so specially
hard because he could think only in Dutch.

Mr. Greene's irritation at being a minor American author
does not justify the main incident of the book, which is a messy
explosion in downtown Saigon, during the shopping hour, put
on by the earnest but unimaginative Pyle in collaboration with
a bandit "general" in the hope of blowing up some French
officers. (The French postpone their parade, and the explosion
merely tears up women and children.) When I reached that
point, most of the way through, I had had breakfast and was
trying to kill the two last deadly hours before Idlewild. I

thought I might as well finish the book so that I could give it to the hostess, a brunette from Rye, New York.

I should perhaps explain here that the book begins with Pyle in the morgue. That is the big gag: A Quiet American. It then goes on to the events that led up to his arrival there. The trouble that starts immediately and keeps on happening is known technically as Who Cares? Near the three-eighths pole, it appears that Pyle, who is a cloak-and-dagger boy attached to the Economic side of the American Legation, is helping the bandit get plastic, which can be used in the manufacture of bombs as well as many other things. I figured the bandit was fooling naïve young Pyle. Not at all. Pyle knew all about the bombs and the contemplated explosion. So did the whole American Legation. The Minister must have O.K.'d it. The way Mr. Greene, through Fowler, tips the reader to this is Fowler is in a café and two young American Legation girls are there eating ice cream—"neat and clean in the heat," a pejorative description for Fowler, who is a great sweat-and-smell man:

> They finished their ices, and one looked at her watch. "We'd better be going," she said, "to be on the safe side." I wondered idly what appointment they had.
> "Warren said we mustn't stay later than eleven-twenty-five."

The two girls go out, and a couple of minutes later the big bomb goes off.

All the Legation personnel had been warned.

At this point, I, as startled as Fowler, remembered something—a miching little introductory note in the front of the book, about how all the characters are fictitious. I turned back to it, not bothering to follow Fowler out of the café and into the horrors of the square, to which I knew he would do stark justice—brusque, brutal, ironic.

"Even the historical events have been rearranged," the part of the note I wanted to see again said. "For example, the big bomb near the Continental preceded and did not follow the bicycle bombs."

Greene was, then, writing about a real explosion, a historical event, which had produced real casualties. And he was attributing the real explosion to a fictitious organization known as the United States State Department. If the State Department had promoted the historical explosion, I thought, it was a terrific news story and a damned shame. We needed a new State Department.

But whether it had or hadn't, anybody who read the book would wonder whether the State Department was engaged in the business of murdering French colonels and, in their default, friendly civilians. In France, which is traversing a period of suspicion, rapidly approaching hatred, of all foreign governments, the effect would be particularly poisonous when the book was translated. I knew that Mr. Greene, like James Hadley Chase and Mickey Spillane, is a great favorite of French readers of whodunits. ("Not for a long time have Anglophobia and anti-Americanism been so much at work in Paris," Stephen Coulter of the Sunday *Times* wrote lately. "It is a rooted French political axiom: 'When in trouble blame the foreigners.' ")

Then I remembered something else. In Paris, where I had been until the day before I began my plane passage, I had noticed, without much interest, that *L'Express*, a bright new newspaper, had already begun the publication of a new serial: "Un Américain Bien Tranquille," by Graham Greene. The serials in Paris newspapers are generally translations of fairly stale books, and they are frequently retitled to appeal to French taste. I therefore had assumed the feuilleton in the *Express* was a book Greene wrote years ago (but of which I had read only a review) about an American who has an affair with an Englishwoman and is punished for the sacrilege. The *Express*, a tabloid, was crowded for news space even at sixteen pages, a format it had struggled for two months to attain. It is a universal belief among French editors, however, that a newspaper must have a feuilleton. The readers demand it, and read it more faithfully than anything else in the paper. I could imagine the *Express*'s hundred thousand readers getting to the two-neat-girls installment and then asking their friends at lunch, *"Tu l'as vu dans l'Express? C'est les Amerloques qui ont fait sauter deux mille français sur des mines atomiques en Indochine."* People everywhere confuse what they read in newspapers with news.

*L'Express* is only a weekly now. "Un Américain Bien Tranquille" was an irresponsible choice for the editors, but they needed circulation desperately. They didn't get it. *L'Express* went two hundred and forty-five numbers before it gave up its struggle to survive as a daily, and it still annoys me to think that a sixteenth of each of at least a hundred was devoted to Mr. Greene's nasty little plastic bomb.

There is a difference, after all, between calling your over-successful offshoot a silly ass and accusing him of murder.

# Lisa Vargo

*Lisa Vargo has taught at Bishop's University, Queen's University, Trent University, and the University of Saskatchewan, where she is now an assistant professor. Her primary research area is English Romanticism, particularly the writings of Mary Shelley and Percy Bysshe Shelley.*

## THE QUIET AMERICAN AND "A MR. LIEBERMANN"

It has been said that England and America are nations divided by a common language. The difficulties Graham Greene encountered in trying to capture the idiom of Alden Pyle in *The Quiet American* suggest how very wide this division can be. Greene seems to have known what he was up against. Toward the end of the novel, Fowler, the English narrator, offers to write a story for an American journalist named Granger whose son has contracted polio. Granger declines the offer: "You wouldn't get the accent right." An examination of different editions of the text from the first edition of 1955 to the Collected Edition of 1973 demonstrates that Greene has continued to work toward getting the accent of the novel right.[1]

Greene was making revisions to *The Quiet American* as early

Reprinted with permission from *English Language Notes* 21 (June 1984): 63–70.

as 1956 when the novel was reprinted for the second time.[2] Near the beginning of the novel Fowler conjures a satirical image of Pyle in America:

> I saw him in a family snap-shot album, riding on a dude ranch, bathing on Long Island, photographed with his colleagues in some apartment on the twenty-third floor. He belonged to the sky-scraper and the express lift, the ice-cream and the dry Martinis, milk at lunch, and chicken sandwiches on the Merchant Adventurer.
>
> (1st, p. 16)

In the first reprint of the novel for 1956, "express lift" is changed to its American equivalent, "express elevator," and "Merchant Adventurer" (the train between Boston and New York) is corrected to "Merchant Limited" (rpt., p. 16). Yet the description still contains an oversight: "bathing" is an Anglicism for what Pyle's family would call "swimming." In another instance requiring correction, Pyle's proposal to Phuong includes an offer to "let her know my blood-count" (1st, p. 96). Greene clearly has the wrong word here; however, the substitution "blood-group" (rpt., p. 96), again seems to be a British term. An American would be more likely to say "blood type."

Some other substantive changes dating from the reprint illustrate the discontinuity between American and English editions.[3] Greene seems to have recognized soon after the novel was published that Fowler's angry description of the Americans in Vietnam "with their private stores of Coca-Cola and their portable hospitals and their Wydecars and their not quite latest guns" contains one definite inaccuracy (1st, p. 32). "Wydecars" is altered in different ways in the first English reprint of 1956 and the American first edition printed in March 1956. In the English reprint Greene changes the reading to "their too wide cars," a nice complement to "not quite latest guns," which establishes a hierarchy of American values (rpt., p. 32). This reading has been preserved in all subsequent British editions.

The American editor takes "their Wydecars" literally; the phrase becomes "their wide cars," which also appears in the first Modern Library edition of 1967 (Vik., p. 32; ML, p. 32). A more curious history of alteration may be found in Pyle's smug confidence to Fowler in the first edition that " 'I feel such a heel, but you do believe me, don't you, that if you'd been married—why, I wouldn't ever come between a man and his wife' " (1st, p. 69). An American would be more apt to say "I feel *like* such a heel"; the British reprint and the American first edition both contain this change (rpt., p. 69; Vik., p. 69). However, "like such a heel" is changed back to the British "feel such a heel" in the Collected Edition (CE, p. 58). Perhaps Greene overlooked this correction when he was preparing the new edition. In a third example of variant readings between English and American editions, an American editor has corrected one mistake in idiom yet to be discovered by Greene or any British editor. The note Pyle leaves for Fowler in Hanoi contains the apologetic explanation that "I shan't get back to Saigon for a week if I don't leave today" (1st, p. 76). The Viking editor transforms "shan't" to "won't," since no American would ever use "shan't" (Vik., p. 76). This revision is retained in the American Modern Library edition, but does not appear in any of the English editions (ML, p. 76).

Because Greene was aware shortly after its publication that corrections in the American idiom of his novel were necessary, he must have been particularly annoyed by A. J. Liebling's April 1956 review of *The Quiet American* which appeared in the *New Yorker*.[4] The review is an indulgence of the whimsy and conceit that characterize Liebling's style, and while it may be effective elsewhere in his writings, here wit merely masks prejudice. Liebling describes the desperate circumstances of having nothing but *The Quiet American* to entertain him on a trans-Atlantic flight. Reading the novel under duress, he becomes irritated by Greene's satirical portraits of Americans abroad, which leads him to point out that Greene has no ear for the American language. He argues that Greene's mistakes in the American idiom confuse the satire as well as the narrative perspective of the novel. Liebling suggests that Pyle's inability to master American idiom indicates that he is actually a French author's idea of an Englishman: "a naïve chap who speaks bad French, eats tasteless food, and is only accidentally and episodically heterosexual" (p. 347). If Greene's "Quiet American" is an Englishman, the British narrator Fowler must have a connection with the United States, since he is able to satirize America too precisely to be an outsider. Liebling spends much of the review presenting plausible explanations for Fowler's past, an activity which, he finds, is more interesting than reading the novel (pp. 348–351). Having destroyed the credibility of Greene's characters, Liebling ridicules Greene's knowledge of politics in Indochina (pp. 353–354). Liebling, it seems, was sufficiently pleased with the review to include it in a collection of his journalism.[5] The alteration of the title from "A Talkative Something-or-Other" to "A Talkative Jerk" removes the only token of generosity from the review.

Greene's first reaction to the review was to glare at Liebling when both men happened to be dining at the same restaurant one evening. This silent protest went unheeded by Liebling, who did not know what Greene looked like.[6] Yet Greene seems not to have been so offended by the review as to have ignored Liebling's advice. Liebling's petty correction of Pyle's use of "sandwich mixture"—("in American, I think a thing like that is called a sandwich *spread*")—(p. 348), is incorporated into the Reprint Society edition of 1957, if not before (RS, p. 91).[7] Greene may well have been led by Liebling's description of Pyle as a "basically English type" to consider further alterations beyond "sandwich spread." A small campaign is undertaken to make Pyle appear less an Oxonian and more like the Harvard man he is. Pyle's description of Phuong's sister as "charming" is transformed to the perfect American banality "very nice" (1st, p. 48; RS, p. 41). When Pyle pays Fowler an early morning visit in the middle of a war zone to proclaim his love for Phuong, he asks if he can move the candle since " 'It's a bit bright here' "; with more accuracy, this phrase becomes " 'a little too bright here' " (1st, p. 67; RS, p. 57). However, Liebling would be quick to point out that Greene overlooks the more obvious fact that Pyle would never describe the boat he came to the camp with as " 'some kind of a punt' " (1st, p. 67). Greene also revises two details in the proposal scene which diminish the English aspects of Pyle's character. The Oxonian Pyle who warns Fowler that he " 'did boxing at college' " is transformed to a Harvard man who " 'boxed at college' " (1st, p. 90; RS, p. 76). In the same scene Greene deletes the overly priggish "Miss Phuong," which, simplified to "Phuong," reduces the degree of caricature in Pyle's presentation (1st, p. 94; RS, p. 79). Not even Pyle would go as far as "Miss Phuong" in a marriage proposal.

Liebling's criticisms doggedly follow Greene to his next revision of the novel for the Collected Edition of 1973.[8] In the Collected Edition, Pyle's admonition to an injured Fowler, " 'Got to save our strength,' " is omitted from the end of " 'Better not talk,' Pyle said as though an invalid" (1st, p. 140; CE, p. 119). The further comment is merely a comic overstatement that is not quite believable. The Collected Edition also contains a softened first view of Pyle, who looks at a Saigon milk bar and says "dreamily, 'That looks like a soda-fountain' " (1st, p. 21; CE, p. 16). The elimination of the adjective "good" emphasizes Pyle's homesickness, a touching aspect of his character, while postponing the introduction of his less endearing habit of recreating the world in America's image.

Liebling sticks to his own territory; he does not mention that *The Quiet American* is not only written in two idioms, but also in two different languages—English and French. While the French in the novel has led to two misprints in the 1974 Penguin edition,[9] the French has not presented a serious problem; only three substantive changes pertain to the French sections of the novel. The first concerns the French pronunciation of "Fowler," which appears in the first edition as "Foulair" and "Foulaire" (1st, pp. 8, 45, 48, 65, 246). While the reprint alters this to "Fowlair" and "Fowlaire," Marcelle Sibon's French translation of 1956, *Un Américain Bien Tranquille*, uses a variety of forms—"Foulair," "Foulaire," "Fowlair," and "Fowlaire"—demonstrating how devilish such small details can be (rpt., pp. 8, 45, 48, 65, 246; Fr., pp. 19, 71, 76, 99, 345). The English and American editions are standardized to different forms. The American first edition uses "Fowlaire" throughout, while the Collected Edition uses "Fowlair" without exception (Vik., pp. 8, 45, 49, 65, 248; CE, pp. 8, 37, 41, 55, 210). In another instance, Greene has turned to a French word in the Collected Edition. When Fowler goes to collect Phuong's belongings from Pyle's apartment, he packs her "small triangular *culottes*" rather than "pants" (CE, p. 22; 1st, p. 27). The Collected Edition also contains a correction of much greater significance—Greene has surprisingly called the dice game, which figures importantly in the novel, "*Quatre Vingt-et-un*" instead of "*Quatre Cent Vingt-et-un*" (1st, pp. 34, 64, 82, 177; CE, pp. 27, 54, 70, 151). Carelessness allows this error to remain undetected through so many editions.

While most of the changes in this discussion have concerned a matter of "getting the accent right," the Collected Edition alone bears evidence that Greene has tinkered with the dialogue concerning the bomb near the Continental, the section of the novel Liebling regards as unjustified. Greene has attempted to make the prose of this "messy explosion," to quote Liebling, a bit more tidy. After the explosion, Fowler muses about Pyle, "Let him play harmlessly with plastic; it might keep his mind off Phuong" (1st, p. 185). In the Collected Edition, Greene intensifies the conflict in Fowler's mind with the addition of "moulds" after "plastic" (CE, p. 158), thus strengthening Fowler's perception of the extent of Pyle's involvement. The balance of Fowler's motives for his betrayal of Pyle is tipped in favor of morality. He acts out of a horror of dead women and children, rather than from the less noble but equally powerful desire to regain Phuong. Greene clarifies the issue further when Fowler confronts Mr. Heng. " 'And plastic

isn't for boys from Boston' " is transformed to the more blatant
" 'bombs aren't' " (1st, p. 226; CE, p. 192). Again Greene reinforces Fowler's decision to set up Pyle for the Communists.
Yet at the same time, Greene's revisions in the Collected Edition attempt to underplay the melodramatic aspects of the
bombing; there is power enough in the recurring image of
the dead woman and child in the ditch. After the bombing in
the square of a righteous Fowler sermonizes:

> "You see what a drum of Diolacton can do," I said, "in
> the wrong hands." I forced him, with my hand on his
> shoulder, to look around. I said, "This is the hour when
> the place is always full of women and children—it's the
> shopping hour. Why choose that of all hours?"
>
> (1st, pp. 212–13)

Greene has eliminated the unnecessary first sentence of this
paragraph to let the action of forcing Pyle to look around the
square speak for itself (CE, p. 182). In the scene with Mr.
Heng, Greene deletes the overly dramatic " 'How many bombs
and dead children can you get out of a drum of Diolacton,' "
leaving the phrase which plays into Heng's hands: " 'What'll
he do next, Heng?' " (1st, p. 226; CE, p. 193). Greene is careful
to bring further authenticity to his speculations about what
Liebling calls "a fictitious organization known as the United
States State Department" (p. 354). Fowler asks Heng about
Pyle:

> "What is he? O.S.S.?"
> "The initial letters are not very important."
>
> (1st, p. 226)

In the Collected Edition Greene adds to Heng's reply: " 'I think
now they are different' " (CE, p. 192).

    The introduction the author supplies for the Collected Edi-
tion of *The Quiet American* suggests that Liebling's ill-informed

remarks about Greene's ignorance on the subject of American foreign policy have continued to irritate him.

> When my novel was eventually noticed in the *New Yorker* the reviewer, a Mr. Liebermann, condemned me for accusing my "best friends" (the Americans) of murder since I had attributed to them the responsibility for the great explosion—far worse than the trivial bicycle bombs—in the main square of Saigon when many people lost their lives. But what are the facts, of which Liebermann needless to say was ignorant?
>
> (CE, p. xviii)

Greene's enjoyment of practical jokes is well-known.[10] Accordingly, his reference to "a Mr. Liebermann" is probably but another of his sharply pointed jests. It is difficult to imagine that Greene would forget the name of such an influential journalist, even after almost twenty years—especially with the sting of Liebling's review still sharp in Greene's memory. Surely the introduction to *The Quiet American* contains the last word on the true identity of "A Talkative Something-or-Other."

Recent bibliographical studies of Greene's novels show that American editors have contributed to the muddled state of the texts of *The Power and the Glory*, *The Heart of the Matter*, *The End of the Affair*, and *A Burnt-Out Case*.[11] Greene has revised these novels at different times; however, further unwanted changes result from the liberal house-styling of the Viking Press. While the threat of an English lawsuit brought about revisions in *Stamboul Train*, Hollywood directors and an American magazine have done worse damage to *The Third Man*.[12] Yet the revisions of *The Quiet American*, occasioned by an American critic, vindicate American intervention in Greene's texts for once, and raise the question of just how much attention Greene pays to critics in the revision of his novels.

NOTES

1. I have examined the following editions of *The Quiet American*:
   (London: Heinemann, 1955), hereafter cited as 1st, with page
   number; (London: Heinemann, 1955; rpt. 1955, 1956), hereafter
   cited as rpt., with page number; (New York: Viking, 1956), hereafter cited as Vik., with page number; *Un Américain Bien Tranquille*, Marcelle Sibon, trans. (Paris: Robert Laffont, 1956),
   hereafter cited as Fr., with page number; (London: Reprint Society, 1957), hereafter cited as RS, with page number; Uniform
   Edition (London: Heinemann, 1960); Library Edition (London:
   Heinemann, 1960); (Harmondsworth: Penguin Books, 1962; rpt.
   1965, 1967, 1968, 1969, 1970, 1971, 1972, 1973); (New York: Modern Library, 1967), hereafter cited as ML, with page number; Collected Edition (London: Heinemann and Bodley Head, 1973),
   hereafter cited as CE, with page number; (1973; rpt. Harmondsworth: Penguin Books, 1974; rpt. 1975, 1976, 1977, 1978, 1979
   [twice]), hereafter cited as Penguin 1974, with page number.

   For a list of different editions of the novel, see R. A. Wobbe,
   *Graham Greene: A Bibliography and Guide to Research* (New York
   and London, 1979), pp. 104–106, p. 192.

2. The novel was reprinted once in 1955 and twice in 1956 according
   to the Uniform Edition. I have only been able to examine the first
   reprinting of 1956. Thus, I cannot determine whether these
   changes occurred in the first or second reprinting. In any case, it
   is safe to say that they were incorporated before the appearance
   of Liebling's review.

3. For more information on this subject, see Philip Stratford, "Second Thoughts on 'Graham Greene's Second Thoughts': The Five
   Texts of *The Heart of the Matter*," SB, 31 (1978): 263–66 and
   David Leon Higdon, "The Texts of Graham Greene's A *Burnt-
   Out Case*," PBSA, 73 (1979): 357–64. Higdon points out that Viking Press printed Greene's novels from duplicate typescripts or
   from English proofs (p. 360). It is possible that *The Quiet American* was set either from typescript or uncorrected proofs, given
   the variant readings with the English first edition.

4. "A Talkative Something-or-Other," NY, 32 (April 7, 1956), 148–
   54. All further references will be cited by page number in the body
   of the text. [Ed. note: page numbers have been adjusted to refer
   to this book.]

5. William Cole, ed., *The Most of A. J. Liebling* (New York, 1963),

pp. 307–13. The foreword to this group of essays, by Liebling himself, makes it clear that Cole merely helped to narrow down the unreasonable number of essays Liebling wanted to include in this collection.

6. This story is told by Nora Sayre in Raymond Sokolov's *Wayward Reporter: The Life of A. J. Liebling* (New York, 1980), pp. 271–73.

7. My conclusion is based on having found these corrections in the Reprint Society edition of 1957. It is unlikely that Greene would have made extensive corrections in this edition; therefore, the changes probably occurred in the second reprinting of 1956, within months after Liebling's review.

8. Greene seems to have made no substantive changes in either the Uniform or Library editions.

9. The dice call is mistakenly given as "four-to-one" (Penguin 1974, p. 68). The name of the game should alert an editor that this is wrong. For a description of the game, see *Grand Larousse encyclopédique* (Paris, 1963), VIII, 944. "*Le cauchemar*" appears as "*Le caucheman*" (Penguin 1974, p. 132).

10. Stratford, p. 263.

11. See David Leon Higdon's essays "Graham Greene's Second Thoughts: The Text of *The Heart of the Matter*" *SB*, 30 (1977), 249–256; "The Texts of Graham Greene's *A Burnt Out Case*," *op. cit.*; " 'Betrayed Intentions': Graham Greene's *The End of the Affair*," *The Library*, Sixth Series, 1 (1979), 70–77; "A Textual History of Graham Greene's *The Power and the Glory*," *SB* 33 (1980), 222–239; and Stratford, *op. cit.*

12. See R. H. Miller, "Textual Alterations in Graham Greene's *Stamboul Train*," *PBSA*, 71 (1977), 378–381, and Judy Adamson and Philip Stratford, "Looking for the Third Man: On the Trail in Texas, New York, Hollywood," *Encounter*, 50 (June 1978), 39–46.

# R. W. B. Lewis

*One of the leading American literary critics since World War II,
R. W. B. Lewis has taught at most of the Ivy League schools,
primarily at Yale University as professor of English. His early
work* The American Adam *(1955) is an acknowledged standard,
and he has written books on Edith Wharton and Hart Crane. He
has also edited numerous books, including Graham Greene's* The
Power and the Glory *for the Viking Critical Library.*

## THE FICTION OF GRAHAM GREENE:
## BETWEEN THE HORROR AND THE GLORY

The story of *The Quiet American*, Graham Greene's recent
novel about the war in Indochina, is told in a smooth but sometimes inaudible undertone that marks a further decline from
the harried and explosive intensity of his best fiction up to
about 1940. A further decline: for even in *The Heart of the
Matter*, an occasional narrative flabbiness marred what was otherwise a novel of greater stature than its large and immediate
popularity might suggest. And less happily still, *The End of the
Affair* revealed what seemed to be a disconcerting shift of narrative intention. The account, there, of a woman of frail virtue
reluctantly dragged towards sainthood was a tour-de-force of

First published in *The Kenyon Review* 14 (Winter 1957), 56–75. Copyright ©
1957 by Kenyon College. Reprinted by permission of *The Kenyon Review*.

considerable brilliance—incipient sanctity seen from without with splendid incomprehension; but one had the feeling that the plot was being manipulated in the interest of a furtive edification. Greene has insisted (in the preface to a book about him by the French critic, Paul Rostenne) that he has no desire at all to preach in his fiction, that he is carried along by the unpredictable energies of his characters and not by ulterior purposes of any kind. But what has happened to Greene's longer fiction since the end of the war is that edification has been creeping in; or perhaps that his strong personal beliefs and dislikes have got ahead of his invention. By a paradoxical law of creation, his recent work has, as a consequence, an air of spurious slickness; for as his attention begins to stray, the force of his imagination is gradually replaced—rather than, as before, merely abetted—by competence. Competence, which is not the same as craftsmanship, is a quality Greene, a sometime journalist, has always manifested and sometimes over-valued. But competence can be as self-indulgent as eccentricity; and in *The Quiet American* it tends to produce not a clear and unprejudiced impression of life but an intricate plot with very little action: sensational doings wrapped in perfunctory attitudes which point towards a moral—this time in the field of international emotions—which the novel has scarcely attempted to beget. And for the moment, the strained and searching author of *Brighton Rock* looks like nothing so much as a tired James Hilton wearing a faint neo-Augustinian scowl.

Greene's congenital slickness is misleading, and it blurs our awareness both of his immense talent and his distinguished literary achievement—especially during the period when, as Morton Zabel (in 1943) was able to say, he was close to becoming one of the masters of modern fiction. It is all the harder to detect even the limited virtues of *The Quiet American*, for what is striking about the latter is precisely what it draws to itself from the imaginary world Greene had already created—that baffling landscape, at once harrowing and seedy, which English critics call Greeneland. Greene's world bears a curious but vivid resemblance to fragments of the historical world. He has always sought to imbed his anagogical nightmares within meticulously described settings—sometimes the dingier sections of English cities, but more usually those portions of the earth which, from the western center, appear remote, primitive, fantastic; there is a close relation for Greene between the dingy and the primitive. His aim, moreover, is not simply to describe surfaces, but rather to evoke the very vitality, the natural activity of a place. In the new novel, it is Indochina; elsewhere it has been Stockholm, Tabasco and Liberia, Brighton, London and the English countryside; and one sometimes feels that the best of Greene's books are the two in which vitality of atmosphere is almost everything—*Journey Without Maps* (1936), a sketch of West Africa, and *The Lawless Roads* (1939) about Mexico. But Greeneland also contains representative characters and recurring dramas, and *The Quiet American* introduces us to further adventures and disguises of the former and another version of the latter.

Although the title figure, a young government official named Alden Pyle, embodies a distinctive American trait as seen from a particularly sour European viewpoint—that stony and abstract piety, that compound of headstrong innocence and the assumption of massive power which is so pronounced in our recent conduct of public and foreign affairs—he is no less significantly the latest addition, with an ominous New England accent, to Greene's long gallery of catastrophic trimmers. He belongs with those persons who, like Ida in *Brighton Rock*, are satisfied not only that they know the difference between right and wrong but that it is the only difference worth knowing: relentless missionaries from what Greene calls "the sinless empty graceless chromium world" sent to bring disaster upon residents of the (for Greene) infinitely realer and more vibrant, though narrower and sparser, world of good and evil, of heaven and hell. At the same time, Pyle is caught up in Greene's representative tragic plot, the story of betrayal and sacrifice which—from his first novel, *The Man Within*, onwards—

Greene has been modelling and remodelling, with endless variations, on the Passion of Christ. Pyle's ignorant energy causes the death of several dozen natives. Because of that, and for more selfish and private reasons, Fowler, the English newspaperman whose fuzzy confession makes up the story, betrays him to an underground group which assassinates him. Pyle is thus another of Greene's characters whose experience—like Harry Lime's in *The Third Man*—gains some ironic and pitiful portion of meaning in the perspective of Holy Week. And it is, after all, Fowler, the unquiet European, whose identity is nourished in the dreadful shadow of Judas.

But despite the presence of these symbolic relationships, *The Quiet American* does not finally engage us on any serious level. Yet its failure to do so may, oddly, be part of the design of the book, perhaps the essence of what action it has. "Am I the only one who really cared for Pyle?" Fowler wonders in the opening pages. The question may be taken as exactly what the novel is all about—what, with suitable changes of name, Greene's fiction has been mostly all about. For Greene's special concern has always been the question, "Who cares?"—has been, that is, the lost but recoverable importance of the human act and the human person. The sense of it, he believes, vanished from English fiction early in the 20th Century; his aim has been to find the terms for restoring it. The point of view which can do so, which can reestablish the reality as well as the value of fictional beings and their behavior, is for Greene, needless to say, that of the religious consciousness. The force of that notion in Greene's work is the main subject of these notes; but meanwhile, I hazard a final inference about *The Quiet American*.

The best that can be said for the novel, and it is probably too much, is that Greene is demonstrating in it, deliberately if all too slyly, the *un*importance of the human act when the religious consciousness is absent to the view of it—a demonstration essentially comic (although never very funny) in nature and intent. The dustjacket maintains that Greene "has entered a new vein"—with this novel—"where religion plays little or no part." One might better say that Greene is here continuing the vein, begun a good deal earlier, where the absence of religion plays a rather vital part. The novel's viewpoint is the non-religious consciousness of Fowler, the narrator, whose religious myopia contrasts with the warm, unstable Catholicism shown by his English wife in letters from home. As seen through Fowler's eyes, no one—neither Pyle, nor Fowler himself, nor Phuong, the toy mistress—appears really lively, or even worth writing about; and if they do not, it may possibly be because, within the bizarre limits Greene seems to have set, they were not supposed to. The passion play, at work behind the dispirited melodrama, is perhaps observable to the initiated reader, but it is not intuited by Fowler. A tired humor thus surrounds Fowler's closing lament: "I wished there existed someone to whom I could say I was sorry." And *The Quiet American* can be set down as a mode of comedy: a satyr play, perhaps, to Greene's major phase, the tragic trilogy of *Brighton Rock, The Power and the Glory* and *The Heart of the Matter*.

# Georg Gaston

*Professor emeritus at Appalachian State University, Georg Gaston is the author of the critical biographies* Karel Reisz, Jack Clayton, *and* Robert Shaw: More Than a Life. *He is also the editor of* Critical Essays on Dylan Thomas. *He lives in Spartansburg, South Carolina.*

## THE QUIET AMERICAN:
## A SECULAR PROSPECT

When Greene wrote *The Quiet American* (1955), he was as fully in command of his craft as he would ever be. In fact, it can be argued that this novel is actually his most flawlessly wrought. It's particularly notable that Greene now manages to avoid the descriptive and metaphorical excesses which occasionally appear in his earlier works, and his use of the first person narrative approach fits in more perfectly with his structural and thematic concerns than it did in *The End of the Affair*. Nevertheless, *The Quiet American* has always been his most controversial and widely misunderstood book. No doubt, that's partly due to the fact that many of his readers weren't prepared to shift from his Catholic themes toward a secular direction. But there is an-

Reprinted with permission of the author from Georg Gaston, *The Pursuit of Salvation: A Critical Guide to the Novels of Graham Greene.* Troy, N.Y.: Whitston Publishing Company, 1984, 55–71.

other, more insistent, reason for the misinterpretations. Many people have misread or downright objected to the novel on the grounds of what they felt were its biased political assumptions. Not surprisingly, this has been especially the case in the United States. When the book first appeared in this country, it was immediately met with a great deal of hostility. Critics left and right charged Greene with having essentially written a petulant tract against Americans and their ambitions in world affairs, particularly in Indochina. Once the Vietnamese war became a fact, and the political commentary in the book was found to have been incisive and prophetic to an astonishing degree, it began winning more and more praise from critics here as well as abroad. However, this new reputation which the novel is enjoying is largely based on an unsound impression which continues to persist, that the book is meant to be primarily read as an anti-war story.[1] It should be made clear, though, that although war and politics are prominent issues in the novel, they serve to poise the ultimate concern of personal salvation.

This issue of personal salvation is concentrated primarily in the character of Fowler, the narrator of the book, and in the way he tells his story. Even the anti-American element which aroused so much criticism when the novel was first published must be seen now as having more to do with the fate of Fowler than with that of the world at large. In other words, Fowler's expressions of contempt for all things American are less symptomatic of his politics than of his intellectual and emotional condition. As a political reporter of long experience, he has come to look upon the United States as the force which carries the most responsibility for the misery of the world because it happens to be the greatest power. To his mind, the United States has actually become the symbol of what was wrong with modern civilization. These views, through their extreme logic, can suggest the mind of an idealist and a cynic, perhaps in a state of serious conflict. If he holds a grudge against Americans it is because of one particular American. It is Pyle, the "quiet American," who arrives on the scene in Vietnam to liberate

Fowler from his emotional and spiritual exhaustion. But Pyle is an unconscious, and paradoxical, savior. He enters Fowler's life suddenly to steal his girl and then to cause more misery in general by getting involved in terrorism. After Fowler witnesses a bombing caused by Pyle, he decides that his rival must be destroyed for the good of all. Thus when a political enemy of Pyle insinuates to Fowler the opportunity to fulfill his wish even though some violence might be involved, he gives in to temptation. After the death of the American, however, Fowler finds himself possessed by sorrow and guilt, the first real signs that he could be headed for a spiritual recovery.

Before Pyle's arrival, Fowler tried to feel satisfied with what life then offered—a loyal mistress, a quiet home, one day flowing into the next. But actually he is even then haunted by deep fears. He is terrorized by life, since it means suffering, and so he has tried to withdraw from it. Instead, his unnatural isolation has resulted in a kind of personal inferno reflected by the hellish setting in which he finds himself.

As is usual in Greene, the setting of *The Quiet American* is exotic, primitive, and violent.[2] Greene's detractors, who like to refer to his chosen settings as Greeneland, may wish to believe that his primary motive is sensationalism and melodrama. Obviously, though, there is a better reason. When he selects a tropical setting, he shows nature as sluggish and decaying but still energetic and impressive enough "to show up the forces of civilization as degenerate, makeshift and ugly."[3] If the scene is urban, it is often filled with images of industrial decadence reminiscent of Eliot's wasteland. The controlling factor of the setting, whether tropical or urban, is seediness. Seediness is ubiquitous because, as Greene sees it, the experience of modern man is filled with rot and squalor. Seediness is a sign of our maladjustment and the deterioration of our civilization. Thus there is in Greene the pull to primitivism, to go back to a time which was chaste in order to begin again. The presence of violence is important because it is the one pure emotion that joins the primitive with the modern world. Unfortunately, the ontology of violence has been debased to the point where it now expresses most urgently the horror of the present century. The setting of a Greene novel, then, functions as an important symbol of the civilization which has created it.

In a less direct way, the setting also functions to make clear the predicaments of the various characters. In *The Quiet American* the political hell of Vietnam serves especially to reflect and dramatize the inner state of Fowler. Vietnam is a land filled with horror. There is the ever-present danger of sudden death, whether in a contested military area or in a public square. If one loses a leg because of a bicycle bomb, it is considered as merely a poor joke. In *The Heart of the Matter* ubiquitous carrion birds hover over the failure and approaching death of Scobie. Here the birds are planes which do not wait for decay to set in; anything that moves is fair game. The flotsam of victims is everywhere, as omnipresent as the junk of war piling up. Knowing all this, Fowler, after he goes to a romantic movie with a happy ending, remarks that if it had been meant for children, "the sight of Oedipus emerging with his bleeding eyeballs from the palace at Thebes would surely give a better training for life today."[4] It is no wonder that Fowler is filled with cynicism, anxiety, and a terror of life, and that he consequently wishes to withdraw from it into a state of quiescence.

The title of the novel is actually ironic, for although Pyle is verbally quiet he is explosive in every other sense. It is Fowler who wishes so desperately for peace and who tries to insist that he is not involved:

> It had been an article of my creed. The human condition being what it was, let them fight, let them love, let them murder, I would not be involved. My fellow journalists called themselves correspondents; I preferred the title of reporter. I wrote what I saw: I took no action—even an opinion is a kind of action (*QA*, p. 28).

As it turns out, though, his wish for a life of radical detachment is futile. He finds out that he cannot really escape just by deciding to withdraw; events and people behind them will always interfere. Because he has a conscience, it will not allow him to rest when he is surrounded by pain. And he discovers that his chosen world of isolation is actually a kind of hell in itself which causes a torturous sense of alienation and a profound malaise which are akin to a living death.

Fowler is an opium smoker, for this drug can dull the pains of conscience for a time and abstract the spectacle of human misery. Eventually, of course, it can lead to the point where life is no longer a torture because it has become insubstantial. But a concomitant result is that the heart is in atrophy. In concrete terms, one will finally become like Mr. Chou: "with the indifferent gaze of a smoker; the sunken cheeks, the baby wrists, the arms of a small girl—many years and many pipes had been needed to whittle him down to these dimensions" (QA, p. 126). Human dignity is reduced to an "extreme emaciation" resembling a "piece of grease-proof paper that divides the biscuits in a tin" (QA, p. 126). In the back of his mind Fowler realizes that Mr. Chou represents himself as he might be, a part of the wreckage which surrounds the ancient opium smoker and which at the same time represents in real terms the accomplishments of that life.

In the course of the story Fowler goes through a process of psychological and spiritual regeneration, but the way is elaborate and agonizing. We can follow this process, however, by analyzing the narrative form, the structure of the story, and the persons whom Fowler encounters.

In *The Quiet American* Greene employs the basic form of the detective story. This is not surprising, since by now Greene was naturally predisposed to the genre. The reasons for this have everything to do with the nature of his art. The aesthetic and thematic conventions of this genre tend to embrace a number of the obsessions which have personally haunted him and

which he has continuously wished to investigate. Of these, terror, guilt, violence, betrayal, and mystery are the most prevalent. The detective story's most obvious element of pursuit also
creates the most interest through suspense; but this element
has a symbolic function as well. It serves to dramatize the emotional condition of being on the run and is an appropriate "an-
alogue of our search for the way out of confusion."[5] To Greene,
the detective story is a modern fairy tale which perhaps is most
effective in expressing the outrageous truth about the twentieth
century, that it is a slide into savagery. In effect, he prefers this
genre because it can serve best to illustrate our times, and
Greene's ultimate interest is always the means of arriving at
precise truth.[6] By pursuing and ferreting out truth, he believes,
life at least becomes less inane if not necessarily less painful.

The protagonist in *The Quiet American* goes through just
such a process. He is the detective who follows the clues which
lead him to the truth. Needless to say, this is no ordinary who-
done-it. The twist is that the clues of guilt lead the pursuer to
himself. At the end of the investigation Fowler discovers that
he is guilty of the crime. Moreover, in a cunning turn-about,
he finds as he follows the personal leads of alienation, malaise,
guilt, and finally responsibility that the someone he had believed dead was still alive. That is, at the vortex of the mystery
he finds himself.

A conventional element of the detective thriller is the confession at the end. *The Quiet American*, though, goes further
because the whole story is in the form of a dramatic confession.
But if Fowler has the desire to confess, does anyone really listen? Is it, as one critic suggests, only a frustrated confession?[7]
In Greene's Catholic novels there are the surrogates of God to
perform this function, and ultimately God himself listens. Yet
if Fowler's last words possibly indicate the wish that there were
a God to whom he could apologize for his life, it is still only a
wish, although such a hope might eventually turn out to be the
first step toward a religious faith. Whether or not Fowler will
finally take a leap to God remains only speculation in the con-

text of the novel; at the time of his final words of confession his vision of life is still clearly secular. Hence it is appropriate that his confession as a whole be directed at the secular parallel of a priest, a policeman who represents political instead of divine power. Vigot is, however, a silent confessor who does not appear to have much success in his efforts, because Fowler never tells him directly his whole story of involvement with the American whose death the policeman is responsible for investigating. That Vigot does not succeed in getting a direct confession is not really important, though; the important point is that Fowler has the compulsion to admit the truth, however painful the process may be. Without knowing it, Vigot actually does force Fowler to continue to reconstruct his story at least for his own analysis, purgation, and atonement after each meeting that the two have until the facts are all in and Fowler can lift his full burden of responsibility.

It is not true that Fowler, as one critic calls him, is an "obtuse narrator."[8] His problem is that he is afraid of what he does know. He is understandably reluctant to reconstruct his story because what waits at the end is something which might destroy his present hold on life. The danger awaiting him as he travels through the jungle of self-discovery is the realization that he has been involved in a murder and that perhaps he will never be able to be uninvolved again.

To dramatize the terror of Fowler and to reflect the analytical, convoluted self-exploration of his haunted mind as it hunts down the clues which will explain its emotional state, the structure of Greene's novel is purposely fragmented. At first one does make the observation that the grand aesthetic structure of the book is quite neat. Like a well-made play, the story falls naturally into the four parts that divide it, with each part organized around a central event. Thus in Part I Fowler meets Pyle. In Part II his life is saved by Pyle. But in Part III the American steals Fowler's girl away and shocks him with the discovery that Pyle has been responsible for a terrorist explosion which kills and maims the innocent and young. Consequently, in Part IV Fowler sees to it that the American is killed. These parts follow each other with relentless logic to an anticipated end; that is, if this were merely a simple story of revenge.

Within the neat exterior frame, the structure, just like Fowler, is complicated. In the first chapter of the novel we find out that the "quiet American" is dead, but it is difficult to suspect Fowler of any direct involvement. We are led to believe that at the very start of the story he is only waiting for Pyle, who has been delayed for some unexplained reason. One cannot know at the time that when Fowler says he wishes he were Pyle he is wishing for death. One is prone to accept Fowler's remark which ends the chapter at face value: "Am I the only one who really cared for Pyle?" (*QA*, p. 22). On the other hand, there are disturbing signs that seem to indicate Fowler is not after all so innocent despite his repeated disclaimers to himself after he finds out about the death. Why does he repeat his claim of innocence, one has to ask, and why to himself? The answer, of course, is that this is an indication he will be the hardest one to convince he is not guilty. Since such thoughts are painful, he smokes opium, which allows him to drift into abstract thoughts of the meaning of Phuong, who "was a certain hour of the night and the promise of rest," and of Pyle, who "had diminished after several pipes" (*QA*, p. 12). But the escape from the ghost of Pyle and the questioning silence of Vigot is only temporary.

In the first scene of Chapter II we are suddenly transported back to the day when Fowler first met Pyle. In the second scene of the same chapter we are jerked back in time and then forward to the morning after Pyle's death when Fowler goes to the American's apartment in order to help Phuong retrieve her things. There he encounters Vigot again, and thus his mind is once more possessed by thoughts of guilt and involvement. In the next chapter we are again jerked back into the past, to the time when, two months after his arrival, Pyle was first introduced to Phuong by Fowler. The remainder of Part I then more or less stabilizes into a chronological sequence of events. Significantly, this orderly pattern continues throughout Part II, as if Fowler were more willing to face time because his mind was under the illusion of greater safety as the crime receded into the past.

Part III begins on a day some two weeks after Pyle's death with another meeting between Fowler and Vigot. Consequently, as we have noted before, Fowler's conscience once again is forced to take up the thread of the story which in the end constitutes a tortured confession, and the agony which is growing in the confessor is again suggested by the inner structure of the book. As the panic of the narrator grows, so does the division of scenes into smaller and more confined units, as if to reflect the narrower bounds of escape. Part I was divided into comparatively large, rather leisurely units of five chapters, each of which in turn was sub-divided into no more than two scenes. Fowler is far from fully confronting his guilt at this stage. But in Part II we find only three chapters, and the central one is divided into four scenes. It is in this central chapter that Fowler recalls the night he and Pyle spent together talking about religion, politics, and sex; so this is when they actually learned to know each other. Even more disturbing to Fowler's submerged conscience, it was during this night that Pyle saved his life. And now in Part III, where Fowler is approaching the critical point in the story at which he becomes involved in the death of the American, the first chapter is broken into five sections, as if to suggest a delaying tactic against the onrush of truth and to reflect a growing hysteria through its jerky structure.

Part IV opens with Fowler's mind once more going back to a meeting which is described at the beginning of Part III. This final encounter with Vigot spurs Fowler into completing his story. Having by now passed the crisis of facing his guilt, he has ceased to resist and is prepared to finish his confession. Again, the structure of the novel functions to reveal his state of mind. In this part we discover that the inner structure has a numerical symmetry. Chapter I has a scene in which Fowler faces his confessor for the last time. Chapter II is divided into three scenes in which he, respectively, relives being at the explosion which shocked him into taking action against Pyle, going to Heng to see what could be done to stop the American, and finally taking the irretrievable step of entering into a conspiracy of murder. The last chapter of the book follows only a quarter of an hour after Vigot has left, as if to tell us that Fowler is now more at peace with time. In its only scene Fowler can finally make his apology for his past guilt.

Once we have analyzed the structure and start to look at the story in its time sequence, we can also begin to recognize that, like the priest in *The Power and the Glory*, Fowler is a fugitive not so much from the forces of law as from the terrifying knowledge that awaits him. He is a secular traveler, of course, and thus he will surrender to the immaterial force which pursues him more reluctantly. Nevertheless, like the priest, he is not only a geographical but also a mental itinerant who continually comes upon people who function as haunting images of his various sides and lead to a full self-knowledge.

We have already seen that Mr. Chou, the opium addict, serves to suggest to Fowler a grotesquerie of the man who withdraws from life. And we have also already seen that Vigot functions as a reflection of Fowler's conscience and an exorcist of his poisonous guilt. The reason why Vigot is so effective, though, is in itself revealing. When we first see Vigot, he too might appear to represent a man who has withdrawn from life because of "his weariness with . . . the whole human condition" (QA, p. 16). Yet although Vigot is weary, he is still interested enough to read Pascal and to wonder about the fate of humanity. He pursues Fowler not merely out of a sense of duty but because he has become involved in the quest for truth and in Fowler's destiny. Fowler is struck by the fact that Vigot after one of their meetings "had looked at me with compassion, as he might have looked at some prisoner for whose capture he was responsible undergoing his sentence for life" (QA, p. 139).

Fowler has some legitimate fear of the law at this time; however, as he comes to understand, what Vigot's look ultimately meant was that he was aware of the fact that we are all serving life-sentences of a sort. As he had earlier told Fowler, in life one does not have the choice to wager once he has embarked and that consequently Fowler was *"engagé*, like the rest of us" (*QA*, p. 138).

The last meeting with Vigot is particularly revealing of the detective's effect upon the mind of Fowler. After Vigot leaves, Fowler is astonished at how much he has been disturbed by failing to verbally express his guilt to him: "It was as though a poet had brought me his work to criticize and through some careless action I had destroyed it. I was a man without a vocation . . . but I could recognize a vocation in another" (*QA*, p. 171). Vigot's having a true vocation, which causes him to be embroiled in the mire of humanity, is what gives Fowler "the feeling of some force immobile and profound" (*QA*, p. 170). As Fowler realizes, Vigot "would have made a good priest" because it was "so easy to confess" to someone who is sympathetically involved instead of shocked by humanity (*QA*, p. 168). Moreover, Fowler is drawn to Vigot because of the latter's comprehension of the desires and motives of a confessor—to purge oneself, to rest from deception, and to see oneself clearly. Fowler, of course, feels a need for purgation and truth, and above all for self-knowledge.

When Fowler originally came to the Orient, it was for a different purpose than self-discovery. What he desired more than anything was peace, and he thought he could find it by escaping from himself. He had been married, had had affairs, and they each ended in disaster. Because he had been terrified of the end of love, he had rushed toward the finish "just like a coward runs towards the enemy and wins a medal"; in each case he "wanted to get death over" (*QA*, p. 103). In the East he again begins an affair; but because he believes that Phuong, as the myth about Oriental women goes, is a creature of loyalty instead of love, he has the illusion of safety. He feels certain that love is no real threat in this affair because of his pre-conception of Phuong that he describes to Pyle:

> It's a cliche to call them children—but there's one thing which is childish. They love you in return for kindness, security, the presents you give them—they hate you for a blow or an injustice. They don't know what it's like—just walking into a room and loving a stranger. For an aging man . . . it's very secure . . . (*QA*, p. 104).

Fowler may deny it, but at first he is a Berkeleyan in his attitude toward Phuong. He has abstracted her into a symbol. To him she is not an independent creature who is capable of surprising acts and feelings; she is only an ambience or emotion, "invisible like peace" (*QA*, p. 45). Only with his growing self-knowledge does he finally come to understand that he "was inventing a character" and that for all one "could tell, she was as scared as the rest of us: she didn't have the gift of expression, that was all" (*QA*, pp. 133–34). What he is discovering is that if Phuong was capable of fear and terror, then she had exhibited a re-markable quality of endurance. Consequently, even though in the beginning of this story Fowler denies that Phuong's name, which means phoenix, applies to her in any symbolic way since "nothing nowadays is fabulous, and nothing rises from its ashes" (*QA*, p. 11), it is precisely her genius for renewal which ultimately beguiles him, because he is seized by a suppressed but powerful yearning for such an experience.

After Phuong leaves him for Pyle, Fowler flies north to re-port on the war and to get away from the spectre of self-pity. There he meets Trouin, a young French pilot who has the wis-dom which is usually the result of many years. Trouin takes Fowler up for a bombing run, and nothing particularly out of the ordinary happens during it. On the return flight, however, Trouin quite suddenly blasts a harmless looking sampan apart.

Fowler is shaken, as he describes it, by the abrupt "fortuitous choice of a prey—we had just happened to be passing; one burst only was required; there was no one to return fire; we were gone again, adding our little quota to the world's dead" (QA, p. 150). Only that night when Trouin takes him to an opium house does Fowler learn about the pilot's deep and painful remorse. Angrily, he exclaims to Fowler and the world which seemed not to understand: "I'm not fighting a colonial war. Do you think I'd do these things for the planters of Terre Rouge? I'd rather be court-martialled. We are fighting all of your wars, but you leave us the guilt" (QA, p. 151). Refusing to dismiss his crimes on professional grounds, Trouin is a victim of his conscience who is willing to carry his guilt about with him. That he does join a quality of compassion with a sense of responsible objectivity is a source of continuing agony for him but is at the same time what saves his humanity.

Trouin's weight of guilt is religious in nature, since he accepts it as a necessary part of human limitations. One cannot remain innocent, detached, and yet human too. As he says at one point in answer to Fowler's declaration of non-involvement: "It's not a matter of reason or justice. We all get involved in a moment of emotion, and then we cannot get out. War and Love—they have always been compared. . . . I would not have it otherwise" (QA, p. 152). This train of thought has truly arrived at the heart of Fowler's moral turmoil, so that later that night he finds himself impotent to enter into the body of a beautiful prostitute because, he realizes, "the ghost of what I'd lost proved more powerful than the body stretched at my disposal" (QA, p. 153). The thought of Phuong is one ghost; but the memories of his lost humanity aroused by Trouin are also haunting him.

Trouin, of course, is not the only one who suggests to Fowler that he cannot choose not to be engaged without losing his soul. Such admonitions, in fact, become a dominant counterpoint to the theme of despair in what amounts to a kind of confessional fugue. We have already seen that Vigot was properly the one to commence the refrain of commitment. The letter Fowler receives from his wife in which she refuses to grant him a divorce sounds the same note. And Mr. Heng, who represents the Communist forces which are eager to be rid of Pyle, sums it up most directly: "Sooner or later . . . one has to take sides. If one is to remain human" (*QA*, p. 174).

Fowler finally accepts the view of this statement, but only after struggling against and experiencing its disquieting consequences. And it is predominantly his relationship with Pyle that makes the truth of it come home to stay, for Pyle in the end functions as an opposing reflection which discloses his true self and as his moral incubus.

Fowler and Pyle are so delineated as to suggest on one level of interpretation a dramatic antagonism between characters of antithetical positions, between realism and romanticism, experience and innocence, and between detachment and commitment.[9] This pattern of oppositions serves at first to make more concrete the characters of the two and to create the drama of a clash of characters. But ultimately this technique points to the more important issues of how the extreme positions of both represent failure and how a mature synthesis is necessary.[10] If this structure of opposition were used to isolate the factual evidence of Pyle's effect on Fowler, then it would appear that Greene is skirting mere melodrama. Fowler's involvement in the death of Pyle, however, does not just get rid of a dangerous rival in love. It is an act which shakes him out of a tired complacency and into guilt.[11] Moreover, on a symbolic level, it forces him into the realization that he had been responsible for killing his savior.

Pyle saves Fowler once from a violent death; but what the American does not know is that he saves Fowler in a spiritual way, too. At the end of Part I there is an evocative allusion to Dante's *Purgatorio*. This reference is appropriate in one sense, at least, because Fowler is truly wandering through circles of infernal despair. Ironically, he is led out of this region by Pyle, who actually does not know where he is going himself since he is blinded by the false light of his political idealism. But a dream which Fowler has suggests Pyle's function in this regard. It begins with Pyle's insistently and repeatedly calling Fowler by his Christian name, Thomas. This summons is in itself significant, for it stresses that Fowler is, as his first name can imply, filled with righteous doubt. In the dream itself Fowler sees himself "walking down a long, empty road looking for a turning which never came. The road unwound like a tape machine with a uniformity that would never have altered if the voice hadn't broken in—first of all like a voice crying in pain from a tower and then suddenly a voice speaking to me personally" (QA, p. 130). If Pyle is misguided, he still is not lost in one sense, for he does have a faith in something outside himself. Most important, though, Pyle's voice represents that of the young calling out in need. Then the dream merges into half-dream, and as it does it gravitates toward a more complete implication of what Pyle means to Fowler:

> Under my breath I said, "Go away, Pyle. Don't come near me. I don't want to be saved."
> "Thomas." He was hitting at my door, but I lay possum as though I were back in the rice field and he was an enemy (QA, pp. 130–31).

In a very real sense, Pyle is his enemy in love and in war. More symbolically, the American threatens his false peace. This dream, then, serves to indicate that, by continuously forcing himself on Fowler's conscience, Pyle awakens it.

As has already been suggested, what Fowler finally awakens to is not Pyle's personal ideas of conscience. Pyle's vision of life has a fanatical gleam. He has entered into the struggle of life with the weapons of innocence and devotion, but they are both tarnished by intellectual prejudice and they consequently serve to destroy him. He is dedicated to a political vision of life; but, as Fowler realizes, he has no real notion of "what the whole affair's about. . . . He never saw anything he hadn't heard in a lecture-hall, and his writers and his lecturers made a fool of him. When he saw a dead body he couldn't even see the wounds. A Red menace, a soldier of democracy" (*QA*, p. 32). Being only able to see in the abstract, he is blind to the essential truth which Fowler eventually understands: "Suffering is not increased by numbers: one body can contain all the suffering the world can feel" (*QA*, p. 183).

Because Pyle's innocence is not based on experience and creative imagination, it is sinister and lethal. Such innocence, which is really the worst kind of adult ignorance, is a terrible disease. It "always calls mutely for protection when we would be so much wiser to guard ourselves against it: innocence is like a dumb leper who has lost his bell, wandering the world, meaning no harm" (*QA*, p. 37). After the explosion in the square, the dangerous extent of Pyle's political chastity comes home to Fowler, and so he decides on a radical step of involvement. He decides to destroy his antagonist; however, he acts not from a motive of vengeance but with an imaginative sympathy. He has tried to make Pyle recognize that there is nothing gallant in atrocity by forcing his shoe into the blood of the victims of the terrorist violence the American has subsidized, but he can see that Pyle does not understand the significance of the act. Thus Fowler concludes: "What's the good? he'll always be innocent, you can't blame the innocent, they are always guiltless. All you can do is control them or eliminate them. Innocence is a kind of insanity" (*QA*, p. 163).

If Fowler were only interested in the economy of pain, he could find sufficient self-justification for conspiring in the death of Pyle. But his conscience haunts him because of a terrible dilemma, for although he fears and hates what Pyle stands for, he nevertheless is the only one who truly becomes interested in the character and the fate of the American. As he will come to understand more clearly through his subsequent relationship with Granger, a boisterous transmogrification of the quiet American, once one has entered the unexplored territory of another human being, he is mesmerized by the vision of human failure—that is, unless he has a lack of imagination. Having arrived at the point where he understands that he must destroy Pyle in order to save others and himself, he nevertheless has some compassion for his victim and he feels like a Judas who betrays someone who was his savior primarily in the sense that the latter needed him. This is why the final words of Fowler's confession have the quality of genuine torment and ambiguity: "everything had gone right with me since he had died, but how I wished there existed someone to whom I could say that I was sorry" (QA, p. 189).

In these words of repentance Fowler's renewed sense of guilt is conspicuous and is actually the clearest sign of his salvation. An important question, however, must still be asked: who is that "someone" of his supplication?

That the question should be necessary is plainly Greene's intent. He has often expressed his complex vision of life through "carefully nurtured ambiguity."[12] He has been, as Philip Stratford says, "irresistibly drawn to frontiers. Where they didn't exist, he invented them; where they did, he assiduously sought out some of the remoter of them; once across, he hearkened back to the place he had left; when caught in some no-man's land, he suffered from it, exquisitely."[13] Fowler is obviously a kind of extension of Greene. He, too, experiences the fine tension between exile and membership. And as he crosses into various regions of the mind, he suffers the agony of abandonment or alienation. At the end of his journey his anguish is particularly acute because he is entering the territory of faith.

It is perhaps possible that the "someone" of Fowler's last words is God. The critic Pryce-Jones, for one, declares that the reference *must* be to God, and his reasoning certainly has considerable merit. As the argument goes, Fowler's attempt to live in detachment is bound to fail because, when he finds himself in a dilemma which requires a moral decision, he feels at a loss due to the fact that he cannot draw on any religious resources. His neutrality is especially certain to fail in a situation of violence, for if he elects not to give spiritual value to life, then he must rate life even higher than the religious person does since he believes this life to be the only one. When Fowler is made to choose sides despite his skepticism, he goes beyond his subjective assumption and, supposing the existence of higher values, takes part in Pyle's death. What can these lofty ends be, asks Pryce-Jones, but those postulated by God?[14] The answer is that there might be other great ends which can be posited by other forms of faith.

The truth is that Fowler seems to be as set in his atheism at the end of the story as he is at the beginning. What is different in his outlook is that he is more inclined to express a reverence of life. In this regard, it should be pointed out that the critical view that *The Quiet American* is a novel about the absence of religion is imprecise.[15] On the contrary, it turns out to be just what Greene calls it, a "kind of morality about religion."[16] In this novel there is a far-ranging exploration of the differences and the affinities between the varieties of religious experience. In his Catholic novels, Greene was more categorical and restrictive on the subject of religion. In *The Quiet American* his "view of human comedy is more tolerant," as one critic puts it, and "his personal religious affiliation less apparent."[17] If in the earlier novels there exists on the part of Greene a tendency to mock religions other than Catholicism, now only the mongrel Caodaists are selected for a certain amount of irony because of their technicolor fabrications. As a whole, the tone of *The Quiet American* is more indulgent because Greene has apparently determined that the form of a faith is beside the point and that the only thing that counts is whether or not a faith is wed to a creative view of life. What saves Fowler, after all, is not a supernatural manifestation but the sight of the blood of Pyle's victims. Grace may or may not be participating in the fate of Fowler. God may or may not be listening to his confession. In the Catholic novels the devastating presence of God's grace is made quite explicit. But in *The Quiet American*

Greene's implicit purpose is to suggest that there are perhaps other forms of salvation.

## CRITICAL MISCONCEPTIONS

As has already been suggested, there remain critics who, due to the influence of the Catholic novels, find it difficult to shift with Greene to new grounds. The Catholic press in particular has had a painful time in adjusting to the drift of those novels which have followed *The End of the Affair*. The unfortunate result has been a certain amount of intellectual acrobatics which has led to some extraordinary, contorted interpretations.[18] What must be understood is that if Greene wrote his earlier novels in a spirit of Catholic commitment with the characters struggling in a demoniacal world, now he writes, in the words of Philip Stratford, as "a recruit to the Foreign Legion" of the church.[19] Beginning with *The Quiet American* he becomes especially concerned with the politics of deontology.

Following Greene's increasing drift into the political arena in his later novels, many critics have predictably begun to stress the existential qualities which can be discovered in his works. Because of his persistent concern with the paradoxes of compassion and because of his grasp of the ambiguity of goodness, not to mention his abhorrence of power politics, the French existentialists in particular have decided to adopt him as one of their own.[20] To be sure, Greene has always been a Sartrian existentialist of sorts, for he has consistently been attracted by the individuals having the courage of risking choice and engagement.[21] Not surprisingly, he has also been labelled a Christian existentialist.[22] As in the case of his Catholicism, however, Greene's beliefs are too unorthodox to be easily categorized. One should recognize that there is a certain existentialist disposition in Greene's novels, for that constitutes a dimension of his world. Yet it is rather futile to try to fit it into a pre-conceived niche, for Greene's form of existentialism is private and primarily aesthetic.

If the critical concern with the form of Greene's existentialism has failed to fit him neatly into a philosophical school or category, it has succeeded in a more important way. The swell of existentialist interpretations of Greene's works has made plain that he has always been searching for a means by which an individual would be allowed to live in dignity despite the apparently absurd pattern life may impose on one.

In this regard, it should be pointed out that one can discover a note of comic absurdity in *The Quiet American*. For example, there is Fowler trying to suppress a sneeze that would give his and Pyle's position away as enemy soldiers hunt in the night for survivors after blowing up the watchtower where the two had been. Or there is the farcical scene in which Fowler is forced to translate his rival's marriage proposal to Phuong. The laughter at the comedy of life is still muted. Absurdity will however, develop as an increasingly obvious theme in the following books, until it becomes clear Greene is persuaded that, in his own words, beneath "the enormous shadow of the Cross it is better to be gay."[23] The nature of this gayety may often be no more than the sad laughter at the comedy of the absurd pattern man's life might follow. Still, in Greene's later eschatologies there is sufficient reason to be gay because the resurrection of the heart is an endless possibility if one is willing to take the risk of human involvement.

## NOTES

1. Representative of a series of such interpretations is an article by Eric Larsen, "Reconsideration: *The Quiet American*," *The New Republic* (August 7 & 14, 1976), pp. 40–42.

2. Two of the most notable exceptions are *The End of the Affair* and *The Human Factor*, but even there Greene attributes to the English settings these qualities to a certain extent.

3. Philip Stratford, *Faith and Fiction: Creative Process in Greene and*

*Mauriac* (Notre Dame, Indiana: University of Notre Dame Press, 1965), p. 7.

4. Graham Greene, *The Quiet American* (New York: Viking Penguin, 1996), p. 182. Subsequent citations in the text.

5. Gwenn R. Boardman, *Graham Greene: The Aesthetics of Exploration* (Gainesville: University of Florida Press, 1971), p. 36.

6. *Ibid.*

7. Arnold P. Hinchliffe, "The Good American," *Twentieth Century*, CLXVIII (December 1960), p. 535.

8. R. E. Hughes, *"The Quiet American*: The Case Reopened," *Renascence*, XII (Autumn 1959), p. 41.

9. Stratford, *Faith and Fiction*, p. 309.

10. Domingues, a professional aide to Fowler, best represents this ideal synthesis.

11. Stratford, *Faith and Fiction*, pp. 309–10.

12. Philip Stratford, ed., *The Portable Graham Greene* (New York: The Viking Press, 1973), p. vii.

13. *Ibid.*, pp. vii–viii.

14. David Pryce-Jones, *Graham Greene* (Edinburgh: Oliver and Boyd, 1970), p. 93.

15. Francis L. Kunkel, *The Labyrinthine Ways of Graham Greene* (New York: Sheed and Ward, 1959), p. 148.

16. Boardman, p. 109.

17. *Ibid.*, p. 108.

18. See, for example, the argument of Hughes, pp. 42 and 49.

19. Stratford, *The Portable Graham Greene*, p. 582.

20. Kenneth Allott and Miriam Farris, *The Art of Graham Greene* (New York: Russell & Russell, Inc., 1963), p. 163.

21. A. A. DeVitis, *Graham Greene* (New York: Twayne Publishers, 1964), p. 117.

22. Frederick R. Karl, *The Contemporary English Novel* (New York: Farrar, Straus and Giroux, 1965), p. 93.

23. Boardman, pp. 116–17.

# A. A. DeVitis

*Professor A. A. DeVitis taught English for thirty years at Purdue University, from which he is now retired. In addition to his writings on Greene, he has published on Evelyn Waugh, Anthony Burgess, and (with A. E. Kalson) a study of J. B. Priestley. His essays and book reviews have appeared widely in leading periodicals. He lives in Florida.*

## TRANSITION: *THE QUIET AMERICAN*

"Only God and the author are omniscient, not the one who says 'I' "

*The Quiet American* grew out of Greene's first-hand experience of Indochina. In the early fifties he had covered the guerrilla war in Malaya for *Life*, savoring the "sense of insecurity, the danger of ambush on the roads, the early morning inspections of the rubber plantation, tommy-gun in lap."[1] Pleased with the article, *Life* had commissioned him to cover the campaign of General de Lattre in Vietnam. That piece, however, failed to please *Life*'s editors and was later published in *Paris-Match*. "I

Reprinted with permission of Twayne Publishers, an imprint of Macmillan Publishing Company, from *Graham Greene*, rev. ed., by A. A. DeVitis, 108–14. Copyright © 1986 by G. K. Hall & Co.

suspect my ambivalent attitude to the war was already perceptible—my admiration of the French Army, my admiration
for their enemies, and my doubt of any final value in the war,"
he writes in the introductory note to the volume in the Collected Edition. The character of Alden Pyle, the quiet American, was suggested by an American attached to an economic
aid mission, whom the French suspected as a member of the
C.I.A., "a man of greater intelligence and of less innocence,"
who lectured Greene on the need of finding a "third force" in
Vietnam, "the great American dream which was to bedevil affairs in the East as later it was to do in North Africa" (xvii).

The End of the Affair had all but eliminated the melodrama
that characterizes so much of Greene's work. So interiorized
was the action that Greene from time to time, to give his characters something to do, had sent them on walks, many of them
in the rain, through, in, and around the common they lived by.
So frequent were these walks that the common becomes symbolic of the reconciliation portrayed at the novel's conclusion
in Bendrix and Henry's friendship. Yet violence was implicit
outside the immediate setting of the novel in the constant
threats of the German rockets falling on the city of London,
and violence catalyzes the crucial scene of Bendrix's death and
rebirth on the staircase.

The Quiet American, like The End of the Affair, also presents an interiorized drama, one not so noticeable, perhaps,
because of the many scenes of carnage graphically and jour-
nalistically presented. It is, nevertheless, the protagonist's emotional and intellectual acceptance of the source of this violence
that gives the novel its meaning. Like The End of the Affair,
The Quiet American makes use of an unreliable narrator whose
motives must be fully appreciated if the novel's theme is to
develop cogently through the action. Greene also employs other
aspects of the so-called impressionist form, as he had done in
the preceding novel: time shifts, dreams, and what Ford Madox
Ford calls a "progression d'effet," that is, a gradual and inex-
orable unfolding of an action whose full meaning is discerned

in the final or penultimate sentence of the artifact. The novel's ostensible theme is revealed toward the novel's end when Captain Trouin says to Fowler, who professes to remain uninvolved in the politics of real and ideological warfare, "It's not a matter of reason or justice. We all get involved in a moment of emotion and then we cannot get out" (152). The ultimate theme is revealed by Fowler's concluding remark, "Everything had gone right with me since he [Pyle] had died, but how I wished there existed someone to whom I could say that I was sorry" (189).

For Fowler the moment of emotion occurs not so much as an electrifying epiphany, as it does for Sarah Miles, but as the last impression of a cumulative series of images of senseless bloodshed—the sight of the woman covering the mutilated body of the child on her lap with her hat. The Pietà image becomes a comment on the existentialist notion of engagement or detachment that animates the characterization as it adds to the dialectic of belief and nonbelief in God, the ultimate theme of all of Greene's works. Alden Pyle, who also sees the carnage brought on by the diolacton bombs that he has made accessible to General Thé and the Third Force, looks at the blood on his shoes and thinks, automatically, that he will have to have them cleaned before he can report the "incident" to his superior. That Fowler and Pyle are conceived as Conradian doubles adds to the dialectical aspects of both the internal and external themes.

Although *The Quiet American* does much more than pay lip service to the philosophy of existentialism, the novel is in reality a further elaboration of the same theme that informs *The Ministry of Fear* and *The Heart of the Matter*. *The Quiet American*—like *The Heart of the Matter* before it—compresses the political issues into the differences that exist among human beings. The ideologies of Alden Pyle, the quiet American; of General Thé, the exponent and head of the cult of power mysteriously referred to as the Third Force; of Vigot, the disinterested French administrator of justice who reads Pascal; of

Heng, the Communist, who forces Fowler to "engage" or to take sides if only "to remain human"—all these are dramatized in the relationships that ultimately form the meaning of the novel. For, although the background is political and although the existentialist philosophy goes a long way toward explaining the anti-Americanism of the book, *The Quiet American* is primarily about human beings involved in a political and ethical dilemma. In his study of the existential premise in the novel Gangeshwar Rai posits that Greene's attitude towards communism as well as to the United States reflects a "hatred for Communism which is hostile to individual freedom and his antipathy towards America . . . stands for present industrialized civilization in which the individual has no place."[2] Be that as it may, Fowler aligns himself with the Communists, for their faces are more human to him than Pyle's.

Existentialism insists on the cult of the individual—on what Sartre calls "le culte du moi." One branch of existentialism, Sartre's, denies God and makes atheism the reigning philosophy governing individual conduct. Under the branch of Catholic existentialism, as defined by the philosopher Gabriel Marcel, God is somehow, and for many rather mysteriously, accepted and what amounts to free will accommodated. Strangely, it is Sartrian existentialism that best defines Greene's approach to Fowler in *The Quiet American* rather than its Roman Catholic counterpart.

At the heart of Sartrian existentialism lies the point that may have attracted Greene, who is always the champion of the individual: the individual's freedom of choice, or his "engagement." The most compelling aspect of Sartre's existentialism is that it demonstrates the essential and indefinable character of man, a process of definition that often produces anguish, "angoisse." For Sartre only a dead man (and here Pyle might be considered) can be judged, for he alone is "defined"; he alone has finished forming himself. Only the dead man has achieved totalization of experience and existence. The living man may evade responsibility, paradoxically "creating" himself as he exercises this freedom. The moment of choice, of engagement, must at last come if the individual is to achieve essence; and the moment of choice, of engagement, may, and in Sartre's novels frequently does, bring death.[3]

In *The Quiet American*, as in classical drama, the sense of history is dynamically superimposed on the actions of those who go about the business of life. The city of Saigon becomes a microcosm that reflects much of twentieth-century political thinking. *The Quiet American* is, consequently and not surprisingly, one of the few major novels that does not directly make use of a Roman Catholic background, although Fowler's estranged wife and Vigot, the inspector of police, are both Catholics. Fowler, a middle-aged newspaper reporter—he resents the term "journalist" because it implies a commitment to the world that he feels he cannot make—is nominally an atheist, although several times he addresses himself to a God in whom he does not believe. Aided in his occupation by Domingues, an enigmatic Christian-Moslem who has the ability to discern the germ of truth in the mystifying reports of offensives and counter-offensives that inundate the city, Fowler lives with Phuong, his beautiful mistress, enjoying his opium pipe and placidly but cynically an uncomplicated existence. Into the "uncommitted" pattern of his life comes Alden Pyle—American, aged thirty-two, Harvard-nurtured, innocent, and full of intellectual idealism and enthusiasm learned from the texts of York Harding, an American economist. Fowler and Pyle respect and discover a reciprocal understanding of each other's basic integrity and goodness, but neither can be referred to as sinless. They come to an appreciation of one another as good men in the scene in which they are attacked by guerrillas as they shelter in a sentry hut on the outskirts of Phat-Diem. Fowler is wounded in the skirmish and Pyle saves his life, for which Fowler is by no means grateful.

Criticized by American reviewers for its anti-Americanism, *The Quiet American* has been misunderstood because of and in spite of the ironic commentary Fowler makes concerning Pyle's commitment to democracy and to action: "He was young and ignorant and silly and he got involved. He had no more of a notion than any of you what the whole affair's about. . . . He never saw anything he hadn't heard in a lecture-hall, and his writers and his lecturers made a fool of him. When he saw a dead body he couldn't even see the wounds. A Red menace, a soldier of democracy" (31–32).

The point that has been neglected is essentially the core of the novel's meaning. What Greene intends to depict in the course of the novel's activity is that idealism, when uninformed by experience, is a dangerous weapon in a world coerced by the cult of power, symbolized by General Thé and his mysterious Third Force. Greene wishes, moreover, to satirize the belief that money alone can secure peace and understanding. The poem from which Fowler reads as he betrays Pyle is Arthur Clough's "Dipsychus," the twin-souled; and its satiric refrain, the reader will remember, is "So pleasant it is to have money, heigh ho!" (177). Equally important, Greene wishes to describe in Fowler the cowardice implicit in living an "uncommitted" life in a world on the brink of destruction.

To fulfill his thematic intent, Greene employs the innocent abroad, Alden Pyle, who is symbolically the opposite of Henry James's innocent, the American sent to a decadent Europe to reestablish the importance of the human act. Greene's innocent becomes a leaven that brings about bloodshed and tragedy, for his limited understanding of good is inadequate in a world corrupted by the experience of evil. Pyle is compared to a "dumb leper who has lost his bell, wandering the world, meaning no harm" (37), and as a hero in a boy's adventure story who is impregnably armored by good intentions and ignorance; indeed he derives from Anthony Farrant of *England Made Me*. To Fowler, Pyle is like his country. "I wish sometimes you had a few bad motives," Fowler says to him, "you might understand a little more about human beings. And that applies to your country too . . ." (133). However, Fowler comments as ironically on his own position as he does on Pyle's. Both men are in fact aspects of goodness, and much of the novel's meaning centers on the genuine friendship that develops between the two. "You cannot love without intuition" (18), says Fowler; and later he asks: "Am I the only one who really cared for Pyle?" (22). Fowler's repressed idealism is informed by experience; Pyle's abstract idealism by inexperience.

The pawn in this game of experience versus innocence is Phuong, whose name means phoenix. In the plot she represents both the enigma of the East and the desire of Vietnam for political status. Her allegiance to Fowler is neither romantic nor materialistic; she is not, however, incapable of loyalty. She leaves Fowler and attaches herself to Pyle—"youth and hope and seriousness"—who promises her the status she seeks. Ironically this to him is Boston—conformity to American social patterns—and he fails her more than "age and despair" (19). What Fowler offers her is the understanding of experience and the tenderness of his kindly cynicism. At the novel's end, after his betrayal of Pyle to the Communists, Fowler is able to offer her the marriage she desires, for his wife agrees in a moment of generosity to give him a divorce despite her Anglo-Catholic scruples.

Although *The Quiet American* fulfills the existentialist pattern, the philosophy that animates the character of Fowler is the same as that which decides the activities of Arthur Rowe in *The Ministry of Fear* and of Major Scobie in *The Heart of the Matter*. Stripped of Rowe's sentimentalism and of Scobie's religious preoccupations, Fowler seems less noble than his predecessors; but he is, nevertheless, propelled by the same compassion. Again this pity is visualized as a form of egotism when Fowler says: "I know myself and I know the depth of my selfishness. I cannot be at ease (and to be at ease is my chief wish) if someone else is in pain, visibly or audibly or tactually. Sometimes this is mistaken by the innocent for unselfishness, when all I am doing is sacrificing a small good . . . for the sake of a far greater good, a peace of mind, when I need think only of myself" (114). When he can no longer deny the images of suffering that "impinge" on his consciousness, to use Ford Madox Ford's term, he acts to forestall Pyle's blundering attempts to bring about a better world as approved by the American ideology he has abstracted from the textbooks of his mentor York Harding. Fowler's action involves betrayal of the man he has learned to understand and, in his own way, to love, and the reader is asked to remember the point that Greene has made in other works—that Christ was more beloved of Judas than he was of his other followers. The Christ-Judas parallel cannot be pressed too far, however, for the novel's predominant tone is secular and controlled by Fowler's all-encompassing narration, which examines critically commitments of all sorts.

Fowler is, furthermore, the most Conradian of Greene's heroes, and there is a curious parallel to *Victory* to be seen in the novel. Although Fowler and Heyst are separated by years of political and social change, they are both fundamentally unengaged souls whose detachment is challenged by emotion. Each avoids entrapments and each egotistically shuns commitment —Heyst because of early training, and Fowler because of the disappointments of experience. And yet both are made aware of the importance of the human act, and each makes a choice—Heyst for life which, ironically, commits him to death. Fowler is trapped by his pity for suffering, first when he sees the dead guard at the outpost, then when he sees the dead child on his mother's knees after Pyle's diolacton bomb explodes in the square. Fowler realizes that uninformed innocence in a ravaged world amounts to pain and suffering that can be counted as dead bodies and mutilated children. After the crucial meeting with Granger, an incident that has been much admired but little understood, Fowler realizes his affinity to Pyle; and he asks, "Must I too have my foot thrust in the mess of life before I saw the pain?" (185–86). He goes into the street, without hope, to find Phuong, who waits vainly for the dead Pyle. Fowler has taken sides to remain human, and the realization of his compassionate spirit overwhelms him. The novel ends with the sentence, "Everything had gone right with

me since he had died, but how I wished there existed someone
to whom I could say that I was sorry" (189). And the irony
needs no comment.

Although *The Quiet American* makes only casual mention
of religious matters, there is in its shadows the same religious
feeling that infiltrates the entertainments and justifies their
ethics. Although Fowler does not believe in God, he nevertheless addresses him. He leaves Pyle's death not to chance, or to
Fate, but to God when, at the novel's end, he wishes there
were someone to whom he could say that he was sorry. The
statement is tentative, and the reader interprets it as Greene
would have him do. What Fowler is searching for is permanence. "From childhood I had never believed in permanence,"
he says, "and yet I had longed for it. Always I was afraid of
losing happiness" (44). The religious sense is also reinforced by
the nature of Pyle's death. He does not die from the knife
wounds that the Communists inflict upon him; instead, he
drowns. The scapegoat and the drowned man and the Judas
motif add the religious note that helps explain Greene's ultimate meaning.

## NOTES

1. *The Quiet American* (London, 1973), ix. Subsequent citations will
   be to the Viking Critical Library edition (New York: Viking Penguin, 1996), with the relevant page numbers incorporated within
   parentheses in the text.
2. Gangeshwar Rai, *Graham Greene: An Existential Approach* (Atlantic Highlands, N.J., 1983), 76.
3. Compare Paul Rostenne, *Graham Greene: témoin des temps tra-
   giques* (Paris, 1949), 218 ff.; and Robert Evans, "Existentialism in
   Graham Greene's *The Quiet American*," *Modern Fiction Studies* 3
   (Autumn 1957):241–48, for differing approaches to the existential
   problem.

# Philip Stratford

*Philip Stratford, born in 1927, studied French and English and taught at the University of Western Ontario, Canada, and is now professor of English at the University of Montreal. In addition to the book from which this excerpt is taken, he is the author of* Marie-Claire Blais *(1971) and also of numerous translations from and into French. He is also the editor of* The Portable Graham Greene, *published by Viking Penguin.*

## THE NOVELIST AND COMMITMENT

In view of the indignation that *The Quiet American* aroused in the United States and its smug reception in England, it is necessary to doubly underline a few facts about the novel as novel. Greene's use of national and political symbols to carry his story stirred popular emotion much more than any of his Catholic novels, and this has obscured both the artistic value of the work and its real meaning. American readers were incensed, perhaps not so much because of the biased portrait of obtuse and destructive American innocence and idealism in Pyle (that portrait had been painted many times before), but because in this case it was drawn with such acid pleasure by a middle-class

From *Faith and Fiction: Creative Process in Greene and Mauriac,* by Philip Stratford, pp. 311–16. Copyright © 1964 by University of Notre Dame Press. Used by permission.

English snob like Fowler whom they were all too ready to identify with Greene himself. English readers who vicariously enjoyed Fowler's spleen, though they could attribute its excess to
Greene, were just as short-sighted, and hypocritical into the
bargain. The point is that Greene is not Fowler any more than
he is Andrews or Farrant, Bendrix or Querry, or any of his other
unpleasant characters. Fowler is a fictional creation made out
of his author's experience and imagination, but neither a self-
portrait nor a mouthpiece. It is fair to expect the total novel
to carry Greene's viewpoint, but fatal to equate Fowler and
Greene, the narrator and the author. That is why, in interpreting the novel, one must avoid quick judgment and use great
care and latitude in establishing Greene's central position as
creator.

In the dramatized debate between Fowler and Pyle it is
clear that Greene condones neither the selfishness of one nor
the other. Fowler's inert non-commitment is no more compat-
ible to him than Pyle's high-principled meddling. As author, he
is not in the position of "diplomatic correspondent"—altering
every situation to fit his thesis—but he is not a detached "reporter" either. He is a novelist, and his approach to truth
through fiction is a paradoxical composite of these two attitudes. As reporter he must record what he sees with dispas-
sionate accuracy. Greene had twice quoted Chekhov on this
need for objectivity: "Fiction is called artistic because it draws
life as it actually is,"[1] and later: "The best artists are realistic
and paint life as it is." But the second quotation continues to
incorporate the idea that "one has to take sides if one is to
remain human." "But because every line is permeated, as with
a juice, by awareness of a purpose," Chekhov goes on, "you
feel, besides life as it is, also life as it ought to be."[2] The idea
of this dual function remained with Greene. He had used it as
a standard for criticism of books and films; he wrote that as a
description of an artist's theme it had never been bettered[3];
and introducing additional terms he wrote: "The mood of the
author . . . should be one of Justice and Mercy, and while

Justice sees and draws the world as it is, the mood of Mercy is aware of what it might be—if the author himself as well as all the world, were different."[4]

The essential contradiction in this dual duty is similar to what Mauriac calls, in theology, "the eternal contradiction between man's liberty and divine prescience," between God's foreknowledge and the human necessity of choice. This contradiction has special significance for the novelist who is at once a God over his creation and, through his characters, a creature in it. It is a contradiction which cannot be resolved, though it can be assumed in the novelist's paradoxically ambivalent attitude. One cannot expect from him either extreme of commitment or non-commitment, and the nearest one can come to an analogy for his equivocal position is in the figure of an incarnate God.

Not less than in the Catholic novels, though not so explicitly stated, the central attitude in *The Quiet American* is a Christian one. It is not embodied in Pyle or Fowler but does briefly appear in two minor characters in the novel, in Captain Trouin, the French pilot, and in Vigot, the French officer at the Sûreté. Although Trouin is the man who tells Fowler, "we all get involved in a moment of emotion," his involvement is not characterized by a shallow sense of justice or partisan idealism. "The first time I dropped napalm," he tells Fowler,

> I thought, this is the village where I was born. That is where M. Dubois, my father's old friend, lives. The baker—I was very fond of the baker when I was a child—is running away down there in the flames I've thrown. The men of Vichy did not bomb their own country. I felt worse than them.
>
> He said with anger against a whole world that didn't understand, "I'm not fighting a colonial war. Do you think I'd do these things for the planters of Terre Rouge? I'd rather be court-martialled. We are fighting all of your wars but you leave us the guilt."

Trouin's humanity is a composite of his clear-sightedness—the cool objectivity with which he views the facts of fighting a losing war—and the obligation he feels not to hide behind the shield of professionalism and wash his hands of responsibility, but to assume the guilt of the crimes to which he is professionally committed. He envies Fowler his escape through opium. For him there is no escape. He is a prisoner of conscience. In this sense of involvement, the phrase "one has to take sides if one is to remain human" takes on not a judicial but a Christian connotation. It is an admission of human limitation rather than a plea on behalf of humanity.

Vigot, the sad police officer who keeps a copy of Pascal on his desk, is another man who holds the difficult balance between justice and compassion. His job is to find the facts, but his purpose is not to total them up into a sentence. Fowler sees in him a man with a vocation. "You would have made a good priest, Vigot," he says. "What is it about you that would make it so easy to confess—if there were anything to confess . . . Is it because like a priest it's your job not to be shocked, but to be sympathetic?" Vigot's methods resemble those of a priest: he does not accuse but listens. He is "silence sitting in a chair." "I had the feeling of some force immobile and profound. For all I knew, he might have been praying." He shows the same kind of humility as another minor character, Fowler's Indian assistant, Domingues, of whom Fowler says:

> . . . where other men carry their pride like a skin-disease on the surface, sensitive to the least touch, his pride was deeply hidden and reduced to the smallest proportion possible, I think, for any human being. All that you encountered in daily contact with him was gentleness and humility and an absolute love of truth. Perhaps truth and humility go together, so many lies come from our pride.

Fowler lies to Vigot about his implication in Pyle's murder and Vigot is obliged to close his file uncompleted. As he goes, he turns and looks at Fowler "with compassion, as he might have looked at some prisoner for whose capture he was responsible undergoing his sentence for life." And he does, of course, leave Fowler sentenced by his own sense of guilt. The whole novel is, in fact, a confession, an answer to Vigot's silent and sympathetic appeal, and it is made with all the humility and concern for truth that Fowler can muster.

Greene's position as novelist is obviously at one remove from this, for he must be true to Fowler's character as well as to the facts that Fowler describes. Hence the falsity of a facile identification between Greene and his hero. His position as novelist is more truly indicated by the painful ambivalence of Captain Trouin or the sadly sympathetic attitude of Vigot or by the humility of Domingues. Or, if it is necessary to identify him with Fowler—and we have said that his creative act depends on his compassionate identification with his characters— one must allow that his identification is not with one side, the non-committal reporter's side of his character, but with this and with the total complexity of the man. He is also, and finally, the Fowler who hesitates—"I don't know. I don't know"—before agreeing to Pyle's death. He is the Fowler who sees his own error in judging in terms of quantity and says, "Suffering is not increased by numbers: one body can contain all the suffering the world can feel." Without leaving his character, Greene shares Fowler's hatred and Fowler's guilt. His one aim as a novelist has been to achieve something of that Godlike understanding which at the beginning of the novel Fowler feels is so far beyond his reach, but which at the end he feels so badly in need of. In this sense, and in the highest sense of the word, Greene has done Fowler justice.

It must be admitted that, comparatively, Greene does Pyle less than justice in *The Quiet American*. But the title is misleading, for this is really the story of Fowler, not of Alden Pyle.

Also, of course, we are bound by the convention of the narrative to see Pyle, not in terms of Greene's personal prejudices, but dramatically through Fowler's eyes. Furthermore, any serious consideration of this novel must take into account two facts. First, there are the many instances in the novel where Pyle's and Fowler's characters are shown to overlap (the whole story is one of the transfer of Pyle's traits to Fowler and to some extent vice versa). Second, when one considers Pyle in the context of all Greene's fiction, one sees him not so much as an isolated caricature of the American, but as a familiar Greene type. In one respect he is very like Greene's pious Catholics who live by the letter and the law of an impenetrable idealism, although he is treated more sympathetically than many of these, than, for example, Louise Scobie, or the aunts in *The Living Room*, or Rycker in *A Burnt-Out Case*. In another way he resembles Greene's earlier adolescent heroes—Andrews, and Oliver Chant, and the young Arthur Rowe, "the Happy Man" of *The Ministry of Fear*. They too were caught up in the excitement of commitment and melodramatically simple rules until experience thrust their feet into the mess of life. It is a standard theme in Greene's fiction and one of those conflicts which as an artist he has left unsolved. It is just unfortunate for the self-conscious that this time Greene happened to give this stock figure American nationality.

## NOTES

1. "Fiction," *The Spectator*, CLI (September 22, 1933), 380.
2. "Subjects and Stories," *Footnotes to the Films*, ed. Charles Davy (London, 1937), p. 57.
3. *Ibid.*
4. "Books in General," *New Statesman and Nation*, XXXIV (October 11, 1947), 292.

# Zakia Pathak, Saswati Sengupta, and Sharmila Purkayastha

*Each of these three authors has taught on the English Department faculty of Miranda House, Delhi University. Saswati Sengupta and Sharmila Purkayastha hold the M. Phil. from Delhi University, and Zakia Pathak had a career in social work before joining the Miranda House faculty, from which she is now retired after teaching for twenty years. Ms. Pathak has written extensively on modern feminist theory. Her most recent essay is "Resisting Women" (co-authored with Saswati Sengupta), which appears in* Women and the Hindu Right *(1995).*

## From THE PRISONHOUSE OF ORIENTALISM

No, it is not our intention to provoke. The metaphor is heuristic. We teach English literature at graduate level at a women's college in Delhi University: for three years to those who major in the subject and to all students of the first year, science and humanities, as a compulsory subject. It is a pedagogical imperative with us that the teaching of literature should negotiate a discursive relation with the world outside the classroom. And texts must be read "ethically":

Reprinted with permission of Routledge, from *Textual Practice* 5 (Summer 1991): 195–97, 202–206.

When we connect the text of the book to the text of
our lives, the world of choice and action opens before
us. . . . The word ethics is a mockery . . . where the
question of the relationship between reading and any
form of action beyond discussing one's reading is never
even raised.[1]

Given the increasing marginalization of literature in the culture, this might appear to be a quixotic enterprise. The problem is compounded by our having to teach a literature that is
not our own.

Said's *Orientalism* was an epistemological intervention in
this fraught/distraught enterprise.[2] To deconstruct the text, to
examine the process of its production, to identify the myths of
imperialism structuring it, to show how the oppositions on
which it rests are generated by political needs at a given moment in history, quickened the text to a life in our world. An
immediate taxonomic impulse—with implications for an indig-
enously constructed canon—was to identify what we shall call
white texts, i.e., literary texts by white writers dealing with the
colonial encounter, and to constitute them as a strategic formation answerable to an orientalizing interpretation. From our
location in this formation we could participate in the major
debates on nationalism, on tradition and modernity which are
engaging this country. A study of the white texts could even,
hopefully, activate our students to consider how a national
identity can be formulated in troubled times. Certainly the
project would enable us to engage with English literature more
authoritatively than had been granted to us before, since it
would create a space from which we could speak as privileged,
first-order critics.

In the course of time, however, this project came to be
riddled with reservations. The concept of a national identity in
the vast, multi-religious, multi-cultural subcontinent that is India has always been contentious at the conceptual and action
levels. It seeks to homogenize differences of religion, class and

caste, region, and gender; differences which, when suppressed, implode within any nationalistic formulation. Yet such a formulation is implicated in our project. The homogenization of differences seems to force upon us a condition of its possibility a binary opposition in which the Occident is opposed by a western-educated, secularized, urban middle class. This class is increasingly being viewed by those outside it—the vast majority in this country—as spawned by our erstwhile rulers and baptized in their image. To construct a national identity on such precarious ground is, on the one hand, to marginalize ourselves in the national debate, as neo-colonialists. On the other hand, it is to remain within the oppositions of colonial discourse, in a structure which we began, in our titular metaphor, by refusing. In fact, we found the driving power of our deconstructive project to be such that it collapses taxonomic categories. Every text becomes a white text. In every text from a Donne poem to *Wuthering Heights* are clues that yield a narrative which might well become narcissistic or paranoid. In such rereadings of the English literary text which privilege Orientalist discourse as an interpretative grid, the whole of English literature may be reduced to a ground on which racial identities are contested. We remain trapped in the prisonhouse.

Finally, to read the text in ways which inevitably construct the west as Other to be exorcised is to be insensitive to the complex and troubled relations which govern the East–West encounter in Indian society today. The prestige of the English language has, if anything, soared since independence. English has now the status of an associative language, recognized by the Constitution of India. After the United Kingdom and the United States, India has the largest English-speaking population. Many religious and political leaders who condemn the hegemony of English from public platforms ensure that their children are admitted to English-medium schools. Recent attempts by the governments of Uttar Pradesh and Goa to withhold financial grants from these schools has led to widespread protest. In the national education system, English is one of the languages in the three-language formula. (And it is still widely held that a language is best taught through its imaginative literature.) The Sahitya Akademi, the Central Government–sponsored academy for the promotion of Indian literatures, has now recognized that English is one of the languages in which Indian literature may be written.

This hegemony of the west in several fields was sharply brought home to us by the response of our students to our orientalizing project. It ranged from resistance to indulgence of the pedagogue. Irresistibly drawn to the electronic and consumer goods made possible by western technology, avidly reading western magazines from *Time* and *Newsweek* to women's and fashion magazines, their perception of the west is marked by desire. The anxiety and threat as they are experienced by the Indian expatriate cannot effectively communicate a warning to those back home because of the obstinate fact of the expatriates' continuing to prefer their domicile there. In fact, the green-card holder seems to have displaced the Indian Administrative Services Officer in the hierarchy of the marriage market. In these circumstances, to sensitize the student to the ugliness of the colonial encounter by constructing the west as Other is to indulge in an artificial exercise that remains confined to the classroom and defeats the pedagogical objective of connecting it to the world.

In the case of texts which remain outside the formation of white texts, we think that the pedagogical imperative can be more effectively served by inserting them into our cultural practices as a means of estrangement or *ostranenie*; as a means by which we defamiliarize our customs and make them ideologically visible. It seems to us that this would be responsible to both the producing and receiving cultures. By historicizing the text in the one, we would escape narcissism and paranoia; by using it as estrangement, we could make it relevant to our culture and retain our space as privileged critics. We quote an example of how this may be done from the experience of our colleague Rashmi Bhatnagar in the course of her classes on

Pope's *The Rape of the Lock.* The rape of Belinda's lock of hair was instrumental in creating a sense of shared humanity across gender.

> Briefly, the students began by recognizing the poet's theme to be what in India is euphemistically called eve-teasing. Meanwhile the massacre of Sikhs took place that winter (November 1984) on the streets of Delhi. When my students, many of whom were victims/spectators of the sadistic violence and humiliation came back to the poem after curfew was lifted, the cutting off of the lock of hair acquired new and painful associations. We remembered how rioters had desecrated the sacred symbols of the Sikhs by forcibly cutting off their hair in public. The poem thus became not only about the desecration of women but obliterated the sexual differential as Gayatri Spivak puts it and became a poem about the desecration that can be visited even on oppressed men. . . .[3]

It will become clear in the course of this article how *Orientalism* functioned for us as a theory of reading which transformed our classroom practice by alerting us to the workings of the colonized consciousness and to our interpellation as the colonized reader. But a certain distance from Said began to formulate as we let the world into the classroom; at this juncture we found the work of the Indian subaltern historians to be a sobering corrective to our uncritical orientalizing of white texts. We hope thus to have escaped the prisonhouse of self and other, east and west, us and them.

It will be obvious that we have not been concerned to propagate taste, create a canon, or otherwise endorse an aesthetic. Our critical practice has been "to release the positions from which the text is intelligible." We believe that the task of criticism is "that of actively politicising the text, of making its politics for it, by producing a new position for it within the field of cultural relations."[4] And we offer as a political reading one that is multiply determined by concerns of race, class, caste, religion and gender; never finished, always in process. . . .

Graham Greene's *The Quiet American* is a compulsory text for all college students of the first year who have studied English at the elective level in school. We shall recount our reading experience with the class of 1988–89.

The political story was of little or no interest to the students. Too young to have experienced the aftermath of the British imperialist presence in India and attracted to the promise of the west as they absorbed it through popular fiction and cinema, its affluence, its life-style, they showed no interest in the history of Vietnam's colonization. *The Quiet American* was for them Phuong's story. Their reading of popular romances included those under the Mills and Boon imprint. Phuong's story promised a reenactment of the myths structuring such romances, beautiful and desired as she was shown to be. She had begun by appealing—ironically—to internalized norms of the domestic angel: "she was the hiss of steam, the clink of a cup; she was a certain hour of the night and the promise of rest." As the story unfolded, however, the expectations it aroused were disturbed. The heroine of their private romance had to be both beautiful and morally worthy; and she had to be physically chaste. But it was too soon evident that Phuong had traded her virginity before the story commenced; and that she was actively co-operating with the two men in the commodification of her body. It did not help Phuong that the end she was pursuing was a permanent relationship of marriage, the teleology of their own dream. It became our concern to show, in the face of their growing resistance to Phuong, how woman's predicament is produced by and articulated through the social and political formation; and to read the collusion of two discourses, imperialist and patriarchal, as constituting her and structuring the text.

Canonized criticism, by western and Indian critics, was predictably of little help in this task. They forwarded the liberal humanist programme of purifying the story from historical dross, reducing Vietnam to a microcosm of the modern world and collapsing the politics into categories of Christian discourse.[5]

The problem of sexuality likewise is given short shrift. Kulshrestha is dismissive: for Fowler "sex is not so much of a problem as old age and death."[6] Gangeshwar Rao simply inserts it into the dominant discourse of non-involvement and scants it.[7] Salvatore comments on the "vulnerability" of Fowler resulting from Phuong's "inability to articulate her emotional needs."[8] This is an instance of how the psychologizing tendency of canonized criticism works in tandem with narrative devices to determine the responses of the "competent" reader, complicit with the dominant discourses of patriarchy and imperialism.

Nor did Said's *Orientalism* offer any help in understanding Phuong as doubly Other: as woman and oriental. Said does not address the problem of sexuality and regrets the lack. Nevertheless, he does make occasional remarks on the theme which privilege racial markers to the exclusion of others. He does not concern himself with silence, for instance, in its gendered form, as gendered resistance. And he tends to essentialize oriental woman in endorsing western notions of the sex she offers as guilt-free and therefore appealing. It was our pedagogical responsibility to return the problem of female sexuality to the social and political formations which produce it; and to scrutinize the discourses of masculinism and imperialism imbricated in Greene's text.

Silence has most often been seen as the repression of speech, the mark of a subaltern subjectivity. "Flaubert's encounter with an Egyptian courtesan produced a widely influential model of the Oriental woman; she never spoke of herself, she never represented her emotions, presence or history. He spoke for and represented her" (Said, p. 6). Phuong's silence evoked a sympathetic response from our students since they inserted it into the patriarchal norms of self-effacement and sacrifice, the sign of Woman, the corner-stone of the family.

We had to demystify these silences. "Within the context of women's speech silence has many faces. . . . As a will not to say, or to unsay, and as a language of its own, it has barely been explored."[9] We showed how Phuong's silences are a strategy to avoid commitment to any statement or programme which might compromise the future she is pursuing: "a good European marriage," with the help of her sister (p. 40). In the opening chapter Fowler asks her if Pyle was in love with her. " 'In love?' Perhaps it was one of the words she could not understand. 'May I make your pipe?' she asked." When a business telegram arrives for Fowler, he asks her if, had it been bad news, she would have left him. "She rubbed her hand across my chest to reassure me, not realizing that it was words this time I wanted, however untrue. 'Would you like a pipe?' " (p. 117). In the concluding chapter, after Fowler has made it clear that he can and will marry her, she jumps off the bed to go to her sister with the news. Fowler detains her momentarily to ask her about whether she misses Pyle. " 'Do you miss him much?' 'Who?' 'Pyle.' 'Can I go, please? My sister will be so excited' " (p. 189). The students reacted ambivalently to the demystification of Phuong's silence. They are avid watchers of the commercial Hindi film which reinforces patriarchal norms and very receptive to the songs from those films, which are widely disseminated over radio, special TV programmes, and radio cassettes; all of which valorize woman's silence. The textual construction of silence had to be confronted with the experiential; and shown to be the ground of a representation which could work against the interests of women as in cases of dowry murders today. Fowler considers himself authorized by his superior age and experience to understand Phuong; yet he understands neither her silence—"she didn't have the gift of expression" (p. 134)—nor the inconsequential nature of her speech: "to take an Annamite woman to bed with you is like taking a bird. They twitter and sing on your pillow" (p. 12). This twitter is a generic attribute of the Annamite women as is evident later in the novel. Phuong's twitter is silence as much as her silence is speech—both are willed acts in the furtherance of her objective. Fowler's self-deception is a measure of her success in the deployment of speech and silence; Vietnamese women, he thinks, do not love as white women do. "It isn't in their nature. . . . They love you in return for kindness, security and the presents you give them" (p. 104). As our students noticed, she gets what she wants: a European marriage.

The first-person narration has moved, in many critical readings, out of the space where authenticity of experience is guaranteed to the space where "authenticity" is revealed as constructed by race, religion, class and gender. The first-person narrator may now be read as the target of authorial irony. Such a reading would argue implicitly for a subjectivity which is fully accessible to itself, freely willing and acting. On the other hand, the narrative consciousness may be read as representing the space where the contradictions which fracture the ego are inspected. This is a choice that must be made by the reader and it is a political decision.

To construct Fowler as the target of the authorial irony turns up the masculinist who for all his sympathy with Phuong, his desire to protect her from the crudities inflicted on her by white men, his frustration at her silence, ultimately settles for her body on which he inscribes the sign of his possession. On the political plane, this choice translates into the twentieth-century Orientalist; sympathetic but outsider; confronting the East as object to be understood in an essentially hermeneutical relation (Said, p. 22). From this position Vietnam remains the picture on the canvas: "the real background held you as a smell does; the gold of the rice fields under a flat late sun; the fishers' fragile cranes hovering over the fields like mosquitoes; the cups of tea on the old abbot's platform . . . the mollusc hats of the girls . . ." (p. 25). The Orient is unchanging (Said, p. 96). "In five hundred years there may be no New York or London, but they'll be growing paddy in these fields, they'll be carrying their produce to the market on the long poles wearing their pointed hats. The small boys will be sitting on their buffaloes" (p. 95).

The Vietnamese people exist as a dismembered race, as bodies flung in the pond at Phatdiem, as a woman with a mutilated baby in her lap. This is modern Orientalism; the Orientalist as representing the Orient and yet "The Orient is all absence, whereas one feels the Orientalist and all he says as presence" (Said, p. 208).

To construct Fowler as a fragmented subject, on the other hand, is to posit a dialectical relation between the personal and political and to avoid reducing them to each other in a metaphorical embrace. The metaphorical relation implies a fully formed subjectivity whereas the dialectic foregrounds a subjectivity in formation, at the intersection of the two discourses of imperialism and feminism. What seems to mark this subject is a sense of unrootedness; this appears to be the price of union. In the consciousness of Fowler represented through the first-person narration, Phuong is without a history; there is a noticeable absence of cultural markers of class, religion, education which suggests that these are invisible for Fowler and that his desire is only for her body. If Phuong has any identity at all it is as an Annamite and a "bird." The "libertine and less guilt ridden sex" which is offered is clearly outside a social and moral formation; that Said valorizes this sexuality is evidence of the displacement of race by gender. Fowler himself ends up as deracinated. His use of pronouns stresses his resistance to being incorporated with the white imperialist ideology. "We've brought them up in our ideas. We've taught them dangerous games and that's why we are waiting here, hoping we don't get our throats cut" (p. 95). This attempt to disengage his identity from theirs only foregrounds the older British imperialism. "I've been to India and I know the harm that liberals do" (p. 96). His political "involvement" in the final instance is presented as his humanization. But it is tragic that the figure he presents at the end is one of exile, confined to his room, smoking endless pipes of opium.

Marriage is the discursive space in which colonialism and

feminism work out. The peripheral figures of Helen, Miss Hei and the woman in the red dressing gown—the divorcee, the spinster and the adultress—represent the threat to the conjugal relation. The marriage that is achieved is between a virtually deracinated white and a decultured oriental. Interracial sex is removed from the pornographic and sensational space it occupied in the literature of empire. But it is attended by no promise, no hope of regeneration; only by images of sterility and death. In the concluding chapter Phuong tells Fowler the story of the film on the French Revolution which she has just seen; the poet is unable to rescue his aristocratic beloved; she is executed by the throngs singing his composition, *La Marseillaise*. "It was a mistake in the story; they should have allowed her to escape," says Phuong. Phuong's escape has a price: "I never remember my dreams" (p. 189).

In the class from which most of our students come, overriding emphasis is placed on physical chastity. It was our endeavour to show how virginity is another form of the commodification of the body and is itself predicated in the power structure. The popularity of romance fiction was shown to be an implicit recognition of the absence of desire and fulfilment in the arranged marriage. Phuong might be a sister under the skin.

A quick look at some sample questions from the examination papers of the 1980s will show how difficult it is to introduce the idea of the literary text as representation. These questions assume a simple correspondence between literature and reality. "Give a pen-portrait of Phuong." "Fowler has passion, Pyle has commitment. Discuss." "Trace the events which lead to the murder of Pyle." "Discuss the theme of eternal truth in the novel." Such questions appear to our students as apolitical, calling only for a close reading. Our attempts at orientalizing strike them as an idiosyncratic tampering with the text. More often than not, we function as a small isolated group whether teachers or students—it needs patience and passion.

Unregarded—until we read Ania Loomba's most generous acknowledgment of the efforts of Miranda House in her unusual recent book, *Gender and Race in Renaissance Drama*.[10]

## NOTES

1. Robert Scholes, "The pathos of deconstruction," *Novel: a Forum on Fiction* 22 (Winter 1989), p. 227.

2. Edward Said, *Orientalism* (London: Routledge & Kegan Paul, 1978). All subsequent citations are from this edition.

3. Rashmi Bhatnagar, "A reading of Pope's *The Rape of the Lock*," in Lola Chatterji (ed.), *Woman, Image, Text* (New Delhi: Trianka Publications, 1986), p. 51.

4. Tony Bennet, quoted in A. P. Foulkes, *Literature and Propaganda* (London: Methuen, 1983), p. 19.

5. See Samuel Hynes (ed.), *The Quiet American: Twentieth Century Interpretations* (Englewood Cliffs, NJ: Prentice-Hall, 1973); Anne Salvatore, *Greene and Kierkegaard: The Discourse of Belief* (Alabama: University of Alabama Press, 1988); M. M. Mahoud, *The Colonial Encounter* (London: Rex Collings, 1977); John Spurling, *Graham Greene* (London: Methuen, 1983); Gangeswar Rao, *Graham Greene: An Existential Approach* (New Delhi: Associated Publishing House, 1983); J. P. Kulshreshta, *Graham Greene—The Novelist* (New Delhi: Macmillan, 1977).

6. J. P. Kulshreshta, p. 148.

7. Gangeshwar Rao, p. 80.

8. Salvatore, p. 58.

9. Trinh T. Minh-ha, "Not you/Like you: post colonial woman and the interlocking questions of identity and difference," *Inscriptions*, vol. 3/4 (1988), pp. 71–7.

10. Ania Loomba, *Gender and Race in Renaissance Drama* (Manchester: Manchester University Press, 1989).

# Brian Thomas

*Brian Thomas has taught at the University of Toronto and is now director of the Writing Workshop at Toronto's Victoria College. In addition to his book on Greene, he has written on Joseph Conrad. His most recent work is on Hardy:* The Return of the Native: Saint George Defeated, *published by Twayne.*

## *THE QUIET AMERICAN*

One always spoke of her . . . in the third person as though she were not there. Sometimes she seemed invisible like peace.

Mr. Chou cleared his throat, but it was only for an immense expectoration into a tin spittoon decorated with pink blooms. The baby rolled up and down among the tea-dregs and the cat leapt from a cardboard box on to a suitcase.

This was not how the object itself would look: this was the image in a mirror, reversed.

From Brian Thomas, *An Underground Fate: The Idiom of Romance in the Later Novels of Graham Greene.* Athens, Ga.: University of Georgia Press, 1988, 25–51. Copyright © 1988 by The University of Georgia Press. All rights reserved.

Greene's novel about the French war in Indochina, published
in England in 1955, in the United States in 1956, had the effect
of appearing to confirm a growing impression that its author's
imaginative attention had begun to shift from a private and
idiosyncratic Catholic vision of reality to a more widely familiar
public and secular one. The subject of *The Quiet American* is
Western colonialism. Writing about the death throes of a traditional European colonial system and the emergence of a new
and sinister American variant, Greene seemed virtually to have
abandoned the religious frame of reference which had for so
long formed the essential ideological and mythopoeic context
of his fiction. The narrator of *The Quiet American* suffers from
a kind of despair and a kind of death wish, but he professes
atheism; there is nothing in Thomas Fowler's story that could
be regarded as miraculous, no question of any of the characters
being driven in the direction either of damnation or of sainthood. Yet the reception of this book was marked by at least as
much uneasy controversy as had been aroused by any of
Greene's "religious" novels; this time, however, the terms
of the debate were political rather than theological.

Especially in the United States, *The Quiet American* tended
to be viewed as a rather odd and somehow unwarranted polemical exercise, a fictional study of modern geopolitical relations
that seemed distinctly lacking in disinterestedness. Greene's
long-standing anti-American bias, something which had previously been considered not much more than a marginal aspect
of a certain authorial crankiness, now appeared to loom in the
very foreground of his narrative and to invite serious critical
address. In the United States, some distinguished reviewers
were soon engaged in impassioned contention.[1] Their arguments had to do chiefly with the portrayal of Pyle in the novel,
his plausibility both as a character and as an American agent,
and the larger related question of the burgeoning American
presence in Southeast Asia. The debate was much concerned
with Fowler's hostility toward Pyle and ultimately with the
question whether Fowler's contempt for America was also

Greene's—whether the narrator was actually to be taken as a lay figure for the author himself. Given that *The Quiet American* does indeed deal in contentious political issues, these are all, of course, legitimately debatable matters; in the United States, understandably, the novel's reception was largely unfavorable. Even in England, where the figure of Pyle tended to be located in a more specifically literary context (that of the tradition of the American "innocent" abroad), Greene's apparently gratuitous invocation of various unflattering stereotypes met with some disapproval.

If *The Quiet American* is to be read simply as a prophetic thesis about the dangers of American involvement in Indochina, then it could be said, perhaps, that Greene has been retrospectively vindicated by the subsequent drama of historical events. The book is not, however, an argument but a novel. And, of course, within a few years of its publication, critics were attending more appropriately to the text as an imaginative structure of words or, at any rate, discussing it by means of questions pertaining more to philosophy and psychology than to politics. At a distance of thirty years, though, it now seems clear enough that while *The Quiet American* is about colonialism, it is also, more simply, a love story and an adventure story. It has certain obvious affinities, that is to say, with romance. As a tale of love and war, it features as one of its chief characters a highly conventional type of romance hero: Alden Pyle undertakes a lonely and dangerous journey down a river to a place that is perceived as a kind of hell, a figurative underworld where, sure of the rightness of his cause, he first rescues his rival from death and then wins from him the hand of the heroine. Even Pyle's black dog, Duke, seems to function as what Northrop Frye calls the hero's "animal companion" in this lower world.[2] And as one of its central symbols, the story features a highly conventional romance emblem, the image of the tower—usually associated, as it is here, with the kind of perilous epiphany or vision or wisdom granted only to the solitary seeker who keeps a vigil or watch from it.

But the novel, viewed in this way, looks more like a romance
that has somehow gone wrong: the "hero," in this perspective,
is eventually betrayed and murdered, whereupon the heroine
returns to her first lover, the very rival who not only has acted
as the betrayer but seems as well to have been given the novel's
last word on the subject of romance itself:

> I . . . went into the cinema next door—Errol Flynn, or
> it may have been Tyrone Power (I don't know how to
> distinguish them in tights), swung on ropes and leapt
> from balconies and rode bareback into technicolour
> dawns. He rescued a girl and killed his enemy and led
> a charmed life. It was what they call a film for boys,
> but the sight of Oedipus emerging with his bleeding
> eyeballs from the palace at Thebes would surely give a
> better training for life today. No life is charmed. Luck
> had been with Pyle at Phat Diem and on the road from
> Tanyin, but luck doesn't last.[3]

Yet despite this intelligently cynical view of a banal and superficial story of adventure, the narrator's own story, although very
different in texture, has essentially the same kind of narrative
shape as the "film for boys" that he derides. The speaker here
is the novel's protagonist; and Thomas Fowler, while he is
Pyle's rival, can no more be regarded as the villain of the piece
than Pyle can be seen as its hero. But Fowler's own story is
informed, as it were contrapuntally, by the structure of the
story about Alden Pyle. *The Quiet American* is not an "ironic"
or mock romance—merely a parodic inversion of a familiar
pattern—in which the "hero" loses and the "villain" wins, but
is in fact a romance of a more sophisticated type than that
suggested by the film. What needs to be accounted for, then,
before anything else, is the sadness and cynicism of the narrating voice.

   We are brought back, in this connection, to the text's con-
spicuously public and polemical narrative surface. As Greene

himself points out, there is "more direct *reportage*" in this novel
than in any of his others: "I had determined to employ again
the experience I had gained with *The End of the Affair* in the
use of the first person and the time-shift, and my choice of a
journalist as the 'I' seemed to me to justify the use of *reportage*."[4] During the period in which the novel was written,
Greene had actually been working as a journalist himself. In
1951 he had traveled in Malaya, covering the insurrection there
as a correspondent for *Life*, and between 1951 and 1955 he had
spent four winters in Vietnam, reporting on the Indochina war
for the *Sunday Times* and *Figaro*.[5] So he had at least a degree
of professional affinity with his narrator. But the sources of the
affinity lie even deeper, as Greene, again, discussing this phase
of his life in relation to another of his protagonists, seems to
suggest:

> In *The End of the Affair* I had described a lover who
> was so afraid that love would end one day that he tried
> to hasten the end and get the pain over. Yet there was
> no unhappy love affair to escape this time: I was happy
> in love . . . the chief difficulty was my own manic-
> depressive temperament. So it was that in the fifties I
> found myself tempting the end to come like Bendrix,
> but it was the end of life I was seeking, not the end of
> love. I hadn't the courage for suicide, but it became a
> habit with me to visit troubled places, not to seek ma-
> terial for novels but to regain the sense of insecurity
> which I had enjoyed in the three blitzes on London.[6]

This fragment of autobiography tells us much about the genesis
of Thomas Fowler. However, the genuinely significant link
which it establishes is not that between Fowler and the author
but rather that between *The Quiet American* and the novel that
preceded it.

There is a kind of continuum of imaginative identity between the protagonists of the two stories. Like Bendrix, Fowler

is by temperament a solitary and isolated man: his perspective, characterized by a profound and almost self-conscious ego-centricity—what he himself refers to as a knowledge of "the depth of my selfishness" (114)—is typically one of detachment and skepticism. These qualities allow him, in his role as jour-nalist, to maintain an appropriate objectivity or "distance." His room above the rue Catinat seems to have much the same sort of symbolic significance as Bendrix's room in south London, the emblem of a withdrawn and defensive selfhood. Like Ben-drix, Fowler is an observer and, in a rather different sense, a professional writer. His predilection for opium and even his relationship with Phuong reflect and indeed underline his need for detachment, a preference for the distant and impersonal viewpoint. Phuong is the ideal mistress for Fowler: making no serious demands on him, she prepares his opium pipe and seems otherwise passive and unobtrusive, without any real needs of her own. Fowler has, in fact, elevated his isolated de-tachment to the status of a sort of faith: " 'You can rule me out,' I said. 'I'm not involved. Not involved,' I repeated. It had been an article of my creed. The human condition being what it was, let them fight, let them love, let them murder, I would not be involved. My fellow journalists called themselves corre-spondents; I preferred the title of reporter. I wrote what I saw: I took no action—even an opinion is a kind of action" (28).

This self-styled neutrality does not of course mean that he is a man without any affective attachments. He loves Vietnam, for example, in much the way that he loves Phuong. At his first meeting with Pyle, he muses on the beauty of the Vietnamese women: "Up the street came the lovely flat figures—the white silk trousers, the long tight jackets in pink and mauve patterns slit up the thigh: I watched them with the nostalgia I knew I would feel when I had left these regions for ever" (18). But even this kind of appreciation has an oddly aesthetic, distanced quality; it is a response to a certain exotic picturesqueness that tends to be conveyed in visually static terms. When he scorns Pyle's merely theoretical knowledge of "these regions," he does so by contrasting it with his own awareness of "the real background"; but his intimacy of understanding is characterized more by visual detachment than by any sense of personal engagement:

> He would have to learn for himself the real background that held you as a smell does: the gold of the rice-fields under a flat late sun: the fishers' fragile cranes hovering over the fields like mosquitoes: the cups of tea on an old abbot's platform, with his bed and his commercial calendars, his buckets and broken cups and the junk of a lifetime washed up around his chair: the mollusc hats of the girls repairing the road where a mine had burst: the gold and the young green and the bright dresses of the south, and in the north the deep browns and the black clothes and the circle of enemy mountains and the drone of planes. (25)

While this kind of reportage is imaginative as well as specific and concrete in its details, it lacks the immediacy of direct, participatory experience. What Fowler offers is essentially a picture, something seen, again, from a certain distance. The repetition of the word "flat" is not perhaps without significance: his Vietnam is often a series of still vignettes which have something of the effect of the picture postcard, even something perhaps of the calendars belonging to the old abbot. And as pictures, they are often curiously silent and remote, suggesting a vision of a reality that somehow seems to lend itself naturally to third-person description. In one sense, Fowler's Vietnam is all "background," an accumulation of physical detail in two dimensions. While his perspective yields a certain loveliness, that is to say, it can sometimes result in an effect as flat in its own way as Pyle's ideological abstractions.

At the same time, however, Fowler's egocentricity manifests itself in quite different terms. Like Bendrix, he is also an abrasive, turbulent figure: if his reporting of the war is neutral, the reportage in his own narrative reflects his sense of the world beyond his room above the rue Catinat as a hostile and violent place, a world fundamentally alien rather than simply exotic. In this sense, his narrative shares the energy of the kind of "hate" that inspires Bendrix's story—and it is from that sort of energy that the much-debated polemicism in the novel derives: Fowler loves Vietnam but hates the war, and if his sympathies are sometimes with the Vietminh, sometimes with the French army, they are never with the Americans, whom, at best, he regards as blundering and foolish idealists. Like Bendrix, too, he has, in spite of his self-centeredness, a desire "to hasten the end and get the pain over": an ambivalent urge toward death that seems at first glance to contrast paradoxically with everything that his room and his opium pipe and Phuong represent to him. Like *The End of the Affair*, *The Quiet American* presents us with an egocentric first-person voice which gives an account of what might be described as a peculiarly "third-person" reality, a world that seems more than usually "objective," in the sense of being set distinctly apart from the central narrative consciousness, and more than usually unresponsive. So the link between that consciousness and what it reports on becomes at once, paradoxically, a relation of both enmity and attraction for the narrator. More or less alone in the rue Catinat, Fowler is not existentially involved with what he sees from his room, but so long as the external world remains alien and unresponsive, it comes to be increasingly the source and object both of erotic longing and of a hunger for annihilation. For all his celebration of a kind of flat loveliness, Fowler is forever flirting with a murderousness that seems to pervade the world of the novel. His paradoxical relationship with Vietnam is summarized in an account of his relationship with Phuong:

> One never knows another human being; for all I could tell, she was as scared as the rest of us: she didn't have the gift of expression, that was all. And I remembered that first tormenting year when I had tried so passion-

ately to understand her, when I had begged her to tell
me what she thought and had scared her with my unreasoning anger at her silences. Even my desire had
been a weapon, as though when one plunged one's
sword towards the victim's womb, she would lose control and speak. (133–34)

The paradox about Fowler's perspective—his need for distance combined with an unacknowledged longing for involvement—is rooted in the psychological processes of a romantic
nihilism. A world that is silent, however attractive it might
seem, is also a world of death. "I came east to be killed" (110),
Fowler complains as Pyle noiselessly saves his life. Like many
another Greene character, this narrator is fond of nineteenth-
century poetry, and his passion for Baudelaire in particular—
*"Aimer à loisir, / Aimer et mourir / Au pays qui te ressemble"*
(18)—says much not only about his implicit identification of
Phuong with her country but also about a profound confusion
of erotic and thanatoptic impulses in his own nature. In his
fashion (a more "decadent" development of an earlier historical
fashion) Fowler is as much a romantic as Pyle. He is the novel's
protagonist, too, as well as its narrator: his querulous viewpoint,
rather than some unmediated oracular voice, becomes the central technical device of the novel, and as in *The End of the
Affair*, one of the things that it signifies is the fact of his ultimate survival. Where Fowler differs crucially from Bendrix as
a first-person narrator is in the curious doubleness of his narrative perspective.

This doubleness is perhaps most clearly exemplified in his
account of the battle of Phat Diem. Fowler begins by observing
the scene from a high and remote vantage point:

From the bell tower of the Cathedral the battle was
only picturesque, fixed like a panorama of the Boer War
in an old *Illustrated London News*. An aeroplane was
parachuting supplies to an isolated post in the *calcaire*,

those strange weather-eroded mountains on the Annam border that look like piles of pumice, and because it always returned to the same place for its glide, it might never have moved, and the parachute was always there in the same spot, halfway to earth. From the plain the mortar-bursts rose unchangingly, the smoke as solid as stone, and in the market the flames burnt palely in the sunlight. The tiny figures of the parachutists moved in single file along the canals, but at this height they appeared stationary. (46)

The cathedral tower is the first of an important sequence of tower images in the novel. What it signifies, clearly, is the type of detachment—the perspective of distance—that we have already seen as one aspect of Fowler's way of looking at Vietnam: the battle of Phat Diem is initially revealed as a silent and static picture, exotic in one sense but oddly flat and "suspended" in another. This view from the bell tower becomes another version, that is to say, of Fowler's vision of the world from his room above the rue Catinat, the prospect of an attractive, but somehow essentially alien, objective reality. However, when Fowler leaves the tower and joins a platoon of paratroopers, the picture of the battle changes radically, suddenly acquiring a dreadful immediacy. Fowler finds himself, so to speak, *inside* the picture: surrounded by carnage, he is all at once in the midst of a whole world of death, translated abruptly and almost literally to a kind of hell:

The canal was full of bodies: I am reminded now of an Irish stew containing too much meat. The bodies overlapped: one head, seal-grey, and anonymous as a convict with a shaven scalp, stuck up out of the water like a buoy. There was no blood: I suppose it had flowed away a long time ago. . . . I . . . took my eyes away; we didn't want to be reminded of how little we counted, how quickly, simply and anonymously death came. Even

> though my reason wanted the state of death, I was
> afraid like a virgin of the act. (51–52)

The obscene picture, it should be noted, is now no longer still, no longer merely a static or visually suspended "prospect": "Another man had found a punt . . . but we ran on a shoal of bodies and stuck. He pushed away with his pole, sinking it into this human clay, and one body was released and floated up all its length beside the boat like a bather lying in the sun. Then we were free again, and once on the other side we scrambled out, with no backward look" (52). The movement from tower to canal is not just a shift from one mode of reportage to another, but also a journey of descent: in joining the patrol, Fowler finds himself engaged in a metaphorical as well as an actual quest for an invisible "enemy" in what amounts to an underworld.

The landscape of this underworld can best be described as figuratively annihilated. The account of the fording of the canal clogged with gray corpses, horrifying enough simply as an instance of direct rather than distant reporting, has an unmistakably mythopoeic dimension as well. There is perhaps an unattributed invocation here of yet another nineteenth-century poet—an echo of the grisly river-crossing episode in Browning's "Childe Roland to the Dark Tower Came." At any rate, the canal is certainly a river in a mythically "lower" world, and Fowler's quest in this realm of "grey drained cadavers" (53), if it is at all like Childe Roland's, is for a tower of a kind very different from the one atop the cathedral in Phat Diem. But the outcome of the patrol seems strangely inconclusive. There is much "waiting" (53), and no enemy actually appears. The only other victims are a peasant woman and her little boy, "accidentally" shot by a sentry as they lie huddled together in a ditch. However, while Fowler has been half hoping all along for nothing but his own death, this image of the dead mother and child stays with him throughout the remainder of his narrative as a haunting emblematic memory. The symbolic picture of a purely random and gratuitous murder, it seems nevertheless to epitomize the whole significance of the patrol's "progress." Despite the picture's horror, what it seems to hint at, in the immediate context of Fowler's temporary and reluctant involvement, is a type of Pietà vision: a sense that all human death, no matter how grotesque or apparently meaningless, may ultimately be a type of ritual sacrifice, an imitation of the Christian story of the Passion.

The particular hell of this novel, then, becomes a place in which the human body itself is objectified and made hideously anonymous by death. Greene returns again, in other words, to the theme of the annihilation of human identity. And in terms, again, of the perspective of the narrator's involvement, death acquires a figurative as well as a literal meaning. The theme of descent in *The Quiet American* always culminates in a nightmare vision of the reification of personal identity, a process of symbolic extinction anticipated early on in the novel by the nameless "grey heap" (34) of a human figure dragged in by Granger to the bar of the Continental Hotel. The vision is anticipated, too, by the swarming mass of female bodies in the "House of Five Hundred Girls" (36)—a scene which horrifies Alden Pyle, whose reaction to this large-scale sexual objectification of physical beauty becomes the initial source of sympathy between himself and Fowler. Pyle's virginal innocence has a touching and appealing quality for the narrator, but more important, it seems to represent for Fowler a version of his own preference for detachment over involvement—at least in the area of personal relations—which he sees as the basis of a genuine kinship between them. Fowler regards Pyle as someone who shares his own horror at the nullification of human identity. At the same time, however, this shared vision of nullity, the kind of figurative void represented by the canal-crossing episode at Phat Diem, would also seem to have a paradoxical attraction for both of them. What Pyle really shares with Fowler is his love for Phuong, and what this means at the outset of the story is that Phuong represents, for both of them, a kind of anonymous nullity that is conventionally beautiful rather than obscene: both see her in terms of the two-dimensional flatness suggested by the perspective of distance, so that her physical presence ultimately modulates, in effect, into a form of invisibility. For Fowler in particular, Phuong embodies "death" in its most attractive aspect, and it is not for nothing that she is so closely associated in his mind with the sort of escape from reality offered by his opium pipe.

Fowler is both amused and moved by the way Pyle dances with her in the Chalet, holding her formally at arm's length like a nervous schoolboy. When Pyle apologizes "for taking Miss Phuong from you" (44), Fowler responds: "Oh, I'm no dancer but I like watching her dance" (44); and he goes on to reflect on the quality in Phuong that seems to be of the essence of her attraction: "One always spoke of her like that in the third person as though she were not there. Sometimes she seemed invisible like peace" (44–45). It is as if Phuong were, at once, simply a beautiful woman's body and, simply, a phantom. Later, when he prepares for sleep after the battle at Phat Diem, he thinks about her, "but oddly without jealousy" (55): "The possession of a body tonight seemed a very small thing—perhaps that day I had seen too many bodies which belonged to no one, not even to themselves. We were all expendable" (55). And here the day's vision of gray anonymous corpses modulates suddenly to a vision of a different kind of physical anonymity:

When I fell asleep I dreamed of Pyle. He was dancing all by himself on a stage, stiffly, with his arms held out to an invisible partner, and I sat and watched him from a seat like a music-stool with a gun in my hand in case anyone should interfere with his dance. A programme set up by the stage, like the numbers in an English music-hall, read, "The Dance of Love. 'A' certificate." Somebody moved at the back of the theatre and I held my gun tighter. Then I woke. (55)

The "invisible partner" here is certainly Phuong. Pyle in the dream "possesses" a body that is not in fact a body at all but something more like a ghost. Fowler watches. In other words, the dream sums up not only the protagonist's affinity with Pyle but his relationship with Phuong, and, in a broader sense, with Vietnam itself.

As we have seen, there are in effect two Vietnams for Fowler: the exotic but flat picture viewed from a certain distance and the arena of proximate death, characterized as a kind of void or abyss, where the familiar sense of ordinary physical human identity becomes an awareness of the nameless nullity of the body. The dramatic reversal of perspective in the whole Phat Diem episode suggests, in fact, that the dreadful vision of "involvement" is precisely the mirror image of the view from the tower. What Fowler's dream suggests is that the bell tower—associated as it is with his room above the rue Catinat and with the perspective of detachment in general—is in fact a tower of solipsistic vision. Like Tennyson's Lady of Shalott, with whom, oddly enough, he might be said to have a certain spiritual affinity, Fowler not only sees his world from a remote height, he also watches it, so to speak, in a mirror. His dream involves something more than the vision of an invisible nullity: it is also a dream about narcissism. Pyle "represents" him in the dream, but the gun in the dreamer's hand is not there only to protect Pyle: "The Dance of Love" may also be a danse macabre, a dance of death, and the invisible partner a solipsistic projection of Fowler's own death wish.

So his descent from the cathedral bell tower becomes Fowler's descent into his own world of dream and death, a kind of hell where Eros and Thanatos seem to merge and to become indistinguishable from each other. The figuratively annihilated landscape just outside Phat Diem is the terrain of Fowler's own quest, the central metaphorical form of the nether region of his own romance. It is not easy to say just what he seeks there, but it would seem to be some ultimate metaphorical form of nullity, an embodied image of the void in terms of which his senses of both repulsion and attraction are conjoined[7]: in effect, his own "dark tower." At any rate, the intrusive movement "at the back of the theatre" which startles him back into the world of waking consciousness turns out to be the sudden appearance of the real Alden Pyle. It should now be clear, of course, that Pyle's daring night voyage down the river to Phat Diem is really a kind of parody of Fowler's descent from the bell tower, a "boyish" (59) version of a much more significant river journey. For Pyle functions, as he does in the dream, as Fowler's romantic shadow double, becoming increasingly a narrative projection of the protagonist in his role as one who is "afraid like a virgin of the act." Pyle's flatness as a character in the novel is much like Phuong's, an effect produced by the flattening tendency of the perspective of distance. And his eponymous "quietness" as a character is also like Phuong's virtual speechlessness.

The duality of the narrative perspective—our sense that there are two Vietnams—is reflected in the novel in a figurative dialectic of speech and silence, or, more broadly, of human noise on the one hand and an unresponsive emptiness on the other. Pyle's quietness has to do with the fact that he is increasingly revealed, despite the innocence of his boyish romanticism, as a death figure. In the context of the narrator's nihilism, silence means nullity, and Pyle is nothing if not a figurative nil or null, a narrative cipher; in the context of the narrator's solipsism, human noise tends to mean mostly the sound of his own narrating voice. The image of the tower in the novel, besides being the emblem of a self-conscious detachment, has a good deal to do with a figurative view of the human voice as something which asserts a vision of human worth in the face of an all-encompassing, ironic silence: speech, in the broadest sense, becomes a kind of watchtower in the midst of a void. Perhaps the most central emblem of all in this novel is that of a voice crying in pain from a tower set in a flat and empty wilderness. Fowler's "tower," that is to say, is also a tower of words—from one point of view, a metaphorically verbal icon in his creed of noninvolvement; from another, a linguistic construct existentially derived from the need to confront the silence of nullity. In both contexts, the novel's structure of imagery pertaining to speech and silence stems from the two aspects of Fowler's narrative viewpoint, each a reversed mirror image of the other. More important, what this dialectic of speech and silence means is that the protagonist's "tower" is also a form of cage, a place not only of vision but of imprisonment.

In the bizarre Caodaist cathedral in Tanyin, to which he goes for its "coolness" (87), Fowler notices that there is no glass in the windows: "We make a cage for air with holes, I thought, and man makes a cage for his religion in much the same way—with doubts left open to the weather and creeds opening on innumerable interpretations. My wife had found her cage with holes and sometimes I envied her. There is a conflict between sun and air: I lived too much in the sun" (87–89). But despite his atheism, Fowler, of course, has his own peculiar creed. The view from the bell tower at Phat Diem offered a pictorial panorama of the war, a vision of a particular battle seen all at once and as a whole. The perspective of detachment has the virtue of comprehensiveness. At the same time, though, the truth that it provides is partial and limited. For all his brave rhetoric about living "too much in the sun," Fowler really lives, that is to say, in his own particular form of cage. As narrator, he cannot escape the confines of language, which seems on the one hand to manifest only a partial truth and on the other to be inadequate to the experience of nullity; and as protagonist, he cannot, as he has learned at Phat Diem, escape the experience of nullity either. He must live, then, with both speech and silence—in effect, inside "a cage for air with holes." This would seem to be merely a linguistic rather than an "actual" construct, but since Fowler is a writer as well as an atheist, it has no less metaphysical substance for him than the construct represented by his wife's religion—certainly no less than that embodied by the "Walt Disney fantasia" (83) of Caodaism. The second tower symbol in *The Quiet American* is the watchtower on the road from Tanyin to Saigon: here, the tower as an emblem of solitary "verbal" vision actually modulates to the image of a sort of cage on stilts. Fowler's narrative viewpoint becomes, almost literally, a point of demonic epiphany.

As Fowler and Pyle drive back from Tanyin, the exotic picture of Vietnam yields to that of a flat and formless emptiness, a whole world of nothing but "drowned fields" (89): "The last colours of sunset, green and gold like the rice, were dripping over the edge of the flat world: against the grey neutral sky the watchtower looked as black as print" (91). With nightfall, there is a perceptible draining away of color and dimension, a reversal of perspective again, characterized this time by an eerie darkness and silence. We are back in Fowler's private night world, not a world of dead bodies but a figuratively annihilated landscape all the same, in which his own identity once more seems threatened. Climbing the ladder to the tower, he tells us that "I ceased for those seconds, to exist: I was fear taken neat" (92). In the watchtower episode, it is as though the picture of reality as a whole had been turned inside out to become a vision of reality as a hole, the prospect of a void inhabited by figurative phantoms, like the white shadows on a dark photographic negative. The interior of the tower which looks out on this dimensionless reality becomes itself an actual image of the construct suggested by the interior of the Caodaist cathedral. The watchtower seems precisely to be a reversed image of the vantage point represented by the bell tower at Phat Diem: a place for "watching" by day is transformed into a place under the threat of external attack by night. In the context of the night world, even the embrasures in the walls seem to serve only a negative function. Fowler is not, however, alone. Besides the two frightened young Vietnamese sentries, Pyle is with him, and as in the dream of the dance of love, the quiet American functions again in the role of Conradian secret sharer. But this time, silence gives way to speech, so that Fowler has the illusion, after his initial terror, that their conversation together has transformed the tower into a more familiar and comfortable environment: "It is odd how reassuring conversation is, especially on abstract subjects: it seems to normalize the strangest surroundings. I was no longer scared . . . the watchtower was the rue Catinat, the bar of the Majestic, or even a room off Gordon Square" (98). But this illusion is soon dispelled by a disembodied "voice" that "came right into the tower with us," seeming "to speak from the shadows by the trap—a hollow megaphone voice saying something in Vietnamese" (105). Fowler has at last found his invisible enemy, or, at any rate, the enemy has found him. It is as if the exterior nullity had suddenly acquired a ghostly voice and speech of its own, a language that is unintelligible yet menacing, and that seems virtually to displace the very air inside this cage: "Walking to the embrasure was like walking through the voice" (105).

More abruptly than at Phat Diem, Fowler's narrative resumes the theme of descent. He and Pyle have no sooner scrambled down from the tower than a bazooka shell bursts on it. Wounded himself now, and lapsing from time to time into a delirious semiconsciousness, Fowler once again finds himself in a world of death. This time, however, it is a world not of mute corpses but of disembodied voices and sounds. But as at Phat Diem, the descent from the tower leads to a type of hell that seems as well to be a type of limbo—an incomprehensibly horrible place in which there is nothing to be done except to wait. And, waiting, Fowler hears a noise that he cannot help but decipher:

> There was no sound anywhere of Pyle: he must have reached the fields. Then I heard someone weeping. It came from the direction of the tower, or what had been the tower. It wasn't like a man weeping: it was like a child who is frightened of the dark and yet afraid to scream. I supposed it was one of the two boys—perhaps his companion had been killed. I hoped that the Viets wouldn't cut his throat. One shouldn't fight a war with

> children and a little curled body in a ditch came back
> to mind. I shut my eyes—that helped to keep the pain
> away, too, and waited. A voice called something I didn't
> understand. I almost felt I could sleep in this darkness
> and loneliness and absence of pain. (108–109)

Again, the movement of descent seems to involve a reversal of
the tower perspective: it is as if Fowler suddenly finds himself
inside an almost surreal world, dimensionless and colorless,
which was apprehended initially as a kind of dark exterior picture. The wrecked tower itself is now a part of this pictorial
negative, and the weeping voice becomes the only thing in it
to suggest that the whole landscape might have any meaning:
Fowler is reminded of the Pietà scene at Phat Diem—the vision of a brutally sacrificed innocence which, if it does nothing
more, locates the dark picture in a mythic context that seems
familiar.

Fowler resents Pyle's subsequent heroics, although there is
something distinctly comic about his resentment. For the
drama now enacted out in the "drowned fields" becomes essentially a comedy of ritual death and revival. Closer than ever
to the annihilation that he both courts and fears, what Fowler
is waiting for is his own extinction:

> In the very second that my sneeze broke, the Viets
> opened with stens, drawing a line of fire through the
> rice—it swallowed my sneeze with its sharp drilling like
> a machine punching holes through steel. I took a breath
> and went under—so instinctively one avoids the loved
> thing, coquetting with death, like a woman who de-
> mands to be raped by her lover. The rice was lashed
> down over our heads and the storm passed. We came
> up for air at the same moment and heard the footsteps
> going away back towards the tower. (111)

Fowler undergoes a form of symbolic death, but he is not at all pleased to find himself emerging alive from the whole ordeal on the road between Tanyin and Saigon. Pyle insists on saving his life; Fowler is not grateful. The rapport that had been established between them in the watchtower was based on a mutual ambivalence about involvement—chiefly the involvement in erotic experience, but in Fowler's case, a fearful wish "to get death over" (103) as well. As at Phat Diem, the protagonist sees himself as "a virgin" afraid "of the act." Now his sense of an affinity, amounting almost to a shared identity, with Pyle shifts for the time being to the unseen figure of the dying Vietnamese sentry, one of the two youths whom, a few minutes earlier, Pyle was prepared quite casually to murder: "I was responsible for that voice crying in the dark: I had prided myself on detachment, on not belonging to this war, but those wounds had been inflicted by me just as though I had used the sten, as Pyle had wanted to do. . . . I made an effort to get over the bank into the road. I wanted to join him. It was the only thing I could do, to share his pain. But my own personal pain pushed me back. I couldn't hear him any more" (113–14). It is as if, having emerged from a strange looking-glass world, a world like a photographic negative, Fowler wished to rejoin his own image there. He is unable to do so. If his quest is for a Browningesque dark tower, then he has found it, but at virtually the moment of discovery, it becomes a literal and ironic *tour abolie*. The epiphany yielded by the watchtower is of nothing other than apparently meaningless suffering and death, yet the object of the quest is not entirely ironic, nor does it disappear altogether: the "voice crying in the dark" stays with Fowler, like the memory of the murdered child and his mother at Phat Diem.

What redeems Fowler in the novel is the capacity for imaginative sympathy that Pyle seems at first to share with him. The rhythm of the narrative increasingly suggests that his brushes with death bring him closer and closer to the kind of involvement that he both fears and longs for. "Afraid of the act," Fowler nevertheless undergoes a process of constant subjection to death—what amounts to a gradual but increasingly radical violation of his detachment. Pyle, on the other hand, remains the boyish adventurer. The quiet American begins to be perceived as the kind of romantic "hero" whose spiritual virginity will always remain intact precisely because he does not recognize that the country of romance is not just an exciting place but one which always tends to swallow up anyone who wanders into it. Pyle cannot extend his imaginative horror at the vision of the reification of female beauty to an awareness that the world he inhabits is also the House of Five Hundred Girls writ large, an enshrouding, figuratively subterranean place in which the urge toward nullity is at least as strong as the urge toward life and freedom. Pyle does not see that he *belongs* to this world, that he is inevitably an agent as well as an observer of nullification. In a way, the relationship between Fowler and Pyle is like a reversed looking-glass image of that between Harry Lime and Rollo Martins: Pyle is like a Rollo who learns nothing from his underground journey. He remains innocent in the sense that he lacks the capacity for guilt, invulnerable in the sense that he lacks the capacity for vulnerability.

Still, he remains Fowler's private symbolic doppelgänger, too, a secret sharer whom the novel's protagonist never seems quite able to shake off or cast adrift. At this stage, Pyle disappears from the story for a while, but at the same time his presence persists as a kind of narrative phantom. "I had not seen Pyle while I was in the Legion Hospital," Fowler remarks: "His absence and silence, easily accountable (for he was more sensitive to embarrassment than I), sometimes worried me unreasonably, so that at night before my sleeping drug had soothed me I would imagine him going up my stairs, knocking at my door, sleeping in my bed" (130). Fowler's sense of having been displaced from his own life by Pyle is in fact part of a larger experience of displacement and bemusement. The pattern of events which now unfolds in his story becomes strange and mysterious to him, as though it were he and not Pyle who had suddenly become the naive outsider, the character for whom the real significance of things had to be deciphered and explained. In spite of his symbolic return to life on the road from Tanyin, it is as if Fowler—continually haunted by a voice crying from a tower—had not actually emerged from the incomprehensible horror of his experience there. We have noticed that the two Vietnams in the novel are perceived as reflections of each other: Fowler still seems in some way to inhabit the mirror world of dream and death, the world of the photographic negative. He is, in short, lost, still spiritually immersed in the drowned fields. The character of the protagonist's experience in the latter part of his narrative corresponds to that of the romance hero who finds that he has wandered into a labyrinth.

In one sense, Fowler abets the process of his own growing bemusement. Trying to recover something of the character of his life before the appearance in it of Alden Pyle, he returns with a kind of vengeance to his opium pipe and to Phuong. But his perception that he has somehow lost his old life is only heightened; even Phuong, whom he correctly suspects of preparing to leave him for Pyle, now becomes an embodied loneliness:

> I made love to her in those days savagely as though I
> hated her, but what I hated was the future. Loneliness
> lay in my bed and I took loneliness into my arms at
> night. She didn't change: she cooked for me, she made
> my pipes, she gently and sweetly laid out her body for
> my pleasure (but it was no longer a pleasure), and just
> as in those early days I wanted her mind, now I wanted
> to read her thoughts, but they were hidden away in a
> language I couldn't speak. (140)

In a broader sense, the whole of the reality with which Fowler must deal at this stage in his story is also "hidden away in a language I couldn't speak": the Vietnam that he has assumed he knows so well becomes increasingly mystifying, even unintelligible, to him. Now, fortunately, the curious figure of Mr.

Domingues comes to his aid, directing him to Mr. Chou's house in Cholon. The ascetic Domingues seems to function here as the kind of enigmatic magus figure who often turns up in romance, the hermetic, oracular wise man or priest who helps the hero out by offering him a clue to the design of the labyrinth. But Mr. Chou and his domestic retinue seem at first to be the very embodiment of the sort of sheer unintelligibility with which Fowler is now everywhere confronted. Mr. Chou is an emaciated opium addict whose memory has been virtually destroyed and who lives with a bewildering ménage of relatives, domestic pets, and assorted "junk" in a "jackdaw's nest of a house" (125) perched above a Cholon warehouse. Quite apart from Chou's addiction to opium, the effect for Fowler is that of having stepped into a distorted looking-glass reality, a grotesque private "tower" in a night world set in a district that is itself like "a pantomime set" (124)—an experiential context held up to the main setting of the novel like a mirror. The old addict himself is unhelpful: "Mr. Chou cleared his throat, but it was only for an immense expectoration into a tin spittoon decorated with pink blooms. The baby rolled up and down among the tea-dregs and the cat leapt from a cardboard box on to a suitcase" (127–28).

Fowler is led away from this impenetrably surrealistic scene by Chou's assistant, Mr. Heng, a character almost as omniscient-seeming and enigmatic as Domingues. Heng shows him the empty "Diolacton" drum and indicates that it is connected in some way with Pyle's unofficial activities on behalf of the U.S. government. The drum, however, "means nothing" (128) to Fowler. Heng then shows him a "mould" whose significance the protagonist also tries in vain to interpret: "This was not how the object itself would look: this was the image in a mirror, reversed" (129). However, Heng gives Fowler an additional clue, directing him to Mr. Muoi's garage. And yet again, the protagonist finds himself at a "level of life" that seems superficially accessible but at the same time peculiarly and profoundly indecipherable:

> In the Boulevard de la Somme you lived in the open:
> everybody here knew all about Mr. Muoi, but the police
> had no key which would unlock their confidence. This
> was the level of life where everything was known, but
> you couldn't step down to that level as you could step
> into the street. I remembered the old women gossiping
> on our landing beside the communal lavatory: they
> heard everything too, but I didn't know what they
> knew. (144)

At last, though, in the shed behind Mr. Muoi's garage, Fowler
discovers the press, the purpose of which explains not only the
Diolacton and the mold but Pyle's connection with them and
with the renegade General Thé. It is not, however, in its literal
or utilitarian capacity that this press initially manifests itself.
The shed contains "one piece of machinery that at first sight
seemed like a cage of rods and wires furnished with innumerable perches to hold some wingless adult bird. . . . I switched
on the current and the old machine came alive: the rods had
a purpose—the contraption was like an old man gathering his
last vital force, pounding down his fist, pounding down . . ."
(144). Before realizing that he is looking at a device for making
plastic bombs, in other words, Fowler again stares briefly into
a kind of mirror. In the light of his own involvement with the
war on the road from Tanyin, Fowler is of course himself a
"wingless adult bird" in a cage—the image precisely reflects
both the ineffectuality and the sense of confined remoteness
inherent in the perspective of detachment—and he is himself
the "old man" who pounds down with his fist, for he cannot
help but recognize that his own impotence in the matter of
preventing the young sentry's death did not diminish the extent
of his own responsibility for it.

Having at last recognized an image of himself, however unwelcome, Fowler begins to recognize as well that another image, that of the quiet American, has come to inform the world
of his narrative and to give it its meaning. No longer entirely

mystified now, he returns to the rue Catinat only to learn that
he has lost Phuong to Pyle. His first impulse is to find a different world, and so he travels to the war zone in the north.
The final tower emblem in the novel becomes the cockpit of a
French dive bomber poised above a northern village captured
by the Vietminh. And this last "tower" is also, again, a cage:
"there was no way to get out: you were trapped with your experience" (149). But the image of a distanced, solitary vision
suddenly acquires a new dimension: the aircraft which offers
such splendid panoramas of the sheer physical beauty of Vietnam is also an instrument of death. The repeated attacks on
the village are followed, almost like an afterthought, by an attack of a rather different kind:

> Down we went again, away from the gnarled and fis-
> sured forest towards the river, flattening out over the
> neglected rice fields, aimed like a bullet at one small
> sampan on the yellow stream. The cannon gave a single
> burst of tracer, and the sampan blew apart in a shower
> of sparks: we didn't even wait to see our victims strug-
> gling to survive, but climbed and made for home. I
> thought again as I had thought when I saw the dead
> child at Phat Diem, "I hate war." There had been some-
> thing so shocking in our sudden fortuitous choice of a
> prey—we had just happened to be passing, one burst
> only was required, there was no one to return our fire,
> we were gone again, adding our little quota to the
> world's dead. (150)

All at once, the two aspects of Fowler's narrative perspective
have converged. For the B-26 bomber in fact represents what
might be described as a "killing tower," and Fowler's sense of
his own complicity in the general ethos of murderousness is
heightened. At Phat Diem, his involvement with "the world's
dead" was indirect, his role more that of observer than partic-
ipant; on the road from Tanyin, he became aware of an element

of personal responsibility, an involvement in a wider death process that, in existential as well as in ethical terms, was much more direct; now it is almost as if he had actually committed murder himself. The only thing he is left with, again, besides a hatred of war, is the memory of the Pietà vision at Phat Diem, a sense of the ritual inevitability of the sacrifice of innocents. But he begins at the same time to see that he has no choice but to identify himself with the killers as well as with the victims. This position is, of course, logically impossible, and in the terms of the novel's moral (as opposed to its figurative) dialectic, Fowler must soon choose sides.

Following the explosion in the Place Garnier, that is exactly what he does. And in the process, like Rollo Martins and Maurice Bendrix, he becomes a type of Judas. Metaphorically, the effect of Pyle's plastic explosives is to shatter the looking-glass reality, the solipsistic world, in which Fowler, obsessively but confusedly, has so long wandered. The "world that I inhabited," he tells us, "suddenly inexplicably broke in pieces":

> Two of the mirrors on the wall flew at me and collapsed half-way . . . A curious garden-sound filled the café: the regular drip of a fountain, and looking at the bar I saw rows of smashed bottles which let out their contents in a multi-coloured stream—the red of porto, the orange of cointreau, the green of chartreuse, the cloudy yellow of pastis, across the floor of the café. The Frenchwoman sat up and calmly looked around for her compact. I gave it to her and she thanked me formally, sitting on the floor. (160)

The surrealistic quality of this scene suggests, oddly enough, that the collapse of the mirror reality has somehow returned the protagonist to a more innocent world. In one sense, it has: since Pyle caused the explosion, then to the extent that Pyle's innocence remains intact, Fowler finds himself once again in a world of the quiet American's devising. But the initial sensation of having suddenly woken up in a garden is quickly revealed as an illusion. By the time Fowler arrives in the square, he discovers a scene that is in many ways more horrifying than that of the canal-crossing episode at Phat Diem:

> The doctors were too busy to attend to the dead, and so the dead were left to their owners, for one can own the dead as one owns a chair. A woman sat on the ground with what was left of her baby in her lap; with a kind of modesty she had covered it with her straw peasant hat. She was still and silent, and what struck me most in the square was the silence. It was like a church I had once visited during Mass—the only sounds came from those who served, except where here and there the Europeans wept and implored and fell silent again as though shamed by the modesty, patience and propriety of the East. The legless torso at the edge of the garden still twitched, like a chicken which had lost its head. (161–62)

Fowler has been returned not to a garden world but to the deathly silence at Phat Diem and in the rice fields adjacent to the watchtower: at the center of the picture what he sees is yet another dead child in its mother's arms.

So, as Fowler's shadow double or secret sharer, Pyle ceases to be the phantom embodiment of the protagonist's sense of his own lost innocence and becomes instead the embodiment of his sense of guilt. Fowler exorcises Pyle's ghost by betraying him, at last becoming, in effect, a murderer himself. This is not to say that Pyle, as a character in the novel in his own right, ever ceases to be anything but innocent: "He looked white and beaten and ready to faint, and I thought, 'What's the good? he'll always be innocent, you can't blame the innocent, they are always guiltless. All you can do is control them or eliminate them. Innocence is a kind of insanity' " (163). Pyle's innocence, like Harry Lime's, is that of a child who has never grown up.

He is a man with all the right ideas and attitudes but with no real passion and no real moral center. He begins as a conventional romance hero but is increasingly revealed as a kind of villain. The trouble with Pyle seems to be that he is not quite human: he resembles his dog more closely than he knows— "They ought to have called him Fido," Fowler muses at an earlier stage in the story, "not Alden" (102). Or, to put the character of Pyle in a different context, he may be said to resemble what is known in the parlance of science fiction as a humanoid. His affinity with Fowler has to do with the protagonist's initial detachment: what they share is a mutual horror at the brutal "mess of life" (186). But Fowler becomes increasingly humanized in the course of his story, increasingly involved in the mess of love and war, while Pyle looks more and more like an amiable zombie, a mindless death figure capable of any sort of destructiveness in the name of an abstract idealism. He is not a romance hero, in fact, because he never becomes involved at all: unlike Fowler, he never really enters into the underworld of romance itself.

Fowler, on the other hand, sinks deeper and deeper into a kind of phantasmagoric night world; but following the betrayal and murder of Pyle, he emerges from it at the conclusion of his narrative as a different man from the detached and querulous cynic he appeared to be at the outset. There is, in other words, an ascent theme in *The Quiet American* as well as one of descent. By the time Phuong returns to him at the end of the novel, he has begun to see her as an actual and ordinary (if exceptionally beautiful) woman, rather than as merely an exotic phantom: her name means "Phoenix" (11), and her almost literal return to physical life coincides with a spiritual rebirth for the narrator, too. In this context, even Fowler's anti-Americanism is suddenly cast in doubt. After having delivered Pyle into the hands of the Vietminh, he describes a meeting with the long-despised Granger: Fowler begins to see that his contempt for his American colleague, whose son turns out (rather conveniently for Greene's purposes) to be dangerously

ill, has always been based on not much more than the limitations inherent in his former detachment. Whereas Granger was
once "like an emblematic statue of all I thought I hated in
America—as ill-designed as the Statue of Liberty and as meaningless" (184), he now looms suddenly before Fowler, "bulky
and shapeless in the half-light, an unexplored continent" (184).
In one sense, the narrator of *The Quiet American* ends by
sounding like a romantic protagonist almost as much in the
F. Scott Fitzgerald as in the Graham Greene manner. And like
the actor-hero of the "film for boys" alluded to earlier, Fowler
rescues a girl, kills his enemy, and goes on to lead a charmed
life.

Yet this is not quite the whole story of the novel's ending.
At the very last, the narrating voice still conveys a certain sadness and skepticism, as well as an additional undertone of guilt.
"Everything had gone right with me since he had died," Fowler
says about Pyle in his final sentence, "but how I wished there
existed someone to whom I could say that I was sorry" (189).
Like the story of Maurice Bendrix, *The Quiet American* concludes with a distinctly pointed ambivalence of narrative mood.
Fowler remains suspicious of what might be described as the
most obvious conventional principle of closure in romance, that
of the happy ending. His own sense of guilt works against his
sense that a new world has ultimately been opened up to him.
As he broods silently about Pyle, Phuong describes a film that
she has recently seen: a story of ill-starred love set during the
French Revolution, which she herself chooses to see as a romance gone wrong. She objects to its apparently tragic climax
and wishes that the lovers in it had been allowed to escape—
" 'to America—or England,' she added with what she thought
was cunning" (188). Fowler then opens the telegram from his
wife, in which she unexpectedly agrees to the divorce he has
so long been seeking. "Here's your happy ending" (188), he
tells Phuong. But for the protagonist, the ending is more mixed:
his guilt about his betrayal and his urge to "confess"—if not
to Vigot, then to the reader of his story—continue to qualify

his bewildered realization that he has indeed gone on to lead "a charmed life."

As in the conclusion to *The End of the Affair*, it is as if Greene felt almost instinctively impelled to revert to one of the elements of a former pattern: a virtually reflexive need to move back toward the familiar ground of the mood of tragedy: "Was I so different from Pyle, I wondered? Must I too have my foot thrust in the mess of life before I saw the pain?" (185–86). The recurrence in the novel of what has been referred to here as the "Pietà vision" confirms the fact, in any case, that irony and "religious" tragedy—an inclination to keep returning to the figure of the innocent sacrificial victim—have always been significant threads in the design of Fowler's narrative. But his bleak urge to confess does seem to coexist uneasily with the Columbus-like glimpse of "an unexplored continent" in the improbable person of Granger. Fowler's consciousness of himself as a Judas tends to shift the emphasis of his story away from the "happy ending," and again, as in *The End of the Affair*, to realign it with Greene's earlier taste for endings of a more ironic kind. *The Quiet American* shares with *The End of the Affair* the sense of its protagonist's discovery of a new life as something equivocal and even flawed. Both these novels, that is to say, may be regarded to some extent as representing a kind of transitional narrative phase between tragedy and romance.

## NOTES

1. Diana Trilling, "America and *The Quiet American*," *Commentary*, 22 (July 1956), 66–71; Dorothy Van Ghent, "New Books in Review," *Yale Review*, Summer 1956, pp. 629–30; John Lehmann, "The Blundering, Ineffectual American," *New Republic*, 134 (12 March 1956), 26–27; A. J. Liebling, "A Talkative Something-or-Other," *New Yorker*, 7 April 1956, pp. 136–42; Orville Prescott, "Books of the Times," *New York Times*, 9 March 1956, p. 21; Granville Hicks, "In a Novel It's the Life, Not the Politics, That Counts," *New York Times Book Review*, 12 August 1956, p. 5; Philip

Rahv, "Wicked American Innocence," *Commentary*, 21 (May 1956), 488–90.

2. Northrop Frye, *The Secular Scripture: A Study of the Structure of Romance* (Cambridge, Mass.: Harvard Univ. Press, 1976), p. 115.

3. Graham Greene, *The Quiet American* (New York: Viking Penguin, 1996), pp. 181–82. All subsequent references to *The Quiet American* will be to this edition, with the relevant page numbers incorporated within parentheses in the text.

4. Graham Greene, *Ways of Escape* (London: Bodley Head, 1980), pp. 164–65.

5. Ibid., p. 140.

6. Ibid., pp. 139–40.

7. The jargon of "existentialism" seems unavoidable in any discussion of the novel. On this general subject, see, for instance, Robert O. Evans, "Existentialism in Graham Greene's *The Quiet American*," *Modern Fiction Studies*, 3 (Autumn 1957), 241–48, and Hilda Graef, "Existentialist Attitudes and Christian Faith: Graham Greene," in *Modern Gloom and Christian Hope* (Chicago: Henry Regnery Co., 1959), pp. 84–97.

# Miriam Allott

A *senior lecturer at the University of Liverpool and chair of the English Department, Birkbeck College, University of London, Miriam Allott has written or edited numerous books and essays. Her first book (co-authored with her husband) was on Graham Greene, followed by casebooks on* Jane Eyre *and* Wuthering Heights. *She also edited* The Brontës: The Critical Heritage *and* The Complete Poems of John Keats.

## THE MORAL SITUATION IN
## *THE QUIET AMERICAN*

When *The Quiet American* appeared in 1955 it was described on the jacket as "a modern variant on a theme which in the last century attracted Mark Twain and other writers: a study of New World hope and innocence set in an old world of violence," a statement which places it in a literary tradition with which it has some important elements in common. We are likely to do it more justice, I suggest, if we look at it in the context of sophisticated moral analysis of the kind associated with some later 19th-century English and American fiction than

Reprinted from Robert O. Evans, ed., *Graham Greene: Some Critical Considerations.* Lexington, Ky.: University Press of Kentucky, 1963, 188–206. Copyright © 1963 by The University Press of Kentucky. Used by permission of the publisher.

if we begin by relating it to certain types of contemporary existentialist thinking.[1] In its concern with the nature of effective moral action, its feeling for the anomalies which surround most human attempts to achieve this, and its assertion nevertheless of certain enduring human values, it reminds us particularly of James and Conrad (both writers with whom Greene is especially familiar). At the same time, in spite of its non-Catholic central characters, it gives a fresh focus to themes which Greene explores in his "Catholic" novels and, as we might expect, it shows a close emotional and intellectual kinship with these books. For a "correct reading" of this novel all these factors ought to be considered.

The notion that active intelligence rather than simple good intentions is necessary for the successful ordering of human relationships barely emerges as an explicit theme in the English novel until George Eliot; and even here the sober vision which this theme encourages is not yet of the kind to instill serious misgivings about the moral consonance of ends and means. Although George Eliot feels that "heroic Promethean effort" is required to achieve ultimate moral good, she places the effort within the limits of human ability and tries to free it from those limitations of temperament to which she is otherwise particularly sensitive. It is clearly no part of her purpose to unsettle her Victorian readers by suggesting that action directed towards "ultimate moral good" can be contaminated by the evil which it is designed to overcome. A more unflinching reading of experience is offered by her successors in the next generation, who confront more squarely than she does the fact that in an imperfect world choice lies between greater and lesser evil rather than between clear right and wrong. Conrad puts forward his "few simple ideas" concerning fidelity and honour, and then shows in his characters' fated lives, and with the help of Marlow's brooding commentaries, that a code of behaviour based on such ideas is at best no more than a fragile defence. James takes the argument several stages further in his own analysis of the moral life. In characters such as Isabel Archer, Maggie

Verver, and Milly Theale, innocence is equated with immaturity, and it is through their experience of betrayal and treachery that these people arrive at a fuller moral vision and come at last to understand the situation into which they have been drawn as much by their own limitations as by their adversaries' selfwill and ambitious cunning. Determining now to retrieve this situation, they take up the instruments whose use they have just learned. So Maggie resorts to deceit in order to counteract the deception practised on herself and her father by the Prince and Charlotte, and Milly Theale relies on the "cunning of the serpent" rather than "innocence of the dove" to make her way through the labyrinth which Kate and Merton, Lord Mark, and Mrs. Lowder, have prepared for her (it is this "cunning" which ultimately helps to bring about Merton Densher's moral awakening and his final separation from Kate).

Graham Greene's handling of his central characters in *The Quiet American* displays a similarly ironical criticism of life, the main difference being that Pyle's naive good intentions and their disastrous consequences carry James's theme of simple good faith divorced from wisdom into a wider area of social reference, while Fowler's behaviour extends the relevance of James's statement about the corrupting effects of experience to a more urgent and far-reaching "international situation" than any which he could foresee. Some prominent nonexistentialist French writers also share Greene's concern about the high price in personal integrity which may be paid by anyone aiming at efficient moral action for the general good, and they explore in a comparable way the ambiguous relationship between "intelligence" and "goodness." Albert Camus, who firmly opposes Sartre's existentialist beliefs, reminds us in *La Peste* that those who dedicate themselves to the conquest of violence find it hard to escape infection by this "pestilence." Again, in Anouilh's *Antigone*, we find Creon depending on violence and trickery to restore order in his troubled kingdom; his destruction of Antigone is forced on him because, in the society which he must hold together by compromise, backstairs intrigue, and the ruthless suppression of criticism, her inflexible—and in this case noble—innocence can only make for disaster.

Graham Greene's kindred themes point to the contemporary relevance of much of his thinking, but the reader of *The Quiet American* is bound, I suppose, to be more immediately struck by its Jamesian affinities, which are especially noticeable in its dramatization of what is primarily an Anglo-American "international situation"; its quasi-metaphorical juxtaposition of representatives from the "New" and the "Old" worlds; and its probing concern both with the motivation of treachery and betrayal and with the nature of an innocence which is dangerous because ignorant. There is a further similarity in the close interdependence of its tragic and its comic elements. It is after he has exhausted the more direct possibilities for social comedy in his "international situation" that we see James beginning to explore differences between the "New" and the "Old," less as a Balzacian social historian than as a moralist for whom the two worlds are convenient illustrations for universally opposed systems of value. The people who find themselves at odds with each other in *The Golden Bowl* or *The Wings of the Dove* illustrate general moral dilemmas of a kind with which contemporary sensibility is still deeply engaged. Yet at the same time that James locks together his victims and victimizers, his betrayed and betrayers, in their mutually destructive embrace he still manages to surround them with a strong flavour of irony. Similarly Pyle and Fowler, the two principal figures in *The Quiet American* who represent the New and the Old worlds, sometimes appear to stand for conflicting systems of value which cut across the artificial boundaries of nationality and race; at the same time they also succeed in conveying their author's strong feeling for comic incongruity. Pyle and Fowler at cross purposes are often as entertaining as, let us say, Sarah Pocock and Madame de Vionnet in that historic confrontation at the Paris hotel; and in association with the delightful and uncomprehending Phuong, whom they both love, they also demonstrate their author's skill in mingling the funny and the sad, a quality which gives special distinction to some of James's most intelligent achievements from the 1890s onwards.

This ironical temper also links Graham Greene with earlier writers than James, a point which he emphasizes himself by his choice of passages from Byron and Clough as epigraphs for his story. The lines from Byron occur in *Don Juan*, Canto I, stanza CXXXII.

> *This is the patent age of new inventions*
> *For killing bodies and for saving souls,*
> *All propagated with the best intentions.*

Like the description of armies attacking from the air in *Rasselas*, the passage can arouse amusement and surprise in a modern reader, who sees in it a longer reach of irony than the author originally intended. However, a little more may be said about its appearance in this new context without straining its significance too far. As it happens, it follows immediately after a stanza in which Byron indulges in some high-spirited satirical junketing at the expense of America. Along with even more libellous statements, Byron suggests that it might be a good thing if the population of America were to be thinned

> *With war, or plague, or famine—any way,*
> *So that civilization they may learn.*

It is hard to ignore the bearing of this remark on Greene's presentation of Alden Pyle, which is also in keeping, both in theme and tone, with Byron's frequent emphasis in his satirical verse on the connection between "good intentions" and, so to speak, the road to hell. In *The Quiet American* Alden Pyle, setting out equipped with simple humanitarian "good intentions" and a totally untutored moral intelligence, ends up helping General Thé to bomb civilians with explosive bicycle pumps, one of the age's newest "inventions for killing bodies." The epigraph from Byron thus underlines Greene's sardonic commentary on a combination of qualities now distressingly prevalent: i.e., the high development of technical skill combined with the low development of moral intelligence, so that the skill too often gets used for "killing bodies" instead of helping to make them good and happy. Alden Pyle, then, has to carry the burden of representing this combination of qualities, while Fowler, as the knowing observer who is intelligent enough to see the menace in Pyle but refrains from taking preventive action until it is almost too late, illustrates the more complex aspects of Greene's argument about moral responsibility. "Innocence is a kind of insanity," Fowler says, thinking of the way in which Pyle is "impregnably armoured" against knowing his own power for harm "by his good intentions and his ignorance" (p. 163). Like the spokesman of *Don Juan*, Fowler inhabits a mental region which is situated at some distance from Pyle's "psychological world of great simplicity," where one heroically asks trusting questions of one's rival in love. "You'd play straight with me, Thomas, wouldn't you?" Pyle asks, but Thomas Fowler knows that human behaviour, whether in love or war, demands more complex formulations than this. In the consequent disenchantment of its tone his narrative has in fact much in common with Byron's wry amusement, his distrust of cant, and his admiration for the civilization of the Old world as against that of the New.

What it does not have, however, is Byron's vigour. Here one sees the relevance of the quotation from Clough which appears above the lines from Byron at the beginning of the book. The passage is taken from *Amours de Voyage* (Canto II, stanza XI) and the spokesman this time is a young man, Claude, who suffers from that paralysis of the will and the emotions which is a continuing theme in 19th-century European literature and which owes so much to the "other" Byron—the Byron, that is, of the verse tales and *Childe Harold*. It unites Russian Hamlet figures, like the heroes in Pushkin and Lermontov, with Flaubert's Frédéric Moreau, and it even emerges as late as "The Beast in the Jungle," Henry James's short story about the man whose destiny it is to be someone "to whom nothing on earth was to happen." But the major factor in Claude's predicament is the sort of scepticism which we associate particularly with the movement of ideas in mid-19th-century England. His creator is an expert on the crippling effects of this kind of doubt and is also skilled in aiming his best ironical effects at his own indecisiveness. It is almost certain that Greene intends us to place Fowler in this context and see him as a "doubting Thomas,"[2] who is endowed with moral sensibility and yet fears, or is too lazy, to act, these characteristics meanwhile providing constantly renewed resources for the free play of his own ironic sense. Clough's hero does not like "being moved," we are told in the lines which Greene quotes:

> I do not like being moved; for the will is
>     excited; and action
> Is a most dangerous thing; I tremble for
>     something factitious,
> Some malpractice of heart and illegitimate
>     process;
> We're so prone to these things, with our
>     terrible notions of duty.

Fowler does not "like being moved" either, and he goes out of his way to assert his lack of involvement. "You can rule me out," he says early in the story, though it is already apparent that he is protesting too much:

> "I'm not involved. Not involved," I repeated. It had been an article of my creed. The human condition being what it was, let them love, let them murder, I would not be involved. My fellow journalists called themselves correspondents; I preferred the title of reporter. I wrote what I saw; I took no action—even opinion is a kind of action. (p. 28)

For all his assumed air of disengagement, however, Fowler cannot permanently refrain from action. Face to face at last with "the malpractice of heart and illegitimate process" which Pyle is led into by his "terrible notions of duty," he finds that he too has his "notions of duty" and must act upon them. One of the various ironical implications here is that these "notions of duty" again lead to "an illegitimate process." The tragicomic temper of this writing sees to it that Fowler's decision to act, which is founded on a sense of moral outrage and the desire to prevent further violence and suffering, should nevertheless result in betrayal, murder and—as the result of yet another ironical twist to the plot—considerable material advantage to himself. As we pursue the windings of the story it also becomes apparent that the author's tragicomic method acts as a necessary distancing device for certain strongly obsessive emotions.

Here it is necessary to take into account Fowler's relationship with Phuong, for one's judgment of the book depends to a great extent on what is made of this part of it. In the first four lines of the stanza from Clough's poem (Greene gives only the last four) Claude tells us,

> There are two different kinds, I believe, of
>     human attraction.
> One which simply disturbs, unsettles, and makes
>     you uneasy,
> And another that poises, retains, and fixes
>     and holds you.
> I have no doubt, for myself, in giving my voice
>     for the latter.

Fowler "gives his voice" for it too. Phuong—who is charmingly drawn: the elegance and economy of the style are nicely adjusted to the subject—represents the attraction which "poises, retains, and fixes and holds. . . ." She is totally different from "the girl in the red dressing-gown" of Fowler's earlier love affair. Sometimes, he tells Pyle, she seems "invisible like peace," while

the girl of the old affair stands for the other kind of human
attraction which "disturbs, unsettles, and makes you uneasy."

> "I was terrified of losing her. . . . I couldn't bear the
> uncertainty any longer. I ran towards the finish, just like
> a coward runs towards the enemy and wins a medal.
> . . . Then I came east."
> "And found Phuong?"
> "Yes."
> "But don't you find the same thing with Phuong?"
> "Not the same. You see, the other one loved me. I
> was afraid of losing love. Now I'm only afraid of losing
> Phuong." (pp. 103–104)

For a reader interpreting the book in existentialist terms it
is naturally hard to believe that Fowler "loves" Phuong.
"Fowler lives with Phuong because she prepares his opium pipe
and satiates his sexual appetites" is one of the views expressed
in the essay referred to in the footnotes; but this is a simplifi-
cation which may lead to our misjudging both the quality of
Fowler's feelings for Phuong and the function of Phuong herself
in the structure of the story. Through her, and through the
reactions which she arouses in Fowler, the author succeeds in
making us see how inevitable Fowler's ultimate commitment
really is. Fowler, we realise, acts as he does because he has
never, in any real sense, managed to remain uninvolved. His
feelings for Phuong help to explain why. They are complex and,
if we may judge by the general effect of his novels, they are
also fairly typical of Greene's own feelings about humanity.
They mingle tenderness, selfishness, compassion, pain, respect
for human dignity, and a bitter sense of the limitations of human faith and love. A passage like the following, even though
it is supposed to voice the thoughts of a nonbeliever, could
have been written by no one but this particular novelist.

Why should I want to die when Phuong slept beside me every night? But I knew the answer to that question. From childhood I had never believed in permanence, and yet I had longed for it. Always I was afraid of losing happiness. This month, next year, Phuong would leave me. If not next year, in three years. Death was the only absolute value in my world. Lose life and one would lose nothing again for ever. I envied those who could believe in a God and I distrusted them. I felt they were keeping their courage up with a fable of the changeless and the permanent. Death was far more certain than God, and with death there would be no longer the daily possibility of love dying. (p. 44)

A strong ingredient in these complex feelings is pity, an emotion which afflicts Greene's characters like a disease. Fowler's clipped reporting does not disguise from us—though it may do so from the imperceptive Pyle—the intensity with which this feeling can work in him. It is present when he recalls the vulnerability of Phuong as he saw her first, dancing with lightness and precision on her "eighteen-year-old feet" and living on simple dreams about security and happiness; when he seeks emotional relief by describing the grey drained bodies of men caught in a crossfire and filling the canal at Phat Diem as "an Irish stew containing too much meat"; and when he thinks of the peasant woman holding in her lap and covering "with a kind of modesty" what is left of her baby after General Thé's bombs have exploded in the square.

It is this suppressed but inextinguishable emotion which binds Fowler indissolubly to his fellow creatures and makes it impossible for him to remain not involved. It is this, too, which finally separates him from Alden Pyle, whose "York Harding" liberalism encourages belief in large clean abstractions like Freedom and Honour which exist on a plane safely out of sight of "the fury and the mire of human veins." It is true that this belief can promote Pyle's daring cloak-and-dagger enterprise in

saving his rival's life under fire because this "is the right thing
to do," an act of heroism which stands beyond criticism. And
yet nothing in the belief is capable of bringing home to its
possessor the enormity of what has happened when General
Thé's bombs go off in the square. "I dealt with him very severely," Pyle says afterwards, and he speaks "like the captain of
a school-team who has found one of his boys breaking his training" (p. 176). His continued association with Thé does not
present itself to him as needing any kind of moral justification.
The General is "the only hope we have" in the struggle for
power, and the Vietnamese he sees as too childlike and uncomplicated to nurse any resentment against the violence which he
and Thé will continue to inflict on them so long as the struggle
for power goes on. It is just after Pyle has uttered these shat-
tering statements that Fowler finally commits himself. He
moves to the window and gives to the waiting trishaw driver
the signal that Pyle must die. "Sooner or later," he has been
told earlier by Heng, a man who will help to bring this death
about, "one has to take sides. If one is to remain human"
(p. 174). In spite of his hatred of political action, he joins at
last in Pyle's cloak-and-dagger game, ranging himself in the
name of humanity beside Heng and his undercover gang
against Pyle and *his* fellow-plotters.

It is at this point, I think, that one becomes aware of the
thematic continuity linking this book with Greene's "Catholic"
novels, where the author is occupied with the allied problems
of pain and of how far man is justified in risking damnation for
the sake of relieving the suffering of his fellow creatures. These
stories are haunted by memories of "the curé d'Ars admitting
to his mind all the impurity of a province, Péguy challenging
God in the cause of the damned." It is Péguy of whom the
priest speaks in *Brighton Rock* when he seeks to console Rose
after Pinkie's death.

> "He was a good man, a holy man, and he lived in sin
> all through his life, because he couldn't bear the idea

that any soul should suffer damnation. . . . He never took the sacraments, he never married his wife in church. I don't know, my child, but some people think he was—well, a saint."

Scobie, in *The Heart of the Matter*, risks damnation by committing suicide to save his wife and mistress from further suffering, and the whiskey priest in *The Power and the Glory*, praying for the salvation of his corrupted child, beseeches God, "Give me any kind of death—without contrition, in a state of sin—only save this child." Like Ivan Karamazov, who challenges Alyosha on the subject of divine justice and can find no justification for innocent suffering, these people find no escape from the ravages of their sense of pity. The extra turn of the screw in their case is their full consciousness of the spiritual peril into which they have been led by their compassion.[3]

This theological dilemma is absent in *The Quiet American*, but the moral and emotional predicament is essentially unchanged: indeed since the author is now depicting man without God, it is possibly even more urgent in its presentation. We sense this urgency when we realise that Scobie's feelings about suffering lead him to incur the risk, but not the certainty, of damnation, while the effect of comparable feelings in Fowler is to make him take on a burden of guilt from which he cannot be set free. For Scobie and his Catholic fellow-sinners there is always the hope of grace; the point of light may appear at the end of the tunnel, the glimmer of dawn may rise in the night sky, the hand of God may reach out to stay their free fall from "the stirrup to the ground." For Fowler, enacting his Judas role, there is guilt and a happiness stained with remorse. A certain emotional resonance in Greene's treatment of this situation calls to mind Tarrou's question towards the close of *La Peste*: "Can one be a saint without God?—that's the problem, in fact the only problem, I'm up against today."[4] Obviously we cannot say of Fowler, as the priest in *Brighton Rock* says of Péguy, that he may be "well, a saint." And yet it is also obvious that among the characteristics which Fowler shares with these Catholics who challenge God in the cause of suffering is his willingness to take the responsibility of wrong-doing for the sake of diminishing human pain.

He also shares with these Catholic characters the longing for peace which is one of the consequences of their burden of pity, especially their pity for the suffering of children. Like Scobie at the bedside of the shipwrecked child and the whiskey priest praying for his daughter—and like Father Paneloux in *La Peste* watching a child's protracted death from plague or Ivan Karamazov torturing himself with stories about cruelty to children—Fowler experiences with the growth of this anguish the growth also of an angry despair. All victims of suffering— the men in the canal at Phat Diem, the young soldiers in the watch-tower—arouse these feelings in him. But it is memories of the child in the ditch ("one shouldn't fight a war with children . . . a little curled body in a ditch came back to my mind") and of the mangled baby in the Saigon square, which trigger off his decision to take measures against Pyle. His desire for peace is accentuated by these feelings about human suffering, and its existence is in itself a measure of how deeply, after all, he has always been "involved." He identifies Phuong with "peace" and loves her for her stillness and serenity, while death seems to him to be "the only absolute value" because it puts a stop to despair. "There can be no peace without hope," thinks Rieux in *La Peste*, as he meditates on the death of Tarrou, the man who had wondered whether one could be "a saint without God."

> Tarrou had lived a life riddled with contradictions and had never known hope's solace. Did that explain his aspirations towards saintliness, his quest of peace by service in the course of others?
>
> (Part IV, Chap. iii)

Fowler's life, too, though lived at a lower emotional temperature, is "riddled with contradictions" and he has "never known
hope's solace," while "service in the cause of others" does not
bring him peace any more than it really does to Tarrou. On the
contrary it gives him cause to long for it all the more. Peace
remains the *princesse lointaine* of his dreams, and his author
may well intend this longing to be felt as an expression of the
love of God. The desire for peace seems to pursue Fowler as
the nameless "something" pursues Pinkie in his last despairing
drive through the dark. Like Tarrou, Fowler appears to be one
of those people who, as Rieux puts it, "desired reunion with
something they couldn't have defined, but which seemed to
them the only desirable thing on earth. For want of a better
name, they sometimes called it peace." (*La Peste*, Part IV,
Chap. iv)

Fowler himself finds another explanation for his longing,
seeing it simply as the manifestation of his own selfish egotism.
When Pyle at the risk of his own life brings members of the
patrol to his rescue, Fowler refuses their aid until they have
attended to the young soldier whose moaning (it is now stilled
because he is dead) had filled him with a sense of anguish and
guilt harder to bear than the pain of his wounded leg. He totally
repudiates Pyle's admiring interpretation of this behaviour. Pyle
sees him, one understands, as another Sidney at Zutphen, but
Fowler merely remarks that he "cannot be at ease (and to be
at ease is my chief wish) if someone else is in pain, visibly or
audibly or tactually." He goes on: "Sometimes this is mistaken
by the innocent for unselfishness, when all I am doing is sacrificing a small good—in this case postponement in attending
to my hurt—for the sake of a far greater good, a peace of mind
when I need only think of myself" (p. 114). There is, of course,
some truth in this, for Fowler, as I have said, is by no means
a saintly figure: largely, he illustrates the ordinary self-regarding
emotions of the *homme moyen sensuel*. Yet the revelation that
his peace is contingent upon the peace of others only succeeds

in further emphasising how inescapably involved he is in the human situation. Moreover his remark about "sacrificing a small good . . . for the sake of a far greater good" acquires an impressive irony when it is applied to his betrayal of Pyle. The possibility of repose recedes even further into the distance once he has sent to his death the man who is at once the preserver of his life and his rival in love. In the earlier part of his story he explains that the human situation "being what it is" he has never been able to experience the "peace of mind when I need only think of myself" (it is only in his opium-sleep that he manages to approach this state): in the later part of his story he indicates that his own actions have done little to bring the experience any nearer.

It is also in this later part of the story, as we should expect, that the possible religious significance of his longing for peace presses itself more noticeably on our attention. It is especially apparent in his final interview with Vigot, the intelligent Roman Catholic police officer at the Sûreté, who keeps his copy of Pascal at his side like a manual for living. Vigot is in charge of the investigations into Pyle's death, and the verbal fencing which characterizes his exchanges with Fowler, although far less elaborate, is not unlike the dialectical duelling which takes place between Raskolnikov and the examining magistrate in *Crime and Punishment*. Fowler certainly shares with Raskolnikov a compulsive desire to unburden his conscience. The similarity in their situations also draws attention to the enormous contrast between Raskolnikov's intensity of feeling and Fowler's cooler response. He does not give himself away, but he comes near to it in the interview which at last closes his association with Vigot.

> . . . "I've got nothing to tell you. Nothing at all."
>
> "Then I'll be going," he said. "I don't suppose I'll trouble you again."
>
> At the door he turned as though he were unwilling to abandon hope—his hope or mine.

"That was a strange picture for you to go and see that night. I wouldn't have thought you cared for costume drama. What was it? *Robin Hood?*"

"*Scaramouche*, I think. I had to kill time. And I needed distraction."

"Distraction?"

"We all have our private worries, Vigot," I carefully explained.

It was strange how disturbed I had been by Vigot's visit. It was as though a poet had brought me his work to criticise and through some careless action I had destroyed it. I was a man without a vocation . . . but I could recognize a vocation in another. Now that Vigot had gone to close his uncompleted file, I wished I had the courage to call him back and say, "You are right. I did see Pyle the night he died." (pp. 170–71)

The dialogue here has the allusive understatement which serves its author well in his plays. Even the film-titles carry their ironic overtones. The make-believe world of *Robin Hood*, where a gay and gallant solution is found for the problem of wrong and injustice, and the mischief-making buffoonery of *Scaramouche*—Fowler provides himself with an alibi for the last hours of Pyle's life by sitting through this film—underline the contrast between sober reality and the boy's adventure-story world in which Pyle had so touchingly and yet so dangerously believed. There is a similar telling allusiveness in Fowler's throwaway remark about "hope." In the unwillingness on Vigot's side "to abandon hope—his hope or mine," especially when it is taken in conjunction with the references to Vigot's "vocation" and Fowler's desire to confess, one sees the police officer assuming at this point in the story the function in Greene's Catholic novels which is often fulfilled by his priests. The reader is surely intended to remember here Fowler's earlier conversation with the Catholic priest whom he encounters at the top of the church tower in Phat Diem.

He said, "Did you come up here to find me?"

"No. I wanted to get my bearings."

"I asked you because I had a man up here last night. He wanted to go to confession. He had got a little frightened, you see, with what he had seen along the canal. One couldn't blame him."

"It's bad along there?"

"The parachutists caught them in a cross-fire. Poor souls. I thought perhaps you were feeling the same."

"I'm not a Roman Catholic. I don't think you would even call me a Christian."

"It's strange what fear does to a man."

"It would never do that to me. If I believed in any God at all, I should still hate the idea of confession. Kneeling in one of your boxes. Exposing myself to another man. You must excuse me, Father, but to me it seems morbid—unmanly even."

"Oh," he said lightly, "I expect you are a good man. I don't suppose you've ever had much to regret."
(pp. 49–50)

The unconscious irony of the priest's reply is brought home to the reader when Fowler, now with something momentous to regret, wishes he has the courage to obey his impulse, recall Vigot and confess the truth.

Although this wish is not fulfilled, it seems on the face of it that Fowler's story will nevertheless have "the happy ending" which Phuong has tried so hard all along not to seem to want: his job is secure; his divorce will come through; he will be able to marry Phuong; she will stay with him now that Pyle is dead. But the shadow of Pyle remains. Even when the wonderful telegram arrives and Phuong knows that she is to have the security which she had earlier sought with Pyle, the shadow is still there. Pyle's copy of York Harding's *The Rôle of the West*—another title obviously chosen for its ironical effect—stands out from Fowler's bookshelves

like a cabinet portrait—of a young man with a crew-
cut and a black dog at his heels. I could harm no one
any more. I said to Phuong, "Do you miss him much?"
"Who?"
"Pyle." Strange how even now, even to her, it was
impossible to use his first name.
"Can I go, please? My sister will be so excited."
"You spoke his name once in your sleep."
"I never remember my dreams."
"There was so much you could have done together.
He was young."
"You are not old."
"The skyscrapers. The Empire State Building."
She said with a small hesitation, "I want to see the
Cheddar Gorge." (pp. 188–89)

These nicely adjusted lines of dialogue at the close of the novel,
their hinted regrets signalizing new areas of sensitivity in the
relationship between Fowler and Phuong (" 'It's like it used to
be,' I lied, 'a year ago' ") show Fowler ruefully admitting that
the memory of Pyle will be difficult to discard. As we see him
last, Pyle is still on his mind.

I thought of the first day and Pyle sitting beside me at
the Continental, with his eye on the soda-fountain
across the way. Everything had gone right with me since
he had died, but how I wished there existed someone
to whom I could say that I was sorry. (p. 189)

Pyle may not always stay in his mind, one feels, but what has
mattered in Fowler's story is that he is capable of feeling this
pity and sorrow for the lost young man; that as an ordinary,
nonpolitical, moderately selfish but intelligent human being he
is moved to act against violence and stupidity; and that he is
impelled towards such action above all by his insight into hu-

man suffering, especially the suffering caused by war and political conflict.

It is easy to mistake the nature of Greene's achievement in this novel, partly because its extreme economy disguises both the range and quality of its feeling and the reach of its ideas. Perhaps it is also true to say that it illustrates how far this author's obsessive themes make for weakness as well as strength. Pity is one of the most urgent of these themes and it is a dangerous one for any artist to handle. It requires stringent distancing devices, and although the author's careful understatement and the operation of his irony go a long way towards supplying these, there are times when one feels that he may be near to an unbalancing subjectivity. All the same, the theme enables him to present with necessary dramatic intensity issues which it would be perilous to ignore. He succeeds in reminding us that we need Pyle's courage and none of his ignorance, Fowler's moral intelligence and none of his indecisiveness, if we are to find a way out of the alarming difficulties which as nations and individuals we are most of us nowadays required to face. He takes us a long distance, I feel, from the moral position implied in a good deal of modern existentialist writing.

## NOTES

1. Robert O. Evans takes a different view in "Existentialism in Greene's *The Quiet American*," *Modern Fiction Studies*, III (Autumn 1957), 241–48.
2. It is quite in keeping Greene's practice to play with the names of his characters in this way. See Philip Stratford, "Unlocking the Potting Shed," *Kenyon Review*, XXIV (Winter 1962), 134 and *passim*.
3. For a fuller discussion of the theme of pity in Graham Greene's novels, see Kenneth Allott and Miriam Farris, "The Universe of Pity," *The Art of Graham Greene* (London, 1951; repr. New York, 1963).
4. Passages from Albert Camus' *La Peste* are given throughout from the 1948 translation by Stuart Gilbert.

# John Cassidy

*Having checked all available sources in the United States and the United Kingdom, the editor has been unable to find biographical information for the author of this incisive 1957 essay. If readers can supply relevant data, it will be included in future editions of this text.*

## AMERICA AND INNOCENCE:
## HENRY JAMES AND GRAHAM GREENE

Seventy-seven years separate the publication of *Daisy Miller*, by Henry James, from that of *The Quiet American*, by Graham Greene. With *Daisy Miller* James made the closest approach in his lifetime to the kind of popular acclaim now enjoyed by Greene; the novel is one of his simplest, and the workings of its author's mind are revealed in skeletal clarity. The transformation in the significance of America and in the writing of novels which has appeared during that time make it startling that the two books should share something of a common attitude to Americans as symbols. The changes of the intervening three-quarters of a century have naturally had their effect on this symbolic use; the position of America in the world has changed, and the value of the symbol has correspondingly al-

From *Blackfriars* 38 (June 1957): 261–67. Reprinted with permission of *New Blackfriars*, edited by the English Dominicans.

tered from that presented by James. Nevertheless there is a similarity, and it seems that Americans abroad can still provide material for an imaginative examination of society and human motives.

James's ambivalent attitude to his native country is, of course, widely demonstrated throughout his novels. Always he finds it difficult to reconcile his admiration for the forthrightness, vigour and pragmatism of a young country, with a feeling of its inferiority before the majestical sweep of European history and the society with which he sees that history so intimately twined. The arts and politics of Europe are superb monuments of humanity, but at the same time there is in them a subtle threat, a danger that their greatness dominates the life of the present and cows it into submission to a dead past. Into this world enter the young Americans, Roderick Hudson, Christopher Newman, Daisy Miller, Isabel Archer. Their conflicts with the subtleties and intrigues of Europe form the substance of the novels in which they appear.

There is a great distance between Daisy Miller, the American girl touring Europe, and Alden Pyle, the member of an economic mission to French Indo-China almost a century later; yet there is something common in their approach to the societies in which they find themselves. Daisy Miller resents and opposes the conventions which she sees governing the private lives of Europeans; Pyle is a cruder, more active missionary (as *The Quiet American* is a cruder and more violent book) not merely critical of his surroundings but determined to affect them positively, through his membership of a disguised political agency. He arrives primed with lectures and York Harding's books and forces all he finds into his prepared mould. "He never saw anything," Fowler remarks of him after his death, "he hadn't heard in a lecture hall."

Daisy Miller and Pyle are both examples of American innocence loosed among the tangles of an older and more complex world. The situation is at least as old as Mark Twain, whose *Innocents Abroad* appeared in 1869, but with James and

Greene its possibilities are so purposively developed that a further dimension is revealed. The nationality of the protagonists is still of real importance as reporting; the books on one level deal factually with circumstances which exist in the world in a way not far from that in which they are here described. But it surely becomes clear that the conception of innocence as used by both writers is something more than an observation of Americans, and is a factor to be examined in its own right.

Pyle is not in Europe but the Far East, where the impact of the strangeness and complexities of life is sharper than that of nineteenth-century Europe, though often of the same kind. He is unsympathetic towards the East, and his distrust and zeal to change it are manifested in apparently unimportant details; he induces Phuong to straighten her "elaborate hairdressing which she thought became the daughter of a mandarin," and he pushes his Vit-Health sandwiches upon the Caodist commandant, having expressed his fears about the local food. The sterile isolation suggested by the latter incident is echoed by the remarks of Fowler about the sterilized world of the American girls in the milk bar, immediately before the explosion of the disastrous bomb. The girls are mere observers, and have the attitude of tourists:

> "Do you think it's a demonstration?"
> "I've seen so many demonstrations," the other said wearily, like a tourist glutted with churches.

Daisy Miller is the weary tourist, too. In Rome she is pleased only with that part of her own world which she can find there:

> "I was sure it would be dreadfully poky. I was sure we should be going round all the time with one of those dreadful old men that explain about the pictures and things. But we only had about a week of that, and now I'm enjoying myself."

Her effect on Roman society is disturbing, if less alarming than that of Pyle's plastic bombs on Saigon, but she like Pyle is killed by a refusal to understand the realities of a different world. In spite of warnings she visits the Colosseum by moonlight, and consequently dies of Roman fever.

Daisy's involvement with Giovanelli, the young Italian, is an affair infected with as much misunderstanding as Pyle's attachment to Phuong. She cannot or will not realize that Giovanelli's English is as fluent as it is because it has been practised upon a great many American heiresses. Pyle refuses to listen to Fowler's attempt brutally to disillusion him, and persists in his gentlemanly behaviour towards both Fowler and Phuong, striving always to live up to his code of "being fair." The behaviour of Daisy Miller is more enigmatic, even ambiguous; Winterbourne is never quite sure about her:

> It must be admitted that holding oneself to a belief in Daisy's "innocence" came to seem to Winterbourne more and more a matter of fine-spun gallantry. As I have already had occasion to relate, he was angry at finding himself reduced to chopping logic about this young lady; he was vexed at his lack of instinctive certitude as to how far her eccentricities were generic, national, and how far they were personal.

This paradox of American innocence is repeated by Greene. Pyle is almost ludicrously innocent in his personal relationships and in his intentions. "I never knew a man," says Fowler, "with better motives for all the trouble he caused." Much of the trouble, of course, is caused by a stumbling incomprehension, like the support of General Thé and the "Third Force"; but the instigation of the bicycle bombs and the single large explosion stems from an innocence as equivocal as Daisy Miller's.

It is this conception of innocence as a paradox which seems central to the understanding of both books. Henry James is concerned with the ancient antithesis of innocence and experience, and skilfully maintains a poise in all his novels which enables him to crystallize the problem and yet to reserve judgment. Greene on the other hand is committed, and his book embodies the view that the modern world holds no place for innocence, which must crumble before reality and involve much in its downfall.

James is inescapably attracted to the evidence of a tested civilization which he finds in Europe, the "experienced" half of his world. The following description of Rome reveals this attraction and the limitations he felt were intrinsic in it.

> A few days after his brief interview with her mother, he encountered her in that beautiful abode of flowering desolation known as the Palace of the Caesars. The early Roman spring had filled the air with bloom and perfume, and the rugged surface of the Palatine was muffled with tender verdure. Daisy was strolling along the top of one of those great mounds of ruin that are embanked with mossy marble and paved with monumental inscriptions. It seemed to him that Rome had never been so lovely as just then. He stood looking off at the enchanting harmony of line and colour that remotely encircles the city, inhaling the softly humid odours and feeling the freshness of the year and the antiquity of the place reaffirm themselves in mysterious interfusion.

The phrases "beautiful abode of flowering desolation" and "mounds of ruin," and the implication of moss on the monuments indicate the twofold approach: enchantment with the beauty, admiration for the achievement, linked with an insistent feeling that all this is past and that it is to the young Daisy Miller walking through it that our attention must be directed. The ideal "interfusion" between the freshness of youth and the antiquity of man is indeed "mysterious," and attainable only in glimpses of a rare perception. All James's art tends towards the cultivation and preservation of sensitive perceptions of this kind.

In *Daisy Miller* the Colosseum is for Winterbourne the epitome of European civilization, and he enters it by moonlight the better to appreciate its grandeur. At the moment of deepest admiration, however, he remembers that the atmosphere of the Colosseum is believed to be dangerous to health. The passage is germinal.

> The place had never seemed to him more impressive. One half of the gigantic circus was in deep shade; the other was sleeping in the luminous dusk. As he stood there he began to murmur Byron's famous lines from *Manfred*; but before he had finished his quotation he remembered that if nocturnal meditations are recommended by the poets, they are deprecated by the doctors. The historic atmosphere was there, certainly; but the historic atmosphere, scientifically considered, was no better than a villainous miasma.

He is appalled to find Daisy Miller in the middle of the Colosseum, breathing its poisonous atmosphere. Within a couple of days she has Roman fever, and a little over a week later she is dead. Giovanelli pronounces her obituary:

> "She was the most beautiful young lady I ever saw, and the most amiable." And he added in a moment, "And the most innocent."

If a fusion is achieved, it is only through the assimilation of such difficult ideas and experiences, which are squarely faced. James never attempts a facile reconciliation of his reverence for historical grandeur with his feeling that history is stifling, even killing. The power of tradition is in direct opposition to the innocence of youth, contorting it to resemble itself; and since tradition is the experience of previous generations, confused, wrong-headed, often evil, it is the destroyer of innocence. The historical atmosphere is seen as no better than a villainous miasma.

Graham Greene surveys the same conflict from the European end. With him it is innocence which is the destroyer, inimical to institutions which, though imperfect, are the result of the cumulative wisdom of the centuries, and are based on an acceptance of man as he really is. Pyle's innocence is insidious because so deceptive. When he enters the Chinese quarter of Saigon, Fowler's instinct is to protect him:

> That was my first instinct—to protect him. It never occurred to me that there was greater need to protect myself. Innocence always calls mutely for protection, when we should be so much wiser to guard ourselves against it: innocence is like a dumb leper who has lost his bell, wandering the world meaning no harm.

Here "innocence" is fairly obviously synonymous with "naivety." The word (often repeated as in *Daisy Miller*) defines itself during the course of the book, and although it emerges as a complex of several meanings, some are excluded. Naivety is a large part of Pyle's deficiency. When Fowler throws at him a derogatory remark about the Black Prince, his distress is evident and symptomatic. "I was to see many times that look of pain and disappointment touch his eyes and mouth, when reality didn't match the romantic ideas he cherished. . . ." Sheer ignorance of much of the real world, combined with a reforming zeal in the tradition of the American "sense of mission," account for his innocence and ineptitude. Freedom from guilt, of course, is another matter, and Pyle's distance from innocence in this sense constitutes the paradox on which the novel is founded.

Daisy Miller's innocence is an honest-eyed directness which challenges restriction. Of Italy she says:

"The young ladies of this country have a dreadfully poky time of it, as far as I can learn; I don't see why I should change my habits for *them*."

"I am afraid your habits are those of a flirt," said Winterbourne gravely.

"Of course they are," she cried, giving him her little smiling stare again. "I'm a fearful, frightful flirt. Did you ever hear of a nice girl that was not?"

She is prepared to live by her own standards, to preserve this uncontaminated kind of innocence, even in the midst of hostile pressures. Her European associates are scandalized, and in the end she is extinguished by the European atmosphere. Innocence had seemed tough enough to survive and conquer, but the establishments of experience have prevailed. The effect of Winterbourne should be noted; of his experience in knowing Daisy he says to his aunt, "You were right . . . I was booked to make a mistake. I have lived too long in foreign parts." He was beginning to be contaminated, and has been brought to self-awareness by his encountering American directness once again. But James has no such simple "message" as this. The passage continues:

> Nevertheless he went back to live at Geneva, whence there continue to come the most contradictory accounts of his motives of sojourn: a report that he is "studying hard"—an intimation that he is much interested in a very clever foreign lady.

For Winterbourne, the appeal of American innocence is limited; he is committed to Europe and experience once more.

Fowler's reaction is not simple either, and with him it is not merely a matter of seeing limitations. He has seen such disaster follow upon the entry of American innocence that he has accepted responsibility for eliminating it, and connived at the murder of Pyle. Only the book from which Pyle drew inspiration for his actions in Indo-China is left.

> Opposite me in the bookcase *The Role of the West* stood out like a cabinet portrait—of a young man with a crew cut and a black dog at his heels. He could harm no one any more.

From now on life is to be uncomplicated by his presence; difficulties disappear, the pieces fall into place. Fowler's wife agrees to divorce him; he is free to marry Phuong. Yet there is something wrong with the apparent solution, as the last sentence of the book indicates: "Everything had gone right with me since he had died, but how I wished there existed someone to whom I could say that I was sorry." There is an added complexity. The murder of innocence has not been simple either, and though it has brought comfort it has also left regret.

Daisy's innocence is tough, obvious and bright, but it succumbs. Pyle's is self-effacing and deadly. Neither can survive; perhaps neither deserves to. The kind of innocence embodied in these two is essentially unreal. In a kind of optimistic humanism they behave as if the world were as they wish it to be, and are broken by the world's intransigence. The point is driven home by Greene with a typical horrific flourish; after the explosion in Saigon Fowler pushes the bewildered Pyle so that he steps into a pool of civilian blood, and tells him, "You've got the Third Force and National Democracy all over your right shoe." The discrepancy between slogan and reality is made crudely apparent.

The notion of original sin seems a long way from the private worlds of Daisy Miller and Pyle, and it is in their lack of recognition of the kind of reality suggested by this doctrine that their failure lies. This is their innocence, as futile among the social delicacies of Henry James as in the rough political turmoil of Greene's Indo-China. For each writer, in spite of the vast gap by which they are separated, the American is a valid correlative for innocence thus defined. As the world has changed, so the spheres of operation have altered almost beyond recognition; and it is not suggested that James and Greene have much in common beyond the theme of Greene's *The Quiet American* and their common recognition of evil.* The comparison is interesting and valuable because of, not in spite of, the clear differences between the writers and between their worlds. The innocent American of fiction remains with us; but he has become quiet, and dangerous.

* See Greene's two essays on Henry James in *The Lost Childhood* (Eyre and Spottiswoode, 1951).

# Judith Adamson

*Judith Adamson is professor of English at Dawson College, Montreal. She has published* Graham Greene and Cinema, Graham Greene: The Dangerous Edge, *and numerous articles in* Sight and Sound, Encounter, Der Monat, Cinema Journal, *and* The Toronto Star. *Working with Greene, she selected and introduced the essays for his last book,* Reflections.

## VIETNAM

In 1951 when Greene stopped in Hanoi on his way home from Malaya to see his friend Trevor Wilson, he knew little about the situation in Vietnam. The British press had only one correspondent reporting on the whole of Indo-China at the time so coverage was scant. Greene arrived for this first visit with the Western liberal's standard view of communism as nefarious. Four winters in Vietnam, a novel and many articles later, he had decided "there is something in Communism besides politics."[1]

The spell of Indo-China was quickly cast "by the tall elegant girls in white silk trousers, by the pewter evening light on the flat paddy fields, where the water-buffaloes trudged fetlock-deep with a slow primeval gait, by the French perfumeries in the rue Catinat, the Chinese gambling houses in Cholon, above all by that feeling of exhilaration which a measure of danger brings to the visitor with a return ticket." Greene drained a magic potion there, "a loving cup" which he has since shared "with many retired *colons* and officers of the Foreign Legion whose eyes light up at the mention of Saigon and Hanoi."[2]

On this first visit he stayed only a couple of weeks but was able, with the help of General de Lattre who put a small plane at his disposal, to see a good deal. He got to Saigon, and in the Southern delta made the first of many visits to the political-religious sect, the Cao Dai, "whose saints included Victor Hugo, Christ, Buddha and Sun-Yat-Sen." He saw "the little medieval state established in the marshes of Bentre by a young half-caste, Colonel Leroy, who read de Tocqueville and struck, with the suddenness and cruelty of a tiger, at the Communists in his region."[3] In the North he went to Phat Diem, the prince bishopric whose army he would rather have belonged to than to the Malayan police, and which would figure in *The Quiet American* (1955).

Eight months later, in October 1951, he returned to write his first report. Between these visits General de Lattre's only son had been killed in an ambush in the region of Phat Diem and, according to Greene, the General attributed his death to Catholic machinations. Being "highly suspicious of Catholicism . . . in a strange sick manner he linked the death of his son with my visit to Phat Diem and the fact that both Trevor Wilson and I were Catholics."[4] The result was that Wilson was declared *persona non grata* and was thrown out of the country before Greene got back in October. He was allowed to return while Greene was there to pack his belongings, but he and Greene, whom General de Lattre "had on one embarrassing occasion and at his own dinner-table accused . . . of espionage,"[5] were put under supervision of the Sûreté. Greene published the story of their experiences with M. Tourraint, who was assigned to keep track of them, in *The London Magazine* (August 1954) as "The General and the Spy," and later in the Introduction to the Collected Edition of *The Quiet American* (1973) and in *Ways of Escape* (1980), where M. Tourraint was called M. Dupont.

On this second visit Greene was commissioned to write an article for *Life* magazine but his "ambivalent attitude to the war was already perceptible—my admiration for the French army, my admiration for their enemies, and my doubt of any final value in the war."[6] *Life* rejected what he wrote, and the report was published instead in *Paris-Match* as part of a joint piece with Raymond Cartier. On this visit Greene saw Colonel Leroy again. He described him as "*le plus heureux des seigneurs de la guerre en Cochinchine*."[7] With American aid, thirty-two-year-old Leroy, who was half French, half Annamite, had created 94 first-aid posts in the territory he administered (there were 96 in the whole of Cochin-China), and had instituted a system of local elections for a consultative assembly. He had also built a lake with a pagoda on it and a zoo. Beside the lake was a bar lit all night by neon lights. To entertain his guests he poured brandy down the throats of the women in attendance and played music from *The Third Man* on a gramophone. There was "an astonishing contrast between this gay and rather bizarre Catholic state and the sombre diocese of Phat-Diem,"[8] Greene said. He and Leroy became friends and when the Colonel wrote about his experience in *Un Homme dans La Rizière* (1955), Greene supplied the introduction.

While staying with Colonel Leroy Greene shared a room with an American attached to an economic aid mission. Though he was more intelligent and less innocent than Pyle, he was to be the model for Greene's protagonist in *The Quiet American*. The two men drove back to Saigon together, as Pyle and Fowler would in the novel, and the American lectured Greene about the necessity of creating a third force in Vietnam which he thought might be led by self-styled General Thé. On Greene's first visit to the country Thé had been a colonel in

the Cao Dai army of 20,000 men fighting in the South, theoretically alongside the French. But between January and October 1951 Thé had left Tay Ninh, the political centre of the
Cao Dai, where they made primitive mortars from the exhaust
pipes of old cars to supplement the arms they got from the
French, and set himself up as a general ready to make war on
the Viet Minh and French alike.

Greene didn't trust the Cao Dai remaining in Tay Ninh.
Thé had assassinated General Chanson, in Greene's opinion
one of the best young French Generals, and when the French
asked the Cao Dai to capture Thé they said they could not
because he had not attacked them. By the time Greene wrote
*The Quiet American* Thé was in contact with the Americans.
Greene speculated that he was responsible for the bicycle
bombs that were going off in Saigon at the time, and the bigger
bombs that went off in the main square of the city. Though
Greene's suspicion was based on several pieces of evidence, he
drew flak from American critics when he fictionalised the connection between Thé and the United States and implicated
Pyle in the bombings. "There is a difference," A. J. Liebling
wrote in the *New Yorker*, "between calling your over-successful
offshoot a silly ass and accusing him of murder."[9]

Greene made two more trips to Vietnam, one from December 1953 to February 1954, the other later in the spring of 1955.
He wrote pieces for *The Sunday Times* on both occasions and
after the 1954 trip published extracts from his journal as
well—in the *Spectator* (about Dien Bien Phu a few months
before the battle began), in the *Tablet* (about Bui Chu, an
Annamite bishopric on the edge of Phat Diem), and in the
*London Magazine* (about smoking opium and his experiences
with the Sûreté). If dividing the journal into pieces appropriate
for different publications puts one in mind of a tinker peddling
his wares, it also shows the necessary ingenuity of the free-lance
writer who makes his living by his pen.

In *The Sunday Times* in 1954 Greene wrote about the Cao
Dai, and the Hoa Hao as he had in his 1952 *Paris-Match* article.

But "what on my first two visits had seemed gay and bizarre were now like a game that has gone on too long. . . ." These armed religious sects no longer seemed naive and charming, but "cunning and unreliable like a smart advertisement."[10] He warned Americans who dreamed of using the renegade Cao Dai General Thé as the leader of a third force that "you cannot fight a war satisfactorily with allies like this." Thé's two hundred pound bombs had exploded among innocent shoppers in the square in Saigon. Another sect leader, whom he did not name, "treated his faulty liver homeopathically with the help of human livers supplied by his troops and the Binh-Xuyen, the private army under General Le Van Vien who controlled the gambling joints and opium houses of Cholon. . . ." These were not men to be relied on.

Nevertheless, Greene believed that many Catholic Vietnamese formed small pockets of resistance to the Viet Minh and should be encouraged. He cited Thui Nhai, a village in the region of Bui Chu in the North which "is almost entirely Catholic, and the Catholics, however nationalist, are absolute opponents of Viet Minh." When the village was attacked its inhabitants continued to fight with the help of Vietnamese troops although two-thirds of the region of Bui Chu had easily been taken. "This small pocket of Vietnam, under its courageous Annamite bishop, was to all intents independent." An old priest there told Greene: " 'We want only peace, to live quietly in friendship, but if the Communists come, we will fight them and kill them. . . .' " These people were united "by their Christianity—not the Christianity of new converts but of men and women whose great-grandparents had survived the Emperor's persecution a hundred years ago, when to shelter a missionary entailed death under the elephant's hoof." Villages like Thui Nhai, where the people were united by a belief for which their ancestors too had fought, had a better chance against the disciplined Viet Minh than the forces that were fighting haphazardly in the Saigon delta led by the likes of Thé. One should not put one's hope on a single village, but "in the break-up of a world there was no point in anything but irrational hope."

The Vietnamese had an ancient tradition of revolt against oppression. In the thirties, under the impact of global depression a strong nationalist movement had developed which had strengthened in World War Two in the face of Japanese occupation. It was this nationalist sentiment which Ho Chi Minh employed to create a broadly based national-communist movement that attracted many nationalists who were not themselves communist. Nevertheless, when the war against French occupation began in 1946, the French were confident about its outcome. They had élite troops, weapons and airplanes. But the Viet Minh had a knowledge of the land, the people and, most important, they had a cause.[11] Greene pointed out that the Catholic population of Tonkin was almost entirely rural and illiterate. European newspapers were useless in pleading France's case. Ho Chi Minh reached them by radio with the message that it was the duty of Catholics to be nationalists, and the admirable behaviour of his highly disciplined soldiers spoke well for him. The Viet Minh often worked beside the farmers in the fields, and in so doing slowly gained their support.

Greene saw an element of idealism in the Viet Minh zone. Peasants were taught to read. They and the troops, officers and men alike, received the same rations. As the French came to rely more and more on napalm, the Viet Minh picked up strength on the ground. A writer who had been a prisoner of the Viet Minh followed the troops about after he was released, setting up village schools. He told Greene he had become absorbed in the idealism of communism. "The weight of the haversack, the sound of the whistle, the flicker of the kitchen fires in the forest, such things can attach a man to a cause—until the weight of doctrine benumbs him with its monotony,"[12] Greene added.

In 1952 military victory or defeat had seemed equally possible to Greene, but by 1954 the war had become political and "revolution can be conquered only by a revolutionary spirit."[13]

At the beginning of the war Ho Chi Minh had been reluctant to use force and had wanted a political solution that would have retained a measure of French influence, but by 1954 Greene felt he wanted something politically unacceptable to the French, probably outright independence. Furthermore, enormous political problems were caused by the weakness of central government in Vietnam, and by the lack of political definition of the various parties. "We in the West are dominated by the idea of adult suffrage, but adult suffrage means chaos or corruption in a country like Vietnam with no political traditions, a majority of illiterate peasants and no political parties, as we know the term." He hoped that an agreement with the Viet Minh might still be made. If it were not, quack remedies would follow. The possibility of partition—"of surrendering Annam and Tongking and establishing a Cochin-China Republic"—had become dinner table discussion, and "the pipe-dream of substituting American for French Union troops might lead to a disastrous temporary peace which would abandon many non-Communist Nationalists to the mercy of Viet Minh—in particular the Catholic populations of the north, Thai-Bin, Bui-Chu and Phat-Diem."

Greene offered a solution. It arose from his belief that independence had been delayed too long around "the counsel tables of Geneva, Washington, Peking and Moscow. . . . The last performance has begun: a country one has loved is about to retire behind the curtain. But because a game is nearly lost, there is no point in not playing the last card of any value (one cannot do more than lose), and that card is complete independence." This he wrote at the end of March 1954, less than a month and a half before the fall of Dien Bien Phu on 8 May and the agreements reached at the Geneva Conference, which partitioned Vietnam along the 17th Parallel and promised country-wide elections by July 1956 to reunite the North and South. The elections, of course, were never held. If Greene's view then was "uniformly pessimistic," he still hoped that Catholics might form a vanguard within a free Vietnam to

withstand the Viet Minh. Catholicism, he believed, could provide that sense of community and tradition he had seen in Thui
Nhai where the militia consisted of the whole population, and
its leader was "a commandant without rank or pay who eats
his mother's rice in return for fighting his father's enemies."
The people there had a cause. They were bound to each other
by their desire to defend their village and way of life, which
centred on the Church.

Dien Bien Phu was an enormous victory for the Viet Minh.
In January, a few months before the battle, Greene watched
the French build their "great entrenched camp on the Laos
border." He heard them boast that " 'this is not a defensive
post, this is a post from which to counter-attack.' " And he felt
"a sense of unreality. There the Viet Minh were able to observe
the arrival of every plane, every movement in the camp from
the encircling hills. They knew our strength better than we
knew theirs. We were like actors in the arena."[14] On 13 March
1954 the battle began. By the time it ended on 8 May, the
French had lost 16,200 men, killed or captured, and the war.
The northern industrial half of Vietnam went to the Viet Minh,
who were thereafter known by the Vietnamese as the side that
drove France away. The North had "leadership, a form of government whereby men rose through their ability, and an ideology which made the system work. In the South there was
only the residue of that eight year old war,"[15] and a new President who had been out of the country for many years.

Looking back on Dien Bien Phu a decade later, Greene saw
the battle as one of the great blunders of the twentieth century.
It was more than a defeat of the French army. "It marked
virtually the end of any hope the Western Powers might have
entertained that they could dominate the East." The French
accepted the verdict. So to a lesser extent did the British. "That
young Americans continue to die in the southern delta of Saigon," Greene wrote in 1963, "only shows that it takes time for
the echoes even of a total defeat to encircle the globe."[16]

Greene's last visit to Vietnam was made a year after Dien

Bien Phu. . . . In a small room in Emperor Bao Dai's former palace, Greene met Ho Chi Minh. Though to see him he "had to resort to a touch of blackmail because it was difficult to get into Hanoi once the French had pulled out,"[17] he was there on a mission—to hand Ho a letter from a Vietnamese whose name Greene has never disclosed. He was able to be of use to Ho in another way as well. At the time there was a rumour among the French that Ho was no longer in charge, and Greene was able to say that this was at variance with what he saw.

As many other journalists had been before him, Greene was struck by Ho's "simplicity and candour. . . . There was nothing evasive about him: this was a man who gave orders and expected obedience and also love. The kind remorseless face had no fanaticism about it. . . . This was a man who had patiently solved an equation. So much love had to be given and received; so many sacrifices demanded and suffered." He was impressed with this national hero who worked fourteen hours a day in the cause of his people. Greene was reminded of a "Mr. Chips, wise, kind, just (if one could accept the school rules as just). . . . I regretted I was too old to accept the rules or believe what the school taught. . . . I could understand the loyalty of his pupils."[18]

Was it because of Ho Chi Minh that Greene's views about communism relaxed, or was this due to the Church's complicity with American involvement in the South, or the experience of a war which, although it had not begun as a communist war, was turning into a communist success story? If Greene found sadness in Hanoi in May 1955 because there were no cafés to sit in and nothing but propaganda films at the cinema, he also pointed out that the peasant does not miss cafés or restaurants or French and American films because he has never had them. Perhaps even the compulsory political meetings, lectures and physical training sessions were better entertainment than he had had before. "We talk so glibly of the threat to the individual, but the anonymous peasant has never been treated so like an individual before. Unless a priest, no one before the Com-

missar has approached him, has troubled to ask him questions
or spent time teaching him. There is something in Communism besides politics."[19]

Greene was impressed with Ho Chi Minh's courage, modesty, patience and sacrifice but, curiously, he showed no personal interest in his politics. He briefly reviewed Ho's
background by listing incidents which he said "had contributed
to the solution: a merchant ship, the kitchens of the Carlton
Grill, a photographer's studio in Paris, a British prison in Hong
Kong, as well as Moscow in the hopeful spring days of the
Revolution, the company of Borodin in China."[20] The
"solution"—communism—Greene avoided in his sparse account of Ho's life, as he did any consideration of how the incidents he noted contributed to the development of a
revolutionary conscience. Ho himself said his political convic-
tions had developed "step by step, along the struggle by studying Marxism-Leninism parallel with participation in practical
activities" until he finally came to believe "that only Socialism
and Communism can liberate the oppressed nations and the
working people throughout the world from slavery."[21] One
senses that Greene may have begun to suspect the truth of Ho's
conclusion, but if he did, he never acknowledged it. . . .

Though Greene had no intention of turning his experiences in
Vietnam into a novel, *The Quiet American* took hold of him
and fiction merged with fact so that the book contains more
direct reportage than any of his other novels. Fowler, the journalist narrator, sees and speaks what Greene saw and wrote in
Vietnam. His first name is Thomas—the name Greene chose
for himself when he was baptised as a Catholic—after St.
Thomas Didymus, the doubter. Fowler too has been to Malaya
and, like Greene, cares deeply about Vietnam. His description
of Phat Diem begins, as Greene's does in *Paris-Match*, from
the bell tower of the Cathedral. The press conference at which
he meets Granger matches one Greene himself attended. His
description of the Cao Dai in Tanyin resembles sections of

Greene's *Sunday Times* articles. The horizontal bombing raid after Phuong has left him for Pyle is identical to Greene's piece "A Memory of Indo-China" in *The Listener*. "I had determined to employ again the experience I had gained with *The End of the Affair* in the use of the first person and the time-shift," he remarked later, "and my choice of a journalist as the 'I' seemed to me to justify the use of *reportage*."[22]

The novel circles back on itself and begins where it ends with Phuong lighting Fowler's pipe. As he tells us about the well intentioned but dangerously innocent American, Pyle, whose absorption "in the dilemmas of Democracy and the responsibilities of the West"[23] leads him to Thé and to murder, Fowler's passivity turns into involvement. When Greene was caught during the fighting around Phat Diem between the French paratroops and the Viet Minh he thought, "how stupid it would be to lose a leg or to be hit by shrapnel for no reason at all, in this country which is not mine, in a war which is none of my business." But by the time Fowler arrived in his consciousness, Vietnam had become his business. In *The Quiet American* he uses the word *engagé* for the first time in a novel, and after many years of advocating the necessary political neutrality of writers, he produces a journalist-narrator who is forced by events to take political action. Perhaps, as Fowler speculates about himself, Greene had to have his foot thrust into the mess of life before he could see the pain. "We belong, to quote the words of Ezra Pound, to a 'botched' civilisation,"[24] Greene himself concluded. Hitherto he had tried to observe with neutrality the bearers of this botched culture—the English in Malaya and Kenya, the French in Vietnam—as they struggled with the changes that had come over the colonial world. But when he ran up against the Americans his detachment dissolved.

This was only partly because of his distaste for American culture. Ho Chi Minh was successful and Greene admired him, but Ho had not converted him to communism. What Greene advocated for Vietnam was political independence which he thought would prevent the country from becoming communist.

In 1965, ten years after his last trip there, he wrote a letter to *The Times* calling for America to negotiate with the Viet Cong in order to prevent the National Liberation Front from becoming the legal government of South Vietnam. "To refuse to negotiate with them is to refuse to negotiate with the future and to repeat the unhappy mistakes of the past,"[25] he insisted. Greene disliked the empty consumerism and naïvety of American culture and he was angry that under its influence the struggle against communism was being lost. In the early fifties he had insisted that the Vietnamese would fight for their country better if they were completely independent than if helped by America. The United States was certainly not unique in thinking it was bringing enlightenment and progress through the benefits of "free enterprise" and American-style "democracy" to Vietnam, but Greene identified it exclusively with this attitude. In his quiet American, Alden Pyle, he allowed his intense irritation with the smug and dangerous expansiveness of American culture to take hold.

"The bar tonight was loud with innocent American voices and that was the worst disquiet," he wrote in his journal in 1954. "They were there, one couldn't help being aware, to protect an investment."[26] At 32, Pyle is "in his element . . . with the whole universe to improve."[27] His goal is the conversion of Vietnam to American democracy in the naive belief that the only reason anyone would not want to live as an American is that he has not been properly exposed to the beauty of the American way of life. If it became necessary to kill innocent people to achieve this goal, "it was a pity, but . . . they died in the right cause. . . . In a way you could say they died for democracy."[28] Pyle's good intentions and his ignorance make him impregnable and dangerous. Where he went, nothing would ever be the same again.

Greene's newly acquired first person voice was well suited to the purpose of exposing Pyle's connection with Thé and America's desire to dominate the world. He no longer moralised as he had in the thirties because, in a sense, everything was

already lost. Before the war he had held on to a past, calmer
scheme of things that he saw slipping rapidly away. "Then we
lived through the Second World War, and I think we were all
strongly impressed with the sense of chaos. After that revolutions, guerrilla warfare . . . disorder rather than an evil fate."[29]
As a reporter Fowler carried Greene's partly despairing, partly
cynical estimate of the human condition into the post-war
world of anti-colonialism, post-colonialism and neo-colonial-
ism. If, as Fowler says, "nothing nowadays is fabulous and nothing rises from its ashes,"[30] Greene nevertheless continued to
record the direction the new world was taking. He wanted to
go deeper, "to be more implicated . . . When one is a rescue
worker, or a reporter, or indeed a writer trying to bring a scene
(however ghastly) to life, one is active, and this activity enables
one to bear the weight of suffering."[31]

Fowler is a seasoned reporter who prefers that title to correspondent because it denotes a lack of involvement: "I wrote
what I saw, I took no action—even an opinion is a kind of
action." Fowler believes that to have opinions is to interfere
like York Harding, "a superior sort of journalist—they call them
diplomatic correspondents. He gets hold of an idea and then
alters every situation to fit the idea." Pyle did this when he
came to Vietnam full of Harding's notions and then got mixed
up in something that was none of his business and did a lot of
harm. Fowler speaks to us often of non-involvement but the
reason for his disaffection is not, as one might expect, non-
interventionist politics. It is cynicism about man. "Wouldn't
we all do better not trying to understand, accepting the fact
that no human being will ever understand another, not a wife
a husband, a lover a mistress, nor a parent a child? Perhaps
that's why men have invented God—a being capable of understanding. Perhaps if I wanted to be understood or to understand I would bamboozle myself into belief, but I am a
reporter," Fowler tells us. To think one understands is dangerous. It is tantamount to belief, and belief is blind. Pyle never
sees "anything he hasn't heard in a lecture-hall, and his writers

and his lecturers made a fool of him. When he saw a dead body he couldn't even see the wounds."[32]

Because he sees human beings as basically isolated, Fowler thinks it moral to report only what he sees. Yet he tells us that even reporting is impossible. He censors himself: "It wouldn't have done to cable the details of his [Pyle's] true career . . . for it would have damaged Anglo-American relations."[33] And censorship is imposed on him: when he and Granger get information at the press conference they are told it cannot be printed. Only opinion is permitted and Vietnam is awash with it, but Fowler regards opinion as "empty privilege" by which humans, in trying to make sense of things, inevitably commit intellectual violence by imposing themselves on others.

Opinions are abstract: reportage is concrete. To presume is to be blind: to report is to remain sensitive to empirical reality. So Fowler watches, and his politics are based on empirical evidence. The peasants "want enough rice. . . . They don't want to be shot at. They want one day to be much the same as another. They don't want our white skins around telling them what they want." Fowler has no interest in "isms and ocracies. Give me facts. A rubber planter beats his labourer—all right, I'm against him. . . . I've seen a priest, so poor he hasn't a change of trousers, working fifteen hours a day from hut to hut in a cholera epidemic, eating nothing but rice and salt fish, saying his Mass with an old cup—a wooden platter. I don't believe in God and yet I'm for that priest." He prefers the French to the Americans because they are at least dying for their colonialism. "They aren't leading these people on with half-lies like your politicians—and ours,"[34] he tells Pyle.

What Fowler does not admit at first is the vulnerability of his position. Over and over he is told "one day something will happen. You will take a side."[35] What that means here is that involvement will come from honest observation whereas nothing will be learned from living with pre-conceived abstractions. Fowler is passive. He allows the ebb and flow of experience to change him, which is what Greene said the process of writing should do. And not only experience changes a writer, we are told. "One is changed by one's own books. The writer plays God until his creatures escape from him and, in their turn, they mould him."[36]

Fowler's great boast at the beginning of the novel is that he has no politics. Until his fourth trip to Vietnam, that was Greene's boast too. Both insisted a writer must not take sides, must expose but not judge. Yet Fowler's language is riddled with anti-Americanisms. He regards America as the place where everything has gone wrong, as did Greene. Even before he visited the US on his way to Mexico in 1938, America had become his symbol of rampant materialism, lack of tradition, cultural naivety and destructive altruism. If Greene admired both the French, who themselves were anti-American in Vietnam, and the Viet Minh, "the temptation to double allegiance tends to disappear before American capitalism and imperialism," he admitted in 1979. "I would go to almost any length to put my feeble twig in the spokes of American foreign policy. I admit this may appear simplistic, but that's how it is. Some time ago there was an article in *The Spectator* about *The Quiet American*, which said that it made little difference whether I inclined to the Right or the Left, since what I truly detested was American liberalism. That wasn't far wrong."[37] In the face of American intervention in Vietnam, apolitical Fowler helps the Viet Minh and anti-communist Greene acknowledges the attraction of Ho Chi Minh. "He was of course a wonderful old man."[38] He was also the first of many revolutionary leaders Greene would meet and admire.

But something else happened to Greene in Vietnam. Along with Fowler and Pyle, he got blood on his shoes. The canal full of overlapping bodies, the woman with the small neat clot of blood on her forehead whose child "lay like an embryo in the womb with his little bony knees drawn up,"[39] the sampan blown apart in a shower of sparks—these images along with Ho Chi Minh's selflessness remained in his memory. Perhaps as Bendrix said it is the subject which chooses the author, but it is not

every author who can look at such a subject squarely and admit
" 'the guilty' . . . is all of us."[40] _The Quiet American_ is Fowler's
apology for facilitating Pyle's death. Perhaps it is also Greene's
for writing an openly political book. It was necessary to expose
the dangers of American foreign policy and "sometimes . . . a
writer can make a sharper impact with his books than if he
signed petitions and tracts. Writing is certainly a kind of
action."[41]

The impressive thing about Greene's reporting from Vietnam is his ability to record what he saw and his refusal, despite
his Catholic and anti-communist interests there, to be misled
by pre-conceived ideas. Despite his opposition to communism,
he is excited by Ho Chi Minh. Despite his support of the
French and Vietnamese armies against the communists, he acknowledges as admirable the discipline and commitment of the
Viet Minh. It would be easy to say that this was because he
was fair as a reporter and refused to be biased by his own pref-
erences. Yet was it? If we look closely at the pattern of his
reporting in the fifties, we see that it followed his liberal pred-
ilections until his fourth trip to Vietnam. He supported the
underdog in Kenya, but he did not support the political aims
of Mau Mau, which he failed to recognise as an indigenous
peasant movement. During his first visits to Vietnam he supported the Vietnamese army against the Viet Minh, and advocated Catholicism as a means of mobilisation; in Thui Nhai
he even praised the arming of children against communism.
Yet after he met Ho Chi Minh, suddenly he acknowledged that
the commissar who preached collectivism treated the peasant
as much as an individual as did the priest, and that the peasant's interests were better taken care of in the North than in
the South where the government was corrupt and anonymous.

Greene had always been interested in the possibility of social improvement but until Vietnam he had never recognised
communism as a move toward it. He had looked to the model
of sacrifice and humility that Christianity offered as a base from
which the emptiness and indifference of materialism, which he

saw as the illness of modern times, could be withstood. In support of this position he had written plenty of anti-communist cant, and shown great vigilance about the oppression of Catholics, and had been a strong defender of the rights associated with the liberal concept of freedom—freedom of speech, of the press, of the right of travel, for example. But his concern for the individual had centred largely on Catholics. And though he was concerned with the exploitation of workers, the unequal distribution of wealth, and the disproportionate political clout that accompanied wealth, he was more concerned with maintaining the liberal façade of freedom than he was in exploring a social order that might guarantee real freedom for all instead of just for the privileged few.

Nevertheless, he was interested in social change in however sentimental a way and in Ho Chi Minh he encountered a man whose life had not only been dedicated to change, but who was effecting it. This was a man whose wispy beard, rubber sandals and frayed uniform held none of the militaristic appearance Greene had previously associated with communism. Greene found in him a reflection of real humility. Moreover, Ho was not interested in proving a political point about the death of capitalism. He fought because he believed Vietnam was unviable if divided and because the French were violating his country's national dignity. In this war of liberation, if Greene admired the French in their defeat, he had no sympathy for the Americans who failed to recognise the determination of the Vietnamese to govern themselves.

Fowler's experience of Vietnam is similar to Greene's and involvement creeps up on him unexpectedly as it did on Greene. Fowler's disgust, however, touches more than America's "private store of Coca-Cola and their portable hospitals and their too wide cars and their not-quite latest guns." He despairs of the human condition. "Let them fight, let them love, let them murder, I would not be involved," he tells himself. Saigon, with its fumeries and whorehouses, is a safe haven for him. If its conditions horrify Pyle with his sterilised view of things, they give life to Fowler. In Vietnam he is away from his wife and the other women he has hurt. Phuong expects little and is expressionless except when Helen's telegram arrives saying she will give Fowler a divorce. Fowler has no idea what Phuong feels: "For all I could tell, she was as scared as the rest of us: she didn't have the gift of expression, that was all." This leaves him free of the responsibility for her that Pyle feels, however laughable it may be. Vietnam suits Fowler because he can take from it what he needs and remain unburdened by emotional ties. In Vietnam he can even indulge himself in the assumption that involvement, political or personal, is immoral unless one is willing to die for one's beliefs. "Death was the only absolute value in my world. Lose life and one would lose nothing again for ever. I envied those who could believe in a god and I distrusted them. I felt they were keeping their courage up with a fable of the changeless and the permanent."[42]

But he is not, he says, "a Berkeleian. I believe my back's against this wall. I believe there's a sten gun over there. . . . I believe what I report, which is more than most of your correspondents do," he tells Pyle. And as it happened to Greene, this radically empirical view which seems to offer protection, traps him in involvement. Fowler "never knew a man who had better motives for all the trouble he caused" than Pyle, but Pyle "comes blundering in and people have to die for his mistakes. . . . In a war like this . . . there is no time to hesitate: one uses the weapon to hand—the French the napalm bomb, Mr. Heng the bullet or the knife."[43] Involvement is suddenly produced from empirical disaffection when that very position of uninvolvement is threatened.

Pyle must be stopped. Heng, the Viet Minh, suggests that Fowler publish the truth about Pyle's and Thé's collaboration. "Or perhaps you cannot?" he asks. Fowler replies, "My paper's not interested in General Thé. They are only interested in your people, Heng. . . . [The police] aren't interested in Thé either. And do you think they would dare to touch an American? He has diplomatic privileges. He's a graduate of Harvard. The Minister's very fond of Pyle."[44]

The press does not, or cannot, do its job. Like the army, it is subject to political decisions that are made elsewhere about what can or cannot be done or told. The young French Colonel tells Granger he cannot say that the American supplies have not arrived. "You can say . . . that six months ago we had three helicopters and now we have one. . . . You can say that if a man is wounded in this fighting, not seriously wounded, just wounded, he knows that he is probably a ' dead man. Twelve hours, twenty-four hours perhaps, on a stretcher to the ambulance, then bad tracks, a breakdown, perhaps an ambush, gangrene. It is better to be killed outright." The press cannot call a spade a spade because "perhaps the American newspapers would say, 'Oh, the French are always complaining, always begging.' And in Paris the Communists would accuse, 'The French are spilling their blood for America and America will not even send a second-hand helicopter.' It does no good. At this end of it we should still have no helicopters, and the enemy would still be there." Captain Trouin adds: "We are professionals: we have to go on fighting till the politicians tell us to stop."[45]

The politicians, however, never see what is happening. They sit at home with their western comforts and send out the Pyles of the world who operate on undigested ideas and create havoc through misinformation. And the press is gagged. So we come to the necessity for the courageous individual act. Fowler turns Pyle over to the Viet Minh, not because he believes in their cause, though he is fair enough to have seen, as Greene did, that the Viet Minh who sits in the peasant's hut and asks him his name and listens to his complaints and gives up an hour a day to teaching him, is treating him like someone of value. Fowler turns Pyle over because, given his own liberal conscience, he has no alternative. "Suffering is not increased by numbers," he tells us. "One body can contain all the suffering the world can feel. I had judged like a journalist in terms of quantity and I had betrayed my own principles." He cannot forget the woman in the square who kept her mutilated baby "covered under her straw hat. I can't get it out of my head. And there was another in Phat Diem." The fact that the first woman was killed by Pyle and the second by the Viet Minh does not enter his consideration. Fowler turns Pyle over because after seeing innocents die he must do something in order to live with himself. "Sooner or later," Heng tells him, "one has to take sides. If one is to remain human." Fowler has "seen too many bodies which belonged to no one, not even to themselves,"[46] and he chooses the Viet Minh.

*Pravda* loved Greene for Fowler's choice. Five columns were given over to the *The Quiet American*, which was called "the most remarkable event"[47] of recent British literary history. But in America the novel upset a lot of people, and when Joseph L. Mankiewicz turned it into a film in 1957, he made his American wise and his Englishman the dupe of the communists. Greene was "very angry, indeed" about the political dishonesty of the film. He almost had to be forcibly held down when he heard that United Artists had given all proceeds from the Washington première . . . to an aid-for-Vietnam drive. He was even more annoyed, according to Michael Redgrave, who played Fowler, when he heard he had been allotted a seat beside Vietnam's ambassador at the London première. But in the end Greene responded with admirable restraint. The film would "make only the more obvious the discrepancy between what the State Department would like the world to believe and what in fact happened in Vietnam." He had better things to do than concern himself with a film that one could almost believe was made deliberately to attack the book and the author. "The book was based on a closer knowledge of the Indochina war than the American director possessed and I am vain enough to believe that the book will survive a few years longer than Mr. Mankiewicz's incoherent picture."[48]

In March 1956, the same month that *The Quiet American* was published in the United States, *The Atlantic Monthly* reprinted a report on Poland that Greene had written for *The Sunday Times* in January of that year. Though he was primarily discussing the Catholic Church and the Pax Movement, Greene supported the social and economic changes made by the communist government in Poland since the war, "many of which were both necessary and admirable." He was suspicious of Pax. Its leader, Piasecki, an anti-Semite and nationalist before the war who had fought both the Germans and Russians during it, had been given the Pax press by the Party. Though the press had the liberty to publish a certain number of books from the West, the vast majority of Polish Catholics were opponents of the Pax movement, and some suggested it had been Russian inspired in an attempt to divide the Church. Nevertheless, there were "among the fellow travellers of Pax . . . many sincere patriots . . . who wish to take part in the social reform of their country and if a debt has to be paid by their Catholicism they try to pay it in the smallest possible coinage."[49]

Although Cardinal Wysczynski had been arrested, Greene thought it probable that the government would regret this act. He might be returned to Warsaw as part of a bargain if Vatican policy did not make such a possibility difficult. Rome "seems . . . as much against the Catholic people of Poland as against the Communist Government," Greene said. If the Vatican wanted Wysczynski returned it would have to recognise that "no one in Poland today . . . wants the return of an emigré government. . . . Nor are any Poles prepared to consider the return of the Western-Territories to a Germany responsible for such immeasurable suffering." The Vatican was addressing letters to administrators in "Germania" and had appointed a German cleric to the Bishopric of Breslau. Perhaps, Greene suggested, if the Church could recognise the reality of the situation, the Cardinal might be allowed to come back to Warsaw. However suspicious Greene was of the use the Party was making of Catholicism through Pax and Piasecki, he had no such harsh words for the communists. He visited Auschwitz. "Every visitor to Poland should be made to visit this camp of death. . . .

No crimes have been committed by Communists equal to what Poland has suffered from Germany."[50]

America and the Church were Greene's antipathies in the mid-fifties, and the accomplishments of communist governments began to hold his interest. For all his previous suspicion, he began to see in communism what so many of his peers had seen in the thirties—the attraction of a political discipline. They had come to it with courage and hope in the face of Dachau and the workless hungry. They believed it to be the only reliable opponent of fascism when the leaders of their own society had lost any sense that they were fighting for anything except to patch up the same kind of world that had produced the chaos. Greene came to this position grudgingly ten years after Auschwitz, his religious certainty gone, if indeed it had ever existed, and with the dangerous and expansive complacency of American materialism surfacing in Vietnam, a country he loved. The attraction for him was the rigour of a discipline which, for all its drawbacks, could effect social change.

In Vietnam something else was involved. The communism of Ho Chi Minh was indigenous. This was a movement of the people themselves toward a certain kind of self-government. Though Greene had sympathised with the Kikuyu in Kenya, he had not seen the underpinnings of a successful revolution there. His attitude to them was tinged with the paternalism of empire, which was precisely what he criticised in government and settler. In Vietnam his sympathy for the failing French shows his paternalism still in place, and perhaps his admiration for Ho Chi Minh was the logical conclusion of that attitude of trusteeship. Ho had fought for and won the support of his people. He was loved and respected by them and with them he was changing the direction of his country. Here was a new "father," an indigenous leader. Surely it was time for the empires to go home.

## NOTES

1. Graham Greene, "The Man as Pure as Lucifer," *The Sunday Times* (8 May 1955). There are various ways of spelling the names of the towns and organisations Greene mentions in his Vietnam reportage. I use the currently accepted forms, and have left Greene's spelling as it appeared in his articles.

2. Graham Greene, *Ways of Escape* (Toronto: Lester and Orpen Dennys, 1980), 131. (Hereafter WE.)

3. Ibid., 132.

4. Ibid., 134.

5. Graham Greene, "Introduction," in Graham Greene and Hugh Greene, *The Spy's Bedside Book* (London: Granada, 1975), 13.

6. WE, 134.

7. Graham Greene and Raymond Cartier, *"En Indochine,"* *Paris-Match* (12 July 1952), 19–30.

8. Ibid. (my translation)

9. A. J. Liebling, "A Talkative Something-or-Other," *The New Yorker* (1 April 1956), 136–42. [Ed. note: See this book, p. 355]

10. Until next endnote all quotations are from: Graham Greene, "Return to Indo-China," *The Sunday Times* (21 March 1954).

11. David Halberstam, *The Making of a Quagmire* (New York: Random House, 1965), 35–6.

12. Greene and Cartier, *"En Indochine."* (my translation)

13. Until next endnote all quotations are from: Graham Greene, "Last Cards in Indo-China," *The Sunday Times* (28 March 1954).

14. Graham Greene, "Before the Attack," *Spectator* (16 April 1954): 456.

15. Halberstam, 38.

16. Graham Greene, "Decision In Asia: The Battle of Dien Bien Phu," *The Sunday Times* (3 March 1963).

17. Marie-Françoise Allain, *The Other Man: Conversations with Graham Greene* (London: Bodley Head, 1983), 89. (Hereafter OM.)

18. Greene, "The Man as Pure as Lucifer."

19. Ibid.

20. Ibid.

21. Jean Lacouture, *Ho Chi Minh: A Political Biography* (New York: Random House, 1968), 31.

22. WE, 140.

23. Graham Greene, *The Quiet American* (New York: Viking Penguin, 1996), 18. (Hereafter QA.)

24. OM, 55, 116.

25. Graham Greene, "Tactical Error on Viet Cong," *The Sunday Times* (23 June 1965).
26. Graham Greene, "Return To Indo-China," *The Sunday Times* (21 March 1954).
27. QA, 18.
28. Ibid., 179.
29. OM, 17.
30. QA, 11.
31. OM, 69.
32. QA, 28, 167, 60, 32.
33. Ibid., 21.
34. Ibid., 94, 95, 96.
35. Ibid., 151.
36. OM, 142.
37. Ibid., 93.
38. Ibid., 89.
39. QA, 53.
40. OM, 115.
41. Ibid., 81.
42. QA, 31, 28, 134, 44.
43. Ibid., 94, 60, 174, 178.
44. Ibid., 173–4.
45. Ibid., 66, 152.
46. Ibid., 183, 174, 55.
47. *Newsweek* (1 October 1956), 56.
48. Adamson, 88.
49. Graham Greene, "Between Pax and Patriotism," *The Sunday Times* (15 January 1956).
50. Ibid.

# Topics for Discussion
# and Papers

## THEMES, SUBJECTS, AND MEANINGS

1. Trace the word "responsible" throughout the book. How does this concept function thematically?

2. Do a similar search for and analysis of the word "involved" and "engaged." Pay particular attention to what Mr. Heng and Captain Trouin say.

3. Do you see Greene trying to show a distinction between innocence and ignorance? Is one characteristic more dangerous or tragic than the other? Explain.

4. A major subject is the role of the press. How does the novel present reporters and how are they seen to function? What are the restraints placed upon them?

5. Does the novel seem to "take sides" in the war? Where do you think Greene's sympathies lie?

6. Attitudes toward the military. Show how Greene presents the professional soldiers on all sides and summarize what you think he is trying to tell us about the role of the military man in a war directed by politicians.

7. Fowler says that he does not believe in God, but Pyle says that he does. Examine the religious aspects of *The Quiet American*.

8. Why does Fowler state at the end that he wishes there was "someone to whom [he] could say that [he] was sorry"? Why can't he? What would he say if he could? Explain.

9. How does this novel evaluate Greene's major subject of "the human condition"?

10. From reading this book, what do you think about America's involvement in the Vietnam War? Do you think that you should read more? Explain.

11. Racism is an important concern in late-twentieth-century Western society. Is Fowler a racist? Is Pyle? In the 1950s, is it important to them? Do they care? Do you? Explain.

12. Is there an existentialist theme in this novel? Compare the views of some of the critics.

## THE CHARACTERS

1. Does Greene's portrayal of Americans differ from the way he presents British, French, and Vietnamese characters? Do you think that this novel is only anti-American?

2. Is Alden Pyle a hypocrite? Do you think that he understands more, less, or about the same amount about the Vietnamese as Fowler tells us that he does?

3. Phuong has been called a "flat" character by some critics. Is she? Discuss the reasons for her motivation and loyalties.

4. Is Thomas Fowler a direct spokesman for Graham Greene, or is his vision in the novel noticeably different from Greene's as shown by Greene's autobiographical writings included in this edition?

5. Discuss Thomas Fowler as a traditional European colonialist.

6. Given your knowledge from the media of American foreign policy that caused military intervention in Grenada, Panama, Kuwait, and Haiti, how do you evaluate Greene's characterization of official Americans working abroad?

## STRUCTURE AND STYLE

1. Examine the novel's events in strict chronological order and evaluate whether Greene's structure makes the novel more or less effective than it would have been if told as it happens. Consider the effect of dramatic irony.

2. Analyze Thomas Fowler as an unreliable narrator. How much can we believe him? How much does he really understand? How honest is he, even with himself?

3. Much of the tension of this novel is created by what the characters say—but even more important may be contained in what the characters do *not* say. Analyze selected dialogues and show how what is not said by various characters contributes to a reader's understanding of what Greene is really trying to show.

## TOPICS FOR RESEARCH

1. Read pertinent selections from volume 2 of Norman Sherry's biography of Graham Greene and discuss autobiographical elements in *The Quiet American*.

2. From the same biography, note the attributed sources of various characters in the novel. See if you can track down more information and expand upon how each of them is portrayed in the novel.

3. Greene presents aspects of various military engagements in the novel. Look at available histories of the war and determine how accurately the actions and results are portrayed.

4. How prophetic do you think Greene was in showing the eventual result of the American presence in Vietnam? Document your opinion by specific references to subjects and themes of *The Quiet American* as compared with the many published reasons for the final outcome.

5. Read some of the numerous studies done about the way the press functioned and was treated later in the Vietnam War and make a comparison with the way the press is treated in this novel.

6. How well does this novel present the Saigon of the early 1950s? There are many available works to consult for background.

7. Based on your reading of U.S. Government publications contained in this text and available elsewhere, show how American policy of the time is or is not reflected in the attitudes and actions of the American officials as portrayed by Greene.

8. Compare the attitudes toward religion in *The Quiet American* with those especially in Greene's *The Power and the Glory* (or another work or works).

9. Where do you think this novel stands in the canon of Greene's works? High? Low? About average? Explain. (This subject would be best treated in a thesis.)

10. Graham Greene could be described as an epitome of male chauvinism in his personal relations with women. Read the biographies and criticism, then determine whether *The Quiet American* is a chauvinistic novel.

11. With regard to number 10 above, read carefully the literary criticism of *The Quiet American* written by women. Do you see a different approach than that presented by men? Can you draw any relevant conclusions about Greene as artist?

12. (For French speakers.) Look at the French publications about the war in the early 1950s. How accurately does Greene present what the French thought was really going on? (You should also look at the French reviews of *The Quiet American*.)

# Selected Bibliography

## I. RELEVANT WRITINGS BY GREENE

### PUBLISHED BOOKS
*Reflections.* Ed. Judith Adamson. New York: Reinhardt Books, 1990.
*Ways of Escape.* New York: Simon and Schuster, 1980.
*Yours, etc: Letters to the Press, 1945–1989.* Ed., Christopher Hawtree. London: Reinhardt, 1989.

### MANUSCRIPTS
1. At the Humanities Research Center, University of Texas, Austin:
   Diary: "Indo-China." n.d.
   "The Fall of Dien Bien Phu": Two manuscripts with revisions. 1963[?].
   Journal: "Saigon" (26 pp.), 30 December–15 January [Wobbe notes 1962–63 with a question mark]
   *The Quiet American.* Manuscript of introductions: 1963, 6 and 19 pp; 1972, 24 pp.
   ———. Page proofs for Collected Edition with corrections. 1972.
2. At Georgetown University, Washington, D.C.:
   Travel diaries of Greene's visits to Vietnam

### PUBLICATIONS AND INTERVIEWS ABOUT INDO-CHINA

1952
"Indo-China: France's Crown of Thorns." *Paris-Match* (12 July).

1953
Broadcast, "A Small Affair." BBC–Third Programme (10 August; repeated 13 August).
"A Small Affair." *The Listener* 50 (20 August): 302–304.

1954

"Return to Indo-China." *The Times* (London) (21 March).

Letter. *The Times* (25 March): 9.

"Last Cards in Indo-China." *Sunday Times* (28 March).

"Indo-China." *New Republic* 130 (5 April): 13–15.

"To Hope Till Hope Creates." *New Republic* 130 (12 April): 11–13.

"Before the Attack." *The Spectator* 192 (16 April): 456.

"Catholics at War: Extracts from an Indo-China Journal." *The Tablet* 203 (17 April): 366–67.

"On Indo-China." Interview with Brian Crozier. BBC–General Overseas Service (10 May).

"Indo-China Journal." *Commonweal* 60 (21 May): 170–72.

"The General and the Spy. Extract from an Indo-China Journal." *London Magazine* (August): 26–29.

"A Few Pipes. Extract from an Indo-China Journal." *London Magazine* (December): 17–24.


1955

"Diem's Critics." *America* 93 (28 May): 225.

Broadcast. "A Memory of Indo-China": BBC–Third Programme (8 September).

"A Memory of Indo-China." *The Listener* 54 (15 September): 420.


1957

Letter. *The Times* (19 January).

Broadcast. "Asia and the West." BBC–London Calling Asia (11 June).


1961

Letter. *The Times* (4 January): 9.


1964

Letter. *The Times* (6 November).


1965

"The American Presence." *New Statesman* 64 (19 March): 448.

Letter. *The Times* (24 September): 13.


1966

Letter. *The Sunday Telegraph* (16 January).

1968

Letter. *The Sunday Telegraph* (7 January).
Letter. *The Times* (22 March): 11.
———. (25 March): 9.

1970

"Withdrawing from Cambodia." *The Times* (11 May): 9.

1971

Letter. *The Times* (17 February): 15.
———. (23 February): 13.

1973

"Introduction." *The Quiet American—The Collected Edition.* London: William Heinemann and the Bodley Head. [Reprinted nearly verbatim in *Ways of Escape.*]
"My Own Devil: the Experience of Opium Smoking." *Vogue* 162 (October): 188–89, 238.
"To Indo-China with Love." *Travel and Leisure* 3 (October–November): 44–45, 87–89.

1975

Letter. *The Sunday Telegraph* (1 June).

## II. BOOKS ABOUT GREENE (WITH MAJOR SECTIONS ON *THE QUIET AMERICAN*)

Adamson, Judith. *Graham Greene: The Dangerous Edge: Where Art and Politics Meet.* New York: St. Martin's Press, 1990. [pp. 117–38]
Allott, Kenneth, and Miriam Farris. *The Art of Graham Greene.* New York: Russell, 1963.
Atkins, John Alfred. *Graham Greene.* London: Calder and Boyars, 1966. [pp. 227–36]
Bitterli, Urs. *Conrad, Malraux, Greene, Weiss: Schriftsteller und Kolonialismus.* Zurich: Bensiger Verlag, 1973. [pp. 109–47]
Boardman, Gwenn R. *Graham Greene: The Aesthetics of Exploration.* Gainesville: University of Florida Press, 1971. [pp. 106–17]
Cuoto, Maria. *Graham Greene: On the Frontier.* London: Macmillan, 1988. [pp. 166–76]

DeVitis, A. A. *Graham Greene*. Rev. ed. Boston: Twayne Publishers, 1986. [pp. 108–14]

Donaghy, Henry J. *Graham Greene: An Introduction to his Writings*. Amsterdam: Editions Rodopi B.V., 1983. [pp. 67–73]

Eagleton, Terry. *Exiles and Emigres*. New York: Schocken, 1970. [pp. 125–28]

Evans, Robert O., ed. *Graham Greene: Some Critical Considerations*. Lexington, Ky.: University of Kentucky Press, 1963. [pp. 188–206]

Gaston, Georg. *The Pursuit of Salvation: A Critical Guide to the Novels of Graham Greene*. Troy, N.Y.: Whitson, 1984. [pp. 55–71]

Hall, James. *Lunatic Giant in the Living Room*. Bloomington: Indiana University Press, 1968. [pp. 121–25]

Kelly, Richard N. *Graham Greene*. New York: Frederick Ungar, 1984. [pp. 67–72]

Kunkel, Francis L. *Labyrinthine Ways of Graham Greene*. New York: Sheed and Ward, 1959. [pp. 148–53] Rev. ed., Mamaroneck, N.Y.: Paul F. Appel, 1973.

Lamda, B. P. *Graham Greene: His Mind and Art*. New York: Apt Books, 1989.

Lodge, David. *Graham Greene*. New York: Columbia University Press, 1966. [pp. 35–37]

———. *Novelist at the Crossroads*. Ithaca, N.Y.: Cornell University Press, 1971. [pp. 111–12]

McEwan, Neil. *Graham Greene*. New York: St. Martin's Press, 1988. [pp. 73–81]

Miller, R. H. *Understanding Graham Greene*. Columbia, S.C.: University of South Carolina Press, 1990. [pp. 106–13]

O'Prey, Paul. *A Reader's Guide to Graham Greene*. New York: Thames and Hudson, 1988. [pp. 102–109]

Pryce-Jones, David. *Graham Greene*. Edinburgh and London: Oliver and Boyd, 1963. [pp. 90–93]

Rai, Gangeshwar. *Graham Greene: An Existential Approach*. New Delhi: Associated Publishing House, 1983. [pp. 74–80]

Sharrock, Roger. *Saints, Sinners and Comedians: The Novels of Graham Greene*. Kent, U.K.: Burns and Oates, 1984. [pp. 197–220]

Sheldon, Michael. *Graham Greene: The Man Within*. London: Heinemann, 1995.

Sherry, Norman. *Life of Graham Greene*. Volume I, 1904–39, New York: Viking Penguin, 1989. [All material is pre-*Quiet American*, but this definitive biography is vital for background.] Volume II, 1939–55. London: Jonathan Cape, 1994 [pp. 359–76; 385–441; 472–88]; New York: Viking Penguin, 1995.

Smith, Graham. *The Achievement of Graham Greene.* Sussex, U.K.: Harvester Press, 1986. [pp. 129–37]

Spurling, John. *Graham Greene.* London and New York: Methuen, 1983. [pp. 55–58]

Stratford, Philip. *Faith and Fiction. The Creative Process in Greene and Mauriac.* Notre Dame, Ind.: Notre Dame University Press, 1964. [pp. 308–16]

Thomas, Brian. *An Underground Fate: The Idiom of Romance in the Later Novels of Graham Greene.* Athens, Ga.: University of Georgia Press, 1988. [pp. 25–51]

## III. ESSAYS ABOUT *THE QUIET AMERICAN*

Allen, Walter. "Awareness of Evil: Graham Greene." *The Nation* 182 (21 April 1956): 344–46.

Allott, Miriam. "The Moral Situation in *The Quiet American,*" in Robert O. Evans, ed., *Graham Greene.* Lexington, Ky.: University of Kentucky Press, 1963, 188–206.

Bawer, Bruce. "Graham Greene: The Politics." *The New Criterion* 8, 3 (November 1989): 39–41.

Brennan, Neil. "Coney Island Rock." *Accent* 16 (Spring 1956): 140–42.

Cassidy, John. "America and Innocence: Henry James and Graham Greene." *Blackfriars* 38, 447 (June 1957): 261–67.

Creasman, Boyd. "Twigs in the Spokes: Graham Greene's Anti-Americanism." *Studies in the Humanities* 14, 2 (December 1987): 106–15.

DeVitis, A. A. "Religious Aspects in the Novels of Graham Greene," in *Shapeless God,* ed. Harry J. Mooney and T. F. Staley. Pittsburgh: University of Pittsburgh Press, 1968, 55–56.

Elistrova, Anna. "Graham Greene and his New Novel." *Soviet Literature* 8 (1956): 149–55.

Evans, Robert O. "Existentialism in Greene's *The Quiet American.*" *Modern Fiction Studies* 3 (Autumn 1957): 241–48.

Freedman, Ralph. "Novel of Contention: *The Quiet American.*" *Western Review* 21 (Autumn 1957): 76–81.

Gaston, G. M. "The Structure of Salvation in *The Quiet American*." *Renascence* 31 (Winter 1979): 93–106.

Hansen, Neils Bugge. "The Unquiet Englishman: A Reading of Graham Greene's *The Quiet American*," in Graham D. Caie et al., eds. *Occasional Papers 1976–77*. Copenhagen: University of Copenhagen, 1978.

Hazen, James. "The Greeneing of America," in Peter Wolfe, ed. *Essays in Graham Greene*. Greenwood, Fla.: Penkevill, 1987.

Hinchliff, Arnold P. "The Good American." *Twentieth Century* 158 (December 1960): 534–37.

Hughes, R. E. "*The Quiet American*: The Case Reopened." *Renascence* 12 (Autumn 1959): 41–42, 49.

Larsen, Eric. "*The Quiet American*." *New Republic* 175 (August 7–14, 1976): 40–42.

Leibling, A. J. "A Talkative Something-or-Other." *The New Yorker* 32 (7 April 1956): 136–42.

Lewis, R. W. B. "The Fiction of Graham Greene: Between the Horror and the Glory." *Kenyon Review* 19 (1957): 56–75.

McCormick, John O. "The Rough and Lurid Vision: Henry James, Graham Greene and the International Theme." *Jahrbuch für Amerikastudien* 2 (1957): 158–67.

Pathak, Zakia, et al. "The Prisonhouse of Orientalism." *Textual Practice* 5, 2 (Summer 1991): 195–218.

Rahv, Philip. "Wicked American Innocence." *Commentary* 21 (May 1956): 488–90.

Rudman, Harry W. "Clough and Graham Greene's *The Quiet American*." *Victorian Newsletter* 19 (1961): 14–15.

Trilling, Diana. "America and *The Quiet American*." *Commentary* 22 (July 1956): 66–71.

Vargo, Lisa. "*The Quiet American* and 'A Mr. Liebermann.'" *English Language Notes* 21, 4 (June 1984): 63–70.

## IV. BIBLIOGRAPHIES

Brennan, Neil, and Alan R. Redway, eds. A *Bibliography of Graham Greene*. New York: Oxford University Press, 1990.

Cassis, A. F. *Graham Greene: An Annotated Bibliography of Criticism*. Metuchen, N.J.: Scarecrow Press, 1981.

Friedman, Alan Warren. "The Status of Graham Greene Studies."

*Library Chronicle of the University of Texas at Austin* 20 (1991): 36–67.

Wobbe, R. A. *Graham Greene: A Bibliography and Guide to Research.* New York: Garland Publishing, 1979.


## V. WORKS OF GENERAL INTEREST

Buttinger, Joseph. *The Smaller Dragon: A Political History of Vietnam.* New York: Praeger Publishers, 1958.

Fall, Bernard. *Street Without Joy: Indochina at War, 1946–54.* Harrisburg, Pa.: Stackpole, 1961, 1963.

Honaker, Keith. *The Eagle Weeps.* Knoxville, Tenn.: K. and W. Publishers, 1994.

Lansdale, Edward G. *In The Midst of Wars.* New York: Harper and Row, 1972.

Malo, Jean-Jacques, and Tony Williams, eds. *Vietnam War Films: Over 600 Feature, Made-for-TV, Pilot and Short Movies, 1929–92.* Jefferson, N.C.: McFarland and Co., 1994.

O'Ballance, Edgar. *The Indochina War, 1943–1954.* London: Faber and Faber, 1964.

Patti, Archimedes L. A. *Why Vietnam: Prelude to America's Albatross.* Berkeley, Calif.: University of California Press, 1980.

Pratt, John Clark. *Vietnam Voices: Perspectives on The War Years, 1941–1982.* New York: Viking Penguin, 1983.

Simpson, Howard R. *Tiger in The Barbed Wire: An American in Vietnam, 1952–91.* Maclean, Va.: Brassey's (U.S.), 1992.

# FOR THE BEST IN PAPERBACKS, LOOK FOR THE 🐧

In every corner of the world, on every subject under the sun, Penguin represents quality and variety—the very best in publishing today.

For complete information about books available from Penguin—including Puffins, Penguin Classics, and Compass—and how to order them, write to us at the appropriate address below. Please note that for copyright reasons the selection of books varies from country to country.

**In the United Kingdom:** Please write to *Dept. EP, Penguin Books Ltd, Bath Road, Harmondsworth, West Drayton, Middlesex UB7 0DA.*

**In the United States:** Please write to *Penguin Putnam Inc., P.O. Box 12289 Dept. B, Newark, New Jersey 07101-5289* or call 1-800-788-6262.

**In Canada:** Please write to *Penguin Books Canada Ltd, 10 Alcorn Avenue, Suite 300, Toronto, Ontario M4V 3B2.*

**In Australia:** Please write to *Penguin Books Australia Ltd, P.O. Box 257, Ringwood, Victoria 3134.*

**In New Zealand:** Please write to *Penguin Books (NZ) Ltd, Private Bag 102902, North Shore Mail Centre, Auckland 10.*

**In India:** Please write to *Penguin Books India Pvt Ltd, 11 Panchsheel Shopping Centre, Panchsheel Park, New Delhi 110 017.*

**In the Netherlands:** Please write to *Penguin Books Netherlands bv, Postbus 3507, NL-1001 AH Amsterdam.*

**In Germany:** Please write to *Penguin Books Deutschland GmbH, Metzlerstrasse 26, 60594 Frankfurt am Main.*

**In Spain:** Please write to *Penguin Books S. A., Bravo Murillo 19, 1° B, 28015 Madrid.*

**In Italy:** Please write to *Penguin Italia s.r.l., Via Benedetto Croce 2, 20094 Corsico, Milano.*

**In France:** Please write to *Penguin France, Le Carré Wilson, 62 rue Benjamin Baillaud, 31500 Toulouse.*

**In Japan:** Please write to *Penguin Books Japan Ltd, Kaneko Building, 2-3-25 Koraku, Bunkyo-Ku, Tokyo 112.*

**In South Africa:** Please write to *Penguin Books South Africa (Pty) Ltd, Private Bag X14, Parkview, 2122 Johannesburg.*